INKED IN ONYX

INKBOUND, BOOK 2

SHANNON MAYER

Adopted by a kindly blacksmith and his horrible wife at the age of four and unaware of her royal beginnings, Harmony has spent the last 25 years in a poverty-stricken village called The Hollow. She was plagued by dreams of a dark-haired stranger, headaches due to repressed memories and magic, all while her two evil step-brothers and stepmother do their best to make her life a living hell (which is a short trip given the wretched conditions they already face). But Harm is a fighter. Plus, she's got her inventions, her best friend Molly, and her trusty falcon Fetch by her side. It might not be a lot, but it's enough to bring some glimmer of happiness to her world until she can figure out a way to escape their circumstances.

As for Molly, she's got her own plans on that front. When she takes one last, forbidden trip over the golden wall that separates The Hollow from the opulence of

Alabaster City in pursuit of a wealthy husband, disaster strikes. An evening in the arms of the Crown Prince turns violent, and the stiletto heel of Molly's glass slipper winds up buried in his chest. Stuck on the wrong side of the wall with a maniacal king who should be dead, an evil sorcerer, and his pack of undead soldiers called "jackals" on the hunt for the woman who fits the glass shoe, Harmony will have to rely on her wits to keep her and Molly hidden until they can plot their escape. And sometimes the best place to hide is in plain sight...

After creating disguises for them both and landing a position as the palace falconer, Harmony is forced to rely on an unlikely group of allies, including charming but secretive second-prince Duncan and The O'Donnellys —a family of smugglers who'd just as soon sell her for parts as help her escape. But danger lurks around every corner. Whispers — those who possess some measure of magic – still exist in Alabaster, and they aren't afraid to use their powers to ferret out the woman with the missing stiletto. As the walls start closing in, Harmony uncovers the monarchy's darkest secrets: The should-be-dead Crown Prince is actually being kept "alive" through black magic, and the people of both The Hollow *and* Alabaster City are puppets under the control of a sadistic sorcerer with a plan that has served him well for nearly a century...

Strip the poor of magic, leaving them too weak to resist.

Keep the rich too comfortable to bother.

Revolutionary spirit ignited, Harm realizes she can't just save her and Molly. She has to figure out how to tear the whole power structure down. And to do so, she'll need an army. When Prince Duncan offers his help, she wants to trust him, but there is no question he's hiding something.

Something big.

As the two grow closer and the Prince professes his love, Harmony's dreams about the dark, handsome stranger only grow more intimate. But, she needs to keep her head in the game if she has any chance of protecting her and Moll. After a series of missteps almost get them caught, Harmony realizes they are on borrowed time. She and the O'Donnelly's stage a rescue of those falsely imprisoned for Moll's "crime", and they finally make a run for it. But the sorcerer's jackals are hot on their trail. Prince Duncan comes to their aid, and we learn his secret. He is a Whisper himself with the amazing yet terrible ability to turn into a mindless fighting machine much like a Viking berserker at the cost of both his physical well-being and his sanity. He defeats the jackals, and they escape to join forces with famed revolutionary, The Speaker. Not quite a Shout, but far more powerful than a Whisper, The Speaker's abilities are second only to the sorcerer's himself. And, he's willing to give his life to tear down the gilded wall that separates the rich from the poor and bring magic back to the people.

Their group travels to a village The Speaker has built in the treetops far away, where there are hundreds of Whispers who have been waiting for Harmony's prophesied arrival to stage their coup. The Speaker gives her a magical jeweler's loupe to help her develop the true strength of her magic as a Tinker, who can see the inner workings of things and patterns that others don't.

But when she's unable to figure out how to truly connect with her Tinker magic, and a pissed off witch from the outside world starts trying to destroy the very fabric of their universe, it seems like a long shot.

Things only get more bleak when they meet up with the sorcerer and his jackals for the battle royale. As fighting reaches a fever pitch, The Speaker insists that Harmony leave so he can finish the job, and he finally reveals the whole truth. His destiny is to die here and take the evil Sorcerer down with him. Hers is to collect three magical items and learn valuable lessons on her journey that will help her defeat the enemy bent on destroying her.

She has both gained some knowledge of her circumstances as well as a magical jeweler's loupe, which allows her to see and manipulate the filaments of magic that make up the world to create even more complex inventions. She has done all she can in

Alabaster, and in order to complete her destiny, she needs to "turn the page" and move on.

Harmony, Molly and Fetch approach The Shadow Abyss and she knows she has to make the leap. But to do so, she must leave both this world and Duncan behind, and turn the page…literally. As The Speaker gleefully gives his life in a blaze of glory, Duncan encourages her to leap for the dog-eared edge of their flat "world" and turn the page, carrying her, Moll, and Fetch to the next tale in their adventure, leaving Duncan behind to rebuild his fractured kingdom…

CHAPTER 1

"*Enemy spotted off the starboard deck! Ready the cannons, and shoot to kill!*"

Water splashed into the air as Moll and I flailed in a desperate struggle to get away from the oncoming pirate ship. I thrashed wildly, treading water as I searched the evening horizon for any sign of hope, no matter how small, but found nothing but a sea of blue as far as my salt-battered eyes could see.

Only moments before we'd defeated the Sorcerer Relyk and his troupe of undead warriors in battle, and this still somehow topped that in terms of danger. Maybe there was a way to turn the page back? But even as I thought it, I knew it wasn't possible. At least not now. As ludicrous as it sounded, I knew one thing for sure:

I was meant to be here.

Daughter, tinker, pirate, mage...

Fetch let out a fierce shriek as a human-sized shape zipped through my line of sight, disappearing when I blinked.

"What the fuck!" I tugged on Moll's leg as I came to a full stop.

An adolescent flying mantis?

My heart stuttered as a cannon boomed to life, the thunderous crack reverberating through to my bones. I raised my arms to cover my face on instinct, dipping lower into the water as Moll let out a choked gurgle.

She pulled frantically at my arm as the first volley ended. "We need to keep moving!"

I cried out, but it was inaudible over the roar of the cannons.

We're going to die. The realization set in within a heartbeat, no longer feeling like a question. And what a place for it to end, after all we'd accomplished.

At least Duncan hadn't come, too. His dream of a better Alabaster wouldn't die. Not today.

A sense of peace washed over me as the first of the cannonballs hit the water with a mighty splash, just ten yards away from us.

"I love you, Harm!" Moll wailed, tightened her grip and yanked me close.

"Love you too, my friend."

I closed my eyes to say a little prayer when a wash of purple flashed behind my lids. I opened my eyes and squinted into the swirling waves of color that had surrounded us like a shield, eclipsing the galleon from view. My breath caught in my throat as I looked up to see the barrage of cannonballs slamming against it high above our heads with a muted *clink* before bouncing harmlessly away like pebbles against a brick wall.

Fetch screeched once again, bringing my attention upward a half second too late as a slim figure swooped down on me from above. Fingers dug into my shoulder before I could react, and I heard a soft, masculine grunt as I was yanked upward, out of the water.

"No!"

My stomach lurched as I shot into the sky, a narrow arm now wrapped around my midsection.

"We'll get you to safety. Just keep still, dang it!" the low voice murmured. A young man...who knew how to fly?

"But, my friend—" I started, cutting off as he gestured behind us.

A second figure was hot on our heels, pulling a wriggling, screaming Molly along with her. And, unlike the guy who'd grabbed me, this one was a female...with gossamer wings. Their pearlescent color changed from pink to peach to brilliant green as they moved.

"A fairy?" I breathed, my brain spinning like a top as it tried to keep up.

"You guessed it in one." He looked down at me to flash a wink.

My heart thumped in my chest as a screech pierced the night and another form came hurtling toward us.

Fetch, and he was on the warpath.

Oh fuck.

"No! Don't hurt him!" I shouted, praying I'd been quick enough as the fairy lifted her hand and golden dust sprang from her fingertips.

The falcon slowed and the fairy's frown faded. "Hurt him?" she said with a reassuring smile. "Wouldn't dream of it."

She blew into her hand, sending the dust curling in Fetch's direction, wrapping around him before fading away.

He'd been ready to defend me from the clutches of what he probably thought of as a much larger bird. But now, his head relaxed and the wings that had been tucked tight as he dove flared out as he fell into an easy rhythm just over head.

"Wh-what'd you do?" I asked, the terror fading, leaving behind a metallic taste in my mouth.

"Soothed him," she called, fluttering her fingers without looking back. "Now let's save the chatter for *after* we get out of here with our skins intact."

Another round of cannon fire added urgency to her words, and the man's grip tightened on my side as he brought his speed up a notch. I gritted my teeth, but the drag I'd been expecting never came. My legs swayed behind us in the wind, but there was nothing pulling me down. Rather than battling *against* gravity, it was as if he'd simply severed its hold on us entirely.

Just as incredible, though, was the endless sea churning beneath us. I'd seen paintings and heard stories, of course, but the scale went far beyond anything I could've imagined. As hard as it was to believe, we truly had toppled through the Shadow Abyss into another world. One with an ocean, and pirates, and fairies.

The thought threatened to overwhelm me, but I fought through the incoming panic.

First thing first, we needed a plan. Unless they'd been expecting us due to some magical intervention or prophecy of their own, eventually, they were going to ask where we came from. I needed to make sure I had an answer ready in hopes of cutting Moll off before she told them the truth.

Once I had an idea of what to say, I launched into the second part of the plan, which was gathering some info on our saviors to get the lay of the land.

"Who *are* you?" I asked after several minutes of trying to think of a more polite way to ask. The purple wall of magic had disappeared, and we seemed to be far out of cannon range now. "And how did you know that we needed help?"

"Peter Pan, and Tinkerbell. You can call us Pan and Tink," the man said, yanking me into a more secure position as if I weighed little more than a sack of flour. "And we didn't know you needed help. You just got lucky."

"What about that ship? Using cannons on two random swimmers seems like overkill."

He glanced over, cocking his head. Then, he let out

a laugh as the realization struck him. "Ah, you thought they were firing at you?"

I opened my mouth to reply, suppressing a wave of embarrassment. "They weren't?"

"Nope. That's Hook and his crew," he said gravely. "Pirates, and the worst of the lot. They've been after us for years."

"Surely you could beat them if it came to a fight, even with the cannons. You can fly. And that magic wall you guys put up earlier was incredible."

"Hook has plenty of tricks of his own. We're at a stalemate… for now. But no more chatter, we're almost home, and there's always a bit of turbulence here. I have to concentrate."

A gust of wind rolled through almost immediately as he said it, and I suppressed a gasp as I glanced down. A small island appeared below us, as if out of thin air. The wind buffeted at my ears as we hurtled toward the green stretch of land. On a normal day, it would've been terrifying, but, after all we'd been through, I felt like I'd used up all of the fear I could muster and was running on empty.

We touched down in a large clearing just a few minutes later. My knees went shaky as gravity regained its hold on me, and I dropped to my bottom with a grunt rather than fight it. Tink set Moll on the ground beside me a second later, and I let myself fully relax for the first time all day as Fetch latched onto my shoulder.

"We made it." I smiled as Moll leaned close to help me to my feet, tears welling up in her eyes.

She wrapped her arm around my shoulder as she let out a relieved breath. "Safe and sound."

"How did you wind up in the water, anyway?" Pan asked with a frown. "There's no land for miles…"

"We were just going fishing." I rushed to tell my fabricated tale before Moll opened her mouth, "and the tide pulled us out further than we expected. Then we got hit by a wave… Rogue. Big one." I spread my hands high and wide to hammer the point home. "It filled our little boat with water and that was the end of that. Good thing you guys came. We'd been swimming for what felt like hours." I gnawed on my bottom lip as I tried to think of how to change the subject. "Where are we, anyway?" For the first time, I noticed the mild weather that was as warm as any summer in Alabaster.

"Welcome to Neverland," Pan said, gesturing all around as Tink fluttered over to stand beside him. I tried not to stare, which was tough, what with this being my first time seeing a fairy or even knowing they existed. She was petite, several inches shy of five feet tall, but her curves made no secret that she was a full-grown woman. Her wide, violet eyes were framed by lush dark lashes, and her golden hair was pulled into a tail high atop her head, which she rested against Pan's bicep.

So they were a couple?

Interesting.

Something about them seemed like a mismatch. It wasn't that she looked older than him, exactly. But Pan's lilting voice and the boyish green cap perched on his auburn hair gave him an air of youthful innocence she didn't have.

There was no chance to dwell on it though, because an instant later, Pan was turning away with a frown.

"Now, at the risk of being rude, Tink and I still have a matter to attend to. Don't worry, though. Tink's magic makes Neverland impossible for outsiders to see, so as long as you're here, you won't run into any trouble—"

He broke off as the door to a large, thatch-roofed house at his back creaked open, revealing a pale, thin boy, who couldn't have been older than seven or eight. "Ah, perfect. Caleb, why don't you and the others show our guests some hospitality until Tink and I get back?"

The boy nodded, smiling as Pan reached down to ruffle his dark hair. "What should we show 'em?"

"They need a change of clothes, so let's start with that. You can grab some from the guest room. We shouldn't be long; we just had a run in with Hook and need to check where he's headed."

Caleb's face darkened at the use of Hook's name, and he nodded grimly. "Good luck." His gaze flitted toward me and Moll, his cheeks going beet red.

"This one can be a little shy," Pan said, chuckling as he nudged the boy in our direction. "Can't say the same for the other two, though…"

"Other two?"

"They'll be here any second, I'm sure. They've surely heard the commotion and they're far too nosy to ignore it." He spared a final glance toward the hut. "Feel free to make yourselves at home while we're gone. As the kids know, only our bedroom is off limits." He waggled his brows, turning to Tink as he said it.

She gave him a playful shove, rolling her eyes. "Stop that, Peter!"

The pair took to the sky in a flash without another glance in our direction, and I watched with awe as they zipped off into the evening sky.

"Hi, Caleb," Moll said, wiggling her fingers at the wide-eyed little boy they'd left behind. "I'm Molly, nice to meet you."

I opened my mouth to introduce myself as well, but my breath caught in my throat as I caught sight of the little girl that had just exited the hut behind him. Freckles dotted her face and her messy, white-blonde hair fluttered in the balmy breeze as she ran.

"Hallo!" she called as she raised her hand in greeting, pausing to elbow Caleb in the ribs. "Are you gonna introduce me, or cat got your tongue?"

It had been clear who she was from her appearance alone, but that voice sealed the deal.

"Cissy?" I croaked as I tried not to let the shock show on my face.

It seemed impossible, but the child in front of me

was none other than our neighbor from The Hollow, Cissy Petway.

CHAPTER 2

"It can't be," Molly whispered.

But it most definitely was. I'd seen the girl a week or so before on the cobbled streets of The Hollow…watched her get snatched by a flying mantis right before my eyes. Caught her as she'd fallen from the monster's clutches.

So what the fuck was she doing here, on the other side of The Shadow Abyss? Unless she'd dove off the edge like we had…

Cissy's face screwed into a scowl as she stopped in her tracks, cocking her head. "How d'you know my name?"

Not our Cissy then, or if it was, she didn't remember us.

"Pan mentioned it earlier," I lied, taking the opportunity to search her face more closely. My heart skipped a beat as I realized she was missing a scar over her right brow. She'd gotten it during an ill-advised sling-shot war with one of the boys in town a couple years back, and I distinctly remembered sewing it up for her. As I looked her up and down, it was also clear that she was a few pounds heavier. Her cheeks had lost that Hollow— hollowed—look, and her shoulders looked a hell of a lot less like a coat hanger. Whatever was going on here, she was clearly not the same Cissy Petway.

Somehow, the girl existed in both worlds at once.

But how? From those horrifying, black voids in the fabric of reality itself to the hints of prophecy that had led me here, it was becoming more and more clear that there were larger forces at play in my life that I couldn't even begin to grasp. If anything, this was one of the *least* strange of such occurrences, and if I let myself fall down this rabbit hole, I wasn't sure I'd ever make it out.

I pushed the matter aside and refocused on the scene in front of me.

Cissy led us toward the house with Caleb in tow. "Come meet Tristan. He's the most recent Lost Boy to come to Neverland."

"Is that what you call yourselves? The Lost Boys?"

Cissy nodded. "Yep."

"Shouldn't you change the name to the Lost Kids or something, since you're not all boys?" Moll asked.

Cissy shrugged and looked away. "It, um, already had that name when I got here." She shoved open the front door and went tromping in with Caleb hot on her tail. "Tristan?!"

I paused at the door, taking a glance down at my sand-caked pants and wet boots.

Moll sidled up next to me and we watched as another boy came trudging into the kitchen toward Cissy. He was a bit older than the other two, maybe eleven or twelve, and looked seriously irritated.

"Thought I told you I wasn't interested. I'm building my bookshelves so quit bothering me."

"Yeah, but I figured you probably changed your mind by now," she answered cheerily. "C'mon, Pan wants us to show these two around."

Tristan scowled, but then turned his attention to us and paused as his gaze locked on Fetch. "Fine... whatever."

Cissy grinned and then glanced toward Moll and me. "What do you want to see first? Our fire pit? Ooh! Maybe our fishin' spot?"

"How about we start with that change of clothes?" I tugged at the hem of the shirt that was plastered to my body with seawater.

Cissy flashed an accusatory glance at Caleb. "Weren't you s'posed to get that for them?"

He flushed, opening his mouth as if to respond, but she cut him off with a wave.

"No big deal." She turned back toward Moll and me. "I'll show you to one of the guest rooms."

I shot a glance at the gleaming, wooden floors and

winced. "Maybe a towel first? I'd hate to drag sand and sea water in…"

Cissy let out a snort. "Don't worry about that. Tink can just throw some pixie dust at it, and it will disappear like *poof*!" She blew into her hand and then splayed it wide. Cissy's nose crinkled as she leaned in closer and lowered her voice. "Don't tell her I told you, but I don't get why she makes us do so much boring chores when she can just use her magic."

"She says it will help us learn 'sponsatility and build character." Caleb was clearly offended on the fairy's behalf.

"Responsibility," Tristan corrected, rolling his eyes. "And, yeah, that's what she says, but I don't see her scrubbing floors to build *her* character."

"Maybe she already has enough character?" Cissy suggested, looking thoughtful.

He let out a snort. "Not likely."

"Take it back!" Caleb glared at Tristan, his little fists balled at his sides.

"What are you gonna do if I don't?"

"Do you guys like hide and seek?" Moll interjected, seemingly out of nowhere.

Cissy and Caleb exchanged a look and Caleb nodded, his fists unclenching. "Yeah, why?"

"Well, I've been wanting to play, but…" She let out a sad sigh and shook her head. "I'm so itchy in these salty clothes, and—"

Caleb stepped forward and grabbed her hand. "Come on!"

Thank the Gods for Moll—she knew how to deal with the littles far better than me. Twenty minutes later, I was sprawled with my legs hanging over the edge of a massive, wooden bathtub full of fresh, hot water, and it felt amazing.

"If I die here, I'm okay with it," Moll murmured from a second wooden tub the kids had dragged in just for us, on the other side of the checkered curtain that separated us.

"Same. I didn't realize how sore I was." A glance down confirmed I was basically one giant bruise from all the fighting and falling.

So much falling.

So much fighting.

I grimaced as memories of the battle at the Sky Tree flooded back. Total carnage, on both sides, all because of Relyk's lust for power. I sent up a silent prayer for Duncan, Sir Crispin, and The Speaker's band of Whispers. But, deep down, I knew that they would be alright. With the sorcerer and Heinrich dead, Alabaster's soldiers would have surrendered quickly, falling in line under their new king.

And what an improvement it would be. He might be a member of the royal family, but Duncan was as good a man as I'd ever met. Under his leadership, the people of The Hollow, The Smudge *and* Little Alabaster would prosper. It was just a shame I couldn't be there to see it.

A wave of regret washed over me as an image of his face shimmered to the forefront of my mind, but I forced it down. Maybe we'd meet again someday. Though in my heart of hearts, I knew that was a foolish hope. He was…somewhere else. Even now I didn't fully grasp what had happened, or how we'd gotten here.

I swallowed a sigh as an image of The Speaker's final stand came rushing back to my mind. We hadn't known each other for long, but I sincerely wished that I could see him again, too. Although it seemed like a lifetime ago, it had been just hours since we'd witnessed him sacrifice himself in a blaze of glory, taking Relyk with him. Despite the grief, there was something bittersweet about it. He'd *chosen* to go out that way, accomplishing his life's goal in his final act, while surrounded by those he loved. How many others could say the same?

I frowned, sloshing a bit of water over the sides of the tub as I reached for the still-damp pouch I'd set on the little stool beside the tub, a wayward thought circling to the front of my mind.

The magical jeweler's loupe. Had it fallen out at some point in all the madness?

My pulse thumped heavily in my ears as I reached for my bag, my hands ghosting over the pockets and through the interior as I tried not to panic. I sucked in a relieved breath as I felt the smooth curve of the brass exterior and tugged the loupe free. Such a tiny thing… yet it had changed the entire outcome of the battle against Relyk, allowing me to finally, truly unlock the magic inside me. I had no idea if I would need it again in this new place, but knowing I still had it gave me a small sense of peace.

I ran my thumb over the glass before slipping it back into the bag, pausing as my fingers brushed against a piece of damp paper. There were a few things in the bag, my incapacitator, a small dagger that my stepmother had given me, and an acorn from the Sky Tree that I'd taken in remembrance of my time there. But I didn't recall a note or—

Maybe Duncan had slipped it to me at some point before I'd left?

I unfolded it as gently as I could manage, letting out a sigh as I saw that, while the ink was a bit runny, it was still readable.

The day will come, so don't be late
  She's in The Hollow, to fulfill her fate
  Fair of face, with boots of red
  Her name is peace, A wizard's dread
  Daughter, tinker, smuggler, spy
  A falcon's heart, a jeweler's eye
  She's the one who holds the key
  To unlock the ring and set you free
  Shine a light and steal the dark
  Help her see, ignite the spark
  She alone cannot succeed

She needs you all to complete the deed
Then prince and pauper, hand and hand
To finish the job, to heal the land
Only then can she hope to turn the page
Daughter, tinker, pirate, mage.

FIGURED since you didn't have a whole lot of time to write it down or memorize it, this might come in handy. I also wanted to thank you for everything you did for our people. Sometimes, it seemed like I'd never find you, but in the end, it was worth the wait.

But as you already know...your work isn't done yet. There are other worlds, and other people who still need saving.

Including yours.

You're probably wondering where to start, and while I don't know much more than you do on that front, I did remember this. Several years back, a woman named Gayelette came to visit me claiming she was from The Smudge. A strong Whisper recognizes another, but I let her keep her secrets because it was clear she had a message that she asked me not to read until I found you:

"When the chosen one is able to turn the page, let her know that her success in this next world relies on her being on time. Outside forces are eating away at the very fabric of reality, and her people need her. The clock is ticking...but also not. She must find it to complete her journey so she can get back home before it's too late."

Not exactly sure what it means, but you'd better get at it. Whatever it is.

-The Speaker

P.S. No pressure, but I'm definitely going to haunt you if you don't do your best to fulfill the rest of your destiny.

I chuckled, wiping a tear from my eye as I slipped the note back into the bag and set it back on the stool. The ending bit had only confirmed what I'd suspected; he'd known he wouldn't make it out of the battle alive from the very start. Yet he was brave enough to do what needed to be done. Now, I needed to take my cue from him and do the same.

And, I needed to do it—whatever it was—pretty fast. Because apparently, my people needed me... But what people? My friends?

"Harm?"

I let my eyes drift shut, the weight of it all bringing me low as I replied to Moll. "Yeah?"

"Do you think that pirate ship was the same one that we saw on the wall of the amphitheater back in Alabaster?"

Still reeling from one shock after another, I purposely hadn't allowed myself to think that hard yet.

But, now that she'd brought it up, there was no point in trying to shove this genie back into the bottle.

"I couldn't see the flag from that distance in the dark, but it sure as hell looked like it."

An image of that massive, terrifying galleon firing cannonballs at us ran through my mind and I winced.

Daughter, tinker, pirate, mage...

Had I already fucked up beyond repair? Was I supposed to swim up and, I don't know, shake hands or introduce myself? Pretty hard to think straight what with all the trying-not-to-drown and attempted murder going on around me.

"What else do you remember about that fairytale book of yours from when you were a kid?" Moll pressed softly.

I pondered the question for a long moment before answering. "Some of the tales, I remember really well. Others, not at all. I didn't want to read the ones that looked scary. Why do you ask?"

"Well, because I'm starting to think we might be trapped inside of one just like it."

CHAPTER 3

An hour later, as we followed the children through the kitchen and back outside, I was still thinking about what Moll had said.

And the more I thought about it, the more sense it made. Crazy, utterly insane sense, sure, but still…

I wish I could've blamed it on the trauma from all I'd done and seen in the past week or so, but Moll had gone through the same, and more. And she'd still seen the connection before I had. The truth that had been right in front of my nose all along…

As insane as it seemed, when we had grabbed that dog-eared fold I had seen with the loupe, Moll and I had turned the *literal fucking page*, thrusting us into a whole new world.

One from my childhood fairytale book and, unfortunately, one I didn't remember at all. The image of the hulking pirate ship at the start of that story had scared me so much as a child that I'd never let my Pawpaw read it to me. Then, once my brothers had destroyed the book, it was too late to go back.

"If I hadn't been such a chickenshit and let him read it to me, we wouldn't be flying blind here," I muttered.

"Stop beating yourself up. You were like what, five years old? There was no way of knowing that the key to unlocking your destiny might have been inside that book and now it's gone forever."

Oof. When she put it like that, it sounded even worse. "Thanks?"

"Sorry," she added, reaching out to give my shoulder a squeeze. "I meant that you were just a kid. And you're not the one who threw it in the creek! That was your brothers' doing. *Not* your fault," Moll whispered as she dodged a sapling that came snapping back at us as we trailed behind Caleb, Cissy, and Tristan.

Once we'd finished our baths, the kids had gotten us clean clothes and some cold, fresh water. Now, me, Fetch, Moll, and the kids were headed to join Tink and Pan by the fire pit for some snacks, storytelling, and the promised game of hide and seek. My bare feet sifted through the soft sand and, although it was still warm from the day's sun, I found myself longing for my crimson boots. I'd done my best to wash them, and only hoped they were fit to wear again once they'd dried.

Duncan had given them to me...

Nope, don't go there.

Thinking about the man who gave those boots to me was a mistake and would only distract me from my purpose here. If he was meant to be a part of the rest of this journey, he'd have come along. I had to trust the process and focus on the here and now.

But, damn, was it hard to not wish he'd come with us. With me…

"Sometimes, we roast sausages, sometimes we roast nuts and fruit. Depends on whether we'd gone and gotten supplies from Blackbriar or are living off the island," Cissy explained over her shoulder as Moll and I sped up to match her near-sprint toward the smell of a campfire.

A soft *thunk* split the air as I stepped through a space in a circle of trees.

By the flickering light of the fire, I got a good look at Tink without the shroud of shock and terror hanging over me, and it stopped me in my tracks.

With her heart-shaped face and cupid's bow mouth, she was the most beautiful creature I'd ever laid eyes on. Her slim shoulders were bare in what could only be described as a mix between a bathing suit and a petticoat that came to mid-thigh. The sage green color would have washed out a lesser woman, but on Tink, it looked just like the rest of her.

Perfect.

Pan stood facing a tree in the distance, arm cocked, knife in hand as I approached. His arm shot forward in a blur, and cheers erupted as the blade buried itself in the trunk with a dull *thud.*

Cissy rushed toward him, holding her hand out for a dagger. "Me next!"

Pan grinned and shook his head. "After we eat you can all have a turn, alright? Our guests are probably starving."

Moll's stomach let out a deep growl, as if triggered by his words, and Pan let out a burst of laughter. "Well, at least Molly is."

Tink shot him a quick frown, and the grin faded as he cleared his throat.

Jealous one, was she?

"Please," Tink said, with a graceful wave of her arm, frown disappearing. "Come sit by the fire and let us feed you!"

It was only then that I caught the subtle scent of cooking spices melding with the wood smoke and salty air. Something with spring onions and roasting vegetables had my mouth watering. We made our way around the fire, where blankets and pillows were strewn about.

"I hope you don't mind. Tristan here has been working on some outdoor chairs for us, but they're not quite finished yet. Right, Tristan?" There was no judgment in Tink's voice, but the boy gave her no more than a clipped nod as if she'd scolded him.

We all sat as Tink reached for an oven mitt on a stone next to the fire and used it to pull the top off the massive pot tucked in the embers. The savory scent intensified, and I let out a groan.

"What is it? Smells like heaven."

"Just a simple one-pot meal I make that the kids and Peter and I all love. It's got wild garlic, leeks, and loads of vegetables. Some we grow here on the island, and some we get from the mainland, like the sweet potatoes and squash."

She made quick work of ladling us each out a portion into lovely little carved wooden bowls, and it took everything I had not to slurp it down the way I would've if Moll and I were alone.

I plucked a morsel of sweet potato from the bowl and held it out to Fetch, but he seemed uninterested, and instead leapt off my shoulder to hunt. More for me. There had to be loads of vermin for him to hunt here with the amount of fruits and vegetables they had on hand.

"Hunt safe, Fetch," I murmured before I poked the bite into my mouth, letting the delicate spices curl around my tongue. Silence reigned as we ate. It wasn't until I finished the last of the stew that I realized none of us had spoken a word in at least five minutes as we relished every bite of our food, which told me one thing;

Every single one of us had known hunger.

The realization gave me the courage to speak my mind. "So, are you all orphans like me, then?" I asked, taking a risk that they'd find the question offensive, but hoping they didn't, and I could get some easy answers.

The children all nodded as Pan and Tink exchanged a glance. Tink tipped her head toward him, as if giving Pan permission to speak.

"Yes. In fact, that's where Tink and I met. The Gentle Hand Asylum for Wayward Youth. It wasn't a good place." Pan's face, which had seemed to be wreathed in a perpetual smile up to this point, grew serious. I tightened my grip on my bowl, knowing in my gut that whatever came next was going to be difficult to hear.

"We had a really evil Headmaster...we called him The Warden because he treated us like prisoners. And he wasn't wrong, I guess. We were definitely stuck there. He was tough on us, especially the boys. We never had enough to eat, and nothing we did was ever good enough." He shook his head and let out a soft laugh. "Funny, when I was a young lad, even younger than Caleb, I remember wishing I could make him like me. Give me a smile or show me some small kindness." He stared into the flickering flames, as if lost in the past, before shaking his head slowly and looking up. "It never happened. But by the time I'd reached my teen years, I realized I didn't need him to like me. I just needed to do my time and get out of there without letting him break me. Even with that...I'm not sure I would've made it if Tink hadn't come along. She saved me."

Tink reached out and took his hand in hers, giving it a squeeze. "You didn't deserve that place, Peter. No child does."

Moll let out a sloppy sniffle, then swiped at her running nose, and I knew she was one more word from full-on, snot-sobbing. She was a tender heart, especially when it came to kids. No doubt she was picturing Peter as a little boy right now, and it was killing her.

"And the kids?" I murmured. "You decided you didn't want to see the same happen to them, so you brought them here. To raise them in the sunshine, food and people who care…"

"Exactly," Tink said with a smile. "These three aren't the first. We've had dozens come through over the past couple of decades. It's given Peter a purpose, and it's been nourishment for my soul, too."

I blinked, still caught up on the earlier part of that statement. Couple of decades? Peter didn't look much older than twenty or so. Tink must have seen my surprise because she wiggled her fingers and shot me a grin.

"We're a lot older than we look. It's the fairy dust, you know," she said as little golden sprinkles shimmered from her fingertips.

I shouldn't have been surprised. This world, like the one we'd come from, clearly had its share of magic. I wanted to ask more about how their magic worked, but I didn't want to seem overly curious. We had to at least try to fit in, like we'd been forced to do in Little

Alabaster after Molly had stabbed King Heinrich with the glass shoe. I was getting pretty good at trying to balance the need for information with the need to hide in plain sight.

Moll, on the other hand...

"So wait, I gotta know. How can you both fly? This guy doesn't even have wings!"

Luckily, neither Pan nor Tink took offense. In fact, he set down his bowl and leapt in the air, whirling, flipping and twirling over the sparks from the bonfire.

"Another thing I love about Tink! She didn't just save me; she shared her power with me, too. I'll never be anyone's prisoner. Not ever again."

He did one more loop-de-loop before drifting back down onto his pillow with a chuckle.

"Cool, huh?" Cissy scratched her nose as she set her bowl down with a clink. "I've been begging her to do me, too. But she says she can't. Peter gots all the extra magic she had. Sometimes he does take us flying, though," she added, looking slightly mollified.

Tristan sat with his empty bowl and head down, sparing a glance up in the sky, likely searching for Fetch, I would guess. Other than that, he remained still and quiet.

I turned and noted that little Caleb had nodded off, having only eaten half of his vegetable stew, and was nestled in his pile of blankets, snoring lightly.

"And why do you call them The Lost Boys?" I asked, lowering my voice as I held my hands in front of the fire, enjoying the warmth and the novelty of not being afraid for my life for a while.

"Well, that's how I felt before Tink," Pan said with a shrug. "Like I was lost. And when we started rescuing needy kids from orphanages over in Blackbriar, we thought it would be a fitting name for them."

"It was meant to be boys only, of course." Tink eyed Cissy with a mock glare. "This one here was a mistake."

"A happy surprise, remember?" Cissy corrected.

"Most definitely. I was only teasing you." Tink turned her attention back to me and Moll. "There were rumors about us over the years, you know. The children at some of the orphanages would climb out onto the rooftops in hopes of being next on the list of the mystical fairy. So Cissy here cut her hair, tucked it under a cap, made sure she dressed like a little boy, and waited."

"Every night for like two whole years," Cissy said with an indignant sniff.

"And when we eventually came around, about a year ago now, she was ready. It wasn't until we got her to the island, and she had her first bath that we realized we'd gotten ourselves a girl. Best thing that ever happened to me," Tink admitted with a soft smile.

Tristan's expression darkened, but Cissy giggled with glee.

I was trying to think of how to segue from talking about the kids to asking about even more pressing matters when Moll piped up. "And what about those pirates chasing you guys? What's that about?"

She was definitely a hammer rather than a chisel, but I couldn't say I was mad at her. My eyes were starting to droop with exhaustion, and we had so little information about where we were. And, if The Speaker's note was accurate, time was of the essence.

"Do you want to tell the story about Hook, or shall I?" Tink asked, arching a brow at Pan.

"Ooh, can Peter? He does it so good!" Cissy said, reaching down to snag one of the free blankets and wrapping it around her shoulders as she hunkered down to listen.

Pan leapt to his feet, so suddenly, so nimbly, that I nearly peed my pants in surprise.

"If you guys insist, I can go ahead and tell you. But hold onto your hats, because it's a doozy. A tale of trickery, treason, and treachery!"

Out of the corner of my eye, I could see Cissy mouthing the words along as Pan spoke. He must've told this one a lot.

"He wasn't always an evil pirate, you see. In fact, for years, we were friends. We'd sail together, go on adventures. Tink even sprinkled fairy dust on him so he could fly solo sometimes. Maybe that's where the seed was planted, and the quest for power was born." He folded his hands behind his back and began pacing around the fire. "I treated him like a brother, and he chose to—"

"Betray you!" Cissy interrupted, her animated face full of outrage.

Pan's mouth snapped shut and he gave Cissy a quick scowl. "As I was saying…he betrayed me!"

Pan looked at Molly expectantly and she hesitated, confused for a moment, before letting out a dutiful gasp.

"No!"

"Yes! It happened on a breezy, star-filled night. Tink and I had just finished supper, and realized that we weren't feeling well. Come to find out that Hook had snuck poison from the Widowmaker's leaves into our drinks, nearly killing us dead. Tink's magic was too strong for that, though. She was able to save herself and revive me. It was only then that we heard the commotion on the beach. We ran out to find Hook, setting sail on the first boat I'd ever built with my own two hands. He'd kidnapped two of our Lost Boys, Miguel and Tommy. The plan was to force them into a life of crime, which was awful enough." Peter crouched and lowered his voice. "But then I realized his betrayal went even deeper than I could've imagined."

Cissy let out a squeak and covered her mouth with both hands.

"Hook had also taken a one-of-a-kind, family heirloom. The only thing I had left of my mother in this world."

"What was it?" This time, the question came from a grudging Tristan, who seemed interested in spite of himself, in spite of probably hearing this story a hundred times already.

"A magical clock," Pan said with a flourish of his hands.

My hands went clammy, and I resisted the urge to turn and gape at Moll. Surely, it was no coincidence that my success in this new realm relied on me being on time. That I needed to find the clock that was ticking...but not.

"D-did you get it back?" I mumbled through numb lips.

"I tried. A fierce battle ensued as Hook and I both drew our swords and parried, feinted and slashed at one another," Pan said, *en garde* as he perched one hand on his hip and lifted the other to brandish an imaginary rapier. "I didn't want to kill him, not at first, but I couldn't let him take my clock and walk away. It was a fair and valiant fight. In the end, though, we both lost. Because Noru, gigantic croc of The Weeping Fen, took the decision out of our hands," Pan's lips twitched into a grin, "Especially Hook's, as he leapt from the water and snatched the clock, along with Hook's left arm from the wrist down, and dragged it back to his lair."

What the fuck...I'd been right not to want to hear this story when I was a child.

"So you're telling me this pirate, Captain Hook, had his hand bitten off by a giant crocodile?" I asked the question as Fetch swooped back down on silent wings, landing lightly on my shoulder. He was clean, but the tiny bulge in his belly told me he'd found his own dinner.

"Yup," Cissy said, eyes wide as she nodded and lowered her voice to an ominous whisper. "Noru, The Ticking Croc."

Molly let out a puff of laughter, but Pan continued, once again as serious as an old man trying to convince a younger generation that he was right, gazing out toward the ocean with a sweep of his hand.

"In order to buy himself time to escape, Hook ran his sword through young Miguel and left him to die before taking off with Tommy. Tink and I had a choice. Try to save Miguel or give chase. Of course, we chose Miguel, who later died from his wounds…rest his soul." Pan's eyes were filled with fire now as he lifted his chin and raised one fist. "To this day, Hook remains my archnemesis as we continue to scour the seas for Noru and the clock. Rumor has it that Hook has killed dozens of men and women in his efforts to get the clock, his heart only growing blacker over the years as he slashes his way from sea to sea, going through anyone who tries to stop him."

"Even with only one hand?" Molly asked.

Cissy leapt up, curling the fingers of her left hand. "He's got a hook now, instead of a hand! Sharp as a dagger, harder than steel!"

Of course he did.

He must've been a formidable foe if even Tink, with all her magic, hadn't been able to put an end to his reign of terror. Didn't exactly bode well for me and Moll trying to join the fray in this hunt for the magical clock.

Because I was a thousand percent sure that was what I needed. And the fact that I found out about it so quickly made me nervous.

Easy to identify?

Check.

Hard as hell to *actually* get my hands on?

Yeah, that's what I thought too.

I touched Fetch's side to reassure myself that he was still there. He could help scout to locate this thing faster. Speed was of the essence, if The Speaker was right with what he'd said in his letter, and I had no reason to doubt him.

I was trying to figure out how to ask exactly what made the clock so magical, but Tink stood and began collecting our bowls, cutting my thoughts short.

"Alright, that's enough about all that. Leaves a bad taste in my mouth, and besides, I'm sure Harmony and Molly don't want to hear the gory details."

To the contrary, I wanted as many details as possible that I could get, but Pan was nodding in agreement with Tink.

"Tink is right," he said with a sigh. "We've kept our guests up late enough. I'm sure they're exhausted after all those hours floating in the sea and trying not to drown."

"But we didn't even get to play hide and seek with Molly yet," Cissy murmured, her bottom lip trembling.

"They aren't going anywhere, sweetie," Tink said, stroking the little girl's hair gently. "I'm sure Molly and Harmony will play with you tomorrow."

Cissy stared down at her feet, digging her bare toes into the sand. "Can we each get a try at throwing the knives before we go to bed like you said? Pretty please?"

"Sure," Pan replied. "Everyone, line up behind Harmony and Molly! Guests first, of course." He bent low, into a deep bow, and presented the small, gleaming dagger on his palm like an offering.

"Thank you, kind sir." I stood, accepting it with a half-smile. I could've told him I had my own tucked in the bag I'd tied around my waist, but something held me back. It was like my brain was still stuck on the story he'd told and the details that for some reason didn't quite fit, though I couldn't put my finger on it. Fetch must've sensed my unrest because he nuzzled close to my neck.

Thanks, little buddy.

"I'll give it a try, but I'm nearly cross-eyed with exhaustion, so don't hold your breath that I'm going to hit *that* tree, or any other."

"Do you want me to watch your falcon for you while you throw?"

I turned, surprised to see the words had come from the oldest boy, Tristan, who now stood behind Cissy.

"I appreciate it, but he's a little shy around new people. He'll more likely take to the skies for a bit."

As I stepped to the line that had been drawn in the sand as a marker, Fetch did exactly that. I sucked in a breath and prepared to throw, more out of politeness than anything. I couldn't wait to get in bed and have a good long think about all that had happened since we'd left Alabaster.

But now that I'd drawn close enough to get a look at the target, my ears started ringing so loudly, I couldn't even think, never mind aim. Because there, nailed to the ashy bark of the tree, was a large poster labeled 'Wanted, Dead or Alive: Captain Hook'. And the familiar, coal-black eyes staring back from the picture below sent a wave of heat through my stomach and a chill down my spine.

Captain Hook—the dreaded, murderous pirate?

Was the very same man I'd been dreaming about for years.

Because of course he was…

CHAPTER 4

I was a stranger in a strange land who had been rescued by a fairy and a flying man-boy, and then brought to some fantastical island. Yet all I could think about was a pirate who I'd never met but came to me in dreams.

Captain Hook.

How had I not realized he and the man Pan had spoken of were one and the same?

No…I'd have remembered if the man in my dreams had a hook in place of his left hand. Was that because things were different in dreamland? Surreal, warped versions of reality?

Or, was it because I hadn't been dreaming of Captain Hook at all, but some doppelganger of the evil pirate instead. One who was somewhere out there in another world, right now, ladling soup out to orphans or building a commune for needy widows?

All night long, I thought about it. About him.

I buried my face in my pillow and let out a groan. Fucking hell...Did a deadlier sounding name even exist?

"Evil McKillface maybe?" I muttered as I squeezed my eyes closed.

All my life, I'd been haunted by the secrets of my past. Wishing I'd known where I'd come from, who my true parents were, and why I'd been sent to The Hollow. Always thinking I was an orphan from Bryngarde or Valencourt.

Now, though? After a week of the universe pummeling me with cryptic answers about who I was and who I was meant to become... After finding out that the man whose eyes made my insides weak—whose voice made my stomach twist in the best/worst way—was a pirate who had murdered a fucking *child*?

Maybe being a woman of mystery was the better option...maybe I could turn the page *back,* and return to Alabaster, stay with Duncan and my friends there. Return to the mew and take care of the other hawks like Shira, or sassy, snow-white Bonnie...

"Are you getting out of bed or what, lazy bones?"

I let out a shriek as I jerked my head from the pillow to find Moll's face four inches from mine.

"Fuck, Moll, I didn't even hear you come in. You scared the shit out of me!"

"I know, right?" she said with a wide grin. "Quiet as a mouse. That's because the weather's so beautiful here in Neverland, you don't even need shoes." She lifted a sand-covered foot and wiggled her toes. "Don't even get me started on the joys of not having to wear that awful fake leg. Check this out," she added, handing me a half-sphere that was brown and fuzzy on the outside and hollow and white on the inside.

I took it from her gingerly and took a sniff. It smelled good, but I was still wary.

"You eat the soft white part," she encouraged, looking far too excited for me to say no.

I sunk my teeth into the tender flesh of the fruit and tore a bite off. "Pretty good," I agreed, savoring the sweet, milky taste before leaning forward on my elbow to take another bite. "What's it called?"

"Coconut. There are loads of trees on the south side of the island, practically bursting with them. You either gotta climb the tree or wait till they fall. I collected eight of them off the ground in the past half hour. You could live off the land here, fat and happy, no problem. It's like heaven. So different than The Hollow."

And by the look on her face, that would be fine by Moll. I searched for a hint of the woman she'd been back in Alabaster and wanted to kick myself when a crease of worry appeared between her eyes.

"Don't look at me like that, Harm." She snatched her coconut back. "The sun is shining, the breeze is balmy, the kids are laughing, and I don't want to think about anything that happened before we got here. Give me one day of peace. One day to pretend that life isn't a pile of shit-stew most of the time, can you do that for me?" she asked, her tone pleading.

It was hard for me to deny her anything, least of all this. She'd been through a lot, more than I had even known—a fact I was still kicking myself for. It was only a couple days ago that she'd finally worked up the courage to tell me the full extent of what Heinrich had done to her.

Even now, I'd give up my own leg for ten minutes in a room alone with the bastard just so I could see him die all over again.

It took a second to tamp down the bubbling rage before I spoke. "We're going to have to figure out how to get to that clock before anyone else does, and it's got to be soon," I murmured.

Her shoulders slumped, and her face fell as I took her free hand and gave it a squeeze.

"But you're right, it doesn't have to be today."

Not for her, anyway. Because it was going to take me some time to figure out exactly how I was going to get us off the island so I could try to beat our new friends and a murderous pirate to the punch when it came to hunting down a giant, clock-eating crocodile.

I also needed to find out what our time limit was exactly. A week? A month? A day?

Fuck. Please don't let it be a day.

I swallowed past the lump in my throat as I tried not to think of Pan's tale about his mother's beloved clock or how shitty it felt to know that I was going to do my level best to steal it right out from under him.

"How about I get dressed and see if our hosts can spare one more set of clothes so we can go swimming in ours?"

She lit up again, her good mood back tenfold. "Yes! That sounds perfect!"

We hadn't managed to see everything the night before, but so far, it was pretty impressive. Plenty of food, a constant, warm breeze, and best of all, unlike in Alabaster, we'd had the chance to get a full night's sleep without fearing we might be woken up by guards dragging us to the gallows.

Judging by her glowing skin and chipper mood so far, Moll looked like she'd taken full advantage of that opportunity. As for me, my head was pounding, and I had more grit in my eyes than was on that beach out there. And it was all because of the man in that damned poster. Hook.

"Still thinking about him, huh?" Moll asked as she plopped down beside me at the edge of the bed. "I have to admit, when you mentioned those dreams to me, I didn't realize he was *that* good looking."

"And here I am, more taken aback by the fact that the man I've spent more hours dreaming about than I can count is actually a murdering pirate," I growled, sparing a glance at the door and dropping my voice to a whisper. "I've been kind of hoping he's like Cissy. In two places at once, you know?"

"Ooh, yeah, that would be good." Her eyes shot wide. "Wait, you don't think that could happen to one of us, do you?"

The thought had occurred to be, but because my brain was close to exploding already, I'd ignored it completely.

"At this point, we have to assume anything is possible."

"Well then we need a special handshake or something. A way that we always know if we're talking to the *real* us or some two-bit phony." She grabbed my hand and demonstrated. "It's two firm shakes, slide up, grip the wrist, then pull back down until we're almost not touching...annnnd sizzle fingers!" She wriggled her fingertips against mine and tossed her hand in the air with a flourish. "No way anyone else is gonna walk up to you and do *that*."

I couldn't argue with her there.

"Now that we've gotten that critical task out of the way, back to Hook. We've got to make sure that the fact that he looks familiar doesn't leave this room. Got it?"

We'd been welcomed and treated like honored guests by two people who were waging an all-out war with the man in question. The last thing we needed was Pan and Tink thinking we knew the guy...or worse, that we were spies working on his behalf or something. After all, how was I going to betray their trust if they didn't trust me?

My stomach roiled and I let out a groan.

"Mum's the word." Moll pressed her thumb and forefinger to her lips, gave them a twist, and threw away the key, but we both knew how reliable *that* lock was.

"Seriously, Moll. It's crucial. Possibly life and death, even."

"Okay, okay. I got it. And I'm sorry for teasing you about him. I was wrong. Not about his looks," she added hurriedly. "Obviously, he's a stone-cold fox. But for teasing you about the dreams. I can't imagine how frustrating it must be to not know exactly where you're supposed to be, and what you're supposed to be doing, but *also* knowing that if you don't get there and do it, the whole world as we know it could end." She looked around the room and lowered her voice to a whisper. "Heck, we don't even know what other worlds exist. Ever since the Cissy Petway thing, my brain has been boggled."

"Same." I swung my legs over the side of the bed and stretched my back. What if there was another Duncan Westerly somewhere here in Neverland…

Another *Heinrich* Westerly? Yet another reason for my insomnia.

Stop borrowing trouble, woman.

I shoved the thought aside and stood just as the pitter patter of little feet skittered down the hallway. A second later, Cissy Petway and Caleb came sliding to a stop just outside our door.

"Do you guys wanna go fishing with us?" Caleb asked, his cute little lisp making my mouth twitch.

"We were just going to go for a swim—"

"Ooh, we love swimming!" Cissy said, elbowing Caleb hard in the gut, causing him to nod in agreement.

"Yeah, we love swimming." He didn't look quite as sure about that as Cissy did, but this Cissy was just like the one back in The Hollow. A hard taskmaster who made sure her minions toed the line. At least some things hadn't changed.

"All right," Moll said, waving the kids out of the room as she made her way towards the door. "We need to let Harmony wake up and get a bite to eat, then you can show us around the island before we do some swimming and fishing. So long as Pan and Tink are okay with that?"

"They will be," Cissy said. "We just have to make sure we collect some firewood first."

"Why don't I help you two, and we'll do it doubly fast?" Moll reached out to ruffle Caleb's dark hair.

Both kids squealed with delight, and the three of them scampered off.

I was bent at the waist, stretching to ease the dull ache in my back from falling out of the sky and slamming into the water at a trillion miles an hour, when a low voice spoke from the doorway.

"Oy."

I jerked upright to find Tristan standing just outside

the room with Fetch perched on one shoulder, looking strangely comfortable.

"I think your bird likes me."

"Huh," I said, surprised. "He does seem to like you."

Fetch hadn't shown the same regard for Tink or Pan, and he and Moll had never reached the 'perched comfortably on her shoulder' stage, even after all these years. He *had* grown fond of Duncan pretty quickly, though…

The thought sent a shaft of pain through my chest, the wound too fresh to dwell on.

Instead, I focused on Tristan, the young man who seemed to have replaced the chip on his shoulder with my falcon. It was then that I noticed the greasy morsel in the boy's hand.

"Ah, you found the way to his heart. He's not won over easily, but catching him a fish is a good start."

"He caught it for me, actually."

I stared at the boy, mouth wide.

"What do you mean?"

"Well, I was walking the beach looking for some driftwood for some shelves I'm working on and saw Fetch flying over the water. I saw a school of mackerel splashing around in the distance, and I let out a whistle and pointed to it. Wouldn't you know, he did a one-eighty, dove down and came up with this sucker right here. Cooked it over an open fire, and that's what we had for breakfast."

Fetch had never been a great fisherman, but clearly, he'd wanted to impress Tristan.

Interesting.

The falcon plucked the last bit of food from Tristan's hand and gulped it down before cleaning his beak on his feathers. Tristan shuffled from foot to foot, head cocked.

"Are you guys gonna stay a while?" he blurted, lifting his head and holding my gaze with an intense stare.

"I'm not sure," I hedged. It was a lie. Fate had brought us to Neverland, but I had that same gut feeling that our time on the island would be short. Guilt poked at me hard as the hope in his eyes died. "It seems like a pretty nice place, with some pretty nice people, so who knows?"

He nodded slowly and opened his mouth to speak, but before he could, another voice chimed in.

"I realize you had a bit of a day yesterday, but we don't want these eggs to get cold now, do we?" Tink sidled up next to Tristan. Not unlike the first time I'd seen her, for an instant, her beauty actually took my breath away.

"Sure, I could eat some eggs, if it's not too much trouble."

"Already made, no trouble. The chickens were good to us this morning so there's plenty," Tink chirped, sparing a glance at Tristan and Fetch. "You should head out and help your brother and sister with the firewood.

Fair's fair," she said with a wink before turning on her heel and making her way back down the hall towards the kitchen.

"Not my brother and sister," Tristan muttered under his breath, the chip sliding neatly back into place on his shoulder. I stayed quiet, unsure of what to say as the boy stroked the downy feathers on Fetch's belly.

There was clearly some jealousy or a family dynamic that I hadn't yet seen a reason for...

And you won't be here long enough to find out about it, I reminded myself grimly.

By the time I scarfed down a breakfast of fresh eggs and fruit, I was feeling a little less guilty and a lot more amenable to spending the day with the children. Molly would be able to relax, and I would be hurting exactly no one as I kept my ears and eyes peeled for any information we might be able to use.

As scary as our original introduction to it had been, I couldn't deny that the aquamarine water surrounding the island was like something out of a dream. In fact, the whole place was kind of like a paradise. The morning passed in a blur as the kids showed us around the northern part of the island, pointing out landmarks and things to look out for.

Like the Widowmaker, a spindly-looking black and red plant with enough venom to kill you if you were stupid enough to be lured in by its vermillion, razor-sharp leaves. And the cave at the far end of the island that was infested with bats. And the little copse of brambles behind the house where the sand wasn't really sand at all. It was more like a trap that would suck you in so the island could swallow you whole.

Apparently, though, the little cove that surrounded Neverland wasn't nearly as fraught with danger as the land or the open sea. As long as we stayed within a hundred yards, we were free to swim without fear of getting eaten by a sea monster, which was nice. And, when we finally hit the crystalline blue water and dove beneath the surface, there were a few moments where I almost forgot that any place else existed.

Colorful fish flitted by in flashes of orange, yellow, and silver. I dove closer to the bottom, reaching out a hand to a creature shaped like a star before pulling away. Safe from sea monsters didn't mean safe from everything. There were definitely things in Neverland that could kill you, and if I hadn't let a reanimated rotting corpse infested with blowflies take me down, I sure wasn't about to let some adorable but poisonous sea star trick me.

I kicked my way to the top, sucking in a breath as my face surfaced.

"You sure can hold your breath for a long time, can'tcha?" Cissy Petway observed splashing water a few feet away.

"I guess I can, yeah."

"Did you grow up next to the sea?" she asked.

Until they'd plucked us out of it, I'd never even seen the sea, but I wasn't about to admit all that. "I didn't, but I did spend a lot of time fishing in creeks and ponds during the summer months."

"Well then, let's make it a contest. Hey, Caleb!" she called, cupping her hand around her mouth. "We're gonna do a fishing contest!"

Caleb kicked and flailed furiously a few yards away, barely keeping his head above water as Moll stood three feet behind him, both hands at the ready in case he went under.

"M-maybe we should swim back to shore and start right now," he sputtered.

I bit back a smile and began to paddle my way back toward the beach.

We dried ourselves off with some towels and then set about catching bait. Caleb, Moll and Tristan worked on trapping minnows in a net while Cissy and I dug for worms.

"Sure, bait fishes are good for catching some big ones," Cissy said, perching the tip of her tongue on her upper lip as she dug deep into the soft dirt by the tree line, "My dad always said, worms ain't fancy, but they're as close to a sure thing a man can get when it comes to fishin'.'"

Her hands slowed and she cleared her throat before looking up at me and forcing a smile. "Oops. He's dead now, and I'm not supposed to talk about him. Don't tell Tink."

A sharp pain stabbed at my chest, but I tried not to let it show as I nodded. "Of course not."

Leave it be, Harm. This is none of your bus-

"Can I ask why?"

"Why he's dead?" Cissy started digging again and shrugged. "He got real drunk and tried to steal our neighbor's cow. Mr. McClachi thought he was a wolf so he sicc'ed the hounds on him and they tore him to pieces."

I bit my lip, trying not to let the image of that form in my mind. "Sorry, I meant why you're not supposed to talk about him."

She screwed up her face and settled back on her bottom. "Tink says men who are mean to little girls aren't worth our tears." She lifted her gaze, eyes glassy. "But he wasn't that mean. Not most of the time. And I really miss him..."

I dropped the handful of dirt I was holding and reached out to take her hand. "I lost my dad too. He wasn't perfect, but man, did I love him. It's okay to miss your father, Cissy. And if you ever need someone to talk to about him, I'm here."

I wanted to bite my tongue off the second I said it. Because I wouldn't be here. The second I got the chance, me and Moll would be in the wind. I was just another adult she was soon to be abandoned by.

Do not get close, damn it.

I moved to pull away and then paused. She had a tiny little mark on the inside of her wrist...

No. Not a mark.

A tattoo.

"What is that?" I asked before I could stop myself.

"That's my magic." She brightened suddenly. "I'm Tideblessed. See," she pointed to the tattoo with one grubby finger. "It's a vine with a droplet of water."

Tideblessed.

"So the vine means…?"

"I'm a Blossom. I can make things grow. Not real good yet, but someday." She looked away and sniffled. "I know it doesn't seem as good as being a Mend, but Tink says it's way cooler, and everyone will think so once I'm older."

I ran my finger over the tattoo and paused. There was definitely something there. An energy…a sizzle under my fingertip.

"And you were given this tattoo when?"

She frowned and laughed. "I was born with it, a course, like all the Tideblessed."

"What about Caleb and Tristan?"

She shot a glance over her shoulder toward the shore where the others were still netting up bait fish, and then leaned closer. "Caleb has one. It's of the sunrise, but it's really faded. I think it might be because his Tideblessing just isn't that strong. And I don't know about Tristan. Never seen it if he has one, and he don't talk much."

"What about Pan and Tink?"

She shook her head. "Nah. Tink's a fairy, and Pan is…" she scrunched her nose. "I don't actually know what Pan is. He's magic, but I never asked if he was Tideblessed. Want me to ask for you?"

"No, no. That's okay. I was just curious."

She cocked her head and stared at me for a long moment. "Did you used to live near Bolton Street?"

I drew back with a frown. "No. Why do you ask?" I wasn't about to tell her I didn't even know where Bolton Street was…or anything else in this place.

"Me and my dad lived there. It's weird…just right this second when you were real close to me, I felt like I knew you…before." She pulled her hand from mine and absently touched her forehead.

On the exact spot of the cut she'd gotten the day the mantis had taken her.

I shivered and waited, my whole body on high alert. Did this Cissy have some sort of connection with Cissy from The Hollow? Would her memories come rushing back?

But she just shook her head and shrugged. "Tink says my imagination is too big sometimes. I gotta squish it down a little."

I smiled and ruffled her hair. "I think a great imagination is a gift, so don't squish it down too much, okay?"

She grinned and then let out a squeal, pointing to a worm poking its head…or tail from the dirt. "There's a big fat one!" She was distracted easily enough, but I found myself dwelling on this new information.

This place had magic users just like Alabaster

except instead of Whispers, here, they called them Tideblessed.

And maybe, just maybe, if a person existed in both worlds, they shared some memories?

Or, Tink was right, and the little girl had a big imagination.

"We've got loads of bait, come on!" Molly called from the beach.

I tucked away what I'd learned to chew on later and gave Cissy a grin. "Ready for me to beat you at fishing or what, little miss?"

The last remnants of sadness after talking about her father seemed to melt away as she shot to her feet.

"I'd like to see you try!"

The rest of the afternoon was a haze of sunshine, laughter, and joy that soothed the ragged edges. Even Tristan had joined the fun. The five of us didn't get back to the big house until the sun was nearly setting, and we piled into the kitchen, sun-burned and giggling.

"I was watching you guys reel 'em in! Seemed like a close race. What's the final count?" Pan asked with a grin.

He was seated on the countertop, legs criss-crossed, watching Tink as she stirred something in a large pot on the stove.

"I supervised, as I don't much have the stomach for it." Molly raised a hand with a sheepish smile. "And Harm had a little trouble with casting into the waves, so we only got three between us. The kids beat us by a longshot."

"I got five and Caleb got three!" Cissy crowed, tucking her thumbs under the straps of her sandy, damp overalls.

Tink let out a gasp, set down her spoon, and pulled her in for a hug. "That's my girl!" She pulled back, her perfect little nose wrinkling just slightly as she let out a chuckle. "Why don't we let the others clean those fish to go with dinner, and we'll get you in the bathtub and into some fresh clothes. You can even try the new gardenia oil I made last week. It smells like paradise."

"We all washed off under the waterfall. I'm clean!"

"My nose is telling me otherwise. You need some soap, my dear."

Cissy stared longingly at us and then at the fish but then gave a grudging nod. "Alright." The two headed off down the hall, leaving the rest of us to finish dinner preparations.

"What about you? How many?" Peter asked Tristan.

"I got eight."

"Nice. I've got to pick some greens for our salad." Peter snatched a basket off the countertop next to him and leapt to his feet. "The big table out front is our cleaning station. The boys will show you where to put the guts and such."

He made his way out the door a moment later and I spared a look at Tristan, who stared after Pan. Fetch was once again perched on his shoulder, and I resisted the urge to reach out and ruffle the boy's hair. He probably wouldn't appreciate the gesture, but I couldn't deny that Fetch wasn't the only one this kid was growing on. He'd come out of his shell as the day had unfolded, offering tidbits of knowledge about the local wildlife that he himself was still learning.

Apparently, he'd only come to Neverland two months before, while the others had been here longer. I'd wanted so badly to know his story. Had his parents died in a tragic accident? Had they left him because they couldn't care for him? Or had he spent his life wondering, just like me? But I forced myself not to ask any of that.

Don't get attached, dummy.

I'd made that mistake last time, and now I was paying the Piper. His price? Pain.

I knew better now. I'd have to be a real fucking idiot to let myself care about any of these people when I knew they were just another steppingstone on my treacherous path to the end game.

I barely heard the little voice in my head that whispered…

It's too late…

CHAPTER 5

"Cissy never has to clean the fish," Caleb said, rolling his eyes as he led the way back outside and tugged the leather cover off what looked like a large butcher's block.

"It'll go fast. Plus, we have Fetch on cleanup." The falcon dipped his head as if he'd understood exactly what I'd said, and was ready for a duty only he could love.

We'd just begun chopping heads and scraping scales when Moll broke into a cheery song.

"Therrrre once was a lady named Mary, who farmed by the sea—it was airy. She milked all the cows and planted her wheat, but goats ate her socks right off of her feet! Soooo, sheee went to the shore for some rest, till a crab pinched her toes—what a pest! It was then that she knew, she needed a shoe—"

"Maybe two!" Caleb cried out.

Moll nodded and beamed. "But the animals weren't impressed…"

Tristan's lips twitched as Caleb erupted into full belly laughter.

As the others started plotting a second song, this one about a mermaid, I found myself softly whistling the tune to the first as I worked. While my time in Alabaster had given me a taste of what it felt like to have enough food, I was still tickled by the gleaming, apricot-colored fillets in the basin and the smell of the soup bubbling on the stove just inside the door.

"We're almost done here. Anybody want to help me make a quick dessert?" Molly flicked a glance around at each of us. "Tristan, do you think your…uh, Tink and Pan would mind if I used some flour, sugar, and an egg or two?"

"They won't mind," Caleb said. "Tink loves sweets. And I want to help but I'm not feeling so great all of a sudden."

As I lay the last cleaned fillet on the block, I turned to see the little boy swaying on his feet, cheeks pale despite a day in the sunshine.

Tristan was rubbing a thick slab of soap on his hands and sudsing up as he pursed his lips and spoke out of the corner of his mouth, for my ears only. "He doesn't feel good a *lot* of times."

Oh no. Was Caleb chronically ill? Or worse? There were some scary things on the island. Maybe something was making him sick? That might explain why his tattoo was fading…

I spared another glance over my shoulder as Molly pressed the back of her hand to the little boy's forehead and frowned.

"No fever. Let's see if Tink thinks it's a good idea for me to bring you supper in bed. I'll even stay and tell you a story, hmm?"

I closed my eyes in an effort to hide the hot rush of tears for the boy. It was probably nothing. Kids were always wiping their boogies on everything and forgetting to wash their hands, passing germs back and forth. I was overtired, overwrought, and *over*reacting.

A good night's sleep, and I'd be right as rain. Of course, that was what I thought yesterday too.

"You got some fish guts on your shirt." Tristan's lips tipped into a ghost of a smile. "I'm gonna start frying up these guys, but there's a whole closet full of clothes in the empty room in the west wing of the house. Tink said to make yourself at home, so help yourself."

I made quick work of washing my hands and then went to hunt for some clean clothes in the sprawling house. When I got to the great room, for the first time, I noticed the second hallway on the wall opposite mine and Moll's room.

"This place is even bigger than it looks on the outside."

I hurried down the dark corridor and made a beeline for the open door at the end of the hall.

Until I didn't.

As I passed a large, ornately carved door to my left, my feet stopped moving of their own accord. Probably the master suite, given that it was the only door on that side of the hall, alluding to a massive space.

Keep it moving, toots. Nothing to see here...

But I found myself frozen in place. Blood rushed to my head as I glanced behind me and reached gingerly for the doorknob. I made to turn it, but it didn't budge. Not that I'd expected it to, really.

Still...

I bent low and reached into my bag for my lock pick when Pan's voice echoed through the house.

"Supper will be ready in ten minutes!"

My heart nearly jumped out of my chest as I shoved the lock pick back, and rushed the rest of the way down the hall. That was beyond foolish. I'd seen exactly how powerful Tink was, and what she displayed so far probably hadn't even scratched the surface. She'd been nothing but kind to me, and I already had to betray her and Pan in the worst way, if I was going to get the clock and fulfill my destiny. Why was I so intent on tempting fate on top of it?

I was still catching my breath when I stepped into the room at the end of the hall, only to lose it again when I got my bearings.

The space was large and empty, but for a single armchair in the corner. The walls, though? They were riddled with countless maps, drawings, and little swatches of cloth and pieces of parchment pinned in place with pen knives.

I spun in a slow circle, trying to take it all in, but it was so overwhelming. My temples started to throb and I closed my eyes as a familiar panic closed over me.

"Nope," I muttered under my breath. "Nope, that's not what we do anymore. Don't fight it, Harm. *Use* it."

I pulled in a shuddering breath and forced my eyes open. Forced myself to *see* through the panic. And then there it was, like…magic. What had been jumbled and chaotic came into sharp focus.

Neverland, and all the waters and land masses that surrounded it. Noru, The Ticking Croc, sightings, plotted points of run ins with Hook, trade routes, and the changing tides and waning moons. Trophies from battles won, notes on battles lost, clues about future plans…

It was all there.

I just had to take a mental picture, and tuck it away in my mind until I needed it…

"Harmony? You alright?"

I swallowed hard at the sound of Pan's voice, wondering if it seemed as loud to him as it did to me. "Yeah, I came in for some clean clothes and just…I've never seen anything like this. It sort of stopped me in my tracks."

Pan crossed his arms and cocked his head as he looked around the room.

"Hmm, it does seem like a lot, now that you

mention it. Shows you how serious I am about getting that clock back, though, doesn't it?"

"It sure does."

"But it's only a matter of time, now." He shot me a wink and lowered his voice to an exaggerated whisper. "We've got 'im now."

"Noru?" I frowned, confused.

"Yup. See, he only comes out when the sun rests, during Ebonfall. Which means we've got two, three days a year where we can get a shot at him. But last time he came out of his lair, we managed to mark him with Tink's magic. She sprinkled some fairy dust onto my arrows. I fired five shots, near miss, every time. But the last one connected and pierced his hide. Got him right in the throat." He shrugged. "Probably didn't even hurt him, but who cares? We *marked* him. He's due to resurface in a couple of weeks, and we will be able to track him. We're going to set a booby-trap like you've never seen." He rubbed his hands together and let out a chuckle. "It's going to be amazing!"

There were times that he seemed as much an adult as I was. Then, there were times that something about the way he acted made him seem as young as he looked. Like now.

"That sounds like a really good plan."

Too good of a plan, actually. And it gave me my timeline. Moll and I had two weeks, until the next Ebonfall, to find Noru and beat Pan and Tink to the chase.

Fuck.

Talk about a ticking croc…

I cleared my throat and managed a smile as I gestured toward the closet. "I apologize if I held supper up. I'm just going to grab those clothes and change, then I'll be right there, okay?"

"Sure. But like I say to the boys, don't dilly-dally. Nobody wants to eat cold fish!"

With that, he waltzed out of the room, leaving me alone with my thoughts.

I dressed in record time, not even looking at what I'd grabbed, then spent another sixty seconds studying my surroundings and committing as much as I could to memory and mapping out the lay of this new land.

Turned out, my best was pretty dang good, now that I'd connected to my Whisper. I'd learned that being a Tinker didn't just mean I had the ability to pick a lock and sense the inner workings of almost any mechanism. It had also allowed me to create mind maps and see patterns in a way others couldn't. I'd figured it out when I was trying to save Billy O'Donnelly from the palace dungeons back in Little Alabaster. I was slinking my way through the falcon chutes and had hit a dead end. Sheer panic was closing in, but I'd fought it off, trying to remember the pattern of chutes I'd seen to that point. Once I pictured it all in my head, the rest of the layout had unfolded before me like a once-hidden map. Clear as a bell. Like I had some hypersensitive instinct of what came next. It was a priceless skill in this moment when I had to process so much information in such a short time. One that allowed me to envision exactly where we were in relation to everything else, and would help us navigate our way out of here.

For once, it seemed like I was in a great position to succeed...

Yup, all I had to do was to stab some new friends straight in the back.

By the time I sat down at the dinner table a couple minutes later, my heartbeat had almost returned to its normal rhythm. Tink was already there with Cissy, who was seated, looking and smelling fresh as a meadow. Tristan stood with a frying pan in hand, serving up helpings of fish and green beans to go with the little mugs of pea soup already beside each place setting.

"Molly is going to eat with Caleb. He's feeling poorly tonight," Pan explained with a wave to the empty chairs as he took his own seat at the head of the table.

"I'm so sorry to hear that. Anything I can do to help?"

"He's got a weak constitution is all. Nothing to be done but let him rest when he needs it," Tink said with an absent smile. "Now let's try this fish you all worked so hard to catch today."

I had to admit, it was delicious, and for a few minutes, I nearly lost myself in the ease of it all. Cissy's laughter, Pan's silly story about a turtle he'd tried to ride the week before, only to get chased off by something called a barracuda. Even Tristan seemed content, especially when Fetch flew in through the open window and perched on his shoulder.

Which was why, between dinner and dessert, I was wrestling with myself in a big way.

Say it and risk suspicion, or don't say it?

Two weeks...

I patted my mouth with a napkin and shot Pan a curious glance. "I couldn't help but notice that huge dark oval at the edge of the largest map on the wall. The Weeping Fen, I think it was labeled? I don't think I've ever heard of it."

Tink's smooth brow furrowed as she forked up her last bite of fish. "Where did you say you were from, again?"

"Blackbriar." My answer was at the ready, what with my spanking new map knowledge. "But we lived in a tiny village and really didn't get out much. My parents kept us very sheltered...before they died, that is."

"Must have been nice to have been protected." Pan's face darkened for a second, but then he rallied and managed a smile.

"Want me to tell her about The Fen, Pan?" Cissy asked, scooting closer and setting her elbows on the table. "I know about it real good."

"Sure, let's hear it, kiddo."

"The Weeping Fen is where monsters be," Cissy said

in a spooky voice, adopting Pan's dramatic storytelling style. "A giant saber-toothed tiger called Belial, big as an elephant. Serpents by the dozens, with fangs the size of me! A hydra known as Gretyl, with three heads that haunts the swamps and caves," she hissed, holding up her fingers like fangs. "And of course, Noru, The Ticking Croc, who rules them all."

"This crocodile rules...them all?" I had never seen one in real life, but I'd read about them in stories. And, while I certainly wasn't in a rush to run into one, I found it hard to believe that a Hydra with three heads would be afraid of a croc, ticking or not.

"You better believe it," Pan said with a grim nod. "He's the toughest bastard around and they all know it. And when he's surrounded by the magic of The Fen, he's even stronger, which is why we have to lie in wait for those rare times he comes out and hope we get to him before that dastardly bastard Hook does. It sounds like I'm telling tall tales, but you have to see this critter to believe it. He's a killing machine. Scratch that. You don't want to see him, because it'd likely be the last thing you ever saw. You'll just have to take my word for it."

But would I?

Late that night, long after the dishes were cleared, and everyone else was fast asleep, I was listening to Molly's low snores from the bed a few yards away. I lay tucked in a perfectly snug nook beneath the windowsill, staring at the night sky, my thoughts running amok.

What must've been a billion stars twinkled overhead, and I couldn't help but wonder if they were the same stars that hung over Alabaster. Was Duncan looking at them too?

Was Captain Hook?

I pressed my forehead against the cool glass with a sigh.

Clearly, the man played some part in my destiny. But it wasn't like I'd had prophetic dreams before. Just because I'd dreamt that he'd…

That we'd…

"Stop that right this instant, you dolt!" I hissed under my breath.

I was just about to climb back into my bed when I squinted, pressing my nose against the glass.

A tiny set of initials were neatly carved into the wood on the interior of the frame.

J.T.

One of the earlier Lost Boys? Or maybe Pan and Tink had kids of their own at some point?

Who knew…and what did it matter? Thinking about the sad tale Pan had told would only make it harder to do what needed to be done. Right now, I needed to make a plan that would allow me to complete my task in this place so I could move on to the next. And eventually, get back home. I had no idea where that might be, but one thing was for sure.

My heart ached for it. Now that I knew there was a place out there for me, the need to be there, to get there was all consuming.

I closed my eyes and focused, bringing forward the mental images I'd stored of the map-covered walls. Then, for the better part of an hour, I studied it all in quadrants. Every drawing, every item, every scrap of information I could recall. By the time I'd opened them, I felt sure I'd filled in most of the blanks. Everything I'd seen in that room tonight led me to the conclusion that Pan, Tink, and Hook himself had spent more than a decade waiting for the rare times—*Ebonfall,* I reminded myself—that Noru left The Weeping Fen in hopes of catching him. The most dreaded pirate of all time, a fairy with magic I couldn't even hope to compete with, and Pan, who had motive to burn.

And each time, they'd failed.

Which meant if I had any chance of getting my hands on that clock before my time here was up, I would have to enter the belly of the beast.

I needed to go to The Weeping Fen.

But first, I needed to steal one of Pan's little boats to get us to Blackbriar and find someone willing to be our guide. I'd just have to wait for my moment, and hope we got far far away from Neverland before anyone even realized we were gone. Because, while he might seem like a child at times, from what I'd seen on those walls tonight?

Peter Pan held grudges.

And he was *not* an enemy to be taken lightly.

CHAPTER 6

The sun was a kaleidoscope of color overhead, and I closed my eyes to enjoy the warmth on my face. When was the last time I'd felt so relaxed...so free?

The water was only a bit cooler than a bath, and I let it cradle me, the gentle waves rolling over my naked body in a delicious caress. Some tiny part of my mind remembered... there was something I should be worried about right now, but I couldn't for the life of me think of what it might be.

"Have you missed me?"

The low, familiar growl made my nipples tighten instantly even as I fluttered my arms so I could stand.

Hook stood in the turquoise water before me, his thickly muscled shoulders and chest on full display for the first time. The breath left me in a rush as I tried to remember every plane and dip, every scar and tattoo. But I didn't get the chance to look for long. He closed the distance between us and laid his right hand on the curve of my hip, gripping tight.

"I've missed you."

You should be afraid, a *way-too-soft* voice in my head whispered. Remember what it is that you're forgetting, Harmony.

But there was no time to remember anything, because his mouth was on mine in a deep, searing kiss. Our tongues danced for a moment, and I reveled in the taste of him, but it was over too soon as he pulled away to press his forehead against mine.

"As much as I try, I can't get you out of my head. It's like you have me under a spell, little sea witch." His breath was warm against my skin as he pulled away and bent his head lower, tracing the tip of his tongue over my collarbone and lower, to capture my nipple between his lips, sucking hard before releasing it with a hiss. "All these years, I've stayed strong...resisted taking everything you've offered, despite the torture you put me through. But I don't think I can bear it anymore. It's killing me as surely as a dagger to the heart."

His mouth moved to my other nipple, his teeth grazing it just enough to send a bolt of lightning through me. A guttural moan tore from my lips, like the sound had been trapped there for a lifetime.

"I want you inside me." The raw desperation in my voice made him freeze for half a heartbeat. His grip on my hip tightened, fingers digging into me like he was holding back something wild...something dangerous. Then, with a low groan, he re-captured my nipple between his lips, sucking

deep. Pleasure shot through me, and I arched my back, plunging my fingers into his black-as-night hair.

His mouth lingered, his tongue batting against the sensitive peak before he lifted his gaze to meet mine.

"Next time, we make it last," he vowed, his voice thick.

"Yes. Next time," I breathed, barely managing the words. I would've agreed to anything if he promised not to stop this time.

The hand that had been on my hip drifted slowly over my pubic bone and lower, cupping me, squeezing just enough to make me gasp. My body burned, every nerve alight as he grinded the heel of his palm against my clit, teasing, torturing. The throbbing ache built to a fever pitch almost instantly, and I rolled my hips against his hand in a desperate chase for relief.

"Please, Hook. I need—" I broke off on a ragged cry as his clever fingers parted my overheated flesh and he tucked two of them smoothly inside me.

"I know exactly what you need, love."

My head lolled back as I arched into his touch. In and out, a slow drag of flesh on flesh, the warm water lapping at my thighs.

"Gods, you're so fucking beautiful," he rasped.

I forced my eyes open to meet his and the naked need on his face...the near agony of it matched my own.

I let go of my death grip on his hair and dunked my hand below the surface of the water. A moment later, I closed it over his thick cock and squeezed. His growl sent another bolt *of lust straight to my core and I pulsed my hips into his fingers.*

"Please..."

It was sensory overload. His velvet-covered shaft, swollen, hard as stone, and throbbing in my hand. His fingers wedged inside me as they worked over my achy flesh, filling me, but not quite enough. The water swirling around us in a sensual dance, like nature itself wanted this as much as we did...

He wedged his knee between my thighs, forcing me to open wider for him. His breath was ragged, and I could hear his heartbeat over the waves.

"You're mine, Harmony."

I shuddered at the possessiveness in his tone, at the way it curled around something deep and primal inside me. I wanted to answer, but then he slid his fingers away and pressed his hips to mine. The thick head of his cock pressing against my entrance.

I wanted to tell him to go slow. That it was my first time, but I couldn't form the words. Not when everything inside me was screaming for him to go fast. Hard. Deep. To give me everything, all at once and end this torture.

His hand slid to my throat, not squeezing, just holding. He tilted my chin up, forcing me to meet his gaze.

"Mine," he growled, the very tip of his cock pushing inside me. "You're mine and always have been. Now and forever." With that, his hips flexed and he filled me with one, smooth thrust.

I gasped, gripping his shoulders, desperate for something

solid to cling to as waves of ecstasy crashed over me. There was a sharp stretch, a fleeting sting, but it was drowned out by the overwhelming fullness, the shocking pleasure of finally being claimed by him.

His fingers tightened around my neck just slightly, his lips parting on a groan. His forehead pressed to mine once again, breath hot against my parted lips, hips rolling in a slow, deliberate rhythm, forcing me to feel every inch of him.

I whimpered, my nails digging into his muscled back as I tried to form words, but my breath came too fast, too shallow to speak. I was drowning.

He set a punishing pace, a relentless rhythm that sent stars exploding behind my eyes. The force of it stole the breath from my lungs, made my head spin.

He slipped a hand between us, pressing his thumb against my clit, and the sensation was instant, electric. My body clenched around him in response, making him groan.

"So good," he murmured, his voice raw with need. "So perfect."

He flicked his thumb, sending another jolt of pleasure through me, and I cried out, unable to hold back the sound any longer. He grunted in response, capturing my lips in a searing kiss, teasing my mouth open as his tongue tangled with mine, demanding, devouring.

The world blurred, faded, until there was nothing but him—his body driving into mine, pushing me to the very edge of reason. The lapping of the water against my back, the sound of skin meeting skin, the echo of our breaths—all of it disappeared into the fire building inside me.

The release slammed into me like a tidal wave, violent and all-consuming. My knees buckled, but he held me, whispering something against my lips as he rode it out, making it last, until the full-body quaking slowed to a tremor. I barely registered the sharp nip of his teeth against my lower lip before he pulled back, his gaze molten with heat.

"Again, little one. Once more for me."

I was still struggling to catch my breath when I let my head fall back only to see a bolt of lightning snake across the cloudless blue sky. A shrill cackle followed by an ominous crack of thunder had Hook yanking me flush against him and hulking over me.

"I'll get you, my pretty...and your little bird too!"

I SHOT UPRIGHT WITH A GASP, the last remnants of my dream-turned-nightmare clinging to me just as surely as the damp sheet wrapped around my waist. My pulse hammered against my ribs as my eyes adjusted to the dim light, and for a few scary seconds, I didn't know where I was.

The wooden ceiling above, the briny air, the distant slap of the waves against the shore—

Neverland. Pan and Tink's house.

I turned my head to see Moll, curled into a ball on her bed, snoring softly.

How could she be so cozy and relaxed when I'd been six feet away, trying not to die of pleasure...and terror?

I let out a low groan and swiped a clammy hand down my face.

The dreams about the dark stranger with the onyx eyes had been sexual at times before, but we'd never... he'd never—

"Fuck," I whispered under my breath, my skin still tingling from the false memory of his touch.

Whether it was seeing his picture and hearing Pan's story or just knowing he was real and feasibly within reach, something had taken them up a whole other notch. And then that haunting cackle and creepy voice. The same as I'd heard when I'd turned the page from Alabaster.

I so didn't need this right now.

My whole body was still on fire, every nerve-ending alight, even as panic clawed at my chest. There was zero chance I was getting back to sleep, so I slipped out of bed and padded barefoot to the window. The indigo sky was painted with the first streaks of pink and gold. By the time I got ready, the sun would be cresting the horizon. Surely, safe enough to go for a walk.

I desperately needed some fresh air.

I dressed quickly, slipping into the same clothes I'd worn the day before and stuffing my feet into my red boots. Then, I tugged my bag over my shoulder and made my way through the house on silent feet.

The second I stepped outside, I sucked in a deep

breath. The cool breeze was heaven, and the last of the lightheadedness faded away.

"Big deal," I muttered under my breath, relieved to have control of my senses once again. "You had a sex dream about an evil pirate and got interrupted by a possibly even more evil witch."

Given the events of the past couple of weeks, it was hardly that strange. But as my stomach clenched and the space between my hips pulsed and went heavy, I knew it was more than that.

Why had it felt so fucking real?

I crossed my arms and marched into the balmy breeze, letting my feet choose my path.

Think about anything else. The call of seagulls, the smell of tropical flowers, sweet on the breeze.

That firm, sexy mouth—

"Arg!" I slapped my hands over my ears, like that would help somehow.

I needed a task to keep my brain from replaying it again and again…

"Count the types of flowers."

So I did, keeping a careful watch for anything Cissy had told me about that could be dangerous. By the time the sun had fully crested the horizon a short while later, my pulse was finally getting back to something close to normal, and I could no longer fry an egg on my cheek. But as I spun in a slow circle and took in my surroundings, resting my hand on the gnarled trunk of a tree, I realized I'd gone further than I meant to. This side of the island felt different. Wilder.

I was about to retrace my steps when I caught sight of a cave, its mouth a black hole against the cliffside, half-hidden by thick vines. The second I laid eyes on it, every instinct told me to turn around.

Instead, I stepped forward, one foot in front of the other. The closer I got, the more resistance I felt. It was subtle at first—like walking against a current. Then stronger, like pushing against an invisible wall. Far more than just instinct, it was doing its level best to stop me.

Tink.

I could sense her magic there, as clear as a fist full of fairy dust.

Which means you should walk away...

I gritted my teeth and pressed forward again, but it pushed back, the force as stubborn as I was, and then I saw it.

A bone.

Long, pale, stripped clean of flesh. A few yards inside the cave, barely visible in the dim light. The size of it sent a chill down my spine—A bear, maybe? But how had it gotten there? What type of animal could have stripped it so completely?

"Careful!" A sharp voice pierced the air.

I looked up to see a blur of fluttering wings streaking toward me, and then Tink was there, her hand gripping my collar as she yanked me back with surprising strength. The force sent me stumbling back-ward, and I pinwheeled my arms to keep my footing.

She landed in front of me, her violet eyes sharp, and her expression tight. "You do *not* want to go in there."

I swallowed, my throat dry. "W-why not?"

She crossed her arms, glancing toward the cave before looking back at me. "Because that's where the carnivorous bats live."

I blinked. "Bats?"

Tink nodded, her lips pressing into a thin line. "They don't usually bother us because they hunt in the dead of night, and sleep during the day." She stepped closer, her voice dropping lower. "They're not typically big game hunters. They go for easy kills—birds, squir-rels. But they are very territorial, and if you enter their lair, they won't care what size you are."

A shiver ran down my spine as I glanced back at the bone tucked away in the gloom.

"Probably what happened to that." She jerked her head in that direction and I swallowed hard.

"A bear?"

"Who knows? Wouldn't be the first time," Tink said grimly, grabbing my wrist and tugging me back the way I'd come. "This side of the island is bad news. You shouldn't be here alone."

I let her lead me back, but I couldn't shake the unease curling in my gut.

When we reached the main path, she let go and flut-tered into the air, blocking my way. "I won't tell Pan about this." Her voice was lighter now. "But don't go wandering over here again, alright? The island's got its rules for a reason. People who break them can get hurt..." She trailed off, her expression unreadable.

I nodded, but I barely heard her. I was too busy wondering what other horrors were secreted away on this island...

Not your problem.

My mission wasn't to uncover Neverland's secrets. It was to get the fuck out of here as soon as possible so I could fulfill my destiny...

A destiny that I had decided fully and with my whole chest did *not* involve getting eaten alive by a flesh-stripping bat.

Amen.

CHAPTER 7

Three days.

It took three more gut-wrenching days of feigning friendship, making memories, and gaining trust before I found my moment. Pan and Tink had flown off the island to check out a new orphanage that was opening in Covington and didn't plan to return until well after nightfall. The kids were busy doing chores when Moll and I had managed to slip off without being noticed.

Despite rationalizing what we'd done with pep talks to both myself and Moll about "the greater good" and destiny, I still felt sick. Moll hadn't made it any easier, fretting about the children, wondering who was going to tell Caleb stories at night once she was gone, and how sad Tristan would be without Fetch, who had become his little sidekick for at least a few hours of each day. But all that had been a mere smattering of precipitation compared to the shitstorm we were in right now.

Jolts of pain shot through my fingers as I latched onto the mast like a vise, sucking in a breath as we approached another massive wave.

"Hold on!" I shouted, a half second before impact.

Water sprayed up in a mist as we smashed directly through it, the impact rattling me down to my bones. I slammed my eyes shut, wincing as the icy water rained down on us from above, covering my already-soaked shirt.

"You okay?" I shouted, a burst of relief rolling through me as I caught sight of Moll.

She let out a groan of frustration, dropping butt-first onto the ship's deck. "How much further?"

I glanced forward, flipping the long-distance lens of my loupe into place. My teeth dug into my cheek as the distant land mass came into view, and I cursed myself inwardly for the surge of conscience that'd led me to take the crappier of the two boats, despite Moll's protest.

"If we're going to steal, we might as well steal the nicer one."

"An hour or so, *tops*." I hoped I sounded more confident than I felt. Sunset wasn't far off, and it would cause serious issues if it grew dark before we found a place to dock.

I'd once spent a day rafting down the creek behind Old Cletus's hut before he'd caught me, but that was where my boating experience ended. The ocean had seemed a million miles away in Alabaster, not something anyone expected to actually see, never mind sail across. The truth was, I was going entirely off vibes.

Not ideal.

"I think I'm going to—" Moll's hand shot up to cover her mouth before she could finish that sentence, and she yanked herself up by the railing, retching over the side of the rocking sailboat.

I pocketed my loupe and strode over to her, setting a hand on her shoulder as she dry-heaved in misery.

Fetch screeched overhead, and the boat began to tilt and sway even more violently, sending plumes of water splashing into my face.

"Hold on!" A terrible crack split the air before I could take my own advice.

Well that can't be good.

The boat lurched sideways, and the world spun around me as I fell to the deck, flailing desperately for something to hold onto. My heartbeat thundered in my ears, and darkness was creeping in from the edges of my vision as I finally caught hold of something.

Keep it together, Harm. You can do this.

The boat whipped sideways once again, throwing me like a ragdoll. But this time, I was ready. I held on with everything I had, my fingernails digging into the wooden railing. I shot to my feet the moment I was able, half-running and half-leaping toward the boat's wheel, which had been spinning wildly, out of control.

My heart sank as I grabbed hold of it. It was loose, moving at the slightest tug of my hands. The rudder wasn't just damaged or out of line. It was completely destroyed, and another massive wave was approaching fast.

Moll shouted something from behind me, but the dozen thoughts running through my head at once drowned out her voice.

How far was the closest island?

Did the monsters of The Fen come out at specific times, like Noru, or were they lurking below us, even now?

Were we about to die?

A flash of feathers to my right pulled me back to reality, and I sucked in a deep breath as Fetch's talons sunk into my shoulder pad. No, we weren't going out like this. Not if I had anything to say about it.

My temples thrummed, half tingling and half pain, as I stared into the oncoming wave. It was only seconds away, but the time seemed to stretch on for an eternity. A wave of energy rolled through me, spreading from my head to the tips of my fingers, and then into the boat's wheel.

A deep calm settled over me as a mental blueprint of the vessel appeared in my mind, as familiar as my own body—maybe even more-so. From the squeaky plank at the very back to the specific knots that'd been used to secure the mast, there was nothing I couldn't see.

Nothing I couldn't *do*.

I loosened the sail with a thought, repositioning it ever so slightly. I gauged the angle of the wind, feeling the way it pressed up against the cloth the same way I could've felt it on my own skin.

Just a little bit more...There.

Our angle was correct, now, taking us toward the nearest island, but it still wasn't enough. Even with that adjustment, each wave was still going to throw us wildly off course if we were sailing completely rudderless. I let my awareness slip down from the mast, refocusing on the ship's rear. It would've been suicide in a normal situation, but...

I sent my energy surging down the rope and into the anchor, vaguely hearing a distant yelp from Moll as I pushed it overboard with my magic. It dropped into the water with a thunk, but I kept my focus on it as I stared down at the wave that was just about to reach us. I used my magic to tug the anchor gently from side to side, somehow certain of exactly where it needed to be to keep us on course.

I was doing it. I was *actually* fucking doing it. This was far beyond anything I'd thought possible, and triumph bloomed in my chest as we rolled easily over the incoming wave, and then the next. The small island grew closer with every passing second, and each wave was tamer than the last. The only challenge left was the landing.

We were going to make it. I could f—

A spike of pain shot through my temples, so vicious it brought me to my knees. My instincts screamed for me to retreat from the boat and pull back into my own consciousness. It was only Moll's voice that made me hold fast. It wouldn't just be me who would die if I failed here.

"Harm?!" she called, unsteady footsteps audible from just behind me.

My teeth ground together, and I forced myself back to my feet.

"It's okay, I'm all good," I lied, my focus already shifting back to the task at hand.

The waves were hitting harder now, and I was barely able to see or think through the haze of agony. But this part didn't have to be perfect. All I had to do was get us to shore in one piece.

Get to shore in one piece.

I repeated the mantra over and over in my head, shifting my awareness back and forth between anchor and sail. I wasn't moving nearly as efficiently as before, and the tips of Fetch's talons poked through the pad and into my shoulder as we hurtled the last few dozen feet toward the shore.

A little bit more—

Now!

I threw my awareness back into the anchor, forcing it down with all the magic I could muster. The boat jerked wildly from side to side, thrashing like a bull with an unwanted rider, but I pressed on, trusting my gut. The anchor sunk into the sand below, and the shuddering grew even worse until I turned the sail abruptly sideways. We were only inches from the shore, and my teeth clacked as the wood of our hull skidded onto the sandy beach.

I released my hold over the boat, dropping to the deck in a trembling heap.

"Holy shit." Moll appeared in front of me as we ground to a halt, her eyes so wide they looked ready to bulge out of her head. "How the heck did you manage that?"

"No clue." I sucked in a deep breath, letting out a laugh of semi-hysterical relief. "But that piece of shit boat barely held it together in the end there." And there was zero chance it was sound enough to get us to The Weeping Fen. Whoever we hired as our guide was going to have to have a ship of their own.

She cracked a half smile, both of us well aware we had barely dodged disaster, and giddy for our good fortune.

"So you're saying this is a good time for an 'I told you so', then?"

"The perfect time."

CHAPTER 8

"There it is!"

The small shanty town came into view just as the sun was disappearing under the horizon, and I breathed a sigh of relief at the sight. We'd taken a rest by the beach, but I was still mentally exhausted from pushing my magic so far. Fetch, who had been flying overhead for a good portion of the rocky boat ride, had clearly reached his breaking point, as he was perched on my shoulder, eyes closed, head tucked close to mine.

We all needed a chance to regroup.

"Let's try to find an inn or something before we start asking around."

"Sounds good. I'm not built for camping," Moll agreed in a near-whisper, sounding as parched as I felt.

"We just have to hope that the gold Duncan slipped me won't do more harm than good." The last thing we needed was people asking a lot of questions, and our money surely didn't look like theirs...

"The type of people we're looking for don't care where gold came from or whose face is on it, so long as it ends up in their pockets," she murmured, her voice breaking as she looked away.

"You okay?" I asked, eyeing her more closely.

"I…I guess. I'm feeling really guilty about how we left. Are they going to end up remembering us as thieves?" She turned away, her voice growing softer. "If they even remember us at all."

I stepped in beside her, pulling her close as we walked. "They'll know better than to believe that. The connection you formed with them was real, and I'm sure Peter will understand once he reads our note."

We'd left behind an apology, along with a small sack of coins for Pan and Tink, explaining that we were sorry to leave without warning, but that we had run into some trouble before they'd found us. And, now that we'd gotten to know them, we didn't want to bring that trouble to Neverland. We had no way of knowing the worth of the boat in this new world, but we'd left enough gold to cover the materials and labor several times over, if my estimate was correct. It was all we could do to ensure we had some left to complete our mission, while also hopefully earning us enough good-will that the pair wouldn't hunt us down for taking their boat.

We crested a low hill, and a seed of anxiety formed

in my gut as I stared down at the empty, unlit town below.

"Wonder why no one is out. It can't be later than six o'clock, right?"

"Early curfew here, maybe?" she suggested as we stepped onto the shanty town's street.

I nodded, glancing around as we strode deeper into the village. The buildings were small, but cozy-looking and sturdy. About the size of the nicer homes in The Smudge, but the half-rotted ship's wheels, fishing nets, and rusty anchors nailed to the walls gave the whole area a nautical feel. "Well, they don't seem to be abandoned. There must be some kind of event going on."

"Quiet!"

Moll let out a yelp, her fists flying upward in an awkward mockery of a fighting stance at the male voice shouting. "What the—?"

I leapt sideways as the door to the house on our right flew open, lifting my arm to stop Fetch from attacking as a figure emerged.

The man's thin lips were curled into a frown, and he spat on the ground as he caught sight of us. "Ruined my nap, you damned outsiders."

"Ruined your nap? You scared us half to death!" Moll shot back with an indignant sniff. "Who naps at a time like this, anyway?"

The little man's frown somehow deepened even further, and he jabbed a finger toward the beach.

"Whoever you're lookin' for, you'll find 'em by the docks. Now shoo!"

I nudged Moll into silence. "How do you know who we're looking for?"

"Doesn't matter who."

"Is there some kind of event going on there or something?"

He cleared his throat loudly, then spat again, this time sending the glob straight into the inside of his own door.

I forced an encouraging smile to hide my revulsion.

"I'm not one to tell tales out of school, but there's a big pirate meeting going on." He paused for a long moment before adding, "The Captain of Captains brings his boys here a few times a year to whip the other crews into shape…Davis or Davy or some shit. Annoying prick who thinks he's the best that ever was."

A chill rolled down my spine as an image of Hook shimmered to the forefront of my mind. Was that his given name, then? Not very intimidating…I could see why he went with Hook.

"Is it open to the public?" I asked, glancing at the empty houses all around. "Everyone seems to be over there."

He scowled. "Look, if you're *that* desperate, fine. You can come in for a cup of tea…But I'm a busy man, I don't have long…And don't bring that damned bird with you, either." A teapot whistled from behind him as if in reply, and he let out a final grunt before stepping inside, leaving the door open just behind him.

"So much for waking him from a nap," Moll whispered with a roll of her eyes. "He must've sleepwalked his way to the kettle then."

I bit back a laugh, keeping my voice low. "Should we go in?"

Moll shrugged. "Why not? It won't even make the top ten worst ideas we've had recently."

"He could be a good source of information," I ventured with a shrug.

"In or out," the crusty old man shouted from the interior of the little cottage. "You're letting out all my hot air."

Somehow, I had the feeling he had loads of hot air left. Plus, it was still warm and balmy outside, but who was I to argue? His house, his rules.

"Go check out the lay of the land," I whispered, turning to Fetch. "See you soon, my friend."

Fetch let out a chortle and then soared off.

I pulled the door shut behind us, making sure to avoid the glob of spittle he'd launched there.

Sturdy barrels lined the walls on either side, but the home was far from the shithole I'd been expecting from a guy who went around spitting everywhere. In fact, each wall was decorated meticulously, with long cords of knotted rope, folded up sails, seashells, and other decorations.

Maybe he was a fisherman, back in his day?

He reemerged, holding a kettle in one hand and pressing a cluster of mugs against his chest with the other.

"Sit," he said gruffly, plopping two of the mugs on the table while pouring tea into his own. When he was done, he threw it back for a sip, then shoved the kettle in our direction as he sat. "Pour for yourself if you want some."

I glanced over at him as I pulled out a chair to sit. Tufts of wispy gray hair gave token bits of cover to his spotty scalp, and his skin was as dry as my leather pouch. He looked at least eighty, and the calluses on his hands and the scar across his jaw showed that he'd lived a hard life, but who knew? Poverty and hard work aged a person. A Hollow sixty was an Alabaster eighty, as the saying went.

He turned, meeting my gaze with milky, blue eyes. *Nearly blind?*

I turned away anyway, reaching for the tea. "Thank you for inviting us in. We traveled a long way to get here."

"I can tell," he said with a scowl.

"What should we call you, by the way? I'm Harmony, and this is Molly."

"Name's Garth…Look, just get to the point. What is it that you're lookin' for?"

I shared a look with Moll, wondering how much to tell the man. "We were originally looking to get to

Blackbriar, but we ran into some boat troubles and ended up here."

"Can't even sail a damn boat," Garth muttered.

Okay, then. Not exactly a charmer.

I took a swig of the tea, swishing it around my parched mouth. A strong, cinnamon-y flavor washed over my tongue, and I savored it for a long moment before trying again. "Seems like you were a sailor at one point?"

He fixed me with a milky stare. "What's it to ya?"

"It's such a neat job," I began.

He leaned forward, closing one eye to scowl at me. "Oh yeah? What's so neat about it, missy?"

Moll cut in with a beaming smile. "We were trying to get to Blackbriar in hopes of hiring someone to take us to The Weeping Fen, considering your experience and knowledge—"

"The Fen, you say?" Garth's eyes widened for an instant before he leaned back in his seat and shrugged, Mr. Nonchalant. "Eh, go wherever youse want. I wouldn't advise it, though. The world is full of inter-esting spots…"

"We need to get to The Weeping Fen, specifically." Molly said, still smiling like an angel. "If you'd rather not help us, we'll thank you for your hospitality and hopefully find someone who will."

He stared at us and let out a long breath that sounded something like, "Save me from idiots." Then, he gestured toward the door. "I'm not one to tell tales out of school," he reminded us, "but David, or whatever that bastard calls himself, brings in Beast Seekers from all over for these little gatherings. He's like a twelve-year-old boy, always looking for tall tales about manticlopses and octocorns or whatever the hell. One of them pirates might be able to help you not get your fool heads bitten off, at least. Why do you need to go there again?"

"We just have a passion for monsters," I said.

"How might one gain entrance to this…gathering?" Moll added, raising her brows expectantly.

"It's for pirates and wannabes only," he grunted.

"What about the rest of the people from town?"

"Hired out to serve food and the like."

"So what if we say we're there for that?"

"You don't exactly look the part…" Garth's eyes traveled up and down my body before turning to Moll. He rubbed his jaw for a long moment, his lips pulling upward in a hint of a smile before disappearing. "You can be a tavern wench, but the other one there will have to try as one 'o those wannabes. I *s'pose* I can make a bit of time for this," he continued, scooting his chair away from the table.

Was he planning to take us over and introduce us? "Time for what?"

He grunted, gesturing toward the hallway with his head. "Follow me. What you two need is a pair of decent disguises."

Moll and I exchanged a look.

He could be leading us into his murder lair, and we'd be fools to follow him like a pair of dumb cows. But the way he'd been almost waiting for someone to walk by to engage with, it seemed more like he was just a lonely—if cranky—old man, desperately looking for a purpose, and we'd unwittingly given him one.

My gut had served us well so far in this new land, and I was going to have to start trusting it again. Right now, it was reminding me that we didn't have a whole lot of knowledge or resources at our disposal. We needed to let this man help us if he could.

Besides, Moll had her incapacitator, and I had my knife. If shit went sideways and we couldn't figure out a way to overpower this man who was old enough to be our great-granddad, we were never making it to the end of this journey anyway.

"Are you coming or you just going to stand there like a pair of numpties?"

Moll shrugged, and I nodded.

Best case, his help would lead to us finding a guide willing to take us to The Fen. Worst, we'd at least have done a good deed, giving an octogenarian serial killer one last hurrah.

There were worse ways to go…

CHAPTER 9

was still wondering if we might've been better off with the whole Garth-winding-up-being-a-serial-killer option. Because my knees were quaking as Moll and I strode toward the torchlit docks an hour or so later.

With a little luck, this excursion could end our whole search, just days after I'd found out about the clock's existence. But, as awesome as that would be, it had just as much potential to go horribly wrong.

After Garth's insistence that 'you'd have to be a pretty sexy wench to get in as a serving girl now that it's already started', followed by a very pointed and rather insulting glance in my direction, we'd settled on a pair of disguises.

Moll would dress up as a girl from the village looking for work while I took a page from Cissy Petway's book and disguised myself as an adolescent boy looking to join one of the crews, complete with tiny dabs of shoe polish Moll had painted on my chin like stubble, and a red silk tie across my waist in place of a belt. And, while I had an easier time of it than Moll had when we'd been forced to cut and dye her hair back in Alabaster, I definitely wasn't happy about waiting a good year or two for it to grow back.

I glanced up at the sky and let out a breath. Fetch surveyed the area overhead, ready to rejoin us once we were finished. Worst case, I knew I could count on him to peck a few eyeballs out if need be, but we were still headed onto a ship full of pirates.

I shot Moll a worried glance, but she seemed to be in a fair mood, considering the seriousness of our current situation.

"You have the knife I gave you? And the incapacitator, yeah?"

She tipped her head in a curt nod. "Yup. For the third time, I'm armed and ready, Mom."

"If you want me to do this alone, I'm happy to find you a place to—"

Molly wheeled around, grabbed both of my lips and squeezed them flat like a duck bill. "What did I say about that? After the last time you pulled some shit like this?"

I stared at her and tried to reply, but the words were nothing but a series of muffled hums.

"Exactly. Me and you are like bread and butter. You go, I go. And besides," she added, releasing my lips. "I'm not afraid." She let me go and I rubbed at my recently pinched lips.

"How is that possible?" I replied, picking up the pace again. "I mean, fear is a healthy response here. This is a scary situation."

We walked for another ten paces before she answered. Pausing, she turned to face me, her expression solemn. "The worst has happened, and I'm still here, that's why. I refuse to let that sadistic fuck break me. And if one of these pirates wants to try me, he's going to find himself right next to Heinrich. In the bowels of the underworld with my knife in his gullet." The fierce light in her eyes died and her lips twitched. "To tell you the truth, the only thing about this particular situation that's scary is your new haircut. Truly hideous…" She snicked her tongue and then doubled over with laughter.

I played along and swung my mouth wide, perching my hands on my hips in outrage. "You're really getting a kick out of this, huh?"

"It's just so…bad. And the funny part is, you let that crazy old man with cataracts the size of dinner plates cut it because you were afraid I was going to mess it up on purpose. You have to admit, that's rich." She reached over, plucked off my cap, and ran her hand through my freshly-shorn hair that stood out in tufts that ended at my chin. "I never bought that 'best revenge is living well' crap anyway, but this seals the deal. The best revenge is seeing someone get a worse haircut than they gave you."

I rolled my eyes, but couldn't help but grin at her, delighted even if it was at my expense. "We're even now."

She looked over, incredulous. "You think that makes us even? After that vow of silence and the fake leg? Pfft. Not even close. You owe me for all eternity. You do make a pretty good boy, though. Not exactly my type, but you have a certain charm that I would consider if my options were limited…"

"You do know that gold from Duncan is all the money I have in the world, right?" I asked in mock confusion.

She chortled as we took our first step onto the wooden dock. "Look, when a lady aspires to a standard of living…"

She trailed off and I followed her gaze, the laughter falling away. Massive ships loomed all around, bearing flags of skulls, blades, krakens, and anchors. Each one was intimidating in its own right, but the one at the very back dwarfed them all.

The Floating City, Garth had called it, and the closer we got, the more apt that name seemed. The moon hung just behind the mast, giving it an eerie, other-worldly feel. A burly man stood just in front of it, next to a steep wooden walkway that led up to the deck.

Despite the bad feeling I'd had in my gut that we

would surely cross paths with Captain Hook, none of the ships looked like the one in the drawings at the amphitheater, or the one shooting cannons our way a few days before.

A surprise, but a welcome one. Walking into a den of thieves and murderers in search of a guide brave enough to take us to The Weeping Fen was bad enough without having to also grapple with seeing the one I'd had dream sex with, who'd turned out to be the worst of the bunch.

I turned back toward Moll. "You looking to win the heart of a pirate today? I hear they have a lot of gold." I gestured toward her chest, which seemed ready to burst free of her buttons.

"Nope. I'm over the whole husband hunting thing. I've got you, and that's enough for me. I'm just using what I got to get us inside this shindig," she said with a shrug, lowering her voice now that the guard was almost in earshot. "One of us had to do it, and it certainly wasn't going to be you." She shot a look at my chest that hadn't even needed to be bound for me to pass as a boy.

"Cruel."

I took one last, steadying breath as we approached the man guarding the ship, who was already eyeing us up and down.

"Names?" he grunted, his gold tooth glinting in the torchlight.

"Harmon," I answered gruffly, "and this is my sister, Molly."

"We're from the village," Moll blurted nervously as she dropped into a low curtsy, leaning forward to show off her ample chest.

"I know we're a bit late," I said, praying that she'd leave the rest of the talking to me, "but I'm hoping to find a crew to join, and my sister here wants to see if you need any more servers."

"Can always use more servers," replied the man, wetting his lips. "Head on up, toots."

Moll and I stepped forward in unison, but he held his arm out in front of me. "Yes?" I asked.

He tore his gaze off Moll for the first time to look me up and down in surprise. "You're looking to join one of the crews, boy?"

"I've dreamt of it since I was a kid." I added more bass into my voice for good measure. Garth had told us loads of the local boys looked to piracy as a way to get rich.

"A little scrawny, no?" he remarked, frowning. "How old are ya?"

"Twenty."

He reached over for the nearest torch, pulling it off of the holder. "Let's see those arms."

I held back a wince, thinking fast. My boobs were small, but they weren't *that* small. If he ended up looking me over too closely, there was a very real chance that he'd see through my disguise.

Maybe I could win him over if I called Fetch?

A tinny plink sounded to my left, and I turned in unison with the guard, looking over at Moll.

"Oh my," she chuckled as she tugged at her shirt.

"What's the matter?"

She flashed him a doe-eyed glance. "One of my buttons popped off and I can't seem to find it…"

"Well, if you need some help, I could—"

"Oh, thank you." She held a hand to her heaving chest.

It only took a few moments before he came up with the good, lofting the pearly button high in the air.

"Got it!"

"So clever!" She glanced at his arms. "And strong, too. I'm sure your crew is lucky to have you. You know, I wouldn't mind hearing of your adventures over a mug of ale, if you'll be staying another day or two…?"

Her acting was terrible, but he was far too addled by her creamy bosom to notice.

It was like a frigging superpower, I realized, suppressing a laugh.

The man puffed out his chest and nodded. "I'll be here. We've just come back from two months at sea, so we'll be staying in town at least a few more days."

Moll nodded, her eyelashes fluttering. "Sounds great. I'll stop and see you after I leave later tonight and we can plan where to meet, then?" She was already backing away toward the wooden plank leading to the ship, tugging at my shirt sleeve as she spoke.

"See you then, Miss. And tell your brother to watch hisself. A lot of us are just gods-fearing, sea-fairing men looking for a semi-honest way to make a living. Others…well, they'd as soon gut ya as greet ya."

The wooden walkway stretched a solid twenty feet out, with frayed rope on either side in the place of railings, and we strode carefully across it.

"Fucking hell," I said once he was out of earshot. "I thought we were screwed for a second there."

She chuckled. "We're lucky there wasn't a woman down there instead checking on those coming to the gathering."

The noise within grew louder with each step toward the enormous warship, and I sucked in a breath as we reached the top of the walkway. A few stray sailors milled around the well-manicured deck, but the crowd was still clearly inside. A line of lanterns against one wall marked the entrance to the cabin, and I glanced over at Moll as we stepped onto the deck.

"Ready?"

"Ready. I'm going to try to feel things out with the kitchen and waitstaff like you said."

"Great. I'm going to do some eavesdropping," I said.

She smiled, looking eager to get inside, but then paused. "Thanks for letting me come. It's a lot better than hanging back alone, worried you're never coming back."

I winced. "It was all I could think to do to protect you. But I get it now, and I won't freeze you out again."

"It's actually pretty fun, too! All the intrigue and such." She flashed all of her pearly teeth in a wide grin. "I feel so alive!"

I could only hope that she felt exactly the same way when this was over. More than feeling it, I hoped we were both actually alive.

Too bad I didn't have her confidence. Now that we were up here, my gut twisted with nervousness and unease. Though she was a good listener, as she'd reminded me when she'd eavesdropped at the Harvest Feast back in Alabaster, she was also impulsive.

"Make sure you stick to the plan, Moll."

She rolled her eyes, but the smile didn't leave her face. "Worry about yourself first, 'Harmon'," she replied, throwing up finger quotes as she said the name.

"Fair enough." I stood up a little straighter as we stepped into the well-lit hallway. The sound became almost deafening as we walked down the stairs, and I had to speak louder to even be heard. A massive dining hall opened at the bottom of it, with enough seating for hundreds of people. A group of pirates at the nearest table looked over as we entered, their eyes lingering on Moll for a moment before going back to their food.

"They're really not doing much to break those stereotypes, huh?" Complete with peg legs, eyepatches, and all, it was like they were straight out of a story book.

Because they are, I reminded myself. The strangeness

of *that* fact still hadn't fully set in. Maybe it never would.

Bouts of laughter exploded from random sections of the room every few seconds, and the entire place smelled of rum and old tobacco. A lone pirate sat on a shell-crusted throne on the far end of the room, flanked by an enormous flag with a kraken in the center. I breathed out.

Not the flag from the amphitheater drawings, thank the gods. And the lone pirate didn't look like the man from my dreams, either.

His black-and-gray beard flowed nearly to his waist and was woven with shimmering gold bits and charms. Hooped gold earrings hung off his stretched-out lobes. He held out a hand, which had a ring on each finger with a spare for the thumb, and the young boy standing by his side passed him a bottle of dark liquid, which he brought right to his mouth.

Davis...or Davy? David, maybe...whatever his name, he was obviously the man Garth had referred to as the 'Captain of Captains', and the owner of the largest ship. And he wasn't shy about showing it off. Even the nobles in Alabaster would've turned their noses up at such brazen displays of wealth.

Gaudy and ostentatious they would have muttered under their breath.

Moll nudged me lightly, gesturing to the right, where a pair of serving women had just emerged from a little side door at the room's edge.

"Guess this is where we part ways."

I took a final deep breath, then nodded. "See you on the other side?"

She flashed me a wink, then scurried off.

I stepped further into the room, moving toward a more crowded section. The tables seemed to be dedicated to individual crews, but different groups of men stood all around the room, drinking and merrymaking.

Members of different crews sharing info and mingling?

I inhaled deeply, trying to release some of the pent-up stress. Still no sign of the man from my dreams, and I wasn't quite sure whether that was a good thing or a bad thing. A chill ran through me as an image of his cold, dark eyes came back to me. There was a depth to them that drew me in, one that went beyond simple lust—not that there hadn't been plenty of that, too.

I pushed the thought aside as a line of young men came into view at the corner of the dining hall. Their eyes flitted from table to table, and a wrinkled man with a thick gold chain dangling from his neck and a peg leg stood at their front, scribbling something down on a piece of parchment. He waved the front boy aside, gesturing for the next to approach.

Signing up new recruits? Could I be so lucky?

He glanced over as I approached, waving me into line. "No meat on those bones..." He scowled, but seemed to shake it off, waving his paper toward the other recruits. "Back of the line, boy."

I dipped my head and did as instructed, glancing over at the boy who'd just signed up. He was already speaking to someone at the nearest table, which was a good sign. I had no idea how these people worked, and I'd been too nervous to walk up to a random crew, but it seemed like this would give me an easy in.

I got to the front of the line within minutes, and the man there scowled a second time as he waved me up. "Name?"

"Harmon...Smith."

"Age?"

"Twenty."

"Height?"

I stood up a little straighter. "Five foot seven."

He squinted one eye at that, then shrugged and scribbled it down. "And what crew are you most interested in?"

"Er—" I glanced around, muscles tensing at being put on the spot. "The Captain of Captains' crew," I answered, gesturing toward the front of the room.

He let out a bark of laughter, shaking his head in disbelief. "You should go tell him that yourself, shrimp. See what he says."

I made a mental note to do the exact opposite of that.

"There're so many people here," I said dumbly, more to break the silence than anything else. "Crazy that he can keep so many pirates in line."

"Davy Brone is an impressive man," he agreed. "Can

think of no other who could've united so many of us under one banner."

"Heard he works with monster hunters, too. You know of anyone like that?" I asked.

He looked at me as if I'd sprouted another head, like Gretyl the hydra. "You want to join a crew of Seekers? Have a death wish then, do ya? Cuz there's no shortage of men here willing to help ya with that."

I cleared my throat and tried another tactic. "My dear old Da always dreamed of going to The Weeping Fen to see the monsters with his own eyes. Then, he went blind and never got to go. I want to be able to go back home and tell him tales of all the creatures, so he'll feel like he was there, you know?"

"How?"

I blinked back at him. "Hmm?"

"Your Da." The man gestured to his eyes with one filthy hand. "How did he go blind?"

"Oh, uh, he was attacked by a swarm of bees…"

The man pulled back in horror. "Fooking hells. In the eyes, you say?"

"Yup. He has this sort of light amber, honey colored irises and I'm thinking that's why…" I trailed off, wondering how I'd managed to back myself into this corner and how to get back on track.

"Look, I know what it's like to want to make your old man proud." He lowered the paper, his expression softening a bit as he locked eyes with me. "'Specially being such a runt like yourself. If you want to get picked up by a crew, you'll have to really make yourself stand out. Once the boss is done with his speech, go 'round and introduce yourself. Let 'em know if you have any special skills or magic that might give you an edge."

"What speech?"

He nodded, gesturing toward the front of the room. "Captain Davy is gonna talk things over with the other captains in a few. Go sit with the other recruits while you wait for that to finish." He gestured toward the table a few feet to our left. "And pay attention. You seem like a bright lad, so maybe you'll be able to pick up somethin' from their conversation that you can use when you're sellin' yerself to the captains."

I nodded in thanks, then stepped away. It had been more like a party than a meeting so far, but it seemed that was about to change. Serving girls drifted in, balancing broad trays of potatoes, ham and other roasted meats on their forearms and carrying foamy mugs of ale in their hands, doing their best not to let them slosh all over the deck.

I scanned the room, my eyes settling on Moll's shoulder-length crimson locks within seconds. Her eyes flitted nervously from side to side and her tray wobbled more with every step she took. I shot her a sympathetic smile as she noticed me but made my way over to the table with the other recruits as instructed, keeping half an eye on her.

She lowered the tray to her table, breathing a sigh

of relief as she set it down with a graceless plop. She turned to head back toward the kitchen, then stopped short, turning to scan the room. Her lips turned upward into a toothy smile as we locked eyes, and she shot me a quick thumbs up.

No disasters so far.

I pulled out my chair and took my seat, the nervous energy was almost palpable. The youngest couldn't have been older than fifteen, and not one of them met my gaze as I scanned the table.

Poor kids. Not one of them looked ready for what lay ahead. The journey from strapping, innocent lad to full on outlaw was often a quick one. Their type had been all too common in The Hollow. Joining up with thieves or worse as boys with nowhere to turn and no other way out of poverty being transformed into hardened criminals before they reached their eighteenth birthday. When pushed far enough, hungry, hopeless people took any out they could to get by. I just hoped they learned how dark this path could get before it chewed them up and spit them out, or swallowed them whole like it had with so many others.

"Oy, listen up you greasy buggers!"

I spun, letting out a breath as the low, rumbling voice split the air.

Adrenaline raced through me as Davy Brone walked toward the center of the room. The chatter died in a flash, to the point that I could make out the stomping of his rugged boots on the ship's deck as he strode forward.

He smiled broadly flashing white teeth and more than a few gold. All eyes were glued to him as he waved over a serving boy to pass him the rum. He pressed the bottle to his mouth and took a healthy swig without a word, keeping the rest of us waiting for him with bated breath. He was clearly a showman, and even though it was a ridiculous display, I couldn't quite bring myself to roll my eyes at it. There was a presence about him— an energy that had given him this position as much as whatever pirating skills he might possess. This was a man who was used to ruling, a man who took his authority as a given.

He passed the bottle back to the boy without a glance, then looked up, scanning the room. "Alright, lads, as much as I'd love to sit here and keep drinking, we've got a meeting to hold." His voice was cutting and sharp, like the scraping of a sword against a grindstone. "First order of business. The damn Blackbriar townies have been on us like barnacles on a ship's ass since last month's raid, and I know a lot of you have been shitting yourselves trying to figure out what to do next. We'll go around, crew by crew, and figure out just that, while also settling any disputes."

Davy glanced around, scowling as his eyes settled on the empty table on the far-right edge of the room.

"Cocky bastard's skipping meetings again, eh? Anyone heard from him?"

A slender, dark-haired man from the table nearest him rose. "He was coming, last I heard. Ran into him on the way here, in fact."

"Bah. It will be dealt with, I promise you that. You start us off, Crick," Davy continued, gesturing toward the man who'd stood a moment earlier. "What're you seein' in the west?"

Crick dipped his head toward Davy. "We've had three run-ins with the Shoalhounds this month alone, so things have been tight." He turned with a growl, jabbing his finger toward a crew a few tables away. "And while we're already skint, we found out that Jack's crew has been homing in on our territory."

The other captain—built like a thumb—rose, twitchy as he flicked a glance between Crick and Davy. He went to speak, but Davy shook his head and pressed a finger to his lips. "Let Crick finish."

Crick wet his lips and rushed on. "I know it's not all mapped out all perfect like, but I'm not talking about something right on the edge of my stretch of water. I'm talking about Hardlock Hamlet, deep in my territory. Screwed up a profitable relationship we had there, too. The mayor was in our back pocket and has paid thousands to stop shite like this from happening."

A breeze flowed toward the front of the room as Davy raised a hand, and the man went silent instantly, taking a half-step back. But Davy's anger seemed trained on the other man.

"Is this true, Jack? Did you knowingly pillage a

town in his territory?" The thundering accusation and unbridled fury had me glad his gaze was not on me. Judging by the sweat beading on Jack's upper lip, he was wishing the same.

"Partly true," the short, stout captain croaked, pulling off his hat to run a nervous hand through what was left of his hair. "The Shoalhounds have been on our tail too, so we stopped there to resupply. They tried to price gouge us, and we can't be havin' people think that's alright, now can we?"

Davy narrowed his eyes, steepling his hands in front of his face in consideration.

"I understand that you feel wronged, but there ain't much else he could do, if what he says is true. We can't have people tryin' to take advantage cos they think we're soft." Crick opened his mouth to protest but thought better of it as Davy continued. "With that said…Jack, have your men deliver a hundred gold pieces to Crick's ship before you leave. And make sure you don't—"

"Captain," Crick cut in, exasperated. "The contract he spoiled was worth triple that on its own. Not to mention, time is money. I'm going to have to go back and spend days glad-handing to regain the mayor's trust. And this ain't the first time he done this, neither. He—"

Clang.

I barely caught sight of the flash of magic when the mug in Crick's hand exploded into a million pieces, scattering across the floor like grains of sand on a beach. My eyes shot toward Davy as a gust of wind whooshed out of the room with a whistle as it passed.

"What the fuck was that?" I whispered under my breath.

"His Tideblessing," one of the other young recruits murmured.

My breath caught in my throat as a slight glimmer pulled my attention to Davy's fingertips. He was Tideblessed. Apparently, he was able to control the wind. Or weather in general? I couldn't be sure. Whatever the case, it was strong magic. For a pirate, that type of power would be highly prized and greatly feared. No wonder he was the leader.

Pain pricked at my temples as I focused on him, sensing the waves of magic pulsing from deep inside him. I shook myself out of it, forcing down my own magic with a start. I'd felt a hint of it when I'd touched Cissy's Tideblessing mark, but not to this extent. When had I learned to do *that*? Everything was advancing so quickly…

But that thought was quickly derailed by another.

If I could sense *his*, there was a chance that others could sense mine, too. It'd be wise to suppress it for now, as best I could.

I heard a flutter behind me and turned as Fetch lighted upon my shoulder. He must've sensed my stress, and I lifted a hand to stroke his feathers reassuringly. His presence instantly calmed me some, but I took a quick look around to see if his presence caused a stir. To my surprise, only a few people even glanced my way. There were at least four parrots in the room, and what with the drama unfolding before us, the few people that noticed had already turned their attention back to the main event.

"If I wanted your opinion, I would have asked you for it."

Davy's gaze could have bored a hole right through the other captain, but his voice was smooth and calm. "Do not interrupt me again." He let the words linger for a long moment, as if daring Crick to take the chance to do just that.

Blood had started to drip down the man's shirt from the dozens of tiny cuts on his neck, face and hands, but he stood still as a statue, barring an almost imperceptible nod of his head.

Satisfied, Davy turned back to Jack. "See that it gets done." He swiped his hands together as if to get the dirt off, the fury disappearing from his expression as quickly as it had arrived. He gestured toward another table. "Now, on to the next. Earl, why don't you—"

My heart skipped a beat as a loud crash cut him short, and I spun to see a man walking through the doors at the room's entrance just behind me. For a second, I could only see his silhouette, and that was enough to make me freeze in place. Tall, with massive shoulders, and a walk that reminded me of a predator. Confident, smooth strides that broadcasted the fact that he was the baddest motherfucker in the room. When he stepped into the lantern light and I could see his face, though, the breath in my chest rattled and died.

Eyes, black as sin, and features that could've been chiseled from stone would have given him away on their own. But the curved, iron hook in place of his left hand sealed the deal.

Captain Hook had arrived.

CHAPTER 10

$\mathcal{H}$ook strode nonchalantly into the silent room, glancing from table to table. I winced as he passed Moll, who had just re-emerged from the kitchen, and reached toward her with his good arm. I pushed away from the table, hand shooting toward my pouch and the incapacitator there, but he just grabbed a mug of rum off her tray and continued on.

"No need to wait on my account, Davy," he said gruffly. "What're we up to?"

"The meeting is already underway." Davy spoke even more slowly than before, and, this time, there was a hint of anger in his voice.

Hook shrugged. "I had business on shore. Figured I'd skip the eating and bullshitting." He took a swig of his drink as he arrived at his table, his ragtag crew trailing just behind him, each one of them looked more intimidating than the last. Closest on his heels was a wiry stalk of a man whose fiery red hair gave Moll's a run for its money.

Hook turned, eyeing the shattered glass on the floor as he slid into his seat. "Ah, did I not come late enough to miss the whining session, then?"

There was clearly some history between these two because despite the way Hook was speaking to him, Davy retreated to his throne and sat back down. Seemed off after he'd threatened Crick's life for the mild disrespect that had paled in comparison to what Hook was giving him now.

"We're holding our meeting, same as always. Airing grievances is part of it," Davy spat. The curtains by the nearest window billowed as a light wind began to swirl around the room.

My muscles clenched and resisted the urge to find something nailed to the floor to hold onto.

"Mind if I give my two cents?" Hook asked, swinging his feet up onto the table and leaning back in his chair. "Got an idea might interest you."

Davy glared at him for a long moment, letting out a grunt of disapproval, then forced a nod. "Better be good."

"Things are getting hot in our neck of the woods. Been seeing patrols all week. Random, uncoordinated attacks they can ignore, but they're starting to see us as a threat to their authority. We've become too much like a united force."

Davy glared at him for a long moment, letting out a grunt of disapproval. "If they see us as a threat, it's because we are one. What would you have us do? Go back to the old times and gut each other on sight?" He shook his head in frustration, "How short a memory you have, Hook. Things are better now than they've ever been, and our way out of this mess is to push forward. They're already stretched thin keeping the peace between Blackbriar and Brinepool, and the few warships they can afford to send after us in the meantime are far from enough to do lasting damage. On the other hand, our forces grow by the year as more crews join up, and young men enlist in droves. Just like I promised at the start of all this, I'm going to shape us into a force that not even the Shoalhounds can match. It's only a matter of time."

"War has been averted, Davy," Hook announced, setting his drink down to reach into his pocket.

"Averted?" Davy asked with an incredulous laugh. "Things have been escalating for six months."

Hook pulled out a note and passed it to the red-haired man, who appeared to be Hook's second in command.

"A letter from the Duke himself," he explained, gesturing for the other man to carry it over to Davy. "Blackbriar and Brinepool have come to an agreement."

Davy held out a hand as Hook's man arrived, and I nearly leapt out of my chair with shock as red-hair handed him the note and then, smooth as butter, but quick as a snake, slid what appeared to be some kind of needle directly into Davy's wrist. His hand whipped back to his side with supernatural speed, and the older man's expression never shifted as he stared down at the note.

Some kind of Tideblessing that let him move faster than any normal person could see. Was I able to see it because of my magic?

I could think of nothing else that would explain it. But there was something strange about it, too. I hadn't felt the magic, not like I had when Davy had used his. But what other explanation was there?

There had been a handful of performers back in Alabaster who made money with sleight of hand tricks, but none who had come close to matching his skill.

Hook locked eyes with his man as he strode back toward the table, and the redhead gave an almost imperceptible nod.

Poison? Was this Captain of Captains already a dead man?

I glanced toward the door considering whether to find Moll and make a run for it. If he figured out what had happened and had time to retaliate, that wind magic could take us all out, and Davy definitely didn't strike me as someone who'd care much about civilian casualties.

Davy tossed the letter to the ground, lips curled in disgust. "Even if this was authentic, what choice do we have?" Davy continued, trying to regain control of the room. "Do we plan on just sitting on our laurels while we take attack after attack?"

"Not exactly...If we wanted to be ruled, we never would've become pirates in the first place." Hook let his legs drop from the table, rising as his first mate returned. "The tides have shifted against you, Davy. Don't you feel it?"

A hint of uncertainty crept into the older man's expression for the first time, and he brought his hand up in front of him, as if preparing himself. "Tread lightly, mongrel, or you'll be sleeping with the fishes before you know what hit you."

Hook took another step closer, gesturing to the room around us. "You lost this fight a long time ago, Davy. You were just too far up your own ass to realize." The rest of his crew rose as well, quickly lining up between their captain and the increasingly-agitated members of the other crews.

Davy's arm shot out, anger flashing across his face. "This is the last time you'll disrespect me, Hook. You'll —What the fuck?" He stared at his hand in stunned silence as Hook closed the distance between them in two strides.

The other crews leapt to their feet as he whipped his saber from its sheath. "Don't say I didn't give you a chance, you stubborn old bastard. But it's time for a change."

My temples pulsed with pain, and I chewed at my lip as I felt the massive well of energy inside him. As if one powerful Tideblessed in the pirate alliance wasn't enough…

Davy staggered back, holding his fingers out yet again, wiggling them frantically, but they didn't cause so much as a light breeze. I focused my eyes on him harder, pushing my own magic to the surface to see if I could sense his again, but there was nothing.

The needle?

"What've you done to me?! Men, seize him!"

Hook let out a harsh laugh, stopping in his tracks as the cluster of guards charged up from behind their king. "A fool till the end."

The first of the men stopped as he reached Davy, hesitating for only a moment before shoving him to the ground and pressing the tip of his sword against his captain's throat. The room exploded with a dozen shouts at once, but Hook's crew kept anyone from interfering.

The rest of Davy's crew stood by, swords sheathed. "You mutinous bastards," Davy spat. "What'd he pay you? I'll double it. I'll—"

"You'd be surprised how little it took," Hook answered, taking another step forward. "Betrayed by your own first mate…That Tideblessing of yours must've been the only thing stopping him. You can only beat a dog so many times before it bites, I suppose."

"Y-you can have it," Davy said, without a trace of the composure or confidence he'd shown just a few minutes earlier. "The alliance, it's yours. You can send me into exile, and I'll never return. I—"

Hook's hand shot forward in a blur, plunging his sword right into Davy's chest. A wave of sick washed over me as blood spurted into the air like a gruesome fountain. He fought and spasmed, clawing wildly to reach his killer, but the struggle didn't last long.

A loud clap pulled my attention back to Hook, who had turned to face the room. "Now that that's dealt with," he started, sounding almost disinterested, "let's get to brass tacks. As your new Captain of Captains, I'll be making some changes. We need to get back to what we're good at, which is being fucking pirates. We aren't some asshole's private army, and we aren't revolutionaries."

The tension seemed to shift as whispers of approval rolled through the room.

"We can still meet to trade information a few times a year, and call a meeting for major trouble, but no more leaders and no more groveling. I go my way, you go yours."

His solution seemed popular among the pirates, but I couldn't quite figure out whether that was a point in its favor or a mark against it.

"What'd you do to him?" Crick asked, speaking for the first time since his glass had been shattered. He looked Hook up and down apprehensively. "Is it true, what they say in whispers about your Tideblessing?"

"I'll let you all come to your own conclusions,"

Hook answered, flashing a half-smile. "Wouldn't want to give away any trade secrets."

Cunning. Better to leave the other crews in the dark about what he was capable of. His first mate had done the heavy lifting here, but there was no reason to share that.

I glanced around anxiously, wondering if anyone else had seen the same thing I had. Magic seemed more common in a world without Relyk around to stifle it, and I couldn't help but wonder at how much power was in this room right now.

"One last order of business before I go," Hook said with a grim look around the room. "You there, with the bird, step forward."

I stood stock still, wondering if he'd really just said what I thought he'd said, or if my mind was playing tricks on me.

His eyes narrowed and his voice dropped to a low, menacing rumble. "Do not make me ask again."

I wet my lips nervously and took a tentative step forward.

"Y-yes sir."

He looked me up and down and cocked his head. Then he gestured toward the redheaded man.

"Xander. Chain him and then find his sister. They're coming with us to the *Jolly Roger*."

CHAPTER 11

"Well, that didn't go to plan," Moll murmured from behind me.

I slowed my pace to let her get close enough that she could hear me whisper over the jangling of the heavy manacles around our wrists.

"Don't worry, Moll. If he wanted us dead, they'd have killed us already. He's keeping us alive for a reason."

And if that reason was for us to wash dishes or scrub the galley, maybe it'd be worth it. It would give us access to both Hook and his crew, and hopefully we'd be able to get a lot more information about The Weeping Fen and find passage—*safe* passage—to get there.

Still, marching down the corridor in chains, flanked by pirates on every side, wasn't exactly a win either.

Briefly, I considered offering a bribe with the gold I had tucked on the inside of my waistband, but I dismissed the idea immediately. All that would do was give them gold *plus* two prisoners. Better to keep my mouth shut and listen and look for a way out when one presented itself. The crews were staying a few days, if the guard we'd spoken to outside of Davy's ship could be trusted.

"Watch your step there, miss," said the red-haired first mate—Xander, Hook had called him—as we reached an uneven spot on the deck. "This room on the left," he added, jerking his thumb toward the open door.

I stepped inside, instantly relieved that it wasn't a cell with bars. Moll made to follow me in when Xander stopped her short.

"No, miss. Cap wants you separated so he can ask you some questions. Your little brother will be in this room, and you'll be across the hall."

I risked a glance at Moll and noted that her cornflower eyes went wide. How I wished that my recent ability to communicate with Fetch worked on human beings. I could only hope that my eyes spoke volumes as I tried to tell her not to worry and to remember the story we'd come up with. Her throat worked as she nodded and backed out of the doorway without argument.

"Have a seat. The Captain will be right with you," Xander said before closing the door behind him.

The second I was alone I blew out a shuddering breath and took in my surroundings. The room was small—nine by nine—and mostly bare, except for a weathered map on the wall and two chairs around a small table. It was a smart play on the captain's part if I did say so myself. He wanted to speak to Moll and I individually so he could compare our stories and sniff out any lies.

But that didn't mean he was on to us. I'd just witnessed him murder one of his own kind in cold blood, which led me to believe treachery was common enough between men like this. For all he knew, a rival crew had sent me to sabotage him, or worse.

Or maybe he somehow found out that you came from Neverland, and he is going to rip your fingernails out one by one until you share its location and give him information about his mortal enemies.

I clenched my teeth so hard my jaw ached as I made my way to the table and awkwardly pulled out a chair with my manacled hands. Maybe he'd be a while, and I'd have a little time to think of a new plan and consider all the possibilities.

No sooner had that thought come into my head than the door swung open, and the hulking form of Captain Hook filled the doorway.

"Harmon, they said your name was, right?" Hook asked, stepping inside and closing the door behind him.

The already small room seemed three times smaller

with him in it. Instead of taking the seat across from me, he chose to stand—towering over me, a move meant to intimidate. Rather than terror, I felt instant resentment at his attempt to cow me.

Fuck him.

But not like the other night...

I set my cuffed hands on the table, folding them together and pursing my lips as I fought the flush building in my cheeks. If he thought I was going to just sit there and let his silence pressure me into running my mouth, he had another thing coming. But I made sure to focus on a spot to the left of his face because I knew if I locked gazes with him, every carnal, delicious dream I'd ever had about him would rush through my mind, and my cheeks would go beet red.

"Is your bird just drawn to violence, or did you call him to you somehow?" he asked abruptly.

I weighed my answer carefully before replying. "He came to me of his own accord."

Hook nodded and then used the gleaming edge of his hook to scratch lightly at his jaw. I could feel the heat of his stare boring into me.

"I think you know what I'm asking." His voice was low and silky, hypnotic, when he spoke again. "Are you Tideblessed, boy?"

I did everything in my power not to let the confusion on my face show, but suddenly my eyes burned like all the hells—like I had to blink or die, except the move would signal weakness or, worse, subterfuge.

I held up one finger, and then tipped my head back, faking a loud sneeze. The move gave me a second to moisten my dry eyes and another to think. Did he want me to say yes or no? Which was less likely to get us killed in this situation?

One inky slash of an eyebrow shot up, a pulse in his jaw started to flicker, and I knew I'd stalled long enough.

If he could sense magic in me the way I could in him then lying would be a mistake. I said a little prayer in my mind as I rolled the dice.

"Yup. You guessed it. I'm Tideblessed." I waited with bated breath, but when he narrowed his eyes in thought rather than yanking the sword from its scabbard, I figured I'd guessed right.

"You can talk to the falcon and he responds?" he pressed.

It seemed like a harmless enough admission. I'd keep my *other* talents hidden, only giving enough away to make myself useful enough to keep alive.

I cocked my head and then shook it slowly, relieved to be able to tell the truth for once. "It's not really like that. It's more that he knows what I want him to do, and I can feel his thoughts. But it's not a conversation the way you and I are talking."

He tugged the chair out and folded his big frame into the tiny seat. When he opened his mouth to speak again, I made the crucial mistake of meeting his eyes. It felt like all the air was sucked out of the room. For a single heartbeat, there was no question in my mind that the dreams I'd had hadn't been mine alone.

Mouths colliding in a desperate, almost savage, kiss.

Needy hands, rubbing, squeezing, sliding…

But the moment of certainty faded as quickly as it had come as he stared at me through cold, distant eyes.

"Prove it."

This time, I did blink. A lot. Because I was so lost in the memory of what I'd let this man do to me in the dark of night, I'd completely lost the plot and had no earthly idea what he was talking about.

"P-prove what?"

"Call the bird." He stood, walked to the door, and shoved it open. "Now."

My stomach dropped to my toes. While I'd sent mental messages to Fetch when he was on my shoulder, when I wanted him to return to me from a distance, I usually just whistled. This mind meld stuff was all pretty new. What if I tried it and he didn't show? For all I knew, he could be too far away and my questionable power didn't even reach that far.

Hook made his way back over to the table, the heavy footfall of his boots echoing through the tiny room. Then, he laid his arm on the back of his chair and pinned me with another hard stare. "Have we met before, Harmon?"

I shook my head. "No, we have not. Not before tonight, sir."

"Then what makes you think I should trust your word?"

"Forgive me, sir, but I don't recall ever suggesting that you *should.* I'm only hesitant to call Fetch to me because, if I fail for some reason, I fear you might decide to cut my head off. And I-I'd rather you didn't do that, if it's all the same to you."

"Call. The. Bird."

I opened my mouth to try and argue again, but saw the set of his firm lips and knew it was a lost cause. So I squeezed my eyes closed and tried to think of nothing but Fetch.

Come to me, my friend. Please...

The second I felt the pressure start to form between my eyes, and the spark of magic in my chest, Hook blew out an impatient sigh and my eyes snapped wide.

"Can you, like, step back a little or turn around, maybe? You're sort of hulking over me and it's—"

His nostrils flared and his face twisted into a thunderous frown.

"You know what, it's fine." I waved a hand. "I'll make it work."

For the next few minutes, I concentrated, using everything I had to draw my falcon to me. Mental pleas, threats, and the promise of all manner of entrails and other delicacies. But when I opened my eyes a sliver to peek at the door, there was still no Fetch.

Fucking hells.

"If you can't call the bird, I've no use of you, and certainly not of your sister. Shall I tell Xander to prepare the plank, then?"

Shit.

"Are you sure he's even on the ship still? Maybe he went out for a hunt and he's too far away. Please, sir, I would ask that you give me and my sister a chance to prove our worth. Falcon or no, I'd be a real asset to your crew."

"Would you?" He stayed down his nose at me, his lips pulling into a frown. "And why is that?"

"Because I *really* need a job, so no one would work harder than me. My father is blind—" I mumbled the next bit, "freak accident with bees—and he can no longer take care of our family. My sister, although beautiful, suffers from a condition that causes her to, um, sleepwalk. I'll be blunt, sir, her eyes are wide open when she does it and it's creepy as hell, so she has no prospects for a husband. Zero. I'm the sole provider for Mother, Da, Molly, and Fetch, my falcon. The hope was to find a pirate crew that I could learn the ropes from and make enough money to support the people I love. That's always been my dream."

The gleaming hook scraped along the wooden table, leaving a jagged scar in its path as he leaned forward—so close I could smell the rum on his breath. "Dreams are just nightmares waiting to happen, boy. So I'm going to do you a favor and deny you yours now."

Something in his dark eyes told of pain like I'd

never seen, and I wished I could turn away. I wanted to reply but knew if I tried to swallow past the knot in my throat, it would have reverberated through the room like a cannon blast.

A *whoosh*ing sound broke the spell, and I turned to see Fetch flying toward me, landing smoothly on my shoulder and nuzzled close.

I'm here.

I reached up to scratch at his neck and blew out a shuddering breath. I had no idea what would've happened if Fetch hadn't been a fucking champion among birds and come through for me, and I wasn't about to question it. He was here now, and that was all that mattered.

"Alright, then." Hook glanced at Fetch and then back at me again before he made his way to the doorway, fixing me with one last, steely stare. "We just lost our crow's nest spotter, and I'm thinking you and the falcon can be of use to me in the short term, so no plank…today, at least." He shifted his weight, crossing his arms over his broad chest. "You'll start as a deckhand, and we'll see how that goes. Your sister can work in the galley. I'll warn you now, though. You'll quickly be cured of the notion that pirating is all gold and glamor. It's a brutal life, Harmon."

I managed to keep my voice steady. "I really appreciate the chance, sir. I promise to make you proud."

The pirate's hook glinted under the warm light of the room's lantern as he tapped it against the doorframe. "I doubt that." He let those words hang in the air for a beat before turning on his heel to leave, shutting the door behind him with a metallic click.

The echo of his footsteps vanished down the corridor, and I let out a shaky breath as relief flooded my chest. Why, though, I couldn't say. I hadn't found us a guide to The Fen, and I was still chained on the ship of a pirate who had proven his reputation within the first ninety seconds of me laying eyes on him. Never mind knowing that he'd killed a child.

That was enough to send whatever lust rolled through me into a shame spiral worthy of a whirlpool to the depths of the sea.

The last thing I should've been doing right now was celebrating. Especially since the reward for all this—assuming we were able to escape, and every other facet of our ludicrous plan went off without a hitch—was to head to The Weeping Fen and face off against a killer croc for a clock that everyone I knew in this place was also trying to get for themselves.

"There's no place like home..."

Gayelette's prophetic words rang so true that my soul fairly hummed with them.

Home.

A place I didn't remember, but longed for with every fiber of my being. The only way to get back there was by seeing this through. And yeah, maybe I'd taken one step forward, two steps back. But I was still in the fight.

"You can do it," I whispered under my breath.

I shifted on the hard wooden chair with a renewed sense of resolve.

One challenge at a time, Harmon, I reminded myself. *One challenge at a time.*

CHAPTER 12

en minutes later, I found myself in a cramped sleeping cabin, stomach in knots as I stared at the door.

Where the hell was Molly?

The crew member tasked to bring me to my cabin wouldn't answer when I'd asked him that—or any other question, for that matter. He'd led me down a maze of corridors and ladders to the bowels of the ship and left me there with a grunt after I thanked him for removing the manacles.

One problem solved, which was a start, at least. As much as I wanted to celebrate the small win, the aftermath of coming face-to-face with a man I'd long thought to be a figment of my imagination shook me to my core. I lowered myself to the lumpy bunk and blew out a sigh.

Daughter. Tinker. Pirate. Mage.

I had to assume that me being here—meeting Hook—was all part of the bigger plan...of my destiny. But why did every step have to be so cloaked in mystery and so fucking terrifying? Was I supposed to use my time here to get information about the clock...or the croc?

Dammit, Gayelette.

I was sick of the journey. Just give me the endgame already.

The door swung open, and I let out a yelp that had Fetch squawking from his perch on my shoulder.

Molly stepped into the room, her eyes wide.

"Look, Harmon." She plastered a brittle smile on her face, giving me a pointed stare. "First Mate Xander was nice enough to escort me back. And we've got our own room, being as I'm the *only female* on deck. Lovely, right?"

I winced, realizing the sound I'd let out when the door opened was anything but masculine. Pushing myself from the bunk, I crossed the short distance to greet the first mate with as much manly swagger as I could muster. I stuck out a hand and squeezed hard when he took it.

"Good to see you again, Xander."

The first mate looked me up and down with narrowed eyes, taking my measure but giving nothing away.

"Captain tells me you'll be staying on for a spell. My advice? Keep your head down, keep your nose clean, and do as you're told. You'll be fine. The crew here has been together a long time, and we like a calm ship. Some are rough-around-the-edges, but they won't hurt you unless you give them cause to."

Molly raised her brows at me and gave a little shrug as I pulled back.

"Rumor has it that Captain Hook is one of the most ruthless pirates around. I'm relieved his reputation has been exaggerated," I added.

Xander's lips split into a wide smile that took years off his sun-weathered face. For the first time, I realized that he was almost boyishly handsome.

"Oh, don't put words in my mouth." His grin widened. "No, Hook's soul is blacker than the darkest night. We're well-fed and well-paid because it keeps us loyal. Period. But if you're not one of us? He'd just as soon see you dead as see you never."

Alright, then.

"I'll be taking your leave now," he added, tipping his hat to Moll. "Someone from the kitchen crew will be down with a hunk of bread and some cheese shortly. Eat and get some rest. You're gonna need it." With that, he turned on his heel to go but then paused. "Lock the door once you're settled for the night. No one will try to bother you, but we can't have you wandering around in the middle of the night and falling off the ship or something. See you at sunrise."

The door shut, and the locks tumbling into place made it feel both final and ominous.

"What the hell was that about?" Molly whispered. "Does he think we're stupid enough to go walking off the side of the ship? Hell, I wouldn't leave this room on a dare, given that this whole place is rife with pirates. Like fleas on a dog!"

"About that," I muttered, pulling off my hat and running a hand through my hair with a grimace. "Look, I know you're gonna be mad, but I was desperate. He was so intense, and I just couldn't stop rambling…"

Molly crossed her arms over her ample chest, her glare sharp enough to draw blood. "Harmony Marie Fallowell, what did you say this time?"

I swallowed. "I kind of…sort of…told Hook that one of the reasons he should keep us alive instead of killing us is that I was the caretaker for our whole family because our dad went blind after a bee attack, and—"

"I don't need the whole story," she snapped. "What I need is for you to tell me what you told him about *me*."

I hesitated.

"Wait! Don't. Let me guess what it is this time," she continued, voice dripping with sarcasm. "I'm a simpleton with a brain the size of a walnut with a death wish to boot, who just wanders around walking off boats?"

"Not exactly," I hedged. "I just… mentioned that I had to get a spot on the crew to take care of you as you struggled to find a husband, what with your terrible sleepwalking affliction."

"What?" Molly's eyes widened in outrage. "I can't believe you told him I have a problem finding a husband! That's even crueler than the vow of silence bit. And, frankly, not even believable. Plenty of men in The Hollow would've loved to marry me."

My lips twitched. Only Molly would be more outraged by the implication that she couldn't land a man more than me saddling her with another feigned affliction.

"I know, but let's not get caught up in the small stuff here. Hopefully, we're going to get some information along with a ride to some nearby island, and then, we're never gonna see these people again. Who cares what they think of us?" I reasoned.

"Fine. We'll put a pin in it." She dropped into the tiny stool by the desk in the corner. "But we are going to talk about this pattern of behavior at some point. Either you have a mean streak, or you're trying to get me back for something I haven't quite put a finger on. Which is it?"

Then, just as quickly as it had come, her annoyance drained away and she leaned forward, eyes lighting up.

"Oh! But I *do* want to hear about Captain Tall, Dark, and Sexy, though. Xander said the two of you were talking in another room. How did it go?"

"Not good, Moll." I sighed. "It went…not good." I hesitated, unsure of where to start or how much I wanted to share yet. It was bad enough that we were stuck on a ship with him. Or at least some version of him. The fact that my brain and body hadn't yet figured out how to separate the humorless, child murdering, cruel pirate from the wickedly handsome dream lover was going to be a major problem if I didn't get a handle on it fast. "I did finally figure out the real reason he took us, though, so that's something."

"And?"

"It's Fetch."

Molly wrinkled her nose and shot the falcon a skeptical glance. "Why? Does he have a taste for rodents or something?"

I glanced at Fetch, who cracked one eye open before shutting it again, clearly unbothered by Molly's barbed words.

"No. I just—" I hesitated. I hadn't told Molly exactly how, since my time with The Speaker and the other Whispers, my connection with Fetch had deepened.

I filled her in as best I could, and when I was done, she stayed quiet for a long moment before shooting me a dubious look. "So you're saying you can actually meet minds with that bird?"

I shrugged. "It's not an exact science yet, but I feel like we're getting better and better at it."

"Great, well then maybe you can ask him why he hates me so much?"

I was about to tell her no—that we had more of a "come here" or "alert, danger ahead!" type of communication, and hers was too complex of a question—but then a sudden sense of knowing flooded through me. A thought that wasn't mine.

It belonged to Fetch.

"He doesn't hate you," I said slowly. "He just feels like you both serve the same purpose. You guys are redundant, and frankly, he thinks he's better at the job."

Molly blinked at me. "We serve the same *purpose?*" she repeated, letting out a laugh. "Okay, well first of all, I'm a person and he's a pet. Second of all, he's like an indentured servant, while you and I are equals and best friends."

She wasn't wrong. But that wasn't how Sir Fetchington Von Buren saw things. Still, if I hadn't been so surprised by Fetch understanding and answering the question—coming from Moll and not me, no less—I would've been a little more careful about how I worded the Falcon's response.

"I think he means you're both basically my family," I said carefully, trying to clean up some of my mess. I lowered my voice and leaned in. "And he's probably a little jealous. He knows how close we are."

Molly pursed her lips, then gave a slow nod. "That makes more sense. Okay, Bird. I guess I'd be jealous of me, too."

"As it stands," I continued, "the three of us are in this together. We've got nobody else, so let's do our best to take care of each other, okay?"

Moll nodded.

Fetch closed his eyes and buried his face in my neck again. "He says yes," I added.

There was a long pause until Moll blurted, "Do you think that Cissy, Tristan, and Caleb will ever forgive us for up and leaving like we did?"

The question may have seemingly come out of nowhere, but I'd been friends with her long enough to know that the thought had been on her mind the whole time since we'd left Neverland.

It was something I'd done my best *not* to think about, because it was more to add to the steadily rising pile of collateral damage that I had no one to blame for but myself.

"Children can bounce back from almost anything," I reasoned. "Look how much they've gone through already, and they're still pretty great kids. I think they'll get over it."

"Cissy won't if she's like our Cissy from The Hollow. She's going to be pissed for life." Molly's mouth wobbled into a smile. "I bet she replaced that Captain Hook wanted poster with a picture of us to throw knives at."

I chuckled in agreement. "She's fiery, that one."

"Poor Tristan, though. He finally found a friend in Fetch, and then we snatched him away—" Molly's expression went dark and she wrapped her arms around her midsection. "But most of all, I hope Caleb is okay. He really wasn't looking well…"

She wasn't wrong. In fact, that last morning, his

skin had been so pale, it was almost transparent, the blue of his veins hinting through. The weight of it all got super heavy all at once, and I was grateful when a knock at the door interrupted us.

"Come in," I called.

A salty looking old man in a used-to-be-white cook's jacket stepped inside, basket in hand.

"Thanks so m—" Molly said to the door that was shut in her face half a second after she accepted the food. "Did he tell the rest of them that they're not allowed to talk to us or something?"

"They probably have a lot of work to do now that we've set sail."

"That's true," she said as we each sat on our bunks and tore into the bread. "And at least Xander seems nice enough—even if Hook isn't. Tomorrow will be a better day."

I nodded. "Once I'm out there working with the crew, I'm sure I'll get the lay of the land and ferret some information out of them. First thing on the list, find out where we're going and what's going to happen when we get there."

I was feeling more optimistic as we ate our meal in silence. Moll might love some lace and finery, but at the end of the day, we were iron hearts, forged in the poverty of The Hollow.

Surely nothing we'd be asked to do the next day could be worse than anything we'd had to do to survive to this point...

I really had to stop telling myself lies.

CHAPTER 13

Halfway through the next morning, I was kicking myself for that optimism the night before.

"What's the matter there, slim? Your belly too soft for this life, boy?" a mocking voice called from behind me as I retched over the side of the ship yet again.

How was it even possible?

Surely the bit of dried beef and egg I'd eaten for breakfast at dawn had come up on one of the first twenty times I'd puked. Although now, I was mainly drive-heaving with a bit of bile mixed in for good measure. Like my body was rejecting my stomach entirely, and the demons inside weren't going to stop raging until that, too, had been given to the gods of the sea as an offering.

The massive galleon rocked left to right again, and I

wrapped my arms around the railing to keep from getting tossed over the side.

This couldn't be normal. How could anyone stomach the constant rolling and pitching? But as I swiped at my mouth and turned, I noted that the stocky man giving me shit a few yards away seemed to have no trouble keeping his balance—or his breakfast from making an encore appearance.

I tried to manage a smile as the ship settled some.

"I've been on plenty of boats before," I called back. "Just don't recall it being this choppy."

"I fear you picked the wrong line of work, little man," he said with a guffaw, flashing a handful of teeth —one of them gold. "Luckily for you, the wind's shifting. Should be only another hour or so of this, then smooth sailing until we hit port."

My pulse kicked up a notch, and I tried to seem nonchalant as the boat rocked again and I held on with one arm for dear life. An hour more of this? I wasn't going to be alive in an hour because I'd have puked all my innards up and made them out-ards by then.

"Port, huh? Where are we heading anyway?"

"Cap shares that info with sailors, not scrubs." He shot a glance up to the sky and let out a sniff. "Better get to it. He expects this whole deck to be swabbed before we break for supper," he said before turning to limp away.

"Hey, I'm Harmon," I called after him. "What's your name, anyway?"

"Trick-Eyed Tom," he called back, squinting against the sun and wind.

That was as good a pirate name as I'd heard. I forged ahead, unwilling to miss the chance to make an ally despite my aching gut.

"How'd you get that nickname?"

I'd barely gotten the words out when he plucked his eyeball out, spun it like a top on the tip of his index finger, then stuck it back in place with a wink.

"No idea," he said with a shrug. "Now stop stalling and get back to work."

I picked up the mop I'd been using and dunked it into the hot water and lye solution, trying my best to ignore the blazing sun overhead. At this rate, I wouldn't have to worry about being forced to walk the plank or getting eaten by Noru, The Ticking Croc. I'd be dead long before that, just from a day of sailing on the sea. I'd considered myself pretty tough, but I had to admit—the situation was humiliating.

As the day progressed, Trick-Eyed Tom turned out to be right. The sea calmed, but by the time the lunch bell rang, I was shaking from head to toe, dizzy from dehydration, sun poisoning, or maybe scurvy? I couldn't be sure. I dragged my sorry ass into the galley and found an empty seat at one of the tables. No sooner had I sat down than Molly came scurrying over.

"Come with me," she hissed, grabbing me by the wrist and yanking me bodily from the chair.

A minute later, I found myself in a small bathroom behind closed doors.

"Your beard is almost melted off." She reached into her apron pocket for some shoe polish she'd squirreled away. "Got to check on that a couple times a day. Now I finally understand why I had to do all the heavy lifting back in Little Alabaster with the disguises and such. You can't stay in character worth shit."

I was too exhausted to remind her that the actual reason she'd needed a disguise instead of me was because she'd stabbed the king with her shoe, and if they found her, she'd have been hung or put to the guillotine on the spot.

"That's better," she muttered as she leaned back, inspecting my face. "Your skin is covered in salt. Going to have to do a deep cleanse later, or you're going to get wrinkles. Now come on, I made lunch. You'll feel better after you eat something."

My pitiful stomach gurgled in protest, but I didn't fight it as she dragged me back into the dining hall. Fetch had flown in to join me, and I wound up just sitting there in an exhausted, near-trance state for a while. It was only when Moll set a plate in front of me —with what looked to be some kind of pie—that I realized the room had filled and most of the other tables were packed, while the three empty chairs around me were notably unoccupied.

Lovely.

I needed to at least get closer to the others if I

wanted to eavesdrop, but I was too wrung out to do more than sip gratefully at the lemon water and nibble on some tangy yellow fruit Molly had given me.

"Who made the eel pie?" a gruff voice called out.

Molly stuck her head in from the galley with a wave and a wide smile. "I did. Do you like it?"

"Tastes like a greasy worm fucked another greasy worm and gave birth to this, wrapped it in paste, and took a shit on it."

"Okay, that's a lot." Molly faltered, then nodded, forcing a bright smile. "Got it! I'll do better next time," she said, tucking back into the galley as quickly as she'd come.

Her cooking skills had never been stellar, but I mentally recorded the man's face, filing it away for later. It was one thing for me to make fun of Moll. It was something else for a stranger to do it—especially in front of all these people, when she was trying her hardest. Ungrateful fucker.

Although, as I took a closer look at the bit of pie on my plate, I had to admit, it did not look appetizing. I squinted...Was it still moving?

I covered that part of the plate with a napkin and went in for some more fruit. Once I'd eaten my fill of everything but the pie—slowly and carefully—and gotten some time out of the sun, I felt a little better and tried to home in on conversations happening around me.

"Old Mick and the gang looted the fancy part of Covington."

"I love it when a scallywag parts a rich wanker like that from his gold."

"Word is they've headed northwest. Once we're done with this job, maybe we could catch them on the high seas and relieve them of that burden."

"Did you mention the idea to the captain yet?"

"Not yet. I was going to talk to Xander about it first."

"She had big, soft bosoms like two pillows. I asked her, 'Could I just nestle my face between them for a while, lass?'"

I was about to stroll around the room when all the chatter suddenly came to a screeching halt. A second later, Hook stepped into the dining hall.

Most of the men muttered, *"Captain,"* under their breath by way of greeting and continued eating. Hook's gaze swept the room, pausing on me before flicking to Fetch—then pointedly looking away as I raised a hand to wave hello.

Molly came scurrying out a moment later with a tray in hand.

"Here you go, sir. I gave you a double portion of griddle cakes, in case you were extra hungry."

Hook accepted the food and turned away without a word, leaving the galley.

The hushed conversation resumed the second he was out of earshot.

Not exactly a happy family, then. That was good.

Maybe one of them would be willing to help us if we needed it.

"Ever finish that deck, swabby?"

I looked up to find Trick-Eyed Tom squinting down at me. "I did."

"Great. Now there's only three others like it that you need to finish before we're done for the day. Better pick up the pace!"

He looked pretty pleased with himself for dropping the bad news on me. But he was the only person who had spoken to me all day, and I wasn't about to let him go that easily.

"Hang on a second, Tom. Can I ask you something? You all seem like a friendly lot. I just want to be part of that. Anything I can do to make them like me?"

"Like you?" He shook his head with a laugh. "You'd have to be part of the crew. We don't take kindly to strangers."

"I thought I *was* part of the crew."

"Not without doing the initiation first."

"Initiation?"

He looked around, then leaned forward. "You'd have to complete The Devil's Gauntlet, of course."

Of course. The Devil's Fucking Gauntlet. Just for once, couldn't it be The Kitten's Paw? Or The Goldfish's Gill?

I swallowed an exhausted sigh. "And what, exactly, does that entail?"

"You seen those red streamers hanging above the crow's nest?"

I had but hadn't given them much thought. They looked like someone had shredded a crimson flag, leaving it in tatters that whipped and writhed in the wild winds.

"Well, when each of us became part of the crew, we shimmied up the mast and pinned a strip of cloth to the top. Represents our lifeblood, it does. A show of loyalty to Cap, and our crewmates. Pirates and scallywags we might be, but these men is my brothers. I'd die for any of 'em. You want to be part o' the crew? You've to do the same. Not that I'm recommending it," he added with a chuckle and a shrug. "Something tells me you've neither the muscle nor the heart for it, but you asked, so I'm answering."

With that, he turned and walked away, leaving me to stare after him with something like dogged determination flickering to life in my chest like a flame. He might be right about the muscle, but he was wrong about the heart.

Iron heart, forged in the flames of poverty, fear and questionable decisions.

I'd made Willy Fallowell fall in love with me, despite everything Druzilla did to keep it from happening. I'd somehow charmed old Bertrand the falconer and turned him into a friend. Hell, I'd even made the O'Donnelly's—a family of smugglers and criminals who valued their own hides above all else—into allies.

There was no quit in *this* girl from The Hollow.

I'd find a way to make these pirates accept me, even if it killed me.

CHAPTER 14

"I quit," I muttered, the words a mere hint of a whisper from my parched lips.

By the end of the day, my blisters had blisters, my tongue felt like a dried-up sock in my mouth, and the flame in my chest had died to an ember.

I stared into the bathroom mirror and winced.

My skin was the color of a ripe strawberry, and my lips were so chapped I could have used them as sandpaper. I nearly laughed when I realized that Moll's new and improved shoe shine—the kind she'd used to fix my beard earlier—had actually stayed on this time.

Quickly, I rinsed my ravaged hands and wiped the sweat off my face.

If I wanted a chance to overhear some dinner chatter, I needed to get to the dining hall. One more hour. Sixty minutes of trying to make some headway, and then I could leave and nurse my wounds. A long bath and ten straight hours of sleep would surely help me get a new perspective on things.

Tears pricked at the back of my eyelids as I dried my hands.

"Nope. Pirates don't cry. Get your ass back out there, Harmon."

I stepped back onto the deck a minute later, just in time to see the others making their way toward the galley. A couple of them shoulder-checked me as they passed.

"Out of the way, swabby!"

The last one caught me full force—and he was a big fucker too. I stumbled, nearly caught my footing, and then tripped on the handle of the very mop I'd left out before heading to the bathroom. It sent me pinwheeling backward, and I landed flat on my back.

The breath whooshed out of me, and for a second, I thought my heart had stopped.

"That had to hurt. Talk about learning a lesson on the job, ay, boy?"

I blinked up at the sky, only to find Trick-Eyed Tom bending over me, a grin stretched across his face.

"That's what you get for leaving stuff out like that," he said. "Bet you'll know better next time."

He reached out a hand as if to help me up, but the moment I lifted mine to grasp it, he pulled away.

"Gotta learn to help yourself if you want others to help you, swabby," he murmured, then continued past me, leaving me sprawled on the deck, staring up at the dusky purple sky. This time, when the flame flickered back to life, it wasn't determination. It was fury.

And it was an inferno.

I sucked in a sharp breath and leapt to my feet, shouldering my way through the crowd of men moving toward the galley. I was heading toward the middle of the ship.

"Fuck the devil and his gauntlet."

I reached for the makeshift belt—made from an old, red tie that Garth had found lying around—and yanked one end until it slipped free from my loops. Time was ticking. I'd already wasted the entire day doing nothing besides helping the insidious Captain Hook clean his poop deck. And for what? Not like the next town of innocents he raided would give a rat's ass that he kept a tidy ship.

When I reached the main mast, I wrapped my bloodied right hand in the belt, then reached for the small dagger strapped to my shin, freeing it from its leather sheath. I tucked it between my teeth, then turned to the rickety rope ladder that led up to the ship's crow's nest.

"Don't look up. Don't look down," I muttered through clenched teeth.

Letting out a shuddering sigh, I tightened my grip and stepped onto the first rung. Agony shot through my palms and fingers as the bristly rope ripped open any blisters that hadn't already been torn.

Focus on the positives, I told myself. At least the other

hand—wrapped in the silky length of fabric Garth had given me—didn't feel half as bad.

One foot at a time.

Blood rushed in my ears, competing with the buffeting winds that had once again picked up as dusk slowly turned to dark.

Six rungs. Seven. Eight.

I stopped counting at forty. The thought that each rung meant another foot or more made me nauseous.

Don't look up. Don't look down.

The mast groaned, shifting slightly, sending the ladder swinging far out and to the left. I squeezed my eyes shut, gritting my teeth tighter around the dagger in my mouth.

Another six rungs. Then my foot slipped. I scrambled, my hands on fire, but surely, I was nearly there? Stopping now would make everything I'd done so far, a waste.

Who knew if I'd ever be brave enough to try again? So I forced myself to think about the things that mattered.

Molly. The Speaker. The vague, but oh so real concept of home. The woman's face that showed up in my dreams from time to time, her wide smile and sparkling hazel eyes. My Pawpaw, Willie Fallowell. His face beaming with pride as I forged my first weapon.

I was eating up the ladder now, my steps growing quicker, surer—even as my shoulder muscles began to cramp and my back spasmed.

Almost there. You can do it, Harm.

Over the sound of my own blood pounding, I heard a violent screech that sent an icy wave of terror rolling over me.

Flying mantis?

No. It was only when Fetch's mind brushed against mine—when I felt his fear and anger—that I realized it was him and he was furious.

It's okay. I'm almost there.

I could sense his rejection of that statement, and that was when I made the biggest mistake of all.

I looked up.

Then I looked down.

I still had another twenty rungs to climb just to reach the crow's nest. Worse than that? Now I could see what I hadn't before. The crow's nest was the end of the road as far as the ladder was concerned. The rest of the way was exactly as Tom had described it.

I'd be scooting up the pole without the benefit of the ladder…or anything else, for that matter.

For a second, I froze. There was no chance I could climb back down. Just the thought had me so dizzy, the world started spinning.

Up. It was the only way.

I closed my eyes and began to sing under my breath.

"Therrrre once was a lady named Mary, who farmed by the sea—it was airy."

The silly little song Molly had made up for the kids on Neverland. I moved to the rhythm.

One step, then two. Three, then four.

I warbled the last note, letting it linger before opening my eyes. Relief flooded in as I realized I'd made it. I'd reached the crow's nest. Using what felt like my last reserve of strength, I pulled myself onto the platform and collapsed flat on my back, trying not to puke.

The wind howled around me, and for a second, it almost sounded like it was calling my name.

Fetch fluttered down beside me, poking at my face with his beak, the distinct feeling of his disapproval prickling at the edges of my awareness.

Then I realized with a start that it wasn't the wind howling at all. It was voices, and they were...cheering?

For me.

"Harmon! Harmon!"

I swallowed hard, fighting through the agony. "I'm sorry, buddy," I murmured. "But I've got to finish this."

There's no place like home.

My whole body was like one, raw, exposed nerve and I cried out as I forced myself up onto my knees first, then onto shaking legs.

The gusts had my eyes watering as I looked up to study the rest of the path that lay before me. In truth, it wasn't that much further. The mast was thin this high up...Thin enough to wrap my thighs around. I squinted as I rose to my tiptoes. Roughly hewn divots peppered the wood above me, and I realized what they were.

Handholds.

With a silent prayer of thanks for those who'd gone before me, I dug my fingers into the wood and squeezed my thighs together.

At a snail's pace, I shimmied up the last few yards of the mast. Every muscle shook with fatigue. Every inch of my skin burned.

What if I didn't make it? What would become of Molly and those I cared about? What if I'd bet on myself, and this time, I was wrong?

I let out a strangled gasp, lifting my hand for the next hand hold—only to feel my fingertips brush against cloth. With trembling fingers, I reached down and tugged the dagger from between my teeth, my jaw aching from holding it so long.

Then, lifting the belt high above my head, I took a deep breath and bellowed the words as loud as I could:

"FOR CAPTAIN HOOK!"

I pressed the fluttering piece of cloth against the others, gripped the pole with all my might, then swung my dagger—burying it to the hilt through the belt and into the wood.

I hung there, panting, as my fingers palsied around the hilt of the dagger. It was only as that initial surge of adrenaline and elation peaked and ebbed that I realized the truth.

There was only one way I was leaving this mast. And it sure as hell wasn't by my own strength.

A great gust of wind battered the material above me, and I lifted my gaze. The crimson flag waved valiantly in the night, my belt now a part of it. It was the last thing I saw before the ship rocked hard to the left and my muscles finally betrayed me and gave way. The last thing I saw before I pinched my eyes closed was the deck I'd just cleaned, hundreds of feet below me.

Maybe Tom would be the one to have to clean it this time, I thought, laughter bubbling in my throat.

There was no time to relish the thought though, because I was weightless and falling, Fetch's screech filling my head…

Nooo!

CHAPTER 15

I was floating through the air, boneless, weightless—until something slammed into my side. I heard the crunch of at least one rib, and the agony in my body coalesced into that one spot.

I'd be dead, so it wouldn't matter soon, but damn, it fucking hurt. I forced my eyes open to get one last look at the dusty purple sky, I watched as the ship went by.

Before I could even process what was happening, I smacked into the water. The sea swallowed me whole, saltwater rushing up my nose and into my mouth. I kicked frantically, trying to get a sense of which way was up, but it was already so dark.

And then—suddenly—Something tightened around my neck. I was being dragged upward.

I surfaced with a series of choked coughs and gasps, my hands flying to my throat, clawing at—what the hell was it? It felt like an octopus tentacle wrapped around my neck.

Falling off a crow's nest and splatting on the deck to impress a bunch of pirates was a bad way to die. But getting my head pinched off by a sea monster?

A thousand times worse.

I clawed and kicked, furiously fighting through the waves of nauseating pain.

"Stay the fuck still," a low voice snarled in my ear.

I instantly went limp, my body recognizing the voice before my brain did. Captain Hook.

And judging by the way he was kicking his feet, tugging me along, he was actually trying to save me instead of kill me.

I was about to make some attempt to thank him through my aching throat when something in the distance caught my eye.

A bulge in the water.

I swiped at my eyes, clearing away salt and sea, blinking hard to get a better look. No—definitely a bulge. And it was coming our way.

Fast.

"Hook, there's something—"

"Quiet, dammit," he snapped. "I'm trying to save you here. The least you can do is keep your trap shut."

"Okay," I croaked. "And I appreciate it—but there's something following us. And it looks really big."

Hook whipped his head around, knocking his jaw into the side of my skull.

"Fucking hell."

In the distance, I could hear voices hollering.

"READY THE CANNONS!" someone bellowed.

The bulge had closed the distance fast—probably less than twenty yards away now. And gaining.

"Come on, Captain, you've got it!"

"CANNONS READY—FIRE!"

The night sky exploded in orange, and a spot just a few yards behind me erupted in a splash of foam and salt water.

A preternatural screech pierced the air.

The bulge grew smaller—then disappeared.

"It wasn't a direct hit," a vaguely familiar voice called from somewhere nearby. "Hurry!"

I let out a wrenching groan as Hook yanked me, lifting me summarily from the water and into what felt like a dozen waiting arms.

I was pulled onto the deck, landing in a wet, hacking puddle as the crew rushed back to help Hook from the water.

"GO! GO! GO!"

I managed to lift my head just in time to see them drag him aboard—

And then a thunderous blow rocketed through the ship. It was like we'd been hit by a boulder beneath the surface.

"Fooking hell! It's a sea serpent. And a big one at that!"

"Good thing we got your legs aboard, Captain,"

someone teased. "Or we might have had to change your name to Peg."

I opened one eye to see Hook, who stood at the rail, staring down at the sea below.

I let out a sigh.

Then, blackness. Everything disappeared as it dragged me under...

"So he's a she, then?"

When I woke, the pounding in my head had dulled to a low thrum, and the low voices sounded around me. I forced my eyes open to find myself in the same spot I'd been, still soaking wet, with Trick-Eyed Tom standing over me, along with a dozen other stunned and concerned faces.

"Back away," Hook snarled.

The men obeyed instantly as he dropped to one knee beside me.

"I hope you're all proud of yourselves," he said, his eyes trailing over me, from my face to the tip of my sopping red boots and back up again. "You sent a fucking female, who's clearly never spent a day on a ship, up the rigging, past the crow's nest, for some foolish display of fealty. I turn a blind eye when you fools do it to each other—you have your free will and chose to be here. Lucky, she didn't wind up dead." His lips pursed into a frown. "We're so close to getting what we've worked all these years for and we need her to work with the falcon. You lot nearly fucked it, and for what? A laugh?"

He turned, scowling down at me, his eyes like an ebony storm.

"Who told you to do that?"

I opened my mouth—then snapped it shut. I shook my head. "No one," I finally managed, surprised that speaking didn't hurt as much as I'd expected.

Hook let out a bitter laugh, pressing his face close to mine.

"Well, No One should get ten lashes for this little trick," he murmured. "And you should get twenty. Count yourself lucky. I'm too tired from dragging your sorry ass out of the water to administer a beating tonight."

He pushed himself to stand.

"Get cleaned up." He shot me a glare. "And don't think this gets you off duty tomorrow."

With that, he stalked off, leaving ominous silence in his wake.

It was Trick-Eyed Tom himself who finally broke it. He bent over me, reaching out a hand. "I'm sorry," he said with a grimace. "I'd not have done it if I knew you was a lassie. But it was mean-spirited, regardless." He let out an incredulous laugh as he shook his head. "I honestly didn't think you'd be dumb enough to do it."

"Dumb enough?" a voice called out. "She's a fucking legend!"

And then, they were singing my praises again.

I reached for Tom's hand, and this time, he actually helped me up. Again, I waited for the brutal pain to come screaming back, but it never did.

When Tom released me and I looked down, my eyes nearly popped out of my head. The skin was whole. A little red, a little tender, but whole.

"What the hell?" I demanded, snapping my gaze up to meet Tom's.

"Captain burned a lot of magic on you today shooting you out of the sky with that wind bullet, like you was a fucking pheasant, girly," he said, wiping a hand across his dripping forehead. "Count yourself lucky that he was able to push you hard enough that you landed in the drink instead of on the deck. He wouldn't do it for most. His soul is black as night, you know."

"Give her some space now," Xander said, shouldering his way through the circle of men and handing me a massive blanket and a tankard of what looked like ale. He stared down at me, assessing, as he murmured, "Hook saved you, but it was Tom who healed you. He's a gifted Mend. And despite his foolishness, he's got a good heart. But tell me, now that we know the truth about you; what's your real name?"

"Harmony." I pressed the cold mug to my lips and took a deep, greedy swallow. The cool liquid on my parched throat was heaven. I let out a sigh as I smacked my lips. "My name is Harmony."

"Well, Harmony…welcome to the crew. Now go dry off and meet us in the card room for drinks. It's a celebration!"

The men exploded into cheers, and as silly as it was, I couldn't deny the swell of pride rising inside me.

You're pleased with yourself because now you can get the answers you need.

But that wasn't the truth. The truth was, it felt good to be part of something, even if it was a ragtag crew of evil pirates, apparently.

And wasn't that some shit?

CHAPTER 16

"Y ou did what?"

Molly's cornflower blue eyes were wide as she stared at me in shock a short while later.

"I climbed up the mast and hung my belt up there with the others," I repeated, keeping my gaze trained on the scarred table in front of me. "Nearly broke my neck, but Hook…he shot me out of the sky with some sort of magic. I don't know if it was a sound wave or a-" How could I even explain it? Like a hard shove, but with no hand doing the shoving.

What type of Tideblessing could do that?

"Get back over here, swabby!" Tom called from his seat at the card table across the room. "And tell Moll to bring another round!"

The other men let out a huzzah in agreement and broke into laughter.

"You realize that's psychotic, right?" Molly hissed. "Harm, you could have been killed. That's more dangerous than anything I've ever done." She folded her arms, shaking her head. "And *I'm* the silly one."

I wished I could argue with her, but I couldn't. Something had gotten to me—whether it was physical exhaustion, or just me being sick and tired of feeling out of control. I wanted to take control of something. Whatever the case, I hadn't had it in me to stop myself.

Which was all well and good, now that Tom had mended me. Because if not, I'd have been useless for weeks, if not months.

The clock is ticking.

I lifted a tentative hand to my rib cage and pressed gingerly. Still a twinge, but nothing like the pain when it had first happened.

I closed my eyes, swallowing back a groan as the memory of him dragging me out of the water flooded my mind. The fury in those dark eyes.

Not because he cared, I reminded myself. But because he needed me. Despite countless dreams to the contrary, that was the only reason he had helped me. I couldn't allow myself to forget it for an instant. I had to make sure I left this ship unscathed—both physically and emotionally—and so far, I was doing a shit job of it.

"You're right, Moll. It won't happen again," I said. "I think it was just the sun that got to me. If it makes you feel any better, you and Fetch are on the same page here. He's not talking to me at all."

In fact, the falcon had circled overhead for a few moments to see that I was all right after Hook had dragged me onto the deck, but I had seen neither feather nor beak of him since.

"I know I didn't make a perfect decision here but cut me some slack. It's been a really tough couple of weeks, and at least the crew accepts me now."

Molly tucked an errant auburn curl behind one ear, blew out a sigh, then rolled her eyes.

"Fine. Whatever. Go get drunk with your new friends," she muttered. "I'm going back to the galley and putting my feet up while I have some chamomile tea to try to soothe my nerves after the scare you just gave me."

She turned and then paused, her eyes lighting with excitement. "Oh! I did overhear Cooky telling one of the crew that the Captain was skipping his usual whiskey in the library and to just bring him a toddy to his room this evening. Maybe there is something you can do with that? A library is good, right?"

Libraries were often treasure troves of information, and apparently, Hook's would be empty this evening. Did I dare try to find it when I was already number one on his freshly crafted shitlist?

Then again, how else was I going to find out about where we were going?

Liar. You know why you want to go snooping, and it has

nothing to do with the next port. You're here risking your neck for one reason and one reason only. Because you can't stop thinking about Captain Hook and why he's been haunting your dreams all these years.

Moll bustled off, and I shoved the thought away as I crossed the room toward where the rest of the crew was gathered—some shooting the shit, others playing cards, and a few throwing darts at a board.

"Rum for the swabby!"

A man I vaguely recalled being referred to as Pip balanced three shots in one hand and gestured for me to take one.

"Thanks," I said with a grateful nod. My stomach was still a bit topsy-turvy, but I wasn't about to refuse —not after working so damn hard to gain their friendship.

The first mate stepped in, plucking the second shot from Pip's fingers and holding it high.

"To Harmony," he announced. "A toast! Next time you scuttle up, may the gods grant you an easier way down!"

The men broke into laughter, and I grinned.

"I don't know," I mused. "I kind of like the adventure of winging it."

The three of us knocked back our rum, and I spluttered but managed to cover it with a cough and the men roared their approval.

"Throat's still a little sore from all the salt water," I rasped.

Xander slipped an arm around my shoulder, pulling me to the side as a couple of the men began crafting a shanty song about my misadventure.

"Cap is pretty pissed with you," he said. "And us, too."

The smile faded from his eyes.

"You didn't have to do that, you know. It's a bit of a miracle you're not dead. Tom's not a bad person. I truly think he didn't expect you to actually follow through on it."

I opened my mouth to respond, but he wasn't finished.

"Still though, I question whether you're ready for this life. It's tough out here, Harmony. And despite the guts you've shown, I think it would help if you developed your magic a little more. That way, you won't have to rely on someone swooping in to save you when you need saving again. And you *will* need saving again."

I wanted to argue. To explain that I was usually the one doing the saving. The pragmatic one. The one with a plan. But all he knew was what he'd seen so far, and my cheeks flushed as I realized that what he'd seen was a dumbass, doing dumbass shit.

Besides—who was I to argue if he wanted to help me?

"I think I'd be less nervous if I knew where we were going," I admitted. "And what we're going to do. Am I going to have to kill anyone?"

Xander shook his head. "No. Especially now that

Cap knows you're not really like us. And as for where we're headed, I'm pretty sure our course is set for Kraken Reef. We'll be there by tomorrow afternoon. He's looking to resupply—but also to find some people who might be able to help us with a mission. He'll be the one to tell you the plan once he's ready."

I was dying to press, but his expression had grown guarded, and prodding further would only make him suspicious.

"If you want to work on your Tideblessing, like I mentioned," he said after a beat, "and you're willing to wake up an hour before dawn, I'm up anyways. Wouldn't kill me to help you some."

I stared at him in surprise. "Help me how?"

He smirked. "I grew up in a traveling circus. My parents were carnies. I picked up sleight of hand skills and used my blessing to become a pretty proficient magician along the way. The tide didn't see fit to bless me with a *whole* lot of magic, but carnival people are the best at making the most of what they've got. And I can show you how to do the same."

That explained how he'd been able to slip a needle into Davy's wrist without anyone seeing. A useful skill, and I was sure he had many others. But I found myself hesitating.

I wasn't Tideblessed. Not really. I was a Whisper, albeit a strange one. I had no tattoo, and didn't even know if Xander's lessons would help me.

Still, it was a generous offer, and who knew…

"You would do that for me? Why? I'm a stranger to you."

Way to look a gift horse in the mouth, Harm. But I couldn't stop the question from coming out of my lips.

He cocked his head, his green eyes studying my face. Then he shrugged.

"You remind me of my daughter, Lorelei," he said simply. His wistful expression told me he hadn't seen her in a very long time. "It's a compliment. She's a peach, that one."

My heart squeezed, and I managed a small smile, but was saved having to come up with a reply, as a moment later a loud voice bellowed my name.

"Come on over, lass! Listen to the song Slim Sven wrote for you!"

A giant bear of a man who I was sure had never seen a day of slim in his life stepped forward with a broad grin.

"It's a work in progress, but here's the start." He cleared his throat, and began to sing, the notes pitch perfect and clear as a bell;

"There once was a lass, on the roaring wild seas,

With soul full of grit, and brass in her knees

She climbed to the crow's nest, brazen and bold,

In a show of great strength, she braved winds so cold!

She pinned her red silk on top of the mast,

We shouted and cheered, but our joy did not last!

· · ·

OH, ho, ho! She took such a fall!

Oh, ho, ho! The shame of it all!

She'd pinned her bright silk, then fell like a stone,

But when the sea came to claim her, it wasn't alone…

INTO THE WAVES did our new friend descend,

Towards a monstrous sea serpent—would this be her end?

Its maw open wide, it came full speed ahead,

Out for first blood, this t'ing wanted her dead!

But our Captain Hook is too clever a man

And he stole that ting's dinner, and the two 'o them ran!

OH, ho, ho! She took such a fall!

Oh, ho, ho! The shame of it all!

She'd pinned her bright silk, then fell like a stone,

But when the sea came to claim her, it wasn't alone…"

My face flushed, and I grinned like a fool. It was nice to be appreciated, even if it was under somewhat false pretenses.

Trick-Eyed Tom climbed up onto a chair and lifted his glass high. "A toast to the lass, courage without end! Raise your mugs, boys, and let's sing it again!"

I set the ale aside and plugged my fingers into my

lips, letting out a sharp whistle of approval as the others stomped their feet and clapped. The men continued to sing and drink, but my mind was elsewhere.

We were headed to Kraken Reef, a place I had seen on Pan's maps. It was pretty large, and if we were going there to resupply, just maybe I'd find a chance to break away and ask around about passage to The Weeping Fen.

I thought about the fury in Hook's face when he thought he'd lost his chance to use Fetch and me as his…ticking-croc searcher. Running off would make me his mortal enemy, but I'd cross that bridge when I came to it. Because at the end of the day, once I'd gotten what I'd come to this place for, I'd turn the page again and be gone. If Pan, Tink, and Hook were all hunting me while I was hunting the croc, so be it. As long as I was faster, and smarter than they were.

My actions today had me questioning the latter, but I had to have faith in my own ingenuity. And if Xander was truly serious about helping me develop my magic, maybe I could even get a leg up on them.

My stomach roiled with guilt, but I shoved it aside.

There would come a day—sometime in the near future—when I'd find a way to right all the wrongs I'd done in order to get me back home to fulfill my destiny. I'd just have to add "using Xander" to the pile.

"I'll be back. I've got to run to the head," I said to Xander, setting my mug down.

He shot me a wave, then turned his attention back to the others.

I took a quick glance around, making sure no one was paying me any mind before I scuttled out of the card room and down the corridor of the ship. Then, I made a beeline for Moll's and my quarters, reaching under the mattress of my cot to pull out the bag I had tucked away there. I was down a knife, which I'd have to replace, but everything else important I owned was still inside.

I reached in and pulled out my magical jeweler's loupe—the one The Speaker had given me. I ran my fingers over the smooth metal, then slipped it into my pocket along with a slim metal pick before tucking the bag back in place.

A moment later, I exited the room, closing the door quietly behind me. The ship was a maze of hallways, alcoves, nooks and crannies. Multiple levels. It would take me an hour or more to walk the entire thing from bow to stern—and that was if I didn't open any doors along the way. I needed a little help if I wanted to get my bearings and find what I was looking for.

I skulked along the hallway until I reached the main corridor at the center of the ship. Lanterns lit the way, but it was still dark and eerie, and my nerves were shot from my multiple near-death experiences today. When a rat scurried by, I nearly screamed before slapping a hand over my mouth.

"Please, gods—let the next place I travel not have rats." Seemed like a small enough ask.

I rolled my shoulders, tipping my head to and fro to loosen the tension. Then, I lifted the loupe to my right eye and closed the other.

I swiftly shifted through the lenses, searching for the one I needed. Once I found it, I paused and opened myself to the familiar sensation that crept in.

First, a tension at the front of my forehead. Next, a warmth spread, like a third eye opening. Allowing me to see what I hadn't been able to see before. The hallways and corridors of the ship became instantly visible, almost like a blueprint. Within seconds, I could see it all, as if the ship had been sliced in half and opened wide for me to study. Like a mind map.

"Gotcha," I whispered, catching sight of exactly what I wanted. I tucked the loupe into my pocket and began heading toward the stern of the ship.

Five minutes later, I was standing in front of a massive pair of double doors. They were as dark and imposing as Hook himself, and I almost reconsidered.

Today is your day, Harm. It had started out shit, but my luck had turned, and who knew if or when I'd get another chance like that?

I reached into my pocket and pulled out the simple lockpick, leaning close to press my ear to the door.

Silence.

I blew out a breath and pulled away, mind made up.

"Let's see what secrets you're hiding," I murmured, slipping the pick into the keyhole.

Whatever they were, he wasn't hiding them very well. I didn't even need to access my magic as the lock *snick*ed open with just a few turns and a jiggle, smooth as butter.

Nice.

I pocketed the pick and lifted my fingers to the doorknob once again, turning slowly. My head hummed as it slid open, and I stepped inside. This was as crazy as climbing the damned mast. I knew it, and yet I couldn't seem to stop myself.

I chewed at my lower lip and stepped into the dark room, gently closing the door behind me.

Moonlight streamed through the porthole against the far wall, and I faltered. The space was massive. Bigger than the dining hall, and every wall was teeming with books from floor to ceiling.

I spun in a slow circle to take it all in. It was only when I finally turned to face the door I'd come through to enter that I came face to face with Peter Pan and Tinkerbell.

Or a drawing of them, at least. The life-sized illustration was mounted on the back of the door and, while there was no question it was them, there was something a little...off about it. Pan's animated face was flat, his eyes lifeless and cold in a way that made his jaunty green cap look juvenile and silly on him. And the way Tink's cupid's bow mouth was twisted into a sneer. I leaned in to get a better look and something shiny halfway down the picture caught the light.

A pair of throwing stars, one buried deep in the center of each of their chests.

If I wasn't so disturbed by it all, I'd have laughed. They hated each other's guts, but apparently, they were more alike than they knew. He threw things at their pictures, and they reciprocated.

If their story was true, what reason would Hook have to hate them? Surely, he wasn't so twisted that he couldn't see they were the wronged party here...

Then again, maybe he was. I didn't know the man at all.

*But you do...*a little voice inside me whispered.

"Nope. A dream isn't knowing someone," I muttered under my breath. "It's just my mind playing tricks on me."

But that tricky mind instantly conjured up another image of Hook staring down at me, his eyes full of longing as he slipped his hand into my hair and pulled me close.

"I'm going to ruin my whole life for you, aren't I?"

"Nope," I mumbled, shaking my head to erase the image. "Stop it. It's not the same guy."

Whether the man in my dreams was a premonition about some Captain Hook doppelgänger who lived in another story somewhere like Cissy Petway who was both here and in The Hollow, or my brain had dragged him up from its depths after seeing a picture of him in my fairytale book and made him into this romanticized hero to create some excitement in the drudgery that was my life in The Hollow, he wasn't real. Not here and not now, at least.

I'd watched the man kill someone in cold blood over politics. And, according to Pan, he'd killed a young boy over this clock...

What more proof did I need?

I turned away from the picture and focused back on the books. I was giving myself twenty minutes. Not a lot of time for a room this size, but hopefully long enough to find something that might help me.

Now where to start...

It only took a moment to see that the books were organized by subject matter. A whole wall dedicated to sailing, navigating, and the sea in general. A second wall filled with books on philosophy. Not exactly the type of reading I'd have expected for a bloodthirsty pirate, but then again, maybe he'd killed this ship's captain and stolen his boat like he'd done to Davy. For all I knew, these books belonged to someone else—

My brain buzzed as I caught sight of the hulking desk in the corner. On it sat a teetering pile of thick tomes.

Monsters of The Fen
Braving The Fen
The Weeping Fen and All Its Secrets
Noru, King of Beasts
Okay, so those *definitely* belonged to Hook. I

hurried toward them and steadied the pile before tugging the bottom one free.

An image of a crocodile was etched into the leather cover. Its jaw gaped wide as it swung its tail at something tucked into the corner.

A ship.

What appeared to be a teeny, tiny, little sailboat. It looked like a toy next to the beast.

I let out a low gasp. Surely, it had to be an exaggeration. I flipped the book open.

The first page I laid eyes on put my most burning question to rest. It depicted a normal sized croc with a picture of Noru below it, and it was clearly intended to be to scale. This thing wasn't big. It was fucking colossal. I leaned closer, straining to read the text below the picture.

The last verifiable sighting of Noru puts the beast at somewhere between 80 and 90 feet long from snout to tail, making it the largest of all the known creatures in The Fen.

There was a load of data in a box at the bottom of the page, but the writing was too small to see in the relative darkness. I took a quick glance around the desk, briefly considering a lamp, but then stopped short. A large, yellowing chunk of what looked like wood or bone sat on the far corner, covered by a domed piece of glass.

What the fuck—?

I could feel my eyes bulge as it hit me. Not wood or a bone.

A tooth.

And it was three times as thick as my arm and twice as long.

Panic curled around me, sending a rush of blood to my head and I grabbed the edge of the desk for balance.

"You're okay," I whispered. "Everything is alright."

"I disagree."

The breath left me in a *whoosh* as I was yanked backward into what felt like a stone wall, and something sharp pricked at my neck.

Hook's furious snarl sounded in my ear as a warm puff of air feathered over my cheek.

"You have three seconds to tell me what you're doing here before I slit your fucking throat, woman."

CHAPTER 17

My heart felt like it was going to pound out of my chest, but for some twisted reason, I didn't want to give him the satisfaction of letting him know how scared I was. I gritted my teeth and croaked out a response.

"You and I both know that, if me dying was on the menu today, it would have already happened, so I'd appreciate it if you'd get the blade off my neck and give me some space. I'm happy to answer any questions you might have. But it's been a rough day, and I'm feeling a little twitchy." A little tremble at the end there, but for the most part, I had done a respectable job of not sounding scared shitless.

I could hear the ticking of the grandfather clock in the corner of the room, and just as loud were the gears in his mind grinding.

"You mistake me. Would it make my task easier to

have you on board? It would. But I can find another way if I have to. Mark me."

A moment later, though, the pressure against the pulse in my neck was gone, and he stepped back. I swallowed a sigh of relief as I turned, resisting the urge to scamper as far away from him as possible. His hair was damp, and I could still smell the soap on him, like clean spices…

Not the same person, I reminded myself. *Cut the shit.*

Moving slowly and deliberately, I perched a hip on the corner of the desk.

"First you climb The Devil's Gauntlet, now you invade my private lair. Is going where you're not supposed to another Tideblessing, or just a talent you possess?"

I was so distracted by his perfectly carved features that it took a moment for his words to sink in. I gripped the side of the desk and held on for dear life, trying to school my features so he couldn't see my reaction to his body having been so close to mine. I opened my mouth to reply, but he cut me off immediately.

"Before you speak, know this. I have a special skill, shall we say, that helps me detect bullshit a mile away. I know you're about to feed me some, but I recommend you save it. If ever there was a time to be honest, it's now. Who are you, really? Because I can't shake the feeling that I've…seen you…have known you before and you're using some sort of magic to trick me or shield yourself…"

There was no way I could tell him the truth. That I'd spent my life dreaming of him. That I didn't know him, but I knew what it felt like to have him inside me? I kept my gaze firmly pinned on his face, refusing to let my eyes drift lower.

My cheeks burned, and I forced a chuckle. "If I could shield myself with magic, I wouldn't have dressed up like a boy with a shoe-polish beard. But I *am* handy with a lock, and I admit to being too curious for my own good."

His eyes once again seemed to burn straight through me, baring me to my very soul.

"A friend of my enemy is an enemy of mine."

"Friend of your enemy? Where are you getting that from? You mean Pan and Tink?"

His eyes narrowed as he cocked his head. "You admit to knowing them?"

"I do." I shrugged. "They helped me and Molly when we ran into some trouble."

"They don't help anyone," he cut in sharply.

"The Lost Boys. They help them—"

"Least of all the fucking Lost Boys, I can promise you that. If you ever decide you want to help me that way, do me a favor and kill me quick instead."

What the hell was that supposed to mean?

My mind instantly shot back to the little hints of strangeness during my short time in Neverland. Tristan's obvious discomfort and the way he kept his distance from both Tink and Pan. Tink's reaction when I'd wandered off across the island to the carnivorous bat caves.

"If you have something to tell me about them, feel free to spill it now. I'm all ears."

His voice dropped to a menacing whisper that was way scarier than if he'd been shouting.

"It's not my motives that are in question here. I'm a bloody pirate and this is my ship. I don't particularly care what you think me guilty of. It's you who needs to justify your existence if you want it to continue. I'll ask you one more time. How did you meet them?"

I cleared my throat and tried again. "Well, our boat capsized and they plucked us out of the water and brought us back to their island."

"You've been to Neverland, then?" Hook asked, crossing his arms over his chest.

"I have." There seemed no point in denying it. "But they're not my *friends*, exactly. They were kind to us, although we couldn't stay. We..." I trailed off and let out a low cough, "borrowed one of Pan's boats while they were gone, and went on our way. I'm sure they wouldn't view *us* as friends right now, either."

"So they didn't send you to me?"

He unfolded his arms and reached out with his right hand. Instinctively, I lifted mine toward it and, before I could pull away, he circled my wrist with his fingers and pressed his thumb against my pulse.

"Tell me the truth, Harmony. Were you sent here by Pan and Tink to spy on me...or worse?"

"I was not," I managed, my throat sticking together. No doubt my blood was pounding. But it wasn't because I was lying. It was because I'd been in this exact position with him once before, in a dream from long ago.

"Do I make you nervous, little one?" he murmured, a hint of a smile tugging at his firm lips. *He reached out and pressed his fingers to the soft underside of my wrist, which jumped and flickered to greet his touch.*

"If not for Pan and Tink, why did you come to the meeting?"

"I was hoping to find someone who could take me to The Weeping Fen."

"Because..."

I couldn't lie. He would surely sense it. I'd seen his magic at work, and it was nothing to play around with. "I need to find Noru before the next time he emerges."

His face went carefully blank. "Why?"

"Because Pan and Tink managed to mark him with some sort of magic arrow the last time he surfaced. They are going to be able to track him and set a trap to catch him. I need to beat them to the punch."

"Fucking hell." Hook's nostrils flared and his jaw went tight, his eyes steely. "She was right, then..."

"Who?"

"It's not important. All that matters is that we get the job done. Your goal is to get the clock, then?"

There was no point in denying it anymore. "Yes. But maybe we can share it?" I hurried to add. "I don't even know exactly what—"

"It doesn't matter. The clock means nothing to me in the long term. If my suspicions are correct, I'll have no use of the thing once it's served its purpose. I'll happily give it over to you and we can part ways."

"And I'm supposed to believe that because you've been such a gentleman so far?"

He drew back in surprise, and I nearly burst out laughing.

"Sorry, I do this thing when I've hit my quota of terror for the day where my brain gets so overloaded that I start speaking my mind. Believe me, I'm still plenty afraid, but some sort of assurance that we aren't going to help you and then wind-up fish food afterwards would go a long way towards building a bit of trust between us."

"I just saved your fucking life."

"Like I said, that was only because you think my connection with Fetch can help you, not because you care if I'm alive or dead," I reasoned with a shrug. He stared at me in disbelief, but I wasn't about to be cowed this time. "At least tell me the plan. If I'm to be a part of it, I should know my role."

"My plan was the same as yours. Although I didn't know how short on time we were, I did know that the window on finding Noru and the clock was closing." He blew out a long-suffering sigh. "We are headed to

Kraken Reef to hire an experienced guide to take me and a small, strategically selected crew to The Fen. I'm hopeful that we can use your ability to communicate with animals along with the Tideblessings of some others to help us find and defeat the croc and any other monsters that get in our way."

"Why now? Pan said it's been years since you betr—" I broke off and tried again, "since your…falling out. Why is it suddenly okay to go now?"

He reached out and touched the gleaming tip of his hook to the glass orb that covered the massive tooth. "Loads of sailors have entered, but few have come out, and even fewer than that in one piece. I've interviewed those still capable of communicating. Going with my usual crew would've put them all at risk with very little chance of reward. Due to the size of the ship needed to navigate those waters, going alone would be impossible, so…"

His meaning hit me like a stone from a slingshot, right between the eyes.

"Holy diabolical fucking hell…You're putting together a crew of people you don't give a fuck about, knowing that it's probably a suicide mission." I let out a harsh laugh. "Ooh, I know! We can call it a 'soon-to-be skeleton crew'! That should give them all the warm fuzzies and get 'em lining up to join."

Hook moved so fast, my eyes didn't even detect the motion before he was on me, pressing me against the desk, forcing me to use my hands to keep from being flat on my back.

"You can say whatever you wish about me as a man. I've done plenty of bad in my life that I deserve the scorn," he hissed, hook pressed against my jaw as he glared down at me, eyes flashing piping hot fury. "But don't ever question my ethics as a captain. Those I lead are my sworn and sacred responsibility. Even you and your fake sister, Harmony Fallowell."

I swallowed hard and tried to focus on his words and not to stare at his mouth. The mouth that had been on my collarbone in a dream just a few nights before, seconds before it drifted lower…

His eyes slid down to my mouth, and it was like I had no choice. My hips flexed almost imperceptibly against his.

He shoved himself backward with a snarl and pointed an accusatory finger at me. "We'll arrive in Kraken Reef by noon. Try not to get yourself killed in the meantime. And if you find a locked door, leave it that way. Am I understood?"

I swallowed hard and nodded. "Aye Aye, Captain."

I turned and rushed from the room like it was on fire. And, judging from how hot my skin felt, it just might have been. It wasn't until I got to my room and closed the door behind me that I realized what he'd called me…

Harmony Fallowell…

How did he know my full name?

CHAPTER 18

I leapt up, suppressing a yelp as a sharp rap at the door rang through the otherwise-silent room.

"One sec," I called, hastily stuffing The Speaker's note into my pouch as I stood.

Maybe Moll had finished those chores she'd insisted on not needing my help with? Or maybe it was Hook…But he'd been busy docking the ship at the city's small harbor last I'd heard.

"Yes?" I pulled the door open, poking my head out into the hallway.

"Just stoppin' by to let you know we're headin' into town in a short while," Trick-Eyed Tom answered in his rough, gravelly tone. "You should get your things together if you want to come."

"Uh, yeah, I'll be there soon."

He moved as if to go but turned back before I had

fully shut the door. "And lass…sorry again for misjudging you. You got more moxy than most of the pirates I've battled. Happy to have you as one of us."

I nodded slowly, a little taken aback. "Thanks." Part of me had wondered if the bloom would fall off the rose, but clearly The Devil's Gauntlet had done the trick.

Tom dipped his head and limped off without another word, and I shut the door behind him. I'd never truly be one of them, but I'd managed to make a reluctant ally out of Captain Hook and get the admiration of the crew in short order, which was a good start.

I strode over to the wooden chest that held the scant pile of clothes I'd "borrowed" from the left over booty that was stored in the belly of the ship, and began rummaging through it. Hook and I had come to an uneasy truce after the conversation we'd had the previous night, but I couldn't shake my discomfort about it. What would happen after he was done with the clock? Would he truly just hand it over? And, more importantly, what exactly did he plan to do with it? Based on his blinding hatred of Pan and Tink, I couldn't imagine it would be anything good…

According to him, though, *they* were the true villains. Destiny had thrust me in the middle of this war, demanding that I pick a side. And, if the right choice was hidden somewhere in the prophecy, I sure hadn't found it yet. Or the answers to how he knew anything about where I'd come from…

A tingle crept up my back as the dream from a few nights before threatened to come rushing back in, but the feeling was quickly replaced by a flash of irritation.

He's a pirate, I reminded myself, forcing the thought aside. *An ally in this mission or not, he still might well be your enemy.*

I let out a sigh as I scooped an off-white shirt and tan breeches out of the chest, tossing them to my bed. While this was all important, I was getting ahead of myself. There was still a long road ahead of us if we were going to survive the journey to get the clock. No point in borrowing even more trouble.

One step at a time.

Moll trudged in a short while later, just as I was about to step through the door. She let out an exaggerated sigh as she caught sight of me, wiping a streak of nonexistent sweat from her forehead.

"I should *not* have offered to do the laundry. Do you have any idea how vile these men are? Skid marks were the least of it. They—"

"Spare me the details," I cut in quickly. "Are you going to come into town with us? I'm sure Xander is going..." I added, grinning at the blush it brought out on her cheeks.

She gave me a playful shove. "You're one to talk. Don't think I haven't seen the way you look at the captain."

"Not even true," I replied, making a mental note to keep my recent dream between me and the gods. I bit back a groan and turned to face my bed to hide my face as heat flashed through my cheeks.

"I can't wait to see what a crew of monster hunters is like," Moll mused, not seeming to notice my meltdown.

"I...I bet they're really skilled," I agreed, sucking in a calming breath. "Probably super tough."

"They've gotta be, with how big those things are."

"I didn't see the whole serpent that came after me yesterday, but just the bulge in the water alone was scary enough. The size of our hut in Little Alabaster. And that's what's in the regular ocean. Imagine what they're like in The Weeping Fen...Pan said that Noru was the king of the jungle, so to speak. The biggest and the baddest."

Moll's expression darkened, drained of any trace of her previous enthusiasm. "I— I'm still finding that stuff you told me about Tink and Pan last night kind of hard to process. If what Hook said is true...if they're bad people...we can't leave those kids with them."

I nodded grimly. "I've been thinking about that too, but it doesn't seem like there's anything else we can do about it right now. Even if we could escape and find a way to sail there, with the invisible shield and all? We'd never find the place. Hook has searched for years, and with a whole crew of experienced sailors and navigators."

If I thought long and hard about the room with the maps, tapping into my magic, I could piece together the general location of Neverland in relation to all the other landmarks. If we wanted to go back there, we'd need more than that. We'd need to figure out a way to home in and pinpoint, or else it would be like trying to find…well, a magically hidden island in a ocean.

I strode over, laying a hand on her shoulder. "We might be helpless to do anything for them right now, but let's use this time to dig a little. I've made some friends, and it seems as if you have, too. Let's see what other people say about Pan and Tink and get to the truth behind this feud. Then, when the time comes, we go in knowing that we will do everything in our power to keep those kids safe. If we need to."

It was as close to a promise as I could make under the circumstances, but it still felt hollow.

Moll gave a tight nod, then sucked in a deep breath. "I hate it, but I know you're right. For now, staying put gives us the best chance of helping them if they need us later." Her expression hardened, and her knuckles went white as she clenched a fist. "But if Hook is right…if they're holding them hostage or hurting them in any way? They are not going to recognize the side of me that they see next."

MOLL and I stepped out onto the dock a short while later, following Hook and Xander's lead as they headed into town. Most of the crew had already gone ahead to the shops and markets to load up on supplies and secure lodging for the night. And, while I'd been apprehensive about what Hook had in mind for the townsfolk when I'd first heard we were heading here to resupply, the crew wasn't here to pillage.

Kraken Reef paid protection money to Hook, and, for all their flaws, the pirates in this world seemed to take that type of thing seriously. A crowd of children of all ages milled around the edge of the dock as we approached, shooting us nervous glances when they thought Hook wasn't looking, and a pair of fishermen hardly seemed to notice us, like this was all business as usual.

"Where's the pub?" I asked, savoring the feeling of solid ground beneath my feet. The steadiness and lack of motion was almost disorienting after a couple days at sea.

"Not far," Hook said, not sparing a glance as he tossed the words over his shoulder.

"Where are we going, exactly?" I called. The houses looked more or less the same as the ones in the shanty town had, but a glance around almost took my breath away. A pair of grassy hills flanked the quaint little seaside village, the reddish light of the setting sun just visible over their peaks.

When Hook didn't bother to reply, the first mate chimed in. "There's a little tavern that the Beast Bane Boys frequent right around the corner. And, if we're lucky, they'll be there. Even if they aren't, the owner should know where they're staying."

"Doubt they'd even bother to open if they weren't. They love a pint…probably account for half the place's monthly sales," Hook deadpanned. "And don't call them that stupid name. It's ridiculous."

I made a quick adjustment to my mental image of the team of monster hunters as Fetch smacked down on my shoulder. "Any luck?"

He clicked his beak, and I could just make out a faint trace of blood on it as he peered down at me. He hadn't had much opportunity to fish for more than small trout in The Hollow, but he seemed to be using the skills he'd honed in the cove surrounding Neverland on the open sea just fine.

Hurried footsteps sounded from our left, pulling my attention away from the bird, and I turned to see a pair of teen boys striding up to us.

"'Scuse me sir," said the taller of the two, a wiry, brown-haired boy who couldn't have been older than fourteen. "I hope we ain't botherin' you, but I wouldn't be able to forgive meself if I didn't try…"

Hook silenced him with a hand. "No openings, lad."

"I know we're young," the stouter, red-faced one cut in, "but we're real strong for our age. Promise we won't be deadweight. We'll—"

Hook's expression darkened. "No. Openings. Now go, before I change my mind and bring you along as crocodile bait."

They paled and their throats bobbed as they backed away, then turned and ran.

"Subtle," I muttered.

Hook didn't look at me, but Xander lifted both brows and shook his head ever so slightly.

The tavern came into view a few minutes later, with a half-rotted sign out front marking it as the "Siren's Den," right next to the carved image of a half-woman, half-bird creature. I sent Fetch back to the skies as a bout of cheering erupted from within. He wouldn't like all the noise, and maybe he'd be able to get an hour or so of real hunting in before nightfall.

Another cheer sounded from within as Hook pushed the door open, but the patrons weren't focused on us.

Most of them stood in a large cluster at the bar's center, with a few disinterested drinkers chatting at the bar on the left side of the room.

The bartender scurried over as we entered the room, eyes wide with surprise. "Evening, Captain. What can I get you?"

"We've got a seeking job we need done. Are the boys around? Guessing they have something to do with whatever's going on over there?" He gestured toward the room's center with his iron hook.

The bartender nodded, scowling. "Taking bets on some game or other, as usual. Let's see if they can keep from smashing my tables and mugs this time."

Hook dismissed him with a wave of his hand, then

made a beeline toward the center of the room. I craned my neck to get a better look as we approached the ring of men, a chill creeping up my spine at what I saw.

A massive hulk of a man sat across from another, leaner guy with dark hair who flashed a roguish grin as he extended his arm toward the table's center. Moll's elbow slammed into my side at the same time I noticed.

"Is that…it can't be—"

"Paddy O'Donnelly," I whispered, as stunned as she sounded. I took another step forward, resisting the urge to call out to him. It was him, no doubt about it, but not the *same* him as I'd met in The Smudge. I scanned the crowd, finding the other three O'Donnelly brothers as we approached.

"No Billy…" I muttered. Like the first time I'd met them in Alabaster, their older sister and matriarch of the family was nowhere to be found. I pressed up to the edge of the crowd to get a better look as the larger man clasped Paddy's hand at the table's center.

Paddy raised his free hand, waving the crowd into silence. "So remember, the first rule is that there are no rules. When I win, this ugly lug is going to serve as my manservant for a week. If he wins…" He cut off, cocking his head as he glanced back at the other man. "What'd I bet again?"

"Fifty." The larger man's face was bright red with anger, and he gritted his teeth, seemingly from the effort it took to not leap across the table and throttle Paddy.

"Oh, yes. Fifty gold, apparently." He frowned, looking the man up and down. "Actually… why not make it a hundred?"

The crowd whooped with glee at that, and the big man flashed him an almost imperceptible nod. "I'm going to rip that arm of yours clean off, little man."

Paddy flashed a look of mock horror. "Ready to watch this bastard get what's coming to him?" he called, "And remember; no outside interference. Other than that, anything goes."

Jacob O'Donnelly strode over to the table, rolling his eyes with irritation as he raised an arm into the air. "Three, two—"

The big man surged into action, grunting as he threw his arm sideways with everything he had.

Paddy's hand stopped just inches from the table, and he gritted his teeth, trembling against the power of his stronger opponent. "Men," Moll whispered at my side, her eye roll somehow making it into her tone.

Why had he even agreed to such a contest? Had he actually thought he stood a—

Paddy's free hand flew from the table's edge, reaching directly under the table, and I winced as it smacked directly into the big oaf's manhood.

And he didn't stop there.

Still managing to keep his hand from smacking into the table, he grabbed hold of the other man's parts, yanking on them with a feral roar.

His wrestling arm surged back to equilibrium, and

then past it, as the big man screamed. And it was only when he had smashed his hand into the wooden surface of the table that Paddy stopped pulling.

His arm shot into the air as the crowd whooped and hollered. On another day, maybe they would've argued over whether this counted as a win. But not today. He'd already won them over with his antics before the match.

"Men indeed," I said, echoing Moll's previous statement with a chuckle.

The larger man rose from the table, lunging at Paddy, but he stopped short as the sudden movement seemed to send a spike of pain through his barely-attached nuts. "Y—you cheated!"

"I won," Paddy corrected. His lips pulled into a smile as he added. "And that's 'you cheated, *sir*' to you, manservant."

CHAPTER 19

"Let's move," Hook said, pushing his way through the whooping crowd.

The room grew suddenly tense as Paddy's opponent closed in on the smaller man, gripping him by the collar of his shirt.

"Call me a servant again, you slippery fucker. See what happens."

Paddy stared up at him, his easy smile slipping away as his hand inched toward his belt. "You lost fair and square. There are no rules, now get that hand off me if you'd like to keep it."

Andrew was already creeping up behind the man, unbeknownst to him, and Jacob was stirring as well, positioning himself to the man's side. I chewed at my inner lip. The bastard was about to get himself killed.

"A threat now, eh?" He shoved Paddy back, sending him crashing to the ground, right over his chair.

"Now!" Jacob spat, a glint of steel flashing from his belt as he charged the larger man. I winced as Andrew did the same, brandishing his own blade.

"Stop." The word of command cut through the air as cleanly as any knife, silencing even the cheering crowd, and the two brothers lurched to a halt as Hook strode forward.

The brute of a man who'd been attacking Paddy whirled, arm pulled back as if to strike him, then stopped, eyes wide. "I—"

Hook raised his hand, cutting him off without so much as looking at him. "Out."

The vein on the man's temple throbbed as he stared back at the captain, but, incredibly, wisdom won out in the end. He flashed a final scowl toward Paddy, then stomped off, shoving through the crowd as he made his way to the door.

I let out a breath, hearing Moll do the same at my side. "Seems like the crew has quite the reputation."

I nodded, scanning the now-silent crowd. The looks of joy and excitement over the impending fight seemed to have been completely overwritten by fear. The tension was thick as smoke on the air, and they began dispersing in waves. What did they know that we didn't?

Scotty strode forward, hoisting Paddy to his feet as the other two O'Donnellys sheathed their blades and moved over to him.

"Thanks, Captain," Paddy said, wincing slightly as Scotty cuffed him on the ear.

"You have business with us, I assume?" Jacob ventured, eyes darting around to look everywhere except at Captain Hook as he took a half step forward.

"Something like that. Let's find somewhere more private."

The brothers led us over to the far corner of the tavern, where a lone table sat empty. A cluster of throwing knives jutted out of a nearby wall, and a cluster of open locks lay strewn over the tabletop.

"This is our spot," Andrew said, stating the obvious.

Not obvious if you didn't already know them, I reminded myself. They hadn't shown even a flash of recognition when they saw me. And, like Cissy, they weren't completely identical to Alabaster's O'Donnellys. They looked a little harder and walked with a swagger that'd been absent in their counterparts in the other world.

Or, in the other *story.*

I suppressed a shiver. No matter how many times this happened, I doubted that I'd ever get used to it. Gods, don't let it happen too many more times. How many stories would I have to leap into, to find my way home? To my real home?

"So, what can we do for you, Captain?" Paddy asked, taking a seat on a rickety-looking chair and waving his hand for Hook to do the same.

"We're heading to The Weeping Fen," Hook

answered gruffly, ignoring the invitation to sit. "Looking for people who know their way around to help us get to the second layer."

A lock dropped to the floor as Andrew looked up, eyes wide. A surprised look flashed across Paddy's face, too, but Scotty interjected before he could reply. "Folks say that only a handful have ever made it out alive after goin' there. What makes you think this'll end up different?"

I tensed, glancing over at a nervous-looking Moll. I'd known it'd be dangerous, but this was even worse than I'd thought.

"Call it intuition," Hook answered, meeting the heavier man's gaze.

"Ain't no one that knows The Fen better than us, but it's gonna cost you a pretty penny," Scotty answered.

Hook raised an eyebrow at him. "Name your price."

"Well," Jacob cut in, stepping forward. "We've heard the news about you…succeeding Davy as Captain of the pirate alliance. Perhaps you could use your new influence to—"

"You heard wrong. Davy's out of the picture, but there's no new Captain of Captains. We'll deal in gold."

Jacob frowned at that but nodded. "Can you give us a bit more information about what you need from us?"

"We're searching for a certain monster, and have reason to believe we can find it, if you get us close enough."

"Well, the Beast Bane Boys are at your service," Paddy said, spinning around to reveal the three sloppily-dyed 'B's on the back of his shirt. Hook rolled his eyes, and I bit back a laugh, but Paddy's expression was more serious when he turned to face us once again.

"What kind of beast are you searching for? Serpent? Saber-toothed tiger? They got 'em all over there."

Hook raised one brow and gave it to him straight. "Noru."

The single word brought a gasp out of Jacob and sent a collective wave of tension rolling through the O'Donnellys. Even Paddy's swagger faltered a bit.

"You want to hire us to kill Noru?" Jacob asked, incredulous.

"My crew and I'll be the ones doing the killing," Hook answered, brandishing his iron hook. "You get us there, and we'll take care of the rest. All I need now is your price."

"Ten thousand pieces," Jacob shot back, crossing his arms over his chest like a challenge. Even his own brothers shared a glance of surprise at the amount.

Paddy sat up straighter, opening his mouth to speak, but broke off as Hook nodded.

"Done. Ten thousand gold pieces. Half up front, and half upon completion of the job."

Paddy leapt up from his seat, holding out a hand, reservations fading fast. "You've got yourself a deal."

Hook reached out to shake it, but Scotty batted

Paddy's arm down a moment before they could seal the deal. "Wait, there's one more thing."

Hook looked over at him, withdrawing his arm and waiting for him to speak.

"We've been to the first layer many times in our day, but the second layer is a different story. We know how to get you in—it's the getting back out that's gonna be difficult. Every time we've met someone halfway sane who says they've been there; it turns out to be a lie."

"Cut to the chase."

Scotty's face wrinkled in annoyance, but he didn't let it into his tone. "We want a map. Or at least a chat with someone who we can confirm has *actually* made it out of there with an idea of how to get in and out."

Hook grunted. "I know a man like you describe. Have already spoken to him about it. What do you need to know?"

Scotty shook his head. "We need to meet this fella, face to face. No disrespect to you, Cap, but it takes a Seeker to know one. And, if he's legitimate, he'll be able to answer the questions we ask."

Hook paused for a long moment, then dipped his head in assent, holding out his hand. "Agreed."

Paddy nudged Scotty out of the way, reaching out to shake Hook's hand. "What's the lucky bastard's name, by the way? The one who got out of deepest part of The Weeping Fen alive?"

"Garth."

"*Garth*?" I asked, all eyes shooting over to me as I

spoke up for the first time in the conversation. "The old man we met the night of the meeting?"

"I didn't realize you knew him..." Hook said, eyes narrowing.

I groaned. "You could say that."

We were headed to the apparently-horrifying second layer of The Fen, and our only source of knowledge about the place was a crotchety old man who seemed far more interested in tea and gossip than hunting monsters.

Perfect.

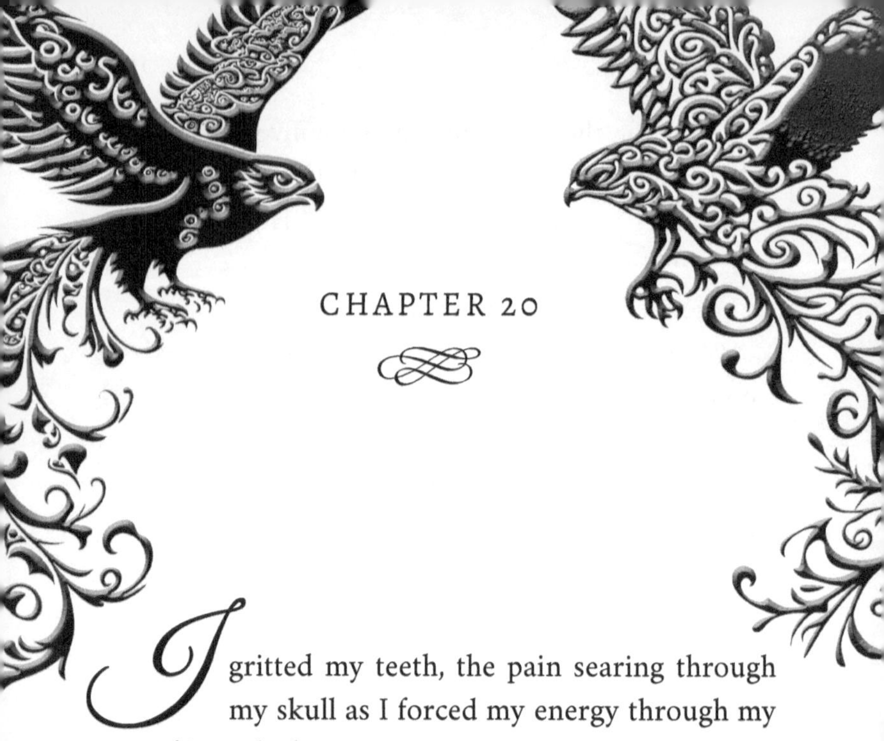

I gritted my teeth, the pain searing through my skull as I forced my energy through my eye and into the loupe.

"Good?" I gasped,

"Hmm…" Xander leaned in, squinting as he stared at me through the loupe like I was some kind of bug in a jar. He stood that way for an unbearably long time before saying, "Yeah, looks good. Go ahead and release it."

Air flooded into my lungs as I took my first breath in what felt like hours. "Gods," I panted, shoving the loupe across the table. "Does the pain ever go away?"

"Pain?" Xander looked up from the notebook he'd been scribbling in and cocking his head. "It can definitely be kind of taxing, but it shouldn't *hurt* to use it."

"Well it does. It's fucking excruciating, actually."

"Hmm…strange." His eyes narrowed in thought.

"Hopefully it'll go away with training. We'll keep an eye on it."

"So what did you see?" I glanced down at the notebook. The haze over my vision had begun to fade, and I squinted over at him. Every Tideblessed could be trained to see magic in others in the way I'd managed at the pirates' gathering, according to Xander. Most magic wasn't flashy like Tink's fairy dust that was a sparkly spray of gold, but more like a pulse of energy and power that required concentration to see. Clearly, Hook had done the work as well, which was likely how he'd noticed my connection with Fetch. Maybe the skill wasn't limited to just Tideblessed. Maybe that was how Relyk had first flagged me as a person of interest back in Alabaster...

"You're strong," Xander continued. "I see so much power in you."

I didn't *feel* strong. Unlocking a ring or steering a ship didn't seem like much compared to what I'd seen from truly powerful Whispers. An image of the shimmering purple wall Tink had managed to conjure appeared in my mind. It'd stretched as far as the eye could see, blocking cannonballs as if they were the wads of paper my step-brothers had loved to spit through wooden tubes at passersby. "I... I've seen people do things with their Whis— Tideblessings that are so far beyond me that it's hard to imagine catching up. What good is tinkering or communicating with my falcon if they can blast me to bits with the wave of a hand?"

"Not everything is a straight up fight, Harm. There are plenty of ways to defeat an enemy before they even know you're fighting." His hand whipped out, faster than I could react, and the tip of his middle finger snapped lightly into my forehead as he flicked me.

I reeled back, shooing him away as I remembered the pulsing, black void rolling through The Speaker's forest, chasing after me as if it was alive rather than just a hole in reality.

"You got away this time, but make no mistake. Soon enough I'll get you my pretty, and your little bird, too!"

My enemy wasn't one I could beat with sleight of hand.

"Is that how you slipped that needle into Davy? The one that kept him from being able to use his magic?"

He grinned and clapped his hands together in miniature applause. "You caught that, did you? That's good. Few would have, if any. I had a feeling that there was something…different about your magic. It's not specialized, like mine or the others. You're a better tinker and falconer than anything else right now, for sure. But I don't think you've even tapped your potential. It's as if you could call on the energy for…well, anything."

I raised an eyebrow. "What makes you think that?"

"Honestly? Carnie's intuition," he answered with a shrug. "But I've never been wrong before."

"Does that mean I can do anything that anyone else can?" I asked, locking eyes with him.

"Not quite, but something close. There'll probably be some things you're good at and others that you can hardly manage, but you have far more than the little taste of magic that the rest of us get. It's exceptional…"

The Speaker had said something similar back in Alabaster, and based on how things were progressing, it was getting hard to argue. My magic, whatever it was, was unknown. And, I was starting to believe it might be something special.

I sucked in a breath, absorbing this new information. Ever since I'd seen the worm holes that followed me throughout my journey in Alabaster, I'd had the sense that my enemy was unfathomably powerful, and I was woefully outmatched. With Xander's belief in my potential, for the first time, I felt like I might have a fighting chance.

"What about your Tideblessing mark…what does that look like?"

I gnawed on my lower lip and shook my head, hoping this confession wasn't going to make waves. "Don't know. I don't think I have one."

He cocked his head and narrowed his eyes. "Interesting. Or maybe you did and it was somehow erased or removed…" His face cleared and he shrugged. "In any case, I'm happy to keep working with you and seeing if we can unlock your potential."

That was a relief. I felt like we were getting somewhere and that something was about to shift when it came to my Whisper, but I couldn't put my finger on what or why.

Xander stepped to the other side of the table, sliding the three cups into position. "One more time."

I suppressed a groan, forcing out a nod. We'd spent the better part of the morning on this same exercise, and I'd thought we were done with it when he'd asked me to focus my energy into the loupe so he could study my magic. But apparently not.

"Is this actually the last time?" I flashed a half smile despite my annoyance. Not like we had anything better to do on our sail back to see Garth.

"Depends whether you see it." He let the coin drop to the table. "Now let's go."

A blur of flesh and the white of the ceramic mug flashed over the coin as he leapt into action, and it never slowed down. His hands whipped from side to side, the glint of the golden coin flashing all around as he slid it from cup to cup.

The ache crept back into my temples as I fixated on him, but the whirlwind of hands came to a stop just before it became truly unbearable.

I held out a trembling finger, holding my breath as I jabbed it toward the center cup. "There."

He lifted the cup with a flourish, and my heart sank to my stomach as he revealed the empty patch of oak that'd been sitting under the cup. But, unlike all the previous times when he'd grabbed the coin and gotten ready to start again right away, he lifted the other two cups as well. Both empty.

"Where's—"

A flash of gold glinted as he flipped his hand over, showing that the coin was sitting on his palm. "Good choice even so." He winked. "I only moved it out of that cup at the last second. Can't have my student showing me up *this* fast."

I rolled my eyes, but slumped into the chair. "Good for the day, then?"

"Today was mostly just about assessing your powers. We'll work on it more in the coming days, but I want you practicing in the meantime." He turned, stuffing his hand into the pouch he'd laid on my bed at the start of the day's lesson. When it emerged, he was holding a braided leather whip.

"What am I supposed to do with that?"

His emerald-green eyes were almost solemn as he unfolded the weapon, letting the spiked tip clatter to the wooden floor below. "You need to learn to defend yourself, and this is the best weapon I know of for someone like you to use. Even if you learned to imbue a sword with magic, you wouldn't want to get into a contest of strength with someone twice your size. But with a whip, you'll be able to keep them at bay, never letting them use raw power to their advantage."

"I— Thank you." I found myself strangely touched by the thought he'd put into it.

He pulled it just out of reach as I moved to take it.

"Don't bother trying to swing it just yet. I'll teach you that part later. For now, just focus on trying to imbue it with your magic. It might be harder than it is with the loupe, but you're more than capable of doing it. Just… spend time fixating on it, getting to know how the handle feels in your hand, learning the sounds it makes when it flexes and bends, memorizing the smell of the leather."

I stared back at him, cocking an eyebrow. "Uhh, okay?"

"I know it sounds stupid, but it really helps." He flicked his coin high into the air, snapping it out of the air with his other hand a few feet above his head without so much as a glance. "I've had this coin since I was in the circus. Can do tricks with her that I'd never manage with a different one."

I nodded, still taken aback by the sudden shift in mood. "Makes sense. I'll work on it in the ways you suggested."

"Let's meet up again in a couple days, then. By then, you should be ready to try swinging it." He held the weapon out hesitantly, letting out a breath as I took it. His lips turned back upward into a smile as I took it, and he clapped his hands together. "Great. We had a productive first lesson. Looking forward to seeing what you can manage when we meet for our next one."

I nodded, squeezing down on the grip of the weapon. It'd looked unwieldy and small in his spindly fingers, but it was quite comfortable in mine. As strange as he'd been acting, the mood had shifted, now, and I decided to leave it for another day.

He turned toward the cabin door, reaching down to grab his pouch off of the bed. "See you then."

"Wait," I interjected, a little more forcefully than intended.

"Hmm?"

"I wanted to ask you a couple questions that have been on my mind."

He drew back and nodded reluctantly.

"Go ahead, then."

"The captain...he's obviously Tideblessed, but I can't figure out what his blessing is. I know it's something with water...and maybe the wind? Some sort of all-encompassing nature thing?"

Xander locked on something in the distance over my shoulder as he scrubbed a hand over his jaw.

"It's complicated. I know you're technically part of the crew now, but it's not information he shares willy nilly. He has too many enemies to be telling the world how to best him, you know what I mean? When he wants you to know, he'll tell you."

He didn't say it in a mean way, but this tone left no doubt; That particular topic of discussion was closed.

"Well, can you at least tell me more about his rivalry with Peter Pan and Tinkerbell...I know he hates them, but he made it seem like it goes deeper than just the battle for the clock. He seems to think they're flat out evil. Is he right?"

He turned slowly to face me, flashing a wry grin. "Moll already tried this—and much more convincingly than you, I might add. It's hard to deny her anything when she puts those big blue eyes on you, innit?" He paused for a moment but continued just as I was about to press. "Look, all I'll say is this: You shouldn't feel sorry for either of them. Pan had a hard life growing up, but the pair of them deserve whatever comes their way. If you want more than that, then you'll have to go back to the Captain. He's the closest thing to a brother I've ever had, and I won't share something with you that he hasn't seen fit to share himself."

Continuing this line of questioning was a risk. I'd made a friend in the first mate, and he was doing me a great favor by mentoring me. I didn't want him to pull away. But I couldn't stop thinking about sassy little Cissy, sweet, sickly Caleb, and Tristan with the chip on his shoulder.

I had to try one more time.

"I get that. But it's possible to love someone who's bad. People do it all the time. Are you sure you're backing the right horse, Xander?" I paused, gnawing on the inside of my cheek as his shoulders stiffened. "There are children involved."

He shot me a hard stare and then opened his mouth as if to answer for a fraction of a second before snapping it shut. "Like I said. If you want to know more, go talk to Hook. That's the last we'll speak of it, lass."

He walked away and I was left watching him go, wishing I'd kept my stupid mouth shut.

I had precious few friends here and couldn't afford to be alienating a single one right now. Did that mean I was going to give up trying to get the information I desperately needed? Absolutely not. It just meant I had to be a little stealthier in order to acquire it.

Hook had secrets that could alter the path of this journey, and I was going to uncover them.

One way or another.

CHAPTER 21

"Lights on, so he's definitely home."

Hook stepped off the cobblestone path and stopped a few feet in front of Garth's door, not bothering to knock as stomping footsteps began to sound from just inside. Air whooshed outward as the door swung open.

"Not interested, so sell your wares to someone who is," Garth growled, his eyes widening as they settled on Hook. "Wait…I might be going senile, but I could've sworn I saw your ugly mug just a few days back."

Interesting. Had he seen Hook the same day Moll and I had met him?

"*Going* senile? A little late for that, old man," Hook answered, shooing him back into the house. "Important business. We need to talk."

"It's a bit late for guests," he started, leaning around Hook to see who he'd brought along, "but I guess I could make a little time for ya. Just make it qui—" He cut off as his gaze fell on me, breaking into a laugh. "Gods your hair is right fucked, huh?"

"Yep, I had a real shit barber," I quipped, hoping Hook didn't notice the red glow blooming on my cheeks. If Moll had been here, she would've joined in, but thankfully, she'd opted to wait back at the inn with Xander.

Hook glanced between us, unamused. "So this is where you got that 'disguise'?"

"I should've let Moll do it," I grumbled.

"Disguise?" Paddy asked, narrowing his eyes at me. "Who're you pretendin' to be?"

I shooed him away with a hand. "Not pretending to be anyone. This is old news."

"Hmm." He sounded skeptical.

Garth groaned, pulling our attention back to him. "Come on in, lads. You're letting out all my hot air."

I spared a final glance at Fetch, seeing that he was still circling overhead, before piling into the house with Hook and the four O'Donnelly brothers. Things looked much the same as last time, but little piles of old books and old mugs of half-drank tea were strewn all around the little house. Garth gestured for us to take a seat, moving over to his own at the head of the table.

"Been on a reading kick?" I asked, pushing a book toward the center of the table as I moved to take a seat.

"Interrogating a man in his own home." He shook

his head disapprovingly. "Kids these days. But yes, if you must know. I've been—"

"We're here to learn more about The Weeping Fen," Hook said, as if the older man hadn't been speaking. He gestured to each of the O'Donnellys in turn. "This is Paddy, Scotty, Jacob, and Andrew. They're Seekers."

"I've heard of 'em." Garth's lip curled downward as he looked them over. "Word around is they're pretty good, too…as far as people of that generation go."

I turned just in time to see Paddy opening his mouth to speak, then cutting off with a soft yelp as Jacob pinched his shoulder.

"The Captain tells us you've been to the second layer," Jacob said. "Is that right?"

"To the very heart of her, then back again." Garth nodded solemnly as he turned to Hook. "So what is it that you need to know, lad?"

I narrowed my eyes and studied the old man's face. Despite his initial, gruff greeting, there was something kinder about how he spoke to Hook. Even his body language was relaxed, less combative. Maybe it was the pirate's reputation?

Something about that didn't quite ring true, though. Why had he called him 'lad'?

"We're taking a trip, and I want to gather as much information as possible," Hook answered. "There are lots of sailors out there spinning fake tales about The Fen, so I brought these fellas to the one man I believe has actually been past the first level."

Garth fixed him with a disapproving glare, his milky eyes threatening to drill a hole right through him. "Can't you just leave that crap behind you? There's more to life than vengeance, and you're wasting precious years on—"

"Just tell us your story, old man," Hook cut in.

Garth leaned back in his chair, crossing his arms petulantly. "And if I don't?"

I had only met Garth a few days ago, but I felt like I had a good read on him. "There was that other guy in town who said he's been there." I shrugged. "Maybe we should try interviewing him, instead…"

The old man's head snapped sideways, and he fixed me with a glare. "Tucker? Bastard's more full of shit than a mushroom farm. Couldn't describe a single creature he saw there beyond the ones even children would know about." He took another glance at Hook, then let out a sigh and leaned forward. "Bah, I guess I can tell you, if you're so desperate…"

Wood squeaked against wood as he pushed out his chair, jumping abruptly to his feet as he cleared his throat.

"Fifty years ago, when I was just a strapping young deckhand, and the pirate alliance was not yet a dream in Davy's head, Captain Meldrick Flannery caught wind of the money that could be made by seekin'. Gave up thievery and started leading expeditions into The Fen. Many thought him the best Captain of our time; decisive, brave, and wise enough to listen to the counsel of others instead of just going off on his own, half-cocked all the time." He fixed Hook with a pointed glance before continuing his story.

"We started small, going just past the outer rim of the place and hauling out some big game hides, plants, and even gemstones. But we didn't stop there. Even the most sensible of men can become greedy when so much coin is involved. We delved deeper each month, still cautious, but always seeking a larger prize. He promised that we'd stop at the very outskirts to that inner layer, but it was like something called to him about it. A last frontier for him to conquer. I talked some sense into him the first few times he brought it up, but eventually it became too alluring. He put together a team of his best fighters, then led us into the second layer. We—"

"Could you be a little more specific?" Scotty cut in, looking skeptical. "You said that you often stopped at the edge of the inner layer before this—what did it look like?"

"It's like an overgrown swampland," he grumbled with a swipe of his hand, clearly annoyed at the interruption, "with a wall of brambles cutting you off from going any further. There were holes you could get through, but they shifted constantly, and you never knew what type of beastie might be coming out of them."

Scotty turned to his brothers with a barely discernible tip of his head.

So Garth's account is accurate so far. Interesting.

"As I was saying…" Garth continued. "We waited for a good, safe-looking entrance to the second layer and took our chance, sliding down a long shaft and finding ourselves in what seemed like a whole 'nother world. More like a jungle than a swamp, with gemstones we'd thought were rare laying beneath our boots with every other step we took. And the monsters," he exhaled sharply. "Saber-toothed tigers the size of this room. Rhinos like elephants, and snakes twice as thick as a man. We tried to leave after slaying one of the big cats who didn't appreciate our intruding on his territory, but the exit-holes never seemed to quite line up; the way back was always just a little too steep, or would shift just as we got to it. Almost like…" He scratched at his bulbous nose and shrugged. "Well, almost like it wanted us to stay."

A chill pricked up my spine at the thought of The Fen "wanting" anything. It was starting to sound like Noru was the least of our concerns.

"So we delved further down instead, pressing into the heart of the place, where the true giants live. It was a difficult trek—"

"I'd love to hear the finer details, but we've no time to spare," Hook interjected, leaning forward. "Tell us about the hydra."

Garth's face scrunched into a scowl, making him look like an overcooked baked potato as he muttered under his breath about 'impatient youngins ruining a good yarn', but he settled down quickly. "The beast ambushed us one night, emerging from a lake and attacking us while we slept. It had a dozen heads, each one of them lethal in its own right. I chopped three off myself, and our crew fought valiantly, but we were no match. It was like battling a dozen monsters that worked in perfect harmony, each of them anticipating the next move of the others. Captain Flannery finally called for us to retreat, but only me and one other were alive to hear it. She wasn't ready to let us go, though. She chased us right up to the edge of the layer. There were three narrow spaces open, and there was no time to spare, so we charged right in, each of us taking a different path." Garth shuddered, looking truly shaken for the first time in his story. "The sounds...If I never hear anything like that again for the rest of my days, I'll die a happy man. The other holes must've closed or been too steep to pass through, because the monster caught up to both of them. Tore the Captain and my crewmate to bits." He stopped abruptly, letting out a ragged breath. "What else d'ya need to know more than that?"

"Satisfied?" Hook asked, glancing at Paddy.

The younger man rubbed at his chin, nodding slowly. "Won't lie and tell you I'm not intrigued. If he's fibbin', he went through a hell of a lot of trouble to learn as much about The Fen as he seems to know."

"He ain't fibbin'," Andrew cut in, shaking his head vigorously. "Stake my life on it."

I couldn't help but agree. Garth might have exaggerated a few of the details for color, but the pain he felt when talking about the death of his crew was real.

A loud crash pulled my attention back to the head of the table, where Garth had slid a book to the ground to make room for a small wooden chest. He flipped open the lid, then spun it around to face us.

"Fib this!"

My ears exploded with pain and my temples pounded as I stared down at a walnut-sized, purple gemstone nestled on a velvet pillow.

Wait, *was* it purple? I blinked twice, shocked to see that the color had morphed, shifting to green.

Paddy pushed out of his chair, the scraping sound dragging me back to reality, the pain in my temples receding. "Is that a maelstrom opal?"

Jacob nodded and wet his lips. "It is. A nice little chunk of it, too."

Hook's hand crept toward his belt as Scotty scooted his chair closer, and I found one hand shooting into my pouch and the other to my whip.

But when Garth snapped the box shut a moment later, the tension seeped from the air in a rush, like a spell had been broken. I let my hands fall to my sides, wondering what the hell I'd planned to do with the whip, anyway. Xander hadn't even taught me to swing it yet, though I knew he'd be proud that grabbing it had been my first impulse after just a day of 'fixating' on it like he'd instructed.

"Mighty fine piece you have there," Paddy said, leaning back in his chair with a hearty laugh. "Gotta admit, I'm a bit jealous, I am. A wealthy patron would pay a pretty penny just for the lore of it, never mind the beauty."

"Lore?" I asked, relieved the pressure in my head was gone.

"They say it's the opals that make the monsters of The Fen so big and strong. They feed off the power of it."

"I can attest to that firsthand. They want to be as close as possible to the stuff. You believe me now or you still think there's a chance I'm lyin'?" Garth demanded, brows raised in a challenge.

"Not a chance in hell. And if there's more like that in the second layer, we're even more committed than before."

Hook rose, wiping his hands together. "What else do we need?"

"I'd like to have him make a rudimentary map of the place..." Jacob started.

"Already done," Garth answered, reaching over to his bookshelf and pulling a large, bound scroll from the top shelf. He tossed it unceremoniously over to Jacob, who fumbled with it a few times before catching it. "If we're bein' honest, you'd all be helpless as a squirrel in the sea without me, even with the damn map, so I *guess* I can make some time to guide you through it. I'll have to check my schedule, but—"

"Absolutely not," Hook growled. "You're too old to sail, never mind actually going there with us."

Garth opened his mouth to protest, but settled for an audible humph. "Talk about looking a gift horse in the mouth…"

"You good with that map?" Hook asked, gesturing toward Jacob. "Anything else you need to ask, get it out of the way now."

"Nothin' comes to mind," Paddy answered, after a moment of deliberation with his brothers. "We'll be heading out in the morning, and we'll meet you all at the base camp at the entrance to The Fen in two days' time."

"Meet us? Why not come aboard my ship and we go together?" Hook asked, his eyes narrowing.

Paddy scratched the back of his neck and wrinkled his nose. "Well, we negotiated a fee to guide you through The Fen, not hold your hands as you sail the seas. I don't want to seem like a naysayer, but word is Pan and Tink are on the warpath more than ever. Why would we risk our necks riding with you lot? It's just not the way the O'Donnellys do business."

"Yeah, it's just not the way the O'Donnelly's do business," Andrew parroted with a snort.

Hard to argue with them, but Hook looked like he was about to try. His jaw went tight, and he leaned close enough to Paddy that I wondered if they bumped noses.

"If you're thinking about fucking with me or mine,

I'll run this hook into your gullet and tear it out through your mouth. If I get so much as a hint that you're playing both sides and talking to Pan and Tink, there is nowhere on the three seas that'll be safe. Not now. Not ever. Is that understood?"

Paddy's trademark dimple and easy smile were nowhere to be found. His Adam's apple bobbed up and down in time with his head.

"Understood."

"Excellent," Hook grunted before backing away. "Then we're off."

"Oh, good. Do me a favor and wait at least a few weeks before coming back to bug me next time," Garth called as we moved toward the door as a unit.

"Can do."

The Captain ushered the O'Donnelly's out first, then me, while holding the door from the inside. And when he stepped outside to join us, Garth shouted a final time from inside the house. "And James?"

Hook held the door open a moment longer, turning to face the older man.

"Don't get yourself killed out there. Not after all I done to save youse."

CHAPTER 22

I needed something to clear my head. A place that I could push some of the worries aside for a few hours. The jumble of emotions—hearing the concern in Garth's voice for *James*.

Which left me standing in the doorway of a building that smelled of coal dust, iron and fire.

The forge was pristine and to say that's unusual is an understatement. Forges were full of coal dust and slag from overheated iron, sweat and blood from the blacksmith and dirt and shit from the horses that came to have their feet trimmed and shod.

Pristine was not a usual descriptor for a blacksmith's shop. But this place was swept, tools were all hanging in their places, the bin of extra iron was carefully stacked, and the stalls where the horses stood had fresh straw and not a bit of shit anywhere.

I hoped I could do what I needed to do here, and

even more, put my current troubles at the back of my mind for a little while. I needed a moment to breathe. Funny how sweating and blistering up my hands working was the place I turned to for respite. Or maybe not so funny, being the Tinker that I was.

"Hello?" I called out into the empty space as I took a step into the forge.

"What you need, ma'am?"

I smiled at the thought of anyone calling me ma'am. I kept walking, looking for the source of the voice. I headed around the back side of the main forge. "I'd like to rent your shop for a few hours, if I could?"

"That's a new one. You kidding, right?"

I found myself thinking of—and missing—my buddy Smitty, back in The Smudge. Why couldn't *this* guy have been a doppelganger? I had a feeling I could've won ol' Smitty over no matter what world he inhabited. Now I had to get this guy to believe in me, too.

Once I found him, at any rate…

Behind the main forge was a small, tidy set up, a table and two chairs, teapot and plate of some sort of golden pastry that had a thick white glaze on it that had to be sweet. The old man who sat in one of the chairs had long white hair carefully slicked back and braided almost to his waist. His knuckles were big for the size of his hands, and he wasn't very big—probably about my height and lean.

Sharp blue eyes narrowed on me. "What do you mean, rent my place?"

I motioned to the second chair, and he nodded for me to sit down.

"My father was a blacksmith, I know my way around a forge, and I'd like to build a tip for this." I pulled my whip out and showed him the bare end.

He took the leather and ran his fingers over the braided end, and I took note of the Tideblessing on his wrist. Flames with a sword inside it. "You'll need something better than raw iron for this."

I touched the pouch of coins at my waist, my earlier thoughts on forging the dagger end of the whip finally coming to the surface. "I am hoping to use a bit of gold, to refine it."

"Gold is too soft, would blow out on the first crack."

I nodded and took a breath to say the thing that I knew he would understand. "I know, but…I have a feeling that it's what this weapon wants."

He arched a single eyebrow. "Not many people would say that."

I shrugged. "You understand though."

"I do." He sat back in his chair. "You think gold fused with iron, eh? I never done it."

Not just any gold, but gold from Alabaster. A place that had been my home for my whole life—or at least my whole life that I could remember—gold that Duncan had given me. And using it here was a way to connect myself to that past, no matter where I went next. Gold could be spent, but a weapon that I was learning to use, and would hopefully be with me for a long time…that warranted the best I could give it.

"It's a gut feeling."

"Hmm. Anything else?"

"If you'll allow me the time, a new knife. Lost mine and could use a backup."

With a tap on the table he stood, spry for the shocking white of his hair. "Smithson Coal's the name."

Of course it was—I had to contain the grin that tugged at my lips.

I held out one hand. "Harmony Fallowell."

He took my hand gave it a firm shake and then turned it over and inspected my palms. "Got some calluses. I don't think your lying about working hard, at least."

"Thank you?"

He held up the end of the whip. "You should start with the dagger. Let your mind rest on how you're going to make *this* work. Cause I want to watch you blend gold and iron into something usable. Not seen it done before. Not sure you can do it."

I stood. "Fair enough. How much for the time and iron?"

Smithson motioned for me to go ahead of him. "Depends on what I learn from you. Knowledge is worth more than gold to me at this point in my life."

"I will do my best."

He followed me to the front of the forge and I got to

work, gathering tools and setting them on the anvil. It was not far off the perfect height for me, being that Smithson and I were of a similar height.

I moved to his scrap heap, so perfectly piled. "You mind if I pull from here?"

"Go right ahead. You're not from round here, are you?"

I didn't need this line of questioning, but I didn't need to answer him—someone else did.

"She's not. She's with us, Smithson." Trick-Eyed Tom stepped into the forge, the door shutting softly behind him.

"A pirate?" Smithson snorted. "Nah, she's too pretty for you lot."

"That she is. But she's tough as nails and loyal. You know that Hook takes loyalty over what anyone looks like." Tom pulled a single stool away from the wall and plunked himself down on it. "That being said, I was curious what she be up to, seeing as she didn't have blacksmith on her application to come aboard."

My lips twitched. "All you wanted was a falconer. Didn't think you needed my entire skill set."

Smithson looked to me and then back to Tom. "You sticking around then?"

"Curiosity."

"Good, you can drink with me."

"Ahh, I knew I liked you Smithson. What you got? Rum? Whiskey?"

"Tea."

A laugh burst out of me as I sorted through the iron heap. "Make him drink it straight, Smithson, no cream or sugar."

A low chuckle from the other room and the clinking of pottery faded as I focused on the iron in front of me. I needed a dagger, but the right iron for the whip was more important so I searched for that first. I let my hands ghost over the bits and pieces.

An old draft horseshoe the size of a dinner plate caught my eye first. There were several nail heads still embedded in it along with dirt. The front of the toe was worn—the horse had worked hard to wear it that much in a single shoeing cycle.

My fingers slid over it and my magic rose to the surface, testing it out. Hard as iron, gritty, and unwilling to give up. The horse had strangely, unknowingly imbued some of its own qualities into the iron.

That was perfect for the whip.

The dagger iron was easier to find. A solid chunk about eight inches long that already had a slight curve to it. My magic kissed along the edges of it, inspecting it. It had started out being molded for a water barrel but broke rather than be trapped like that. I shook my head. What the fuck was happening to me? Iron didn't have...wants. Did it? I wrapped my fingers around the metal and it seemed to warm to me. I couldn't think too much about it, or I'd get sidetracked.

"Which for which?" Smithson asked.

I looked up to see the two men sitting with tea mugs in their hands. Tom looked totally unbothered by the fact that he was drinking tea instead of rum. He held up his mug. "Smithson makes his own…tea…it's got a kick, especially when heated."

I held up the eight inch chunk. "Dagger." Then the horseshoe. "Whip."

"Interesting choices. Proceed."

I turned my back to the men and focused first on the dagger as Smithson had suggested. If they wanted to sit there for the next few hours while I worked, that was their issue.

The low hum of their voices was in the background while I stoked the coal and started to turn the blower handle, pushing more air into the base of the forge and bringing the heat up. I slid the eight-inch chunk into the coal and grabbed a set of tongs. The three hammers I'd set on the anvil were waiting for me and I let my mind wander as I worked on the dagger's shape.

My magic was shifting and changing what felt like every day. It didn't frighten me, but I was trying to understand what I could do and what I couldn't with it. Like Xander had said, a little bit of everything really.

Like a jack of all trades. Even this time, as I forged the dagger my magic was actively bleeding into my movements, down my arms and into the tools and metal. The form of the dagger came quicker than ever, as if the metal was working with me, moving into the shape I wanted.

The spine of the dagger curved, following a wicked swoop on the business side of the blade. I didn't fold the metal as I had before—I didn't need to. This blade was all business and wouldn't break even if I jabbed it into a stone.

It…hell…it wanted to be made.

What felt like a moment passed and it was done, the edge sharpened and the handle made of a solid chunk of white ash wood.

I turned the dagger over in my hand, my magic reaching toward it as if it were its own living thing and with it, little designs emerged from the flat edge as I stared.

Flames licked up from the tip of the blade to the handle, etching into the iron. "Wow."

I blinked and looked up to see both men staring at me, eyes wide and cups dangling from their fingertips.

"What?"

"I've never seen a blade made in less than an hour, never mind a blade that looks like that." Smithson breathed out. "No cost to use the forge. Do the other now."

The door banged open before I could turn away, and a wide shouldered figure stepped through. Damn it, why did he have to show up? "Tom, you in here?"

"Yeah, Hook. Watching our Harmony."

Our Harmony. A blush of warmth flowed through me. Tom claimed me as if…as if we really were family. The warmth tugged at my heart and my eyes blurred a little. I would have to leave this place, sooner over later, but to know that someone thought of me as part of their people...it touched me. Not even Druzilla or my pseudo brothers had ever claimed me. Only ever Pawpaw and Molly.

And now Tom.

"What is she doing now? Causing Smithson grief?"

The warmth didn't fade despite Hook's sharp tone.

"No, she's amazing," Smithson waved his hand toward me. "Whatever her Tideblessing be, I don't know. But I'd offer her a full partnership if she'd take it."

"No." Hook's tone brooked no argument. "She belongs to me."

The three of us stared at him and he didn't stammer.

"She's part of my crew, is she not, Tom?"

"Yes, boss, she is." Trick-Eyed Tom didn't miss a beat. He stood and offered his seat to Hook, then came over to me, and kissed me on the cheek. "You come see me when you're done. I'll heal those hands up right quick."

I looked down to see the blisters forming on my palms. Callouses were all well and good but to have those blisters that quick...the speed of making the dagger had done it.

"Thanks, Tom." I kissed him on his cheek right back and he guffawed and gave me a wink.

I could almost feel the anger radiating off the third

man—Hook was not pleased. Which just made me smile.

Tom left and Smithson motioned for me to go on again.

But it was Hook who put the limit on it. "Time's wasting. You have an hour."

I could have argued but I wasn't going to bother—an hour would have to do.

"If she can make that knife in under an hour, she can make that cap for her whip in thirty minutes."

"Like to gamble on it?" Hook offered.

"Damn straight. That woman there is a treasure. I'd marry her if I wasn't an old codger. She's got magic in her veins like I've never seen."

It was my turn to blush. "Smithson, you talk like that to any woman, you'll have a wife in no time."

"Phaw."

I turned away and did my best to ignore the sensation of Hook watching me. Not that this was private or anything—I mean I'd apparently put on a show for Tom and Smithson, but the weight of Hook's dark eyes was a palpable thing.

I picked up the horseshoe and got to work.

I pulled two gold coins from my hip pouch, paused and looked to Hook as a thought rumbled through my mind. "Can I trade you a gold coin for a gold coin?"

Hook frowned. "Why?"

"I just...I think I need two different gold coins." Again, I couldn't say why, just that it was a feeling. As much as I needed part of this to be from Alabaster and my world there, I needed a piece from this story too.

Hook flipped me a gold coin that I caught in the air, then I tossed him one of my own. He'd surely wonder at the inscriptions on it, but gold was gold. It would spend the same.

I laid the two coins side by side. One had the castle and motto of Alabaster, "To the Strong go the Spoils." The other was stamped with a skull and crossbones, the words "The Pirates Life till Death" etched around the rim.

A third coin. I needed a third coin. I frowned. It wasn't the right time to build this particular cap for the whip. I took two Alabaster coins and started the process.

Neither man questioned, though again I could sense Hook watching my every move. Just like in the dreams, I couldn't escape the weight of his presence, but there was no time to waste.

I heated the horseshoe enough that I could cut it in half, and stuck one end into the water barrel.

I'd use some now and keep the rest for later.

Neither Hook nor Smithson said a word as I began to process the two metals together.

It was not an alloy that I'd ever heard of being done and I knew that my bold statement that I could do it, and would do it, was all that had gotten me this opportunity to work in Smithson's forge.

Heating the horseshoe up, I straightened it out and

flattened it. Then created a divot on each end, just big enough for a coin. This was where it got tricky.

Gold melted fast.

Iron didn't.

I took a breath and wove my magic down through my arm, and into the gold coins. A headache started right behind my eyes, but I pushed it aside as best I could. Pulling my jeweler's loupe out, I set it over my right eye.

My magic was wrapped around the coins tightly as I carefully put the iron-that-used-to-be-a-horseshoe back into the coal. Keeping the gold coins protected while I heated the iron took all my concentration.

Bringing the metal back out, I bent it over, folding it on itself. Over and over, I repeated the process, losing count of how many times I bent and blended.

Like making bread, I kneaded the two ingredients together, watching as the gold slid through the iron in veins, and then further, coloring the entire thing.

Releasing my protective hold on the gold, a burst of colors rose up from the forge and I quickly pulled the newly minted bit of metal out as it sparked and spit.

"Flux," I barked as if Smithson was the apprentice and I the master.

But he grabbed the can of flux that would help weld the metals together and tossed it to me. I sprinkled the white crystals over the metal and began to shape the piece into the cap for the whip. Thinning it out first, the gold-iron alloy moved like liquid under my hammer and the shape came together quickly.

The tip was as sharp as any arrowhead, and the cap would cover four inches on the end of the whip. I thinned out the bottom four corners, pulling length from them so that I could weave them through the leather. That would stabilize it, and give it better balance too.

Still…

"Something is missing." I whispered, feeling the push and pull in the metal, trying to find just what was wrong. I put my hand over the nearly finished cap, my eyes throbbing and my head responding in tandem.

"Oil?" Smithson offered.

I shook my head and pushed my magic deeper into the metal. Something else. "No, I can't quite pin it down."

I knew that if I'd used the coin from Hook, there would have been something missing too. But this was different. Like an ingredient that would be needed to even have the basic model of this done. I kept my hand over the whip cap and let my magic move through it, searching for the missing link.

Accuracy. Brutality. Violence. Blood. That was missing?

Ingredients that didn't make sense.

"You have five minutes left." Hook said. "Then I will drag you from here, slung over my shoulder if I must."

I lifted my eyes to glare at him, and my eyes drifted to his hook. Iron. Accurate. Brutal. Bathed in blood?

That was what was missing. A piece of something that already imbued the traits I needed.

The pattern in the hook opened itself to me, showing me clearly what was there. I nodded. "I need a piece of your hook."

His laugh was sudden, as he threw his head back, and filled the forge.

Smithson flinched. I didn't so much as budge. I knew what I knew.

Getting a hold of himself, Hook stared at me, his laughter fading. "You're shitting me." He held up his missing hand. "You want a piece of me?"

"No, I am not kidding, nor am I shitting you. I don't need the whole thing, just like..." I looked around for a file. "A filing."

"It won't ruin the integrity of your weapon, Captain," Smithson said. "And if it's all the same to you, I'd like to see this through on her end, I've never witnessed this kind of magic. I can always make you another hook if you are worried."

He talked about my magic like it wasn't of their world.

Which of course, it wasn't.

Hook stared at me. Not angry, not furious, but thoughtful. "I do not know what to make of you."

"Thank you."

"It was not a compliment."

I flashed him a smile. "To me it is."

He must have wanted to see this forging through too, because without any more argument, he let me file a bit of his hook over the finished product. I put my hand over his wrist to steady him, feeling his heart beating steady under my fingertips.

I made the mistake of looking up at him.

His eyes were already dark and yet they seemed to deepen into a land of midnight hours and hidden secrets. His heartrate kicked up, thumping harder against my fingers.

Hard to think when we were frozen, staring at one another as the space between us heated more than any forge I'd ever touched.

"Get it done," he growled, his voice husky and thick with something like desire.

Shit.

"Yes, on it." My stupid voice wasn't much better than his, breathy and full of something I'd almost call need. Fuck my life and my stupid hormones.

I gripped him a little tighter and made one pass across the middle of his hook, the metal protesting only a little.

The smallest amount of iron, a single piece only, fell and sunk *into* the cap of the whip, absorbed into the metal as if it had been liquid and not solid.

I let go of Hook and stared at the cap. "That's it." I turned to thank him just in time to see the door just before it slammed shut.

Hook was gone.

"Never seen the captain run from anything before. Funny that it would be a slip of girl like you," Smithson mused.

I swallowed hard and stared at the door. I'd sent him running, huh?

Did that mean I unsettled him as much as he unsettled me?

CHAPTER 23

My mind was still reeling a short while later as I stood in front of the inn, staring up into the night sky for any sign of Fetch, but it was another name that had branded itself in the forefront of my mind.

James.

Garth had called him that, and I couldn't deny it felt better…more fitting than Hook at times, in spite of the obvious, and his prickly personality.

"Not after all I done to save youse…"

Had Garth been the person to help Hook and his friend after his hand had been taken by Noru, or had the old man saved him at some other time?

One thing was for sure, I wasn't about to ask. There was no point. Hook wouldn't tell me anyway. We might be allies for now, but he'd decided to trust me exactly as much as he had to, and not one speck more. How

249

did I know? Because I'd left the forge right after he did, and when I got to the inn, he was nowhere to be found. Apparently, he'd stopped to get something from his room, ran into Xander at the bar and told him not to wait up. That he had some more business to take care of. Then, he'd headed off down the street without another word.

Tired of being kept in the dark, I'd made the snap decision to give Fetch the most complex directive I'd ever attempted; To see if he could find Hook walking and then come directly back to the inn and lead me to him. Fetch had taken off, and I'd been holding my breath ever since. Something deep inside me sensed that the key to unlocking all the secrets hidden within this fairytale hinged on this very moment. I just had to hope that Sir Fetchington Von Buren chose friendship over spite and did as he was told.

Ten minutes later, I found myself wondering if he'd been even more angry about the whole Devil's Gauntlet debacle than I thought, or if I was just being impatient.

"Definitely that second one," I murmured under my breath.

I had barely walked into the inn before turning around and walking right back outside, body humming with pent up frustration.

Fetch was quick, but he wasn't a miracle worker. I had to calm my tits and find a little patience.

I'd just sat on the curb to settle in when the familiar

flutter of wings sounded overhead. I looked up to find Fetch hovering with an expectant gleam in his eye. Despite his lack of reply when I'd given him the command, he'd heard me. And although he still wasn't exactly being his lovey-dovey self, he'd done my bidding.

"You're such a good, smart bird," I cooed as I leapt to my feet.

With a quick glance around to make sure no one was watching, I followed Fetch as he led me down the still-bustling street, past the butcher shop, past the bakery.

We'd gone at least two miles, and the lights from the lanterns flanking the main street had grown dim in the distance. I squinted, trying to see what lay ahead as the cobbled road gave way to a roughly hewn path.

"Well, shit," I mumbled. I'd assumed Hook was going to talk to another prospective crew member or maybe pick up some supplies. But when Fetch slowed and then twirled into a dive right above a quaint, feminine little cottage, I froze in shock.

Had I just followed Captain Hook to his fucking *mistress's* house?

Not that I cared if he had a mistress. It was just, I'd gotten so excited, thinking I was going to get some good information. Now, though, for some reason, the idea of sneaking closer to peek through the window and confirm my suspicion made my stomach roil.

Was she young and beautiful? Did he *love* her?

I was about to turn and go when Fetch made a loop and perched on something in the front yard. Squinting to get a better look, I realized it was a sign:

Gayelette's Forchuns. Garr-un-teed to come true, or your next 1 is free!

The relief that poured through me was so dizzying I had to bend at the waist to steady myself.

Of course I was relieved. Gayelette was the one person who seemed to have all the answers—even if she wasn't quick to give them up.

It had nothing at all to do with the fact that she was unlikely to be Hook's mistress…assuming this was the same Gayelette. And given her advertised profession, I could imagine it was no other. I tried not to get my hopes up as I snuck across the tiny yard, to peer through the window.

Would this Gayelette even remember me or be able to help? Or would she be like all the other doppelgangers in this new world—the same as her namesake in Alabaster, but somehow different? Would her memory of me be gone, too?

I took a shaky breath, steeling myself against disappointment. As I peered into the dimly lit room through the dusty glass. There were colorful tapestries covering the walls and lush plants in pots on nearly every flat surface. In one corner, a rack of spices hung drying, their fragrances mixing with the faint smell of incense. At the center of the room Gayelette and Hook sat across from each other at a small oval table. A crystal ball rested between them, the sole item on a brightly patterned tablecloth.

Gayelette's familiar face made my stomach give a nervous flop. This was definitely the same woman I'd met in Alabaster, though here in this place she'd fully embraced her profession as a fortune teller. A gold scarf covered her hair, and enormous emerald hoop earrings—large enough to fit around her wrists—dangled from her lobes. Her lips, painted crimson, curved slightly as she studied the shining orb before her. Rings adorned every one of her gnarled fingers so that you could barely see the skin beneath.

Her words carried softly through the partially open window. I strained to hear:

"...something, something, prophecy...something, something, magic."

Then, more distinctly:

"...Harmony something something."

My heart stuttered. They were talking about me. No way was I missing out on what either of them had to say.

Especially Gayelette.

Moving as slowly and carefully as possible, I pressed upward on the worn wood of the window frame, inch by painstaking inch. It took a full two minutes before I opened it just wide enough to squeeze my ear (and half my head) inside.

"Why didn't you just tell me that when I was here

two days ago?" Hook asked, clearly agitated as he raked his hand over his face.

"That's not how it works, I'm afraid," she replied.

Classic Gayelette. Hearing Hook suffering the same treatment I had made my lips twitch. Served him right.

He let out a bitter laugh. "How it works is that I pay you, and you tell me what I want to know."

She wiggled her index finger in the air, clicking her tongue. "No. You pay me, and I tell you what you *need* to know."

"It's the same thing, woman. You're picking nits," Hook growled.

"I'm not," she shot back. "It's a hard lesson to learn, but the most important part is the journey. *That's* where we grow. If I told you everything now, you wouldn't be prepared to complete the task required of you. And when you reach the endgame, you'd be a help to no one. A useless tit, if you will."

Hook let out a low, frustrated growl. I didn't want to sympathize with him. But she'd given me the same line back in Alabaster, and though I understood her point, it wasn't helpful or satisfying.

Hook's voice dropped slightly. "You still believe, with the crew I've assembled, that we have a chance to make it in and out of The Fen safely? I have enough blood on my hands, Gayelette. I do not need more."

Her ringed fingers slid over the crystal ball. "I can't guarantee the outcome, but I can tell you the right players are in place. The rest is up to you. Yet a more important question remains." She leaned forward, resting her hand on the crystal ball. "What happens afterward? Win or lose, I see nothing but more darkness beyond the day of reckoning between you and your enemies. Why is that, Captain James Tyler?"

His jaw tightened, and he stared Gayelette down in stony silence.

"There are people counting on you in ways that have nothing to do with the fairy and her lover," she continued. "You need to embrace the fact that there is much more to live for than vengeance—or never-ending darkness will be the only thing waiting at the end of the road. For you and countless others."

She was beating the same drum as Garth about Hook's obsession with revenge, so he obviously wasn't holding his cards very close to his chest. But it also had me wondering...if Pan and Tink truly were the wronged party here, why would a man dedicate his whole life to retribution?

Hook opened his mouth, but before he could speak, Gayelette's gaze shifted—straight to me.

"And you," she said, without breaking eye contact with Hook. "Come on inside and join us. You're letting the flies in."

I froze, but it was already too late—I was caught. I pulled away from the window just in time to see Hook whirl around, his eyes narrowing when he spotted me.

"Son of a bitch," he muttered. "You're unbelievable."

Feeling more than a little sheepish, I wiggled my

fingers at him in a pathetic greeting then made my way around to the front door on quaking legs. I was going to pay for this, somehow, some way. Still, a surge of relief washed through me at seeing Gayelette's weathered face again. After wiping my feet on the mat, I stepped inside.

"Hello," I said with a grimace. "I was just passing by and overheard—"

"Save it," Hook snarled. "You keep asking me to trust you, but you continually prove yourself unworthy of the same."

"Harmony has a destiny, same as you," Gayelette interjected gently, placing her hand over Hook's clenched fist. "The future of her people hangs in the balance. Give her some grace, Hook. She truly does mean well, and she is also fighting to save many lives, whether she knows it fully or not."

"Y-you remember me, then?" I asked Gayelette, sliding into the last empty seat at the table, leaning away from Hook.

"Of course I do. How could I forget? Harmony Fallowell from Alabaster, blacksmith, tinker, and falconer."

She offered me a smile, and I felt heat creep up my cheeks as it dawned on me where Hook had gotten my last name.

"You were here the day we boarded the ship at the pirate's meeting, weren't you?" I said to Hook. "That's why you showed up late. That's how you knew my last name."

He tipped his head in a curt nod. "Gayelette told me that 'Harmon Fallowell…'a falconer," He turned to the old woman with a frown, "And *his* sister would be part of the crew needed to get the clock from Noru. When I saw you and your falcon, I understood why." His gaze flicked back to Gayelette. "But you could have told me she was female."

"You both have to believe that I'm giving you all the information that's required, at the time that it is required," she replied, unruffled. "If you were looking for two females, you wouldn't have even noticed them. Trust the process. And regarding trust, for the time being, you're going to need to trust each other. Both of you will fail in your mission to get the magical clock if you don't—because you're inexorably tied, whether you like it or not. Deep down, you've always known this. Hence the dreams."

At the mention of dreams, I dropped my gaze to the vibrant pattern on the tablecloth, desperate for a change of subject as my cheeks flamed. "I've met others from Alabaster here, but they don't know me at all. Why do you?"

"Because I am not truly of this realm, or the one that you came from, any more than you are," Gayelette explained softly. "I come when I can spare the magic to do so, and I stay as long as I'm able to help guide you. But then I must return to my home."

"And where is that?" I asked, a strange flutter sparking in my chest.

"C'an Saas, child." Her knowing eyes met mine. "The same as yours."

C'an Saas.

A jolt of energy snaked through me, as if I'd been struck by lightning. C'an Saas was my home. I felt that truth in my bones the second she spoke the word.

"You knew me," I whispered, balling my trembling hands into fists as I tried to keep my voice steady. "Before I was sent away to Alabaster as a small child. You knew me, didn't you?"

She inclined her head, a sad smile tugging at her lips. "I did. And I knew your parents as well."

My world spun on an axis that I couldn't balance on. I pressed my hands to the table to keep from falling over. Knowledge of my past, of my parents was right here in front of me. I sucked in a ragged breath and tried to speak.

"Please," I croaked, unable to hide the emotion cracking my voice. I reached for her hand, gripping it desperately. "Tell me their names. Tell me something—anything—about them. How did I get here? Why did they send me? Are they still—"

"No, child," she cut in gently, shaking her head. "I'm so sorry, but they left the mortal world long ago. Your mother and father were king and queen of C'an Saas. They loved you more than anything in this world and the only reason they sent you away was because a powerful witch named Almira had waged a war to take the throne and won. If you stayed, she'd have killed you. She's still out there, and she wants nothing more than to keep you from returning to C'an Saas."

My stomach twisted with a mix of terror and determination. "How do I…?"

"Your success relies on using all the magic in you," Gayelette continued. "Building it, growing it, strengthening it. But you must wield it carefully. Almira is watching from afar, waiting for any chance to strike—and she uses your growing power to find you."

My thoughts spun like a top, flitting from moment to moment.

The gaping holes with the ragged edges that seemed to appear wherever I went.

The chewing sound as if something were eating away at pieces of paper…

"She's the one who sent the worms." Bile rose in my throat as it came together in perfect clarity. "They're bookworms…"

Eating the pages.

"Bookworms?" Hook murmured, eyes narrowing as he shifted his gaze to Gayelette.

But the old woman ignored him and smiled, a touch of pride in her tone. "You're connecting the dots now, child. That's good. But with that knowledge comes more danger. The closer you get to fulfilling your destiny, the bolder and more desperate she will become."

Things had suddenly become so real now, and just within reach…or closer at least. Home had a name. C'an Saas. And when I got there, I would learn who I was. Where I'd come from. *Who* I'd come from.

"Take care, girl. There is still a long, dangerous road ahead of you. Almira will stop at nothing to destroy you."

I swallowed hard and straightened my shoulders, the strength of my Pawpaw, of my friends, of my belief in myself snapping my vision into sharp focus. I was not alone in this, and it was in the bonds of those I loved and who loved me that would see me through this—that's how I knew that one way or another, I would get home.

"Let her fucking try."

CHAPTER 24

I was standing on the deck before the sun broke through the night, channeling my magic down the smooth handle of the whip, wincing as I urged it to flow all the way down to the tip I'd just added. My head throbbed with pain, but I pushed it back, focusing in on a single thought.

C'an Saas.

My home, *outside* this story I was in, and the place I desperately needed to get back to.

The magic snaked down the whip a little further, slipping through the coarse, woven leather. I could feel every nick and scratch, as if I was rubbing a hand across my own skin. Just a little further…

My vision went white as a searing pain spiked through my skull; a dozen times worse than what I'd felt a moment earlier. The magic kicked back into me in a wave, as if the whip and I went from being a single, unified, thing back to being separate once more.

I tossed it to the large crate at my side, panting heavily. I'd been just inches away from imbuing the whole thing with my magic, far closer than I'd ever gotten before. But it wasn't good enough. Not when I was beginning to understand what Almira was capable of. If I was ever going to be able to return home, I simply had to do better.

Almira. I had a name now, a name to focus on, a name to hate. The reason I was cast out from my real home.

We'd left town the previous morning, and I'd spent every waking hour between that, and this fixated on getting strong…growing my magic. My destiny was becoming clearer with each passing second, but the road ahead seemed to grow more daunting in equal measure.

Just a few weeks earlier, I'd never even seen a Whisper stronger than a potions vendor or show magician, and now I was here and there was magic everywhere I looked. There was magic in *me*.

Relyk's power had been incredible, and he wasn't as strong as the witch hunting me.

What did that make Almira in terms of a threat? She had the strength to manipulate entire worlds. Perhaps even enough power to destroy them, given enough time.

As for me?

I was out here, struggling to channel my new-found magic into a whip, while doing my level best to not think about Captain James-Fucking-Hook.

Our last meaningful conversation played over in my mind

"You can run but you can't avoid my questions forever," he called as I rushed ahead toward the Inn.

We'd left Gayelette's place and the last thing I'd wanted to do was talk. Not when I had so much thinking that needed doing.

She knew my father.

My *mother*.

I was a fucking *princess*? Molly would absolutely die when I told her. Maybe I wouldn't tell her for that reason.

Once I made my way back home to C'an Saas, would I meet the real Gayelette? Would she tell me all about my parents? Did I dare to hope that there might even be pictures? Keepsakes?

Nope. I'd drive myself crazy letting thoughts like that take hold. Instead, I thought about the back and forth with Hook as I ran from Gayelette's.

"Running away isn't going to change anything," he *drawled, far closer than I'd expected him to be given that I was basically sprinting down the cobbled street. "I need to know what she meant about the bookworms. And who is this Almira?"*

I didn't slow.

"Listen, Princess. We have no choice here. We have to

combine our magic and work together to get the clock. She said it herself."

"Fine," I shouted, wheeling around to face him and wishing I didn't as he hulked over me, nearly blocking out the moon behind him. "I'm perfectly willing to do that. But she dropped some life-changing stuff on me back there, and I could use one fucking minute of silence to process it all. Is that really too much to ask?"

"You don't want to talk, we won't talk," he said with a shrug. "I'd prefer it that way. But then you need to stop getting in my business. No more following me or breaking into my quarters. We work together to meet our own ends. We don't need to be friends, and I don't need you tailing me like a stray dog with a bad haircut."

Stray dog...bad haircut indeed. I cursed softly, sucking in a breath of the fresh ocean air, as I did my best to stop thinking about those biting words and the man who'd said them. As unsettling as it had felt at first, I was starting to actually enjoy the gentle rocking of the waves. And the sky...The brilliant oranges, reds, and purples of the rising sun shimmered across the endless expanse of sea, more beautiful than any painting.

"You're early."

I spun, my adrenaline spiking as I caught sight of Xander standing a few feet away. "Gods, how the hell did you get so close without me hearing you?"

He flashed a cocky half-grin. "Good to know I haven't lost my touch."

"I'm still working on finding mine." I let out an exasperated huff as I picked up the whip once again. "I feel like I've put so many hours into this, but I still can't fill the thing with my magic."

He raised an eyebrow. "How far did you get?"

"Around here." I gestured to a spot a few inches away from the end. "And it takes so much of my concentration that I doubt I could wield the thing without leaving myself defenseless."

He held out a hand and I passed it over, a little surprised by how weird I felt about parting ways with it. There was a long pause as he just stood there, tracing the weapon with his fingers, but he eventually grabbed it by the handle.

"Watch."

I groaned internally, but focused my vision on him, pushing the magic into my eyes just in time to see his energy beginning to flow into the whip. The gentle glow flowed into it like poured honey, moving slow and steady through the first foot or so of the whip before coming to an abrupt halt.

"Right around here is the benchmark for the first year," he said. The rest of the twelve-foot whip remained untouched by his magic.

"What?"

"The average student would be able to imbue the whip to about here, given a year of practice," he said, meeting my gaze.

"A year?" I asked, incredulous.

"You're no average Tideblessed, of course." He grinned. "And I'm no average teacher. But you need to realize that this all takes time—and you are pushing hard."

I nodded, speechless as I let the magic flow back out of my eyes. Surely, he was exaggerating.

"I won't ask you to show me what you managed just yet, since I'm sure you're tired, but we can get into some of the basic forms, if you like."

"Forms?" I blinked stupidly, and the fatigue of practice made me slow. What was he talking about now?

"Sets of choreographed movements, for learning the proper technique to use when swinging your weapon." He gave the whip a final squeeze before handing it back to me. "You'll be able to incorporate magic into it with time, but it'll still come in handy without that."

"How do you know all this?"

"Come." He turned, waving for me to follow as he strode toward a more open spot on the ship's deck. "Carnies and whips go hand in hand, monster tamers before there were monster hunters." He faced me as he reached into his pouch.

His two hands flashed into motion in unison, with one blurring toward his pocket and the other tearing his own whip from his pouch. Fetch cawed overhead, hardly audible through the thumping in my ears as I braced for an attack that never came.

Instead, a flash of gold burst into the air, almost too

fast to see with the naked eye, and his whip disappeared entirely, shooting through the air like a bolt of The Speaker's purple lightning.

Thunder seemed to crack overhead as the whip snapped, blasting directly into the glint of gold. He eased the end of the whip down somehow, and I pressed magic into my eyes instinctively, watching as he guided the whip's tip right into his open left hand.

I stared down, heart pounding as much from shock and excitement as from the scare he'd given me. The coin was still there, impaled on the barbed, iron tip of the weapon. He tugged at it and the now-ruined coin popped right off.

"Bullseye." He flashed a smile as he flicked it over to me.

I fumbled with it for a moment, managing to catch it in the end. It was still warm from the impact, and, as he'd said, the face of whatever man had been pictured on the thing was pierced straight through the center, as if by a dart. "That was…amazing."

"The crowds liked that one. So did—" he broke off, a familiar sadness washing over his features. "Doesn't matter. Let's get started. It'll take some time, but you'll be able to do the same, once you master everything I have to teach you."

"This isn't your favorite coin, right?" I asked, glancing up at him in horror as the thought occurred.

"Lucky Lucy? Gods no." His hand shot back to his

pocket. "Hmm…I can't seem to find her, though. Could you check your pockets, too?"

I reached down to do as instructed, despite my confusion. "Why would it be in—?" I cut off as my finger rubbed against a cool piece of metal. I pulled it out, as taken aback as I was impressed. "When did you do that?"

"A magician never shares his secrets." He took it and slipped it back into his pocket with a grin. "Now let's get into the basics. If we move quickly, I'll have time to show you one of the forms so you have something to practice in your free time."

He launched into a long lecture, explaining everything from the start. The proper grip, the way I should stand, and even how I should breathe as I worked my way through the form. I stayed captivated throughout, still awed by his demonstration. If I could replicate such a feat, I'd at least be able to defend myself against some pretty serious foes. Nobody wanted a metal spike through the face.

"Okay, last thing. You'll feel the urge to get that crack with your wrist, but in the long run you'll get more control if you focus on the elbow." He demonstrated in slow motion, producing little more than a light snap. "You see the motion, right? There are times when it's right to use the wrist, but don't let it become a crutch."

I nodded, glancing sideways at a flash of movement in my peripheral vision.

"Finished up helping with breakfast and wanted to come watch for a bit," Molly said, swiping her hands on her oil-stained apron.

"You really should consider joining her." His tone suggested that it hadn't been the first time they'd discussed the idea.

"Nope. I've got my incapacitator if I need it, and I have a feeling I'd just make a fool of myself with the whip. I'm known for many things; beauty, charm, wit… But most certainly not coordination."

Xander chuckled. "Suit yourself. Maybe you'll change your mind once you see what we're up to. You got here just in time for the good part."

"Don't let me slow you down." Her eyes twinkled as she leaned back against the mast and motioning for us to continue.

"Try to follow my movements carefully. My teacher called this the first form," Xander said. Each step and motion happened as quickly as if he was submerged in molasses, but, somehow, the whip still let out a sharp report every time he cracked it.

There was something calming, almost meditative about the movements as they flowed together. A step to the side, then a swing straight ahead. A step back, with a flourish, then cracking it directly behind his back. And it continued on in that way for well over a minute before he came to a halt.

"You won't remember the whole thing at first," he

said. "Start with the first third of it, and practice until it becomes muscle memory."

He took me through it a few more times, isolating just the first third and having me go through the motions with him.

"I think I'm getting it," I said, having burned each movement into my brain as deeply as I could.

"Excellent. We'll check back in on it tomorrow morning, so even if you have a few things wrong it's no harm done."

"It starts like this, yes?" I showed him the first step.

He nodded, stepping toward Moll and holding out an arm. "But wait one second. There's one more piece to this. Molly can help."

She stepped into him, and he pulled her in by the waist, leading her over to a spot a few feet in front of me. There was a casual closeness I hadn't seen before, and the air between them seemed to buzz with electricity.

It took everything I had to hold back a grin. I'd never seen this from her before. Not even with her on-again, off-again boyfriend, Stefan the butcher. I'd never seen her laughing so freely with any man. She genuinely enjoyed Xander's company. And, if anyone deserved a little window of joy, it was her. Poverty had forced her to be extremely pragmatic when it came to dating, looking more for a way out than for a person to spend her life with. We might be in the middle of a shitstorm but at least *that* was over now…For good, if I had anything to say about it.

"You stand here," he explained, his fingertips lingering on her waist for the briefest of moments before he stepped away. He moved to my left side, taking a moment to gauge the distance. "It's a form for fighting multiple enemies," he explained. "Whenever you're going through the motions, imagine a person in each of these spots. If you do it like you're just swinging at air, you'll just be building bad habits that we'll have to fix later. The whip should crack right through your imaginary enemies. Ideally heart, face, or balls."

I nodded, glancing over at Moll, who seemed too focused on mooning over Xander to even hear what was being said. I held back a laugh, deciding that I'd monopolized enough of his time for the day.

"That makes sense. I, uh… just remembered. I have some cleaning to do. I'll see you later, alright?"

"Sure. Sounds good." He glanced over at Moll, then back to me, flashing a quick wave.

I hurried away, hoping I hadn't made things awkward between them.

Fetch drifted back down to my shoulder as I walked, clicking his beak as he stared down at me. "What's up, my feathered friend?"

He cawed in that very un-falcon-like way he sometimes did, leaping off my shoulders. Rather than going back into the sky, he stayed low, leading me toward the back of the ship while circling back a few times to be sure I still followed. A loud rustling sound came through as I approached the cluster of barrels strapped to the ship's rear, just barely louder than the whooshing of the waves below.

What the hell was going on? Had some kind of wild animal gotten aboard?

Movement flashed and I held out my whip on instinct, not that I knew how to use the damn thing. But what emerged wasn't an animal at all.

It was a sweaty, red-faced Garth. Our gazes collided and he went stock still like a possum, as if I wouldn't see him so long as he didn't move.

"Fucking hell, Garth! You nearly gave me a heart attack! What are you doing here?"

He stayed frozen in place, visibly cycling through what I could only imagine were a dozen different excuses before settling on one so insufficient, it had to be the truth.

"Well, I wasn't about to miss out on all the action, was I?"

CHAPTER 25

*H*ook pounded toward the dining hall, each footfall booming like thunder, his anger thickening the air like a thundercloud.

"It's like you get a kick out of wasting my time," he snapped, his gaze fixed on Garth from the moment he entered the room. "Ebonfall is only a few days away. We have no time to bring you home and still have a shot of making it in and out of The Fen before then." He tensed, then unclenched his fist, turning away in disgust. "But you already knew that, didn't you? Part of your plot so you'd force my hand. Old fool."

Garth stared down, unwilling to meet his eyes as he took another swig from his mug of water—the first he'd had in the full day since we'd left town because he'd been in such a hurry to catch us, he'd not taken any supplies with him.

"I'm as fit as I've ever been. I'm not gonna slow you

down." Even his usual grumbling had no fire in it. He sounded more ashamed than anything.

I'd taken him down below to recover from the heat exhaustion, and had been dreading Hook's arrival since the cook had gone up to fill him in a few minutes earlier.

"You won't get the chance to slow us down," Hook growled. "We're dropping you off on the way. We'll have to veer a few kilometers off course, but it's doable. You'll stay at Tilly's Inn until we get you on the way back. Assuming you don't die of the shits or catch the rot while you're there, that is. Tilly is a terrible cook and an even worse housekeeper."

"Bah." Garth spun sideways, waving a dismissive hand. "Can't be more depressing than having to stare at your ungrateful mug days on end."

I held back a gasp, my gaze flitting between the two of them. I'd never seen anyone dare to speak to Hook that way—barring Davy, who'd talked his way into an early grave.

Hook's face went ruddy with anger but rather than exploding as I'd expected, he let out a mirthless laugh. "I've got enough on my plate without having a useless old man to babysit."

Garth's face fell. "Ah, fuck off, will you?" But his heart wasn't in it. Hook's comment had clearly stung. Rather than apologizing, Hook did shockingly, exactly as Garth asked, storming out of the dining hall, fury radiating out of him like a hot forge, the door rattling on its hinges as he slammed it behind him.

Rage from Hook. Embarrassment from Garth. Because he *was* an old man. And we all knew it. But to be reminded of it…that was a low blow.

I had to jam my lips shut as a flash of anger of my own surged up to match it.

It's none of your business, Harm.

But that was a hard pill to swallow when I could still picture the sick look on my father's face when Druzilla dared to say something this hurtful. There was little worse you could say to a man Garth's age.

"That went sideways fast, didn't it?" I murmured, trying to break the awkward silence but regretting it as soon as the words left my mouth.

Garth got up from his seat without replying, hobbling right past the cook's counter to grab a bottle of rum from the cabinet. He tore it open with his teeth and a grunt, throwing back a gulp of the stuff straight from the bottle.

My vision blurred as I careened sideways, ears ringing from the tooth-clattering rumble that rolled through the ship as it pitched hard—someone angry was steering apparently.

Three guesses who, and the first doesn't count.

I managed to catch a piece of the countertop to keep myself upright as I looked around frantically, finding no sign of Garth.

Where the hell did the old man go?

And then I spotted him. He was on the ground, his back pressed up against the wall.

"Are you okay?" I called, my heart thumping as I scrambled over toward him.

"Someone really needs to teach the bastard to steer a ship," he groaned, sending a flood of relief rolling through me. "Damn near killed me, he did. Maybe that was what he was going for—quicker than dropping me off at Tilly's."

"Stay on the floor in case that happens again." I ignored his groans of protest as I pulled his head away from the wall. "Are you hurt? Did you hit your—"

A deafening ringing split the air, the vibrations physically shaking the deck. Garth's eyes went wide, and he reached to his waist for a sword that wasn't there.

"That's the alarm! We're under attack!"

"Stay here." I sucked in a frantic breath. "Keep low, I'll be right back."

And, for once, he had no smart comment to make in response. He just dipped his head in a curt nod of agreement. "You should stay here, too. You'll get yourself killed out there, lass."

"Just stay put." Magic buzzed within me, and I let it come bubbling to the surface, as I strode away not waiting for a reply.

I pushed through the door, taking quick stock of the situation. Barrels and crates lay strewn around the deck by the dozen, and footsteps and shouts sounded from all around, mostly above.

I dashed up the stairs and toward the front of the ship, reaching for my connection with Fetch at the same time. He flew just overhead, barely keeping pace with the ship as he watched something in front of the bow.

"Whirlpool!" Xander shouted, the word striking my ear the moment I saw the thing, pulling us in from just a few thousand feet away. And we were headed right toward it, having twisted off course from the suction.

I reached for my magic, not even sure what I planned on doing with it, but a gruff shout broke me out of it.

"To your stations!" Hook dashed past me, hardly breaking stride even as the ship began to tremble and rock. "Harmony, get below with Molly," he called, unable to spare even a glance over his shoulder as he heaved mightily on the wheel, struggling against Mother Nature herself.

I wove my arm through the railing, ignoring him as I gathered my strength. Whatever this whirlpool was, the magic at its core was palpable, oozing off it with each passing second. Had Pan and Tink really gone this far? Had they done this?

A spike of pain shot through me at the thought, and I tore my loupe from my pocket, pressing it to my eye as I stared onward. *No, not Pan or Tink*, I corrected, sucking in a breath. It was far, far worse.

A twisting void of midnight black lay at the heart of the whirlpool, sucking in a lake's worth of water with each passing second and driving all of this. The wind whipped up around us, whooshing right into my back as we tried desperately to change course.

Whoever was causing all this, they were not of this world. And they were doing everything in their power to drag us to a watery grave.

Almira? Was it possible this whirlpool was her doing?

I gritted my teeth against my raging headache, forcing my magic to the surface as Hook barked orders at various members of the crew. If I could just channel that same surge of power I'd managed when crash landing Pan's little boat, then maybe—

I pulled free of my body, my awareness sinking into the ship itself. But, this time, I could sense no way out. I ran through a dozen options, from using the anchor to turning the sails, each idea seeming less promising than the last.

Is this where our story ends?

Hook roared wildly as he threw his weight into the wheel once again. "Tom," he yelled through gritted teeth, "loosen that sail! And Xander, toss the anchor over our port bow. We're gonna spin this thing."

A way out I hadn't considered? I didn't see it, but I leapt at the opportunity nonetheless, doing both in unison before the crewmates had even begun to move.

The ship lurched sideways, groaning once again, and I sent my energy to the wheel, lending Hook as much strength as I could muster and praying that the rudder didn't give out.

Just a little longer...

"Get ready, lads!" The wind seemed to pick up even further as we whipped around, somehow spinning to face directly away from the whirlpool. Hook yanked the wheel the other direction, keeping us steady for the time being as the wind gusted, pressing into the wrong side of our sail.

It was an impressive maneuver, sure, but what good did it do us?

The question didn't linger long, as a new source of wind slammed into the sail on the other side, seemingly out of nowhere. My heart skipped a beat, and I cursed as the lapse in concentration sent my awareness flying back into my body.

I blinked through a mist of salt water, barely able to make out Hook, standing at the wheel with one arm raised in the air. Magical power surged from his fingertips, clearly visible through my jeweler's loupe, and gathered right behind our sail, blasting us forward as quickly as the whirlpool could pull us back. No, *faster* than it could pull us back.

We slid gently over the next wave, moving in what felt like slow motion, but picked up speed before we reached the one after that. I gripped the railing tight, staring over the side and staring at the whirlpool behind us, blinking in case my eyes were deceiving me, then breathed out, what felt like for the first time since I'd seen the dark swirling water.

"Fucking hell, Cap," Tom said, whooping. "I always knew you were crazy, but this takes it to a whole new level."

Hook grunted in answer, sending up a final blast of magic before slumping over the wheel. He forced himself up a half second later, waving for Tom. "The danger has passed. Come take the helm, and make sure we take a wide berth around the whirlpool."

The captain's eyes fixed on me, and he strode in my direction as Tom relieved him. "That magic of yours is something. I felt it working in tandem with what I was doing."

"A compliment?" I asked, in a tone of mock surprise. "That's new."

He shrugged, lips twitching in something that could've been the start of a smile. "Don't get used to it."

If my magic was 'something', then what did that make his? He'd pushed a whole damn ship out of a magic whirlpool that'd been ripped into the sea by someone on a higher plane of reality.

Moll's voice broke me out of the thought. "You good? I was looking all over for you, but the ship started spinning out and I had to stop and hold onto something."

I turned, letting out a breath. "Barely. We almost didn't make it out of a whirlpool."

I expected her to be shocked, or even fearful, but

her attention was elsewhere, those big, blue eyes fixed on something off to the side. She lifted her finger slowly, pointing toward whatever it was, her jaw hanging open.

I turned, joining her in stunned silence as I stared up at the stars. An orange flame wove through the sky in a serpentine pattern. It took a moment to see that its path wasn't random. Jerky, halting letters had begun to form in the sky.

S
U
R
R
E
N
D
E
R
H
A
R
M
O
N
Y

Surrender Harmony.

Then, a cackle echoed from what seemed like the heavens, so wicked, so unhinged, and loud enough that it filled my ears and my skin broke out in goosebumps.

I could feel the stares of my crew mates and knew I had to say something...explain...but my vocal cords were locked tight. Instead, we all just watched in silence as the embers flickered and died, leaving behind barely visible remnants of the words.

"Terrifying," Molly hissed.

"I've seen plenty o' magic in my day. I ain't never seen nothing like that, though. Tink's grown stronger," Tom added in a hoarse whisper.

"No way. Even Tink can't fly that high. And that was no whirlpool like I've ever witnessed," Xander muttered, swiping a shaky hand over his sweat-slick brow. "If Harmony and Hook hadn't managed to navigate around it, I fear we'd have fallen straight to the bowels of hell."

If only that was the worst thing.

At least hell was a place. If we could get there, there might be a way to get back. Everything in me knew that if we fell through one of the wormholes, or in this case, the whirlpool, we'd cease to exist on any plane. But how to explain that to these people I'd come to think of as something like friends?

I couldn't, because talking about the worms and Almira and where I was really from would only open up a whole other can of the critters, and I hadn't even explained the whole truth to Hook yet.

I could feel all eyes on me, though, so I couldn't just stay silent. "It wasn't Tink and Pan," I admitted, wrapping my arms around my waist as a chill rolled through me. "It was someone else. A very bad w—" I paused, hesitant to say the word out loud, "Woman who wants me dead."

"No comma." We all turned to Trick-Eyed Tom, who shrugged. "Surrender Harmony. No comma. So is she asking for your surrender and bad at punctuation, or is she demanding that we hand you over to her?"

It was a fair question that I didn't know the answer to, but it broke some of the tension as Molly blurted out a laugh.

"Imagine? Makes her seem much less scary if you think about her back in her lair that wreaks of sulfur and evil and she's wringing her hands in fury. 'All that and I forgot the comma? Stupid!'"

That got a wide grin out of Xander, and he stared at the woman like she'd just invented cheese or something equally miraculous. "You're so funny. How did you get to be so funny?"

Molly blushed as she dropped into a curtsy, but before she could reply, Tom was talking again.

"Doesn't matter neither way. Harmony and Molly are part of the crew, and we'd never surrender either of them, right Cap?"

Hook's gaze was still locked on the sky as he started to walk back toward the helm. "Get the bird in the sky to scout for more...*whirlpools* in our path," Hook called, voice devoid of emotion as he eyed me, hard.

Just when I thought the frost between us had begun to melt a little...

It was hard to blame him, though. From his perspective, my presence had put his entire crew at risk. "Look, I didn't know that she could—"

He cut me off with a wave of the hand, his lips curling downward in a mixture of disappointment and borderline disgust.

"Enough." He turned back toward Xander. "We'll have to take it slower than I'd hoped, so no time for a detour. Garth will stay on board and then we'll leave him behind when we reach base camp at the entrance to The Fen. Next person who defies me or questions a single command walks the plank straight into the drink, and that includes the old man and both women. Test me if you dare."

He was gone an instant later, leaving all of us staring after him in dead silence.

Alright, so maybe I was wrong. Maybe 'Hook' was more fitting than 'James' after all. But I couldn't stop thinking about the man in my dreams. The one with the wicked smile, who was tough as nails...until he touched me. The one I'd thought was finally going to show himself after our magics had worked together so well, just like Gayelette had told us to.

I shoved the thought away with a grimace.

If James was in there somewhere, he was buried deep and did *not* want to be found.

I'd be gone from this place within days—assuming we lived, of course. The best thing to do in the meantime would be to keep my head down, get the job done, and leave well enough alone. Because trust was a fickle thing, especially when it came to men. Duncan had earned it back in Little Alabaster when he'd helped us hide in plain sight, and again when he'd risked his life to help us flee.

I needed to stop being a drama queen. Hook might not be Prince Charming like Duncan, but he would never surrender me to Almira.

But as much as I wanted to believe that with all my heart, there was a little voice inside my head that wouldn't stop whispering…

Are you sure?

CHAPTER 26

"I can't stop thinking about it."

I rolled to my side to face Moll, who was lying in her bunk, staring at patterns from the lantern light dancing on the ceiling. After a long day on the ship with everyone snappy and clearly on edge, we'd both been more than happy when night had fallen and we got to climb into bed. But after laying here in silence for over an hour, it was clear sleep would be a long time coming for both of us.

I could almost hear her thoughts churning.

"Which thing?" I asked softly.

"Oh, the fire in the sky wasn't great. But I was talking about the wormhole masquerading as a whirlpool...the massive, gaping blackness. It chills me to the bone, that." She turned her head and met my gaze, eyes full of worry. "What's to say she didn't send them to do the same to Neverland yesterday or the day before, thinking you were still there? What if the kids aren't okay?"

"Gods." I pinched my eyes shut, stomach sinking. With everything else going on, it was something I hadn't even considered. But that was Moll for you, always thinking of the children. Even back in The Hollow when we had nothing to give, she found a way to do what she could. Started her own little school where Cissy Petway and the rest of the street urchins could learn to read, do basic math...and apply eye shadow, in the unlikely event the need might arise.

"Can the worms do that to people, do you think? Eat through them, if they find a way to munch on the exact right spot in the book?"

I wanted to reassure her that was impossible, but what did I know about Almira and her magical book worms?

"Maybe, but it mustn't be that simple or she'd have already had them eat me," I reasoned. "I'm guessing it's not an exact science."

"Based on the places we've seen them, though, we can assume that she has some idea of where you are, and even where you're going at points. She could have locked on the position when we were in Neverland..."

She was right. And there wasn't a single fucking thing I could do about it. I gnawed at my lower lip and tried not to drown in my own guilt.

"Shit. I'm sorry," Moll said, swinging her legs over the side of the mattress with an apologetic little smile.

"It isn't your fault, Harm. I'm feeling anxious, is all. I'm sure the kids are fine."

"The best way to protect them and everyone else in this book is to get the rest of the items and knowledge I need to defeat Almira and get us out of here as soon as possible. Which is exactly what we're on the path to doing by getting the clock."

She nodded and let out a sigh. "You're right. No point in dwelling. Let's talk about some good things instead, shall we?"

"Love to. What have you got?" I tucked my hand under my pillow.

"Well, first off, you're a princess!" She let out a laugh and shook her head. "Imagine that, of the two of us after all my years scheming to marry a lord? And, more importantly, you know where you come from now. That's huge!"

From learning about the witch Almira to the fact that Gayelette had known my parents, I'd filled Moll in on everything I'd learned at the old fortune teller's home with Hook the other night, after lights out. It had seemed easier to do it in the dark and I'd just kinda blurted the words before I could take them back. Moll being Moll, she'd lit a candle and stared at me with wide eyes as I'd stuttered and spluttered and explained my way through the crazy story that seemed more than fantastical. It sounded impossible.

And Moll, being Moll, she'd believed me without question and then hugged me tight as the unexpected tears had hit me. I'd been so worried she'd...I don't know, decide not to be my friend maybe? But my worries had been for nothing.

Hook though, I wasn't sure what he thought about the whole story.

James, my brain corrected helpfully.

Well, I'd told her almost everything...the dreams, those I'd kept to myself.

"I wonder if, when we finally get to C'an Saas, it's all going to come rushing back to you. Memories of your childhood, and your family..."

I could only hope.

But something about Gayelette's demeanor when she spoke of it made me think things weren't exactly peachy there under Almira's rule. Why would all these people—from Molly and me, to The Speaker and his tribe, to Duncan, to Hook and his crew—have been called on to risk so much if things weren't an absolute shit sandwich in C'an Saas? I couldn't wait to get there, but part of me was also terrified by what I'd find.

Was I going from bad to worse?

But bigger than that...

What if I failed my people?

"And how about cutey-cute-cute First Mate Xander?" Moll added, her cheeks going pink. "He's a lovely distraction."

"I'm so glad you think so. He's helping me with my magic, too. We can add that to the list of good stuff."

"We also got to see the O'Donnellys again. I know

they're sort of not good guys, but it's nice to see familiar faces, and that Paddy is a hoot."

"He is. I do still wonder if there's a Billy somewhere here. Maybe I'll try to find a way to ask when we're making our way through The Fen."

Moll laid back down and tugged the blanket tight around her. "I'm just going to force myself to keep thinking about all the positives. Plenty of food, we're together...things could be way worse."

I was about to agree when a strange, low sound echoed through the room. Like the tapping of metal on glass...

I flicked a glance to the porthole and shot to my feet so fast, blood rushed to my head, leaving me disoriented.

"Someone," or some*thing*— "is out there," I whispered, pointing toward the pane of glass as the chowder in my stomach from dinner seemed to curdle.

Moll sat up, the color draining from her face.

Tap tap tap.

I reached for the whip on the table beside me.

I'd just closed my fingers around the handle of the whip when the porthole popped open.

"I knew it!" a familiar voice called through the now open space. "Tink kept saying I was being naive again, but I knew you guys didn't really want to leave and that he kidnapped you!" Pan's smiling face came into view, and I nearly collapsed with relief that faded as fast as it had come.

He obviously wasn't here to murder us, which was a plus if I was trying to embrace Moll's recent optimism. But that was where the positives ended.

"Peter!" Moll hissed, rushing to greet him. "How are the kids?"

"They miss you two, I'll tell you that much! They were so sad when you were gone." A crease formed between his eyes as he flicked a gaze between me and Moll. "Are you okay? He didn't hurt you, did he?"

"No, we're fine. How is Caleb? Any better?"

He shook his head, lips twisting. "Not good. But once you're back, he'll be a lot better. He's been crying for days, which I'm sure isn't helping his condition." He bobbed up and down as if the howling wind made it hard to tread air as he hovered. "Did Hook make you write that silly note? I can't believe he thought I'd fall for that. Did he ever say how he found Neverland after all this time? Tink shielded it so well."

"Peter…" Moll began. I stepped closer and gave her forearm a covert pinch, and she went silent.

We needed to tread carefully here.

"Tink didn't come with you?" I asked carefully.

"Nah. She's mad," he said, rolling his eyes. "She has a short fuse, but she'll get over it once we get back. Besides, I don't need her. I'm not here for a fight. This is purely a rescue mission, so we should hurry before someone spots me. If you can sneak out onto one of the decks, I'll scoop you up and we'll be on our way."

I stared into that open, innocent face, and it was

incredibly hard to imagine that this was the person both Xander and Hook claimed was basically a monster. Almost as hard as it was to believe that Hook was the black-hearted villain they—and he—made him out to be.

Either way, though, time was up.

"Sure. Let us just grab a few things…" I tugged at Moll's fingers. "Wait right there."

Pan hovered in the porthole while we made a show of packing what little we had as I reached out for the space in my mind reserved for my falcon.

Fetch, if you can hear me, I need you. Pan is here. Distract him, but don't hurt him if you can help it.

He must've been hunting close by because I'd barely thought the words when I heard a screech in the sky.

"There's that bird," Pan said. "I was just about to ask him. Hook probably wanted to use him to—"

Fetch dive-bombed Pan, flapping his wings violently as I shoved Moll toward the door.

"Go! Run and get help!"

She shot a worried glance to the porthole where Pan and Fetch were tussling, and laid one hand on the knob. "Are you sure we shouldn't go with him? The kids—"

"Once we have the clock, we'll go back for them. Go now!"

She flew out the door, shouting Xander's name, calling for help.

I rushed back toward the open porthole, Moll's incapacitator in hand.

Go, I tried to tell Fetch. *I can take care of the rest.*

But a shaft of pain shot through my shoulder so great, it brought me to my knees.

I gasped, trying to catch my breath as I looked up to see Pan holding Fetch by one mangled wing. His impish face was a mask of pure rage, and I swallowed back a rush of bile.

Go for his eyes, I commanded, any thoughts of mercy drying up under the heat of my fury.

"Let go of my fucking bird!"

Pan turned his attention back to me. "Or what, you lying cunt?" he sneered, any trace of the person I thought I knew stripped away.

Fetch used the opening I gave him to reel up and strike at Pan's face with his razor-sharp beak. Pan let out a howl and released his hold on Fetch, slapping a hand over his cheek.

"You better go while you still can," I said, the grinding pain in my shoulder making it hard to speak. "I hear Hook and the crew coming down the hallway now, and we both know you're nothing without Tink's power."

I was bluffing. Not only was the corridor silent, I also had no real knowledge of Pan's fighting abilities. Apparently, my words hit their mark though, because he let out a low growl and then flitted backward a few yards.

"We don't need you, or that stupid bird," he hissed, blood running through the splayed fingers covering his eye. "We're going to get the clock with or without you. Count on it. And once we do, I'm going to find you again and make you wish you didn't betray me."

Footfalls sounded in the distance, and Pan must've heard them as well, because he was gone an instant later.

I let out a low sob as I tried to reconnect with Fetch, but all I felt when I tried was his agony.

"Help, please!" I hollered as I shot to my feet. My steps were unsteady as I rushed to the door.

"Are you alright, lass?" Xander called in response. But it was Hook who made it to the door to meet me.

His gaze was liquid ink as he looked me up and down and let out a low growl. "Did he hurt you?"

I shook my head wildly. "But he hurt Fetch. Someone has to get him. Peter broke his wing and tossed him into the water. Please!"

"On it." It was Trick-Eyed Tom who spoke, but I only caught sight of the back of him as he sprinted down the hallway in the other direction.

Hook shouldered past me and stalked to the porthole, smashing his hand against the wall with a snarl. "He and that succubus bitch thought they would take you from me, did they?"

I blinked at him and shook my head, the throb in my shoulder making it hard to think straight.

"You mean Tink? No...she wasn't with him. She

seemed to know we were lying to them. Called Peter naive for thinking we were ever his friends. I think he was hoping to have me and Fetch in their corner in case they needed help with Noru."

"What do you mean, succubus bitch?" Moll asked, wheeling around to face Xander when Hook didn't answer immediately. "What does he mean?"

Hook swiped a finger over the blood speckling the porthole and then turned and pinned me in place with a grim stare. "Xander, take Molly to the galley and pour her a stiff mug of whiskey. Harmony and I need to speak in private."

I knew Molly wanted to argue but a subtle head shake from Xander had her closing her mouth in silence.

Hook stalked to the open door, past them both.

"You and me. The library. Now," he growled, not bothering to see if I followed.

"I'm not going anywhere unless it's to see if Fetch is okay," I shouted at his retreating back.

"So long as he's not dead, he'll be right as rain. No better Mend than Tom."

I'd been on the other side of that magic after The Devil's Gauntlet, so I knew it was true, but it wasn't until the pain in my shoulder faded and then abruptly disappeared altogether that I let out a long breath.

Tom's magic had already begun to work.

"Fair warning, woman," Hook called over his shoulder. "If I don't hear you fall into step behind me within the next five seconds, you'll regret it."

Well, shit.

"Want me to come with?" Molly whispered, catching hold of my sleeve as I forced my feet into motion, whole body sizzling with some strange mix of nerves and anticipation.

"Nah. He doesn't scare me."

Or, at least not for the reasons he hoped. Somewhere along the way, I'd come to accept that he wasn't evil—that maybe the story about him murdering a child wasn't the truth...or at least wasn't the whole story. Seeing Peter tonight, hearing how he spoke, made me doubt his stories about Hook. And Hook's men had too much respect for him. Not to mention Garth's clear affection for the man. I felt it in my gut... he wouldn't hurt me. And while I had no doubt he'd hurt plenty of others, he'd had his reasons. I'd finally picked my horse when Pan had come calling. But it was time to pay the piper. I was going to have to come out with at least some of the truth if I wanted Hook to trust me. And the truth sounded like the rantings of a certified lunatic.

I'm real...but I'm not entirely sure you are. See...you're all actually characters.

In a book.

Okay, so maybe I wouldn't lead with that part.

By the time Hook closed the door of the library behind us a minute later and made his way to his desk, I had already planned how to handle things. I'd feed him tidbits, and hope it was enough to satisfy him.

If he's anything like our dreams, he's never satisfied, the helpful little voice in my head chimed in.

Shut up, I shot back.

"Let's start with what happened earlier, shall we? The fire in the sky."

"Right. That was the witch Gayelette was talking about. Almira," I began, ignoring his gesture to sit and pacing in a restless circle instead. "Thinking on it, I wonder if she found me because I've been using a lot of magic while practicing with my whip."

All true.

"The witch from some far away land called C'an Saas." He jerked a thumb toward the thousands of books behind him. "I've sailed all three seas. I have over a hundred maps of the world. And when she said it the other night, I spent hours poring over every one of them. There is *no* such place. So what the fuck aren't you telling me, Harmony?"

The damnable grandfather clock ticked in the corner of the room like a heartbeat, punctuating the silence, ratcheting up my nerves.

Tidbits weren't going to work. He was not one to be left in the dark, and wasn't going to stop until I bared my soul.

Also like in our dreams.

Shut UP!

I hesitated one more moment and then shrugged. "Fine. I'll show you mine if you show me yours."

I wasn't going to be the only one with my bare ass hanging out here.

Quid pro quo, motherfucker.

He stared at me for a few tense seconds, threw his head back and let out a bark of laughter. "You've got balls, I'll give you that. My mortal enemy comes to *my* ship to rescue you, and I'm just supposed to trust that you're not going to betray me? Do I look like a complete idiot to you?"

"No. But trust is a two-way path," I shot back, my spine stiffening. "You want me to hate Pan and Tink as much as you do, but you won't tell me why. And still, I didn't let him take us. Not to mention that I nearly broke my fool neck pinning my belt to your stupid flag to show my loyalty, and still got nothing in return. Sure, I was able to get some information because I followed you to Gayelette's, but you've been about as forthcoming as a stone." I crossed my arms over my chest and lifted my chin. "If you want me to show my cards, it's got to be a fair exchange. If you tell me about Pan and Tink, I'll tell you what I know about your world...and mine."

If stares were knives, I'd be full of holes, but I held strong, not blinking until he pounded the desktop with his fist.

"Damn you, woman."

He stalked over to one of the bookshelves behind

him lined with what looked like hundreds of thin, leather-bound journals. The ease with which he laid his hands on this one in particular let me know it wasn't the first or even the tenth time he'd done so. This was clearly something he'd read often.

He lowered himself to the massive chair behind the desk and glared at me. "Sit the fuck down. You're making me twitchy."

"Ha! You have a lot of nerve. Your attitude makes everyone twitchy, all the time. Have you considered switching the rum to some warm milk or maybe thought about taking a nap every once in a while?"

We both stared at each other, and I only faltered when his eyes drifted to my heaving chest.

Son of a bitch—

"Fine. Boss man says sit, I'll sit." I flopped into the chair, crossed my arms over my chest, and waited.

He let his fingers linger on the cover of the book and let out a long breath. "What did Pan and Tink tell you about me?"

"That you were friends. That you stole his mother's magic clock and tried to kidnap some of The Lost Boys."

That you killed a boy. But I couldn't get that final accusation past my too-tight throat.

He let out a bitter laugh and studied me through heavy lids.

"Is that their story then? My dastardly nature caused me to betray them and steal his beloved mother's clock?" He nodded slowly, glancing at the giant crocodile tooth on his desk. "I guess that makes sense. How could they tell you the truth?" His eyes locked onto mine, searching. "The question is, do you believe them?"

It took me a minute to find my voice.

"I don't know what to believe," I admitted.

But as soon as I said it, I knew it for the lie it was. I'd always felt something around Tink that bothered me. I couldn't quite put my finger on it, but it was as if the exterior didn't match what was brewing inside. A smile slightly too brittle. A word to one of the boys a little less than sincere. That sad little exchange with Cissy about her dad and how Tink didn't allow her to talk about him.

And Pan had seemed a little off, too. Even before tonight, there were times when he was almost ludicrously boyish, like a twelve-year-old trapped in a man's body. Then, there were other times when he seemed...disconnected somehow. Once I'd seen how he'd looked at Fetch, though, my doubts had disappeared.

There was a vein of evil in him, running deep beneath the surface.

"There's so much about my life lately that has me in a tailspin. A prophecy that's clearly incomplete, a ruthless enemy that I've never even met who wants me dead...and the one person trying to help me fill in the gaps can only talk in riddles. Every step I take comes with a price that others wind up paying. And every step I take feels like a wild fucking guess. I'm tired of guessing. I need to know the truth about Pan and Tink because I need to feel sure about *something.* Please, James."

He drew back for an instant, and then let out a sigh, nodding.

"I'll start at the beginning then, because it matters. Once upon a time, there was a boy named Peter Pan…"

CHAPTER 27

*T*he Gentle Hand Asylum for Wayward Youth,
fifty years earlier...

PETER STEPPED into the mess hall and made a beeline
for the giant pot of gruel, letting out a sigh of relief.

The workday was done. His hands stung from the
lye, and his back ached, but there was a chance he
might get to see Tink later tonight, and that made
everything—*anything*—bearable.

He spooned a helping of gruel into his bowl, then
headed over to the table where his friends were already
eating. "Any good?"

Jack nodded eagerly, "A bit of salt in it today."

"Headmaster was happy because we did such a
good job cleaning this morning," Peter said as he shov-
eled a bite of the gluey slop into his mouth. Sprinkling

a bit of salt on shite didn't make it any better in his book, but he wasn't about to take the wind out of Jack's sails.

"Except Eddie," Jack added, his lips pursing in short-lived sadness. "But there's nothing to be done about that."

"What's his sentence again?"

"Three days."

Peter glanced over his shoulder, fury bubbling in his empty gut as his gaze found the headmaster. The old man leaned down over one of the younger girls, a skeletal hand shooting forward to snatch the paper she'd been drawing on. He held it up, face twisting in anger as he chewed her out for "wasting school resources on her nonsense."

The blood pounding in Peter's ears reminded him to turn away before he said something the shriveled old bastard would surely make him regret.

It's not worth it. Just a couple more years, and you'll be long gone.

Byron Archibald's job as headmaster was to serve as both parent and teacher, but he somehow managed to fail at both. More *tormentor* than mentor, the beady-eyed twat seemed dead set on making life a living hell for every orphan here, and poor, simple Eddie had gotten the brunt of it lately.

Jack laid a hand on Peter's shoulder, bringing him back to reality. "You good?"

"Yep," Peter replied, slurping a final bite of porridge

before pushing his chair back to stand. "I'll catch you guys in a bit."

The other boy's voice dropped to a nervous whisper. "What about your bowl?"

Peter waved the concern aside, looking back to make sure the headmaster was still occupied before dashing the rest of the way out of the room, bowl still in hand. He leapt nimbly over the creaky bottom step, then crept the rest of the way up the stairs.

He turned down the hall, listening for footsteps as he tiptoed up to the bulky, wooden door to the right. A low grumble rose from his stomach, but he pushed the feeling aside as he rapped lightly on the door.

Movement rustled from inside, and a low voice called out, "I'm almost done, sir! Just a few more lines and—"

"It's only me." Peter slid the food port open and pushed the bowl into the slot. "So jumpy."

The younger boy looked up from the page he'd been scribbling, which was, no doubt, filled with hundreds of blithering apologies—one of The Warden's favorite punishments to dish out. His eyes lit up as they locked onto the food. "Gods, thank you," he said, dropping his pencil and scrambling over eagerly.

"You need to eat fast," Peter said, seeing how unnecessary the words had been as the other boy ignored the spoon, bringing the bowl right to his lips and tilting it back to dump in what was left of the porridge. "The Warden's been keeping you hungry, eh?" he muttered, using their nickname for the malicious Headmaster.

The boy pushed the empty bowl back through the port, wiping a glob of gruel from his upper lip with a groan. "Haven't had a bite since he put me in here. Has he said how long I'll be here, by the way?"

Peter chewed at his inner lip, pausing for a moment before answering. "Two more days."

Eddie's hands shot upward, latching onto his mop of blond hair. "*Fuck.*"

Fuck, indeed. The kid's belt was already on the first hole, barely holding up his loose trousers as it was. If he was here much longer, he'd be nothing but a bag of bones.

Peter squashed down the rising rage and managed a grin for his friend. "I'll do my best to sneak food whenever I can. Gotta go, or I'm going to wind up sitting right beside you."

Peter let the port swing shut behind him, beginning his march back down the hall. *Probably best to hide the bowl and bring it back la—*

A loud creak cut the thought short, and terror sent a spike through his chest as he broke into a sprint. But where was there to even go? The Warden would check the common room first, so...

Peter shoved the door to the storage room open, closing it behind him as he crept toward the window. He avoided looking down, sucking in a breath.

No time to waste.

His hand shot upward, latching onto a protruding brick. Fear turned into relief as he yanked on it with everything he had, latching onto the next brick.

His fingertips brushed the top of his next handhold, and he yanked himself up again, his heart thumping heavily in his ears. One screw up, and he'd be dead, but he'd never felt more alive.

Now this *is freedom.*

He latched onto the roof, springing upward a final time with a spinning leap as pure joy tingled at his scalp. It wasn't quite flight.

Not yet, he reminded himself as he landed on the roof with a gentle thud. One day, it would be, and he'd taste true freedom.

A cold gust of wind sent a chill up his spine, and he whirled, grinning. "Tink?"

Light blotted out the stars for the briefest of moments, and he raised his hand in greeting as the love of his life appeared in front of him. She blushed, and her butterfly wings came to a stop as she reached out to cup his face.

"I've missed you. How have you been?"

"Great." And somehow, it didn't feel like a lie. All the struggle and pain he'd been through in the weeks since their last meeting seemed to fade as it always did, carried away by the wind. "And you?"

She shrugged, ignoring the question as she pulled him toward the chimney at the edge of the roof. "The stars are beautiful tonight."

Peter nodded in agreement, but his gaze never left Tink. "Not as beautiful as you."

The light in those brilliant, violet eyes faded and her smile trembled for the briefest of moments before she broke into a giggle.

"You must not be seeing the right stars."

"Show me, then."

And she did. For the next hour they lay side by side, hands clasped, staring upward as they named constellations and told stories of distant places far more interesting than this. And, for that time, thoughts of the orphanage, The Warden, and everything else were the furthest thing from Peter's mind.

One day, *this* would be his life.

"Ooh, that one almost looks like a—," he started, cutting off as he heard a soft snore at his shoulder.

He grinned, pressing his nose into her hair and breathing in the smell of honeysuckle as his own eyes drifted shut. There would surely be consequences for it tomorrow, but they seemed unimportant compared to this. He'd wake her first thing in the morning, then sneak into his cot before the breakfast bell.

A soft rustling and a whimper at his side had his eyes snapping open again.

"Tink?" he whispered, going silent when he saw that she was still sound asleep.

And yet…

Her body began to shift and writhe, going fuzzy at the edges. Little craters began forming on her porcelain skin, and her features began pulling closer together, bit by bit.

Peter scrambled back, voice catching in his throat. "T—Tink?! Are you okay?"

She reeled, her now-sunken eyes shooting open in a flash of purple, and she pulled back in panic as her face began to blur once again. "Please tell me you didn't see. You—"

He tugged her back, his hand going to her cheek. Most would have considered her true form hideous; he could tell that much. But somehow, he couldn't bring himself to feel the same. Even if she wasn't the fairy he'd thought she was, she was still his Tink.

"Shhh. It's okay, Tink. You don't have to do that," he said as her face smoothed out, beginning to return to its normal form. Then he leaned forward, going for a kiss.

And, for a half-second, she moved as if to return it, then pulled back, shoving him away. "No! How is it okay? Don't you get it. That...that is what I look like. I'm *hideous*, Peter. Aren't you angry that I deceived you?"

He laughed softly, a deep peace washing over him. "Look at me."

And she did, looking terrified and amazed in equal measure.

"I love you for you, Tink," he said, his hand settling on her chest. "For what's in here. And no matter what, you'll always be beautiful to me."

She stared back at him for a long moment, tears welling up in the corners of her eyes as her chest began to glow with warm, orange light. "You really mean it, don't you?"

"Of course I mean it," he said, leaning toward her for another kiss. "You're still my Tink, and I'm still your Peter."

Her trembling hand went to her chest, her gnarled fingers pressing right into it, as if it was made of water rather than flesh and bone. And when they emerged, she was holding a glowing ember of pure energy.

"Will you take it?"

He couldn't speak, or even breathe, so he settled for a nod, and she pressed it into him, as if fusing a tiny piece of her soul into his.

"I am yours," he managed after a long moment. She was changing back even as he said it, and, this time, he didn't stop her. She'd already seen that he didn't mind, but it'd take time for her embarrassment to fade, and that was okay.

"And I am yours." She paused for a long moment as her face returned to the heart-shaped perfection he knew and then gestured outward into the surrounding city. "So let's leave this place, then. You should come with me, Peter. We can run off to somewhere far away together."

He turned away, guilt twisting his stomach in knots. "I'm not ready yet, Tink. We can't just have you using your magic to take care of us. People will start to notice, and that could put you in danger. You know how cruel people are. They don't understand your kind, and we can't have you ending up like the rest of them. I need to be able to take care of you, and I'm not sure I'm strong enough to do that yet. In just a few months, I'll be old enough to work side by side with one of the craftsmen as an apprentice. I'll learn a trade. Until then, I'd only be a burden to you."

If she knew half of what went on at the orphanage, she'd have insisted they leave a long time ago. But he was so close to the end now. As much as he'd love to walk away and never look back, he needed to see it through.

"You wouldn't be a burden, Peter. You'd—"

He held up a hand. "I can't, not until I'm sure I can build a good life for us. The other boys need me, anyway. They'd be lost without me…"

"Well, we can't have you leaving behind a house full of lost boys, can we?" She flashed a sad smile before pressing her face into his chest. When she pulled back, her expression had hardened some. "There's one more thing, Peter, something important…"

"You can tell me anything."

A loud crash broke them out of the moment, and Peter sprang to his feet, his magic welling up to the surface as the Headmaster's spindly form came into view.

"Damn kid. I knew you were hiding somewhere.

How *dare* you?" the man roared, tearing the belt from his pants in a smooth motion.

Peter turned toward Tink in a panic, opening his mouth to call for her but closing it when he saw she had disappeared. Thank god. He could bear whatever came next so long as she wasn't there to see it.

He whirled back toward The Warden, raising his arms to cover his face. "I'm sorry, sir. It won't happen again, I just—"

The belt snapped forward in a blur, connecting with his jaw like a lick of fire.

"Do you know how much time I wasted looking for you? Fucking *useless* gobshite!"

Peter's face screamed with pain, but he repressed the urge to fight as the belt came down once again, cutting into his neck. *He'll pay for this,* he reminded himself for the hundredth time. *One day, The Warden would get a taste of what he dished out.*

Peter used that thought as fuel as he fought back the rage, terror, and shame that welled up inside him.

He bit back a howl of pain, determined not to give the bastard the satisfaction even as the belt rained down again and again. Agony radiated from every inch of his body, but still he stayed quiet, even though he knew it'd only be worse for him in the end.

"You ungrateful, motherless bastard," the Headmaster bellowed, tossing Peter headfirst into the chimney. "Clearly I've gone too easy on you until now, but that all changes here and—"

A blinding flash of light from behind lit up the chimney, followed by a deafening crash, and Peter whirled on him, cringing back with his hands raised in front of his face. But his jaw dropped at what he saw.

A shimmering tower of blue flame had consumed the Headmaster where he stood. His face contorted as if he was about to scream, but the skin bubbled and melted from his face before he could let it out. It scorched him through to his very core within seconds, transforming him into a horrific, motionless statue.

Peter stared in stunned silence as his tormentor's body fell to the ground.

"You *bastard*," Tink roared as she charged toward them, letting out a feral scream, her magic surging even higher. Shimmering blue flames shot from her fingertips in waves as she roasted The Warden's already very-dead body into ashes. Tendrils of flame licked at the building's wooden roof, igniting it as well.

Peter's vision went black at the edges as he lurched toward her, trying to stave off the shock threatening to swallow him whole.

"Tink, stop!" he pleaded, his lungs burning from the greasy, acrid smoke that had already begun to fill the air.

She turned, wild, violet eyes softening as she met his gaze.

"You have to stop now," he whispered, reaching out and squeezing her shoulder with an icy hand.

Horror washed over her face as looked around, as if

noticing the fire around them for the first time. "Hell, Peter, we need to get out of here! The whole place is ablaze!"

"The others!" Panic clawed at his throat as he caught sight of the ocean of fire that now lay between them and the door.

"Peter. It's too late for that." Tink's fingers closed over his wrist, and he let out a shaky breath.

"We can't just leave them," he said, less sure, now.

Her fingers snaked up his arm, going all the way to his chin. She grabbed it, standing on her toes to kiss him. "Let's go, Peter. We can leave all this behind, forget this place even existed."

He opened his mouth to protest a final time, then slammed it shut. *No. You have your Tink, and that's all that matters.* "Let's go."

"I shared my magic with you when our souls touched," she said, her index finger pressing into his chest. "Just put your trust in it, and jump."

He stepped up to the building's edge without the faintest bit of fear, feeling the newfound energy bubbling up to the surface.

They stepped off the edge and a wave of pure, unbridled joy washed over him as they flew toward the stars in the distance without so much as glancing at the devastation he'd left behind.

CHAPTER 28

*H*ook closed the front cover of the journal and looked up for the first time since starting his tale.

"You wanted to know the truth about them. That's where it all started."

"Awful," I croaked, swiping my hand over my runny nose. "So much pain. What they did was terrible, but they were children, and—"

"*He* was a child," Hook corrected with a grimace. "She was and still is immortal, and was no child when they met, except for by hobgoblin standards. She's at least fifty years older than Pan. She knew exactly what she was doing when she met him. Using his love for her to get what she wanted. Giving him the care and attention he was starving for. But she was starving, too."

"How do you mean?" And why did he keep calling

her all these names…hobgoblin… succubus? She was the epitome of a fairy in every child's book I'd ever seen.

But before I could ask, Hook had begun to speak again.

"Tink's kind require a constant stream of external energy to preserve their magic, which is why they were killed off en masse decades before. All except her. The glamour spell she uses to make herself look like that alone would drain her within weeks if she didn't replenish that well. Where better to get it than from a group of energetic, Tideblessed little boys who no one would ever miss..."

It was like every molecule of air was sucked from the room and for a second, my vision went hazy. Thoughts of Caleb, Tristan, and Cissy ran through my mind.

"What are you saying? The Lost Boys...they take them so she can drain them of their magic?"

"Not just their magic. She drains them of life."

I closed my eyes and gritted my teeth. "Caleb...that's why he's so sick."

"It took me nearly a year to figure it out, and another still to plan how to get us out of there. How fucked is that?" His lips twisted into a sad smile. "Because it wasn't me she was draining just yet, I waited a whole year to make my move."

When his meaning finally hit me, everything before it paled in comparison. "You were one of them. You weren't a friend of his, you were one of The Lost Boys," I managed through numb lips.

"I was. James Tyler."

J.T.

"You carved your initials into the windowsill!"

"I did. I was brought to Neverland when I was around twelve years old. They fed me. They took care of me. I had friends there, and wanted so badly for it to be as perfect as it seemed. But nothing ever is, is it? Once Miguel's Tideblessing mark began to fade and he grew ill, I finally knew for sure. It took months to plan our escape and figure out how to make sure they could never hurt anyone like that again. That's where the clock came in."

His eyes were unseeing, as if he was no longer here with me, but was there, in the past again as he continued.

"It was so strange. It made a ticking sound, but the hands never actually moved. I offered to try to fix it for them, and Pan lost it. I knew then, it held magic that they needed. It wasn't until later, after me, Tommy and Miguel tried to escape that I learned the whole truth. When Tink gave him a piece of her heart, he was able to use some of her magic, but she was unable to share her immortality with him. He continued to age, and they knew being together forever would be impossible unless that stopped. So, she spent years gathering as much energy as she could—leaving a trail of bodies in her wake, I'm sure—and she used every bit of it to separate Pan from his shadow."

His shadow? I stared at him in confusion. What would that have accomplished?

Before I could ask, Hook was answering my question. "Our shadows are the vessels for our souls. Once she separated Pan from his, she trapped it inside the clock. As long as that clock doesn't advance, Pan's soul is forever stuck at the age he was when she first severed it. This makes him, like her, effectively immortal in that time cannot kill them, and the only way *I* can kill them is if the clock is running again."

"You stole it to figure out a way to get it working, but before you could, Noru threw a wrench in the works. Makes sense."

"I've been trying to get the clock back and restart it ever since, knowing that, when I do, Pan and Tink will finally come face me. Then I can finally end this for good."

I was quiet for a long moment as all of this new information sank in.

How in the hell had I not noticed that Pan didn't have a shadow? I'd been looking so hard for clues and digging for information, but I'd missed something huge, and it had been right in front of me.

I swallowed hard and asked the question that had been dogging me since I'd heard about Miguel's death. Taking a breath, I dove right into it.

"Pan also said it was you that killed Miguel. Is that true?"

His face went blank, and he looked off into the distance. "No, he was telling the truth about that. Tink hadn't finished draining Miguel, so my magic continued to develop. I hid it as best I could, and spent the better part of that year honing my own skills, and became an adept swordsman. Pan helped train me. Despite my youth, I got the best of him in the fight, and was about to deal him a killing blow when he yanked Miguel in front of him like a human shield. I didn't have the skill to avoid running Miguel through."

"Pan killed him, then. Not you," I spat, grateful for the rush of outrage that took sadnesses' place for the moment.

"That's not the way the universe looks at it."

"How can you possibly know that?"

He set his ebony eyes on me, and the weight there was more than I could bear to look at.

"I just know," he said flatly. "You'll have to trust me on that."

"And you also know about their history at the orphanage…about Tink's giving Pan a piece of her heart…how? Did you steal the journals from Neverland when you stole the clock?"

"Not exactly, but something like that." He paused and then looked away. "I've done all the talking I'm going to do for now. Either you believe what I've told you, or you believe those two. It's your turn. Who are you really, Harmony Fallowell, and where is C'an Saas?"

I chewed the inside of my cheek for a moment. This was the tricky bit. I was still trying to figure out how to explain it all in a way that didn't make him think I was crazy, or upend everything this man knew about his own life and existence. I might despise him at times, but the thought of hurting him unsettled me in a way I didn't want to look too closely at. Especially now that I knew what he'd been through. And something told me we'd only scratched the surface on that.

I thought about starting the night of the palace Jubilee. Telling him about Moll and Heinrich and Relyk and The Speaker. But part of me knew if I didn't say the hard part now, I was never going to have the balls to say it.

So for the second time that night, I just dove off the deep end and spit it out.

"The reason C'an Saas can't be found on your maps is because we're living inside a fairytale book right now," I blurted in a rush. "I was sent into this book by my real parents in order to protect me from the evil witch, Almira, in the hopes that I would someday grow wise and strong enough to leave the book and return home to save my people. The man who adopted me found me in the woods of a place called Alabaster with a fairytale book tucked into my blanket to help guide me, and a falcon at my side, I think to watch over me. Once I grew up and learned the lessons I needed to in that story and retrieved the item that would help me succeed, I was able to turn the page and leave it behind for this one. I believe I have one more destination before I can get back home to C'an Saas. In order to get there, I need the magic clock."

I didn't know what I expected him to do, but, when he threw his head back and started laughing, I knew it definitely wasn't that. And for the first time ever, it wasn't that derisive, humorless laugh. He was full-on belly cackling, to the point that he had to pause to wipe his eyes. Long enough that I feared that I had broken his sanity.

Then, he rose to his feet in one, smooth motion and made his way to the same book shelf he'd taken the journal from. This time, he selected a thick tome tucked at the very end of the row.

"Look familiar?" he rasped, tossing the book onto the desk between us.

It landed with a heavy *thud,* and I stared down at the cover in stunned silence.

Fairy Tales of the Ages.

The same book that I'd had with me when my father had found me, only instead of the page edges being gilded in gold, these were shrouded in black.

"I don't understand," I whispered, reaching out to trace the familiar, spiky script of the title with my finger. "How?"

"That's an amazing question. I'm guessing Gayelette knows, but apparently she didn't think it was important to tell either of us. All I know is this." He dropped heavily into his chair again and closed his eyes. "I was found wandering around on the streets at around the age of five, dragging this book along with me. Whether by a trick of magic or by my own mind trying to protect itself after being left behind, I had zero recollection of my life before then," He tapped his hook against his temple and opened his eyes. "It was a blank slate. And whoever found me left me on the steps of the orphanage and took the book with them to sell, I'm sure. I never forgot it, though, and feared I'd never see it again. Imagine my surprise a couple months ago when I walked into a bookseller's shop and saw it sitting on the counter. More tattered and worn than I remembered, but still intact. I paid handsomely for it, and doubled the amount to have the seller have his bookbinder repair it. Picked it up from him two weeks ago and nearly demanded my money back."

"W-why?" I managed, lifting the cover open and slowly flipping through the pages.

Snow White, just as I remembered. Little Mermaid. The Ugly Duckling. And then, Cinderella. Only that one...looked different.

"Because," James continued softly, "I opened the book to find that I couldn't even read the words. The ink seemed to be alive. Writhing and moving, ever-changing. Except, when I turned the page to an earlier tale, it was fine."

What did it all mean?

Was Hook sent into this book from C'an Saas, same as me? Was that why he'd plagued my dreams since I could remember…Because we'd known one another in a past life?

He continued to speak but his voice became background noise as blood buzzed in my ears and I began to read;

Once upon a time, there was a girl named Harmony Marie Fallowell…

"It's not," I whispered. "My middle name isn't Marie. I don't have a middle n—"

Molly. She called me that whenever she was mad at me, or wanted to make a point. Said all mothers know that if you want to get your children's attention, you need to use all three names, so she'd given me that one.

This wasn't the Cinderella story I vaguely recalled from my childhood before my own book of fairytales had gotten destroyed.

This was *my* story.

With trembling fingers, I leafed to the last page and swallowed a gasp.

And Duncan Westerly, King of Alabaster for a day, became known as Duncan the Just. He restored power to the people and—

The rest was exactly as James said. A mass of swirling letters and ink that made no sense, and shifted with each passing second.

My head thumped like a drum as I tried to digest it

all. I had so many questions, it was hard to even know where to begin.

"Do you know me?" I demanded finally, my voice sounding as raw as my insides felt. "Did you dream of me, long before you ever met me?"

His face went stony and he pursed his lips into a hard line, but it didn't matter. I already knew. Part of me had always known.

I flipped to the next page, hoping to find the answers there but beyond the title and the image of a pirate ship that had followed me from the last world to this, I found more of the same garbled mess. I thumbed through, nearly frantic now, until he laid his hand on mine for an instant.

"Don't bother. My guess is that our fate isn't yet determined and whatever belongs there is still being written."

I looked up and met his gaze and realized with a start that he was smiling again.

"Are you crazy? Don't you wonder where you came from? Why you were put here?" I demanded, incredulous. "Fucking hell, I've never once seen a genuine grin on your face, and this...*This* is what tickles you? Finding out you're trapped inside a fucking book, in a story without an ending?"

"Nope. That's not the part that tickles me, Princess." He leaned in, setting his hook on the desk between us. "What tickles me is that, if I'm stuck in a story, then this hell is temporary. When you finish writing this tale and turn the page to the next, I'll cease to exist." He dropped back against the chair and blew into his fingers. "Gone."

It was a gut punch.

Because that was when I realized that he'd stuck around all these years—steeped in his childhood trauma—for one reason and one reason only. To exact his revenge. Once he'd done that? It wasn't just that he'd be lost…in a dark place without a purpose.

It was that he had no plans to remain above ground.

Fucking hell.

Captain James Tyler Hook had a date with death.

And he couldn't fucking wait.

AN HOUR LATER, I was sitting at the table in my room staring down at the words on the page as they blurred again into a pile of gobbledygook. I flipped to another lens on my jeweler's loupe and tried again.

If possible, it made it even worse.

I let out a groan and tossed the loupe beside the book and pressed a hand to my aching back.

"My eyes are crossing, I'm so tired."

"I hate to say it, but I think you're wasting your time. You'll be able to read it when things become clearer. We obviously haven't learned the lesson or gained the knowledge we need here yet to see it," Moll reasoned with a shrug as she stepped up behind me.

"Who are you now, Gayelette?" I shot back. "If we just stopped trying every time we run into a locked door or a blocked path, we'd never have gotten this far. I gotta do my thing, even if it turns out to be a waste of time."

I wasn't about to tell her that deciphering the book was also a great way to put off telling her what *else* I'd learned in James' library earlier, about Pan and Tink, and about young Caleb's "illness."

"I think our time is better spent getting some rest. We'll be getting to base camp soon enough and then it's going to be go go go. If it were me—and I get it—it isn't," she said, holding up both hands in surrender, "but if it *were*, I'd focus all my energy on the tasks closest at hand." She ticked them off. "Get the clock from Noru without dying, go back to Neverland and make sure the kids are alright, and *then* we check the book again and see if it can give us some clues as to what comes next. You're spinning your wheels for nothing. Especially since…"

We might be dead before then anyway.

She wasn't wrong. I let out a sigh and closed the book, running my hands over the buttery soft, leather cover. But if there was nothing to decode right now, and the other option was to think about James and his death wish? That meant it was time to get Moll up to speed.

"Jame—uh, Hook and I talked about something else as well. It's troubling, Moll." I turned to face her fully and leaned over to pat her mattress. "You should have a seat."

"We just spent the first part of tonight making a mortal enemy of a magical flying man-boy and his freaky fairy girlfriend *and* are on our way to fight a crocodile the size of a barge in fucking Monsterland. How much more troubling can it be?"

I stared at her in silence, and she slowly lowered herself to the bed, the smirk sliding from her face.

"Tell me. Is it the children?"

I steeled myself and forced a nod. "It is. They're alright for now, as far as I know, but Hook shared some things about Pan and Tink."

Sick of being in the dark myself, I didn't pull any punches. I let it rip, explaining about their tragic past, and lives lost at the orphanage. About the clock, and the truth of what happened between them and Hook. And about how the pair lured young boys to Neverland, using their energy so Tink could keep the two of them both strong and immoral. When I was done, I reached out and took her icy hand in mine.

"Nothing has changed." I squeezed until she met my gaze. "Do you understand me? Everything is going exactly to plan. We're going to get the clock and then rescue those kids. The only difference between now and two hours ago is that we know who the bad guys are."

For a second, I thought I'd lost her. She looked

about one stiff wind away from a total, emotional breakdown.

But then something happened. Her posture straightened, her blue eyes, so full of despair a moment before, went cold with determination.

"You know what this means, right?"

"Tell me," I encouraged with a nod.

"It means there is no room for error. We *will* kill Noru and get that damned clock. There is no option to die trying this time, Harm. Promise me. I don't think I could take it if…"

She trailed off and pressed her fist to her mouth.

Even if I was able to get us back to the general area of Neverland, I had no idea how we would find it behind Tink's shield, but because Moll had already suffered so much…because I loved her more than anything, in this story or any other, I did the unthinkable.

I made a vow I wasn't sure I could keep.

"I promise."

CHAPTER 29

etch dove off my shoulder, zipping toward a copse of trees as I stepped on solid ground for the first time in days.

"You called *this* a town?" Moll asked, turning to Paddy with a raised brow.

And she *did* have a point. With a dozen or so makeshift huts—if you could even call them huts—the place looked more like somewhere you'd spend the night while hunting than somewhere people chose to live.

"Looks like no one's 'round right now," Paddy answered, scratching at his nose. "You should see the place in the spring, though. Dozens of lads milling about."

"There goes my bath," Moll groaned.

Paddy gestured toward the ocean. "Water's right there."

"At least we'll get a good night's sleep," I said, cutting in before Moll could snap back at him.

"About that…" Xander slowed his pace a bit. "Cap says we're gonna head in tonight. Made good time here and don't want to waste any daylight. We'll sleep in The Fen."

"Sounds good to me. Provided we stay in level one, me and the boys'll find you a safe enough place to rest." Paddy shielded his eyes from the sun as he turned to our left, staring off into the distance.

The Fen was something like a large island covered in swampland, though the O'Donnellys assured us that wasn't quite accurate. The massive canopy, formed by the tops of thousands of trees, seemed to jut out of the ocean itself, just barely visible through the blanket of red-tinged mist that clung to it. I pressed a hint of magic into my eyes, jamming them shut at the almost blinding flash of red. The entire place was oozing with magical energy, a nexus of power that put even Relyk to shame.

As terrifying as it was, there was a beauty to it, too. An untamed wildness that we were here to face, and hopefully conquer. How many had come here before us with similar goals?

How few left? One that we knew of—Garth.

Moll looked nervous about the prospect of sailing there at night, but it seemed to fade as Xander stepped in beside her, laying an arm over her shoulder.

"Back in my day, we didn't need no fancy town to

camp out in," Garth said. "Just us and our ship. The way it should be."

Hook glanced back, narrowing his eyes at the old man. "We're leaving the ship here along with the vast majority of the crew."

Garth sucked in a ragged breath before answering. "Where's the sense in that?"

"We can't go tromping through like an army, can we? A small group will attract less notice from the beasts in The Fen," Hook said. "Plus, we'll need people to keep an eye on you to make sure you don't try to follow us."

The older man stomped up to the front of our pack at that, huffing with every step. "There ain't a chance in hell that you're leaving me behind, James," he declared.

Hook ignored him, turning toward the rest of his crew as we reached the first of the huts.

"Alright, lads, time to get set up. You'll have to move the boat somewhere safer once we set out, so make sure you bring out enough of the supplies to last a few days. O'Donnellys, direct them to where we can set up, if you please. Don't want us stepping on any toes if more Seekers come to camp while we're still in The Fen."

A cacophony of ayes and yes sirs followed, and the glorified campground began buzzing all around, leaving Hook, Xander, Garth, Moll, and I in a small pocket of inactivity.

"I'm comin' with ya," Garth said, glaring at Hook as

he turned back toward us. "Ain't nothin' you can do about it."

"I'll have the lads tie you up and hold you down until I leave, if I have to," Hook snapped. "It's simply out of the question."

Garth sucked in a few deep breaths, his face going from bright red to a less alarming hot pink. He shook his head in annoyance. "I'm an old man, and I ain't gettin' any younger. I *need* to do this. I can feel it in my bones."

"Probably the arthritis," Hook grunted.

Garth scowled, swiping both hands down the front of his face. His expression darkened, growing more somber, and he stared off toward the red mist in the distance. "When I tell you I'm not long for this world, I don't just mean because I'm getting old, lad."

I winced, a wave of self-consciousness washing over me, and I turned to walk away, with Moll and Xander stepping right behind me. *Definitely* not a conversation I should be hearing.

"I'm dying, James," Garth continued, not bothering to wait for me to get out of earshot.

"Damn it," Moll said, leaning closer to Xander as Hook and Garth's voices grew too quiet to hear.

"So sad. He's a good man," I agreed. "Wonder if Hook's gonna cave and let him come."

"He will," Xander answered, his tone firm with certainty.

"What makes you so sure?"

"In all my days, I've never seen him deny a man his dying wish. This feels much the same."

I nodded, though I was far from convinced. James clearly cared about the old man, and taking him along *would* put him in serious danger. My fingers dug into my palm at the thought. Old or not, it was a selfish ask, given what it'd do to Hook if he died.

If he does *come, I'm going to try my best to make sure he makes it out of there safe and sound,* I promised myself.

The question was, why did I care so much about something that would hurt James?

Don't get distracted with matters of the heart. Not now.

I glanced out at the red mist once again. Noru, the eighty-foot crocodile, was somewhere in there, along with countless other monstrous beasts. And I had a feeling it was going to take every bit of concentration I had to get us out.

"Have you noticed it yet?" Xander asked as he and Moll stepped up beside me.

"It's such a ridiculous amount of magic," I said, glancing over at them.

Moll's face scrunched up into a squint, and she shook her head in annoyance a moment later.

"Not being able to see what you guys see is irritating, even if it *is* still an amazing sight. Do you think the energy is coming from the monsters?"

Xander shrugged. "Hard to say. But I wonder if it's not the other way 'round."

"You think Noru may've just been a normal croc at

some point?" I asked, the thought occurring to me for the first time.

"Or Noru's ancestor," he said with a shrug. "I'll tell you this much, though; he wasn't half that large when he took Hook's hand."

"How do we even fight against something like that?" Moll asked.

"*We?*" Xander asked, spinning toward her. "You know you're staying behind with Garth, right?"

"Harm and I stick together," she said, in a tone that made it clear that she was simply informing him.

"Not this time you aren't. You'll—"

She whipped her hand up, flicking him in the dead center of his forehead. "I'd never forgive myself if something happened and I wasn't there to help. I'm going."

He stared back at her, dumbfounded, and I couldn't help but feel the same way.

"How the hell did she actually manage to flick you?" I asked. "Aren't you supposed to have crazy reflexes or something?"

"You're not going to argue with her about this?" he demanded. "You have to know it's ridiculous."

"We already had it out over this." I threw up my hands. "And it's hard for me to argue when I know I'd do the same if I was in her shoes."

A low fluttering sounded from just behind me, and Moll let out a yelp as Fetch touched down on my shoulder.

A wash of crimson settled over her face, and she turned back toward Xander. "Look, I may scare easy, but I won't run. I have Harm's incapacitator, and I'm pretty nifty with a slingshot, when push comes to shove."

He scowled. "A lot of good a slingshot's going to do against a crocodile the size of a warship."

"And you, with your whip and those little coins are *sooo* much better?" She pushed away from him, then stomped off. "I'm coming. Don't let me hear another word about it."

"That means she likes you," I said once she was out of earshot.

"Dang. How does she treat the guys she *doesn't* like?"

I chuckled, "Give her some time. She understands, and I'm sure she appreciates your concern. But she hates feeling like she's being underestimated. I've been guilty of it too. She's a lot more capable than you think."

"I'm sure she's quite capable, but what lies ahead is going to take more than that. What we need is *magic*. And lots of it."

"These won't be the first monsters she's fought." The image of her stabbing the reanimated Heinrich appeared in my mind. "She may not have a Tideblessing, but make no mistake. Moll *is* magic. Just not the way we are. She's unbreakable. Unstoppable. She has been through so much to get to this point, and she's overcome everything the world has thrown at her. I'm not saying I agree with her decision, but I've doubted her before, and I won't make the same mistake again. This is something she needs to do."

Xander cursed softly, turning away from me. "I'll see you in a few."

"Didn't catch anything, bud?" I asked, turning toward an irritated-looking Fetch.

Footsteps thumped from just behind me, and I had only spun halfway around by the time a pair of arms caught me around the shoulders.

"Thank you," Moll whispered, barely audible over Fetch's indignant squawking despite the fact that her face was pressed against my neck.

"You heard?"

Her forehead brushed against me as she nodded wordlessly, squeezing me even tighter. "Been waiting for you to realize," she whispered, after a long moment.

I gave her arm a gentle squeeze. "Xander's just trying to look out for you."

She pulled back, sighing softly. "I know."

I turned to see how the crew was doing with their unloading, only to see Trick-Eyed Tom striding up from behind us.

"We're gettin' ready to depart," he called, waving us over. "Cap's gonna say a few words to the boys." He hobbled off without waiting for an answer, calling the same out to a group of men who were just stepping off of the ship.

Just a few minutes later, we were all gathered in

front of the largest hut, with Hook standing at our group's center. "Alright, boys. Xander, Tom, and I'll be gone for a few days, so Cooky's in charge until we get back. I don't expect any problems as they don't know our plans and they have some of their own, but I want constant lookouts checking both sea and sky for any sign of our enemies. If a week passes and you've gotten no word from us, you sail off, no questions asked, you hear?"

A collective grumble of disapproval rolled through the dozen or so members of the crew. "Ain't no way we're leavin' you, Cap," one called.

Hook scowled even more deeply than usual, then sighed. "If I come back a week from now and you're still here, I'll have the lot of you strung up for insubordination." He went silent for a long moment, looking solemn. "You know, sailing the sea with you all these years…there's no ragtag bunch of smelly scallywags I'd rather have done it with."

"Why're you sweet-talkin' like this is the last time you're gonna see us?" another voice called, the rest of the crew having gone completely silent.

Hook's somber expression gave way to one of pure determination. "We'll see each other again, alright. I'll kill this croc with my bare fucking hands if that's what it takes. And, once I do, you lot are going to get me to Neverland so I can do the same to those soulless flying fuckers who've wreaked havoc for so long. Who's with me?"

"Huzzah!" the men shouted and cheered, thrusting their fists in the sky.

Captain James T. Hook tried to play the villain, but he wasn't fooling the men who believed in him, or me. The man had the heart of a lion and the soul of a hero. The world needed him in it.

And once we got through this, I was going to find a way to make him see it...

CHAPTER 30

ater sloshed beneath us as the skiff thudded into the edge of the strange, otherworldly swamp. I swiped a hand across my sweaty forehead, careful not to spook Fetch as I held the torch up, taking in our surroundings. Gnarled trees stretched high into the sky all around, and the thick red fog that'd concealed the place from the outside had faded completely.

I sucked in a deep breath, doing my best to calm my pounding heart. A dark energy emanated from the swamp itself, brushing against the edges of my awareness even as I did my best to shut it out. And the sensation only grew stronger when I focused on the heart of the place—the second layer, where the true monsters lurked.

"Alright, lads and lasses," Paddy said, hopping over the edge of the skiff and landing in the swamp with a thunk. "Keep the volume to a whisper, and don't stray far from me and the boys. The place has a way of getting you all turned 'round."

He still had some swagger and confidence to his tone, but it was tinged with something else.

Terror?

"Did we really have to come here at night?" Moll asked, creeping toward the edge of the boat as the others began to pile out.

"Wouldn't be all that much brighter, even if it was high noon anyway," Scotty answered, the skiff rocking as he stepped awkwardly over the side.

It was too high to get a good look at the overly-thick canopy that lay high above us, but a chill crept up my spine at the thought of it. The tree coverage wasn't nearly dense enough for such a thing to exist. According to Garth, vines and branches wove together up there, forming a solid dome that blotted out all but the faintest pricks of moonlight.

Hook gave Garth a hand as he moved to make the jump, keeping the older man steady as he landed on the muddy ground. But he ignored Garth's word of thanks, waving him forward as he waited for the rest of us to exit. Whatever had been said during their private conversation, it'd gone just like Xander had predicted. Garth had given the captain enough to change his mind about letting him come along, but he clearly wasn't happy about it.

I stepped out of the boat next, accepting Hook's

arm as I landed, and suddenly felt glad for the dark as we locked eyes, sending a flash of heat to my cheeks.

"No risks," he grunted.

I dipped my head in assent, turning away from his gaze as Xander helped Molly to the ground beside me.

Paddy waved us onward without any further conversation, leading our trek while his brothers took up positions on each side. Andrew had the rear, and he walked just behind Moll and me, with his head on a constant swivel as he searched for any sign of danger.

The muddy ground gripped my shoes with every step, and a dull ache began to creep into my temples, regardless of how hard I worked to suppress my magic.

"So why does Noru ever leave, if he has access to all this?" Moll asked. "They say he's the king of this place, so can't he just eat the other monsters?"

"He does feed on the other monsters," Andrew answered. "They say he hardly eats, when he's in the outside world. It ain't about food."

"So what is it about?" I asked, yanking my foot out of the muddy ground that sucked down on my shoe with every step.

"No one knows. It's different than the other beasties, though. It's like he actively seeks humans out, just to kill them."

"And when, exactly, are we planning on running into him?" Moll asked, sparing a nervous glance over her shoulder as a soft plunk dropped into the lake at our left.

"Don't worry. He only comes to this layer on his way out for Ebonfall," the boy replied, pausing for a second before adding, "as far as anyone knows."

I let out a humorless chuckle. "Very encouraging."

Another plunk.

He held up a finger, and I went silent when a low hoot split the air. If I hadn't seen him do it right before my eyes, I would've assumed it was just an owl, but the other O'Donnellys brought the group to a sudden halt, and the boy zipped past us to meet up with Paddy, his footsteps effortless and silent despite the thick muck.

"We gettin' close to the second layer?" Tom asked.

"Quiet," Scotty grunted, his voice low.

The brothers convened for a brief moment, then continued moving, with Andrew creeping to the back once again. "Eyes peeled for monsters. Something's off to our left."

I nodded slowly, goosebumps flaring up as I held my torch a little further in that direction. I squinted, trying to make something out in the inky blackness, but saw nothing.

Moll pulled closer into my side, gripping the incapacitator in her free hand. "What do you think it is?" she whispered.

"If we're lucky it's some kind of big fish. If not..." Andrew didn't elaborate.

"If not?" I cut in, hurrying him along.

"If not then maybe it's a—"

Movement flashed in front of my eyes, whipping

through the air a few inches in front of my face like a cracking whip, and things erupted into chaos. "Move!" Andrew spat, whipping his dagger from its sheath.

Fetch stirred at my shoulder, and I willed him to stay put with a thought as I ran, ignoring the shooting pain in my skull. I dashed forward, with Moll right at my side.

The O'Donnellys, on the other hand, leapt into action, waving their torches in wild arcs as they urged us onward. "Keep it moving," Scotty shouted, his voice barely audible over the splashing sounds that were now erupting all around us.

Hook and Xander ignored the command, sprinting their way to the rear of the group. "Fuck," Hook spat, tearing his blade from its sheath.

I spared a glance over my shoulder to see a trio of elephant-sized frogs hopping after us. Spikes jutted out from the tops of their heads, and I winced as one opened its mouth, revealing a line of razor-sharp teeth.

My hand shot to Moll's wrist on instinct as they bellowed in unison, and I pulled her along as I broke into a full-on sprint. Garth panted heavily just in front of us, but, to his credit, he kept up the pace, staying nearly even with Tom.

"Sharp turn!" Paddy shouted, taking a hard left as we passed a massive willow tree.

And we followed suit, the pounding in my skull growing stronger and stronger as we charged through the woods, which grew denser with every yard we traveled. *Too dense for the frogs?*

A tree rumbled and cracked just ahead, putting a halt to that notion as one of the massive beasts leapt right into our path. Raw bloodthirst seemed to ooze off of the monster, washing over me in waves. And it wasn't based on any visual signs. Somehow, I could feel him, on a deeper level than any of my normal senses.

The frog's essence, laid bare for me to see. My temples screamed as I focused in on it, but I ignored them, delving even deeper—like I'd done with the ships. If I could feel his essence, then I could—

A bloodcurdling roar split the air, like a mix between a lion, a bullfrog, and a human scream. Now, it had to be now. I mentally lunged forward, even further into his mind. He pressed back desperately, eager to keep me out, but I smashed into him with everything I had, blasting down his defenses. I reached inside, driving a single thought straight into its brain.

RUN!

The frog's eyes lit up in terror, and he whirled, leaping right back to where he'd come from. The ground rumbled under his weight, and he landed in the water with a plunk a second later.

I sucked in a ragged breath, using every ounce of willpower I had to force my legs to keep churning.

"Gods, Harm," Xander said, his voice coming from just behind me. "I'd heard that the Tideblessings were stronger here, but what I just felt goes beyond that."

I nodded, hardly able to muster a reply.

You just need to keep running. You just need to keep running.

I repeated the mantra over and over, putting one foot in front of the other.

Time hardly seemed to pass as we ran, and the mantra morphed into empty words rumbling through my exhausted brain. Every footfall rattled my teeth, and a thousand little nodes of conscious bloodlust seemed to close in on me from all around. The minds of monsters? But the nodes closest to me were different, a tiny circle of safety in the storm of blind rage.

They ranged from indifferent toward me, as was the case for the O'Donnellys, to concerned and loving, in the cases of Moll and Fetch. And Hook's? I shuffled through them, fixating on his little node of awareness.

The tsunami of pain and guilt that greeted me washed away everything else, threatening to suck me right into it. I delved deeper nonetheless, searching desperately. What else was there? What were his feelings toward me? What—

His mind snapped shut like a trap, hurling me out as quickly as I'd arrived. I scrambled wildly as my knees gave out, and I would've been sent sprawling if not for the sturdy arm that gripped my shoulder from behind.

I spun, heart skipping a beat as Hook stared down at me, his face unreadable. "Up. Gotta keep moving."

And I did just that, tamping down on my magic

with everything I had. But, no matter how hard I tried, I couldn't stop it completely. Something about this strange, terrible place had it bleeding out of me like an open wound. And there seemed to be nothing I could do to staunch the bleeding.

Paddy's torch slowed to a halt sometime later, and I hardly had the energy to feel relieved as I came to a stop, sucking in a gasping breath. I let a dribble of the magic out, goosebumps pricking up on my arms as I probed the darkness. "They're still... coming," I managed. "Need to run."

Paddy waved his torch, striding to the center of our little group to meet back up with his brothers. "The bastards have alerted half the beasties in this layer. It's more than just them that're after us."

"So what do we do?" Moll managed, panting nearly as hard as I was.

"Our group is too large to hide out for long," Jacob said, nibbling at his fingernails.

Hook strode to the center of the group. "Then we go straight to the next layer."

Jacob winced. "Don't be so hasty. It takes time to find a suitable entrance. We—"

A heavy thump rang out as Scotty clapped him on the back. "It takes time we don't have. The Captain's right. We find the first entrance we can and go, then worry about the consequences later."

A jolt of pain spiked through my forehead, that

horrible sense of bloodlust pricking at the edges of my awareness yet again. "They're close."

Jacob opened his mouth to say more, but Paddy silenced him with a hand. "We have no choice. Now let's find an entrance, boys. And fast."

Andrew darted past him without a word, his torch illuminating the massive wall just ahead, and a horrible sense of foreboding settled over me as I looked it over. Thorny vines wove together into a single, impenetrable mass that stretched as far up as the eye could see, and lichen hung in little streamers, flowing in the cool breeze.

He dashed along the wall's edge, moving right while Scotty moved left, and it didn't take long for him to call out. "Got one!"

Fetch clicked his beak on my shoulder as we hobbled toward the sound, his nervousness coming through to me as clearly as the frogs' rage and aggression had. "Not far," I whispered.

"You good?" Moll asked, grabbing my arm.

"There's so much magic here," I said. "It's hard to shut it all out. I can feel every animal in the place."

She leaned in further without another word, and we strode the rest of the way to Andrew, arm in arm. A chill crept up my spine as I watched the vines and brambles twist and writhe like little snakes around the gaping hole the boy had found in the wall. Pure, unmitigated horror rolled through me as I stared at the twisted, unholy perversion of nature. A thing that shouldn't be, but was, nonetheless.

It wasn't like the wormholes, but close enough that it had me reeling.

"So who's up first?" Paddy asked, glancing nervously at it.

I tugged Moll forward despite myself, trudging toward the entrance. The frogs were closing in, and there was no other way out of all this. I peered into the sloped tunnel of shifting vines, leading down into a realm of unknown horrors, but Hook blocked my path with an outstretched arm before I got too close.

"See you on the other side," Hook said, striding up to it and gripping one of the writhing vines with his good hand as he stepped through, then sliding down the viny tunnel, his torchlight disappearing in the blink of an eye.

A bellow tore through the air from behind, and Paddy swung his torch toward the sound, gesturing frantically for the rest of us to enter.

No use in waiting. I strode the last few steps forward, sucking in a strengthening breath before charging into the unknown, with Moll tight at my heels. My torch puffed out like a candle as we slid down the tunnel, and I clenched my teeth to suppress the terror as the walls writhed and stretched against my back, carrying us deeper. Fetch cawed, his anxiety palpable as I held him tight against my chest.

I thudded into the ground a few seconds later, my

knees smarting from the impact, and leapt forward just in time for Moll to land behind me, her hands going on my shoulders as she struggled to regain her balance.

I reached around, pulling her forward as I blinked, my eyes adjusting to the darkness. "Hook?"

"Right up here," a voice called.

I followed the sound, eyes fixed on the dim rays of light that were coming from a side passage. A shiver rolled through me as a vine slid up against my arm, and I winced as another thud sounded from just behind us.

"Gods that was weird," Paddy said, shuddering.

Pain blasted through my head as I turned the corner, my vision going white as light flooded into view. A dozen colors at once, fusing into a blinding white. Just like—

"Maelstrom Opal," Moll whispered.

I nodded, gritting my teeth through the pain as I stepped into the cave. Hook was already there, shielding his eyes as he looked up at the ceiling. "Garth said there was a lot of the stuff, but I didn't expect *this* much."

I tamped down my magic, finding more success than I'd had earlier. It'll get easier, I told myself in an attempt at reassurance. The ground was still muddy and damp, but the viny ceiling was completely crusted in the Opals, shimmering with every color at once like light shining through a prism.

A thump sounded from behind us, but it was almost

completely drowned out by the rumble that split the cavern ahead. "What the—?"

A furry mass emerged from a nearby cluster of trees, and I reeled, inching back toward the tunnel. A bear? No, worse than that.

The big bear's saber teeth glinted in the gem-light as it looked over, stalking toward us.

"Back in the tunnel!" Paddy shouted, moving to take his own advice as a little head poked over the side of the massive beast's furry neck.

"Paddy fookin' O'Donnelly, is that you?"

CHAPTER 31

I stared up, my exhaustion and pounding headache fading to the background out of sheer amazement. "Billy?"

The oldest and only female of the O'Donnelly clan spun to the side, sliding deftly off the giant beast's muscular shoulders to stand. Her cheeks were streaked with some kind of mud she'd used like warpaint, and her tawny hair was tangled and wild. Yet, somehow, she pulled off the look in a 'badass warrior bitch' kind of way.

"Who the hell're you?" she asked, her eyes flitting between Hook, Moll, and I. "My brothers pay you lot to help them come get me?"

"Something like that," Paddy answered, stepping tentatively closer. "But...how've you been?"

She closed the distance between them in a stride, bonking him upside the head. "Took you long enough to come after me." She flashed a grin, pulling him into a hug that said whatever she was talking about was forgiven.

Footsteps sounded from behind me, and I spun to see Tom, Garth, Xander, and the three remaining O'Donnellys stepping out from the cave.

"Well, I'll be damned," Jacob marveled.

"I told you she'd be fine," Andrew replied, dashing forward to throw his arms around her, seemingly unworried about the thousand-pound saber tooth bear standing just behind her.

"Of course I'm fine," she answered, looking confused as to why anyone had thought otherwise.

"Care to fill us in on what happened here?" Xander asked, interrupting the little reunion.

Paddy winced, his eyes darting toward Hook as Billy explained, "We were in the first layer looking for opals a few months back and I got forced down here by a particularly nasty jackalope that *someone*," she shot a pointed glance at Scotty, "should've seen coming. Been hunting and gathering to survive ever since."

Xander gestured toward Paddy. "And you all have been planning a way to come here and find her ever since? *Before* we agreed to pay you 10,000 gold pieces to get us down here? While you acted as if you were only in it for the gold?"

I winced as Paddy threw his hands up in surrender. "Look, we do what we gotta do."

The Captain took a step forward, raising his iron

hook to silence Xander before he could say more. "Water under the bridge. Now let's get a move on. We don't want to be stuck down here for any longer than necessary."

Of course he wouldn't care *why* the O'Donnellys were all here, or if they came with us. He had no plans for what came after this, anyway. The money was meaningless to him, as long as he accomplished his goal.

End Pan and Tink.

I turned away, doing my best to push past the wave of despair that fell over me.

He was a spirit of vengeance, his eyes constantly fixed on that goal. Even now, I could feel the fury, just barely below the surface of his carefully held facade. The single-minded desire to get the clock and kill the two who'd wronged him and killed so many others.

Xander opened his mouth to argue, but shut it as he met Hook's gaze, dipping his head. "Alright. We've got a crocodile to catch."

"A crocodile?" Billy asked, cocking an eyebrow. "Only one beastie like that 'round here, and I know you can't be talking about him. Unless you're stupid."

"Noru," Hook answered. "We're looking for Noru."

"Gods damn it all," Billy muttered under her breath. "Well, we're guides, and I have no problem guiding you to Noru. But you'll have to do the fighting on your own."

"That was the plan."

"And I don't mean to be morbid but have you and my brothers made arrangements to get them paid in the case you…aren't able to pay them out once this is over with." She didn't wince once but kept her eyes locked on Hook.

He laughed dryly, producing a small, rather wet-looking envelope from his coat. "Present this to my crew, and you'll get your payment. No more dallying, though. We need to move."

A sharp stab of pain in my forehead pulled my attention upward, and I looked up at Fetch, dumbfounded. "Did you just…bite me?"

He clicked his beak, shaking his head back and forth as if in pain.

"Your wing?" I asked as we began to walk. I let a trickle of my magic dribble out, probing him with it. There was pain, but it wasn't from his wing.

"Want me to take a look?" Tom offered, slowing down to let us catch up.

"It's not that," I said, chewing at my inner lip as I sealed my magic back up. "It's this place. The magic here, he can feel it, same as I can."

"Very odd," Xander remarked. "I do feel it, from the Opal, but it's not nearly as pronounced as it seems to be for you. Your magic is so strange…it reacts to this unlike anything else."

Made sense, given that it was magic from an entirely different world. But I'd save that conversation for a different day. "I'm getting used to it, and I feel much stronger here."

"That should come in handy when it's time to face Noru," Xander said.

Billy let out a sharp breath. "Have yet to meet the Tideblessed who'd be more than an afternoon snack for that fucker. I wish you the best, I really do, but you're up against forces even we don't fully understand. The entirety of The Fen bends to his will."

"And he's going to bend to mine," Hook cut in.

Billy shrugged. "I'd love to be proven wrong. The bear that'd been walking alongside us nuzzled at her face, and her arm snapped up in a blur, flicking him directly on the nose. "Out of here. Shoo!"

And, for whatever reason, he turned tail and ran. Gods only knew what she'd done to earn that type of respect from the beast. "If even she's saying we can't beat him, maybe we are screwed," Moll muttered, her eyes pinned to the ground.

I bumped her gently with my shoulder. "We'll handle him. Don't worry about it."

"You won't be getting close enough for it to be too dangerous," Xander said, his voice firm. "The O'Donnellys can help you get out if things go poorly for us." Moll opened her mouth to protest, but he cut her off with a shake of his head. "I'm not budging on this. I'll have them drag you out of here if I have to. I want your word."

She scowled, but nodded, nonetheless. "Fine."

"You can still shoot at it with your slingshot or something," I suggested. "It's not the kind of thing you can just run up and stab to death."

"Wise choice, lass," Scotty grunted, striding past us as he made his way to the front of the pack.

"How'd you survive down here for all this time?" I asked Billy, changing the subject as we squeezed through a particularly-dense section of jungle.

She pressed her index finger to her temple. "Wits. The beasts of The Fen have strength and size, but I have smarts. I've stayed by the edge, heading into the jungle to hunt only when I run out of meat."

"And you haven't found a way out in all this time?" Moll asked, glancing nervously in the direction we'd come from.

"It's like the place doesn't want me to leave. Most of the tunnels are too steep to climb up, and every time I think I might have a good one, it closes before I can use it. Maybe we'll have better luck now that there are so many of us."

My fingernails dug into my palm, feeling a sudden wave of claustrophobia despite the size of the place. She'd managed to survive for quite some time on her own, but a group our size would attract more attention. Even if we did manage to kill Noru, our struggle wouldn't be over. We'd still have to find our way back out.

A reddish gleam caught my eye, distracting me from my worries, and I leapt toward it, leaning over to scoop it up. "Maelstrom Opal," I marveled, gritting my teeth as I held my magic at bay as I stared at the ever-shifting gem. The pain was nothing like it'd been in Garth's room, but it was still uncomfortable to look at.

"They fall from the ceiling, sometimes," Billy said, glancing back at me.

"We should grab some on our way out," Tom suggested. "Probably worth a bloody fortune."

Garth glanced over at me, a dark expression on his face as he sucked in a ragged breath. "We had loads of them, before that hydra came for us."

Billy whirled on him. "You've been here?"

"Many years ago. Though it hasn't changed a lick."

"At least there's hope, then. How'd you make it out?"

"Got lucky. Me and the two other survivors all ran through our own exit. I was the only one who made it out."

She nodded. "Let's hope it doesn't come to that."

"One step at a time," Garth said. "But where is the beast? Can't be too far, as far as I can remember."

"Haven't seen him in person, thank the gods," Billy answered, "but we're a mile or so away from the zone where the biggest beasts—" She cut off abruptly, holding out an arm as she slowed to a halt.

My heart thumped in my chest, and I let the magic trickle out once again, sending out feelers for nearby life. A dozen little nodes of energy appeared in my mind's eye, not counting the members of our party. But, this time, there was none of the bloodthirst. I probed at one, getting a distinct image of some small, woodland critter. A squirrel? Or maybe a chipmunk?

I breathed a sigh of relief. "I don't feel anything," I said. "I think we're good." For whatever reason, it somehow seemed safer here than it had on the first layer. Maybe there were fewer monsters?

I expanded my search a little further, wincing slightly as I sensed a presence closer to the edge—some kind of strange wolf creature. Steering clear of it, I probed inward instead. Maybe I'd be able to feel Noru if—

A pair of blood red eyes fixed on me in this magical realm, seeming to stare through me, all the way down to my soul itself. I reeled, trying to suck the magic back into me, but it yanked me back, its crimson gaze never wavering.

Die.

Die.

Die.

It came through as a feeling rather than a word, but I understood it as clearly as if he had spoken it. An instant later, a bone-rattling rumble split the massive cavern.

I let out a slow, shaky breath.

"He's here."

CHAPTER 32

Tiny flecks of maelstrom opal dropped from the ceiling like rain, but I couldn't peel my focus away from those piercing, predatory eyes. As if being an eighty-foot crocodile wasn't enough, he had some kind of strange magic, too, or at least an awareness of magic.

Fetch screeched, shooting up from my shoulder and into the sky, and, as Noru's presence receded, I fixed my attention on the falcon. He'd sensed Noru, too, as clearly as I had. And, in the same way, I could feel his frantic search for the monster, even from down on the ground. And it didn't take long.

The mass of scales and raw, tangible hate pulled himself free of the lake at the center of The Fen, dragging himself toward us step by step. I could just make out his battle-scarred back and tail through Fetch's eyes, but what struck me most was the sheer size of him. Trees quaked as he passed, with one snapping in half as he struck it with a lazy swipe of his tail. To call him a crocodile didn't do him justice. He was more like a dragon from my book of stories, just with squatter legs and a longer snout.

A gentle pressure on my shoulders brought me back to my body, and I blinked, seeing Hook's face just in front of me. "Go," he said, with a determined, and almost excited look in his eye. Moll tugged on my hand as he gestured toward Billy. "She'll take you somewhere a bit safer, and you'll—"

"I'm not going," I said. "We're going to do this together." And, in the speaking of those words, the fear somehow gave way, leaving behind only a cold, emotionless calm. After seeing Noru, and feeling his mind, it was harder than ever to believe we had a chance in hell at winning. But that simply wasn't an option.

So much was hinging on this. The lives of the kids, the people of C'an Saas, and my entire cosmic destiny, all hanging in the balance. Moll squeezed down on my hand, giving me a nod as she pulled away to follow Billy, Garth, and the O'Donnellys.

"Get him, Harm."

"Of course," I said, Fetch's claws smacking back down onto my shoulder pad. Whatever strange shift had come over me seemed to have extended to him, as well. The beak clicking and nervousness had fled, and, giving him a good look for the first time since we'd been here, he looked somehow…stronger.

Larger, even?

At his advanced age, it should've been impossible. But that didn't stop it from being true. His talons pressed into my shoulder right through the pad, and his beak seemed longer, with a reddish hue at the tip.

But I had no time to consider it, as Noru's rumbling footsteps came into earshot. "Not far now," I said. "What's the game plan?"

Hook scowled, opening his mouth to argue, but turned around instead. "You've clearly unlocked something new with your magic, so stay back and support Xander and I from the back. Tom, same to you."

I glanced over to see Tom nodding in agreement, his eyes lighting up with that same, eager fire I'd seen in Hook's. "Got it, Cap."

Hook exchanged a wordless glance with Xander, his magic welling up to the surface as we waited for the inevitable. I had yet to see his abilities in full effect, but whatever they were, he felt incredibly strong. If Xander's magic was a sleek, well-forged dagger, Hook's was a full-on broadsword.

I only hoped he knew how to make the most of it as well as Xander could. He'd been strangely cagey about his abilities from the start, and I felt a little flash of anticipation at the prospect of getting to see him fight up close. Maybe he was like me, and could do a bit of everything? But no, Xander had seemed far too surprised by my abilities for that to be the case.

A nearby tree cracked and broke, and I focused on my own magic as the monster's snout came into view, huffing furiously. If we could just keep our distance, we could wear him down over time. Crocodiles weren't exactly known for their speed, after all.

Or so I thought.

His jaws snapped together wildly as he broke into a full-on charge, dashing toward us at a speed that seemed to defy the laws of nature. How the hell could legs that short carry him that fast?

I had no time to ponder as he came fully into view, his jaws snapping in a wild lunge at Hook. The captain's good hand disappeared in a blur as he snaked out a slash with his saber, slicing the monster across the cheek.

Pain surged through the beast, smacking into me like a physical force. I scrambled desperately for footing as my legs gave out, and I gritted my teeth through the rest. The entire place seemed to sing with Noru's every emotion, buffeting me with as much anger, hate, and pain as I could manage. But fortunately, the others didn't seem to be experiencing the same.

Xander's whip snaked out, smashing into the beast's skull before it could recover from the previous attack, and I moved on reflex to do the same as the thunderous crack rang out. "Take that, you ugly bastard,"

Tom shouted at my side, taking aim down the sights of a crossbow.

I lashed out with an attack of my own, lunging as far forward as I dared before sending my whip screaming toward the other side of his face.

Never give him a chance to recover.

If only it was that easy.

The light from the opals above glinted off yellowing teeth as his mouth shot open, hurling himself at me like an arrow from a bow. Fury and hate pressed up against me, and it took everything I had just to throw myself to the side, praying he missed as Fetch sprang from my shoulder, surging into action.

Get back, I willed him, but he didn't listen, charging right at the beast like the crazy fucking bird he was. Until Hook appeared, that is.

He leapt in between Noru and me, letting out a guttural roar as he threw his arm to the side, blasting a storm's worth of wind and lightning right into Noru's gaping maw. And, somehow, the eighty-foot bastard felt it, throwing his head back in pain as he skidded to a halt.

I grabbed my fallen whip then scrambled to my feet, forcing down my terror as I readied my magic once again. My energy crackled as it surged all the way through the whip, filling it to the very tip.

I snapped it forward as the croc recovered, and I cursed as it bounced right off the beast's exposed neck. A blur flashed through the side of my vision, and

Xander appeared, lashing out with his own whip and drawing the beast's attention. Noru snapped at him, but the razor-sharp tip caught the beast across the face. With a flick of his wrist, Xander hooked the whip around Noru's eye ridge, then yanked it downward in a fluid motion. A horrible, wet crunch sounded as it ripped free a hefty chunk of flesh—eye included.

I winced as Noru bellowed in mind-numbing agony, the emotion flooding into me in waves, but I resisted, and kept my eyes open this time, preparing myself for another attack.

But there was no opening as he rolled and spun, his tail whipping and teeth gnashing in all directions out of pure, unbridled rage. Time seemed to slow as Xander leapt backward a half second too late, the very tip of the beast's tail catching him square in the ribs. With a loud crack, he went flying backward, slamming into a tree. My heart lurched as he lay there, motionless.

In that moment, Garth and Molly sprang into view from their hiding place behind a nearby willow. Billy and the O'Donnellys followed suit, shouting and clanging weapons against the rocks, trying to draw Noru's attention away from Xander. Despite his rage, the crocodile swiveled his massive head, snarling at the new targets.

"Come on, you slimy son of a bitch!" Molly roared, brandishing the incapacitator and setting off the charge, creating a flash of light and a series of *pops*.

Garth hurled a chunk of stone at Noru's flank as the brothers whooped and hollered, searching for rocks as well.

It did no damage to the beast, but it did give Hook time to launch into another attack of his own, summoning a vortex of wind. Lightning crackled around his iron hook, bolts of it slamming into Noru's side in tandem with the wind. The beast roared, staggering under the onslaught, but Hook's breathing turned ragged, his magic faltering just slightly. He was clearly burning through the last of his storm magic reserves.

"Damn it," Hook wheezed, sweat dripping into his eyes as the storm fizzled out, but he wasn't done yet. He lunged forward at blistering speed, leaping out of the way of Noru's teeth and jabbing his saber right into the beast's neck. The sequence repeated a half dozen times, and he dodged each of the monster's attacks, weaving around bites and tail swipes to stab him over and over.

Blood oozed from a dozen cuts, and the heat of his anger and pain throbbed hotter and hotter in my mind, but Noru fought on, wounded but not down, the vast bulk of him seemingly unstoppable.

If I didn't do something, this could only end one way. Hook was as skilled as anyone I'd ever seen, but this wasn't a battle of skill. A single slip up meant certain death, and, regardless of how determined he was, his body could only keep this up for so long.

Blood pounded in my ears as I called on every bit of magic I could muster, remembering the vision of those terrible, red eyes. How could I possibly hope to win a battle of minds against that? The memory of connecting with him earlier—feeling that raw, unbridled hatred—sent a cold chill through me. But we didn't have a choice.

I planted my feet, inhaling deeply as energy flooded my veins, flickers of light dancing over my skin. The headache was instant and nearly unbearable, but I gritted my teeth against it. Just a little more magic, and maybe—

Noru pivoted on powerful haunches, allowing Hook to stab him as he fixed that horrible, one-eyed gaze on me. His jaws opened wide, and my heart seized. Not enough time—

Tom lunged forward from my side, screaming at the top of his lungs. "Come on, you overgrown lizard!" he snarled, hurling himself straight at the beast, his sword held high. And I didn't even have time to scream as Noru clamped down with a sickening crunch, snapping him in half in a single bite.

"No!" I shrieked, horror arcing through my veins. But, as the crocodile lowered, preparing to charge once again, I was ready. Tom's sacrifice had given me the precious few seconds I'd needed.

I let out every bit of magic I had, slamming it into him in an all-out mental assault. It felt like ramming my skull into a brick wall, but I kept pushing anyway.

Those terrible, red eyes appeared in my mind's eye, and I stared right into them, blasting him with a single, desperate command.

Stop.

Stop.

STOP!

In the split second before he would've reached me, Noru froze. His entire body trembled, limbs seizing up as my magic found purchase in his mind. His rancid breath washed over my face as he let out a hiss, but there he stood, rage giving way to raw terror as his muscles stopped responding.

"James!" I screamed, voice tearing raw. "Finish it!"

He didn't hesitate, lunging, blade in hand. With one final slash across Noru's throat and through the thick artery, the monster's eyes rolled. I could sense the fury and bloodlust fade along with his lifeforce as a river of blood gushed everywhere, bathing Hook's boots in crimson.

The croc collapsed in a thunderous crash, his jaws slacking open. A strangled gasp escaped as Tom's upper half tumbled out, a mangled and broken mess, but I could sense the faintest flicker of life. My head pounded, and I sucked in a gasping breath as I dashed forward, but Hook was already there, dropping to his knees beside our crewmate.

Tom let out a rattling breath as a thin trail of blood trickled from his lips. He looked at Hook, eyes clouded with pain.

"Xander," he croaked, fingertips glowing with energy as he threw his hand sideways.

Summoning the last of his magic, a stream of energy arced through the air, flowing directly into Xander's fallen form. The first mate coughed, regaining consciousness, but Tom had nothing left.

"Tom!" I choked, tears streaming down my face as Hook cradled the dying man. Tom's eyes flickered to Hook's.

"Kill me before it's too late," he whispered, voice shaking. "You need to be the one to do it."

"No," Hook rasped. "I can't do it, Tom."

"Cap…let this be the last thing I do for my crew. Please." Tom's hand flopped weakly against Hook's coat. "End it."

Pain twisted Hook's features, and, for a moment I thought he'd refuse. But Tom's pleading gaze was unwavering. Hook swallowed, then pulled him close, setting his blade at Tom's throat. It was over in a single, merciful slash.

Hook stood, face carved from stone as he sheathed his blade, then ripped into Noru's massive belly with his iron hook. After several gruesome seconds, he tore out the clock, covered in gore, the ticking echoing in the sudden silence.

I pressed a hand to my mouth, swallowing the rising bile.

A snarl echoed from somewhere nearby—then another, and another. The roars of beasts thundered through the cavern, as if Noru's death had unleashed chaos in its purest form. I felt my senses ignite: dozens of monstrous presences creeping closer, drawn by the bloodshed and the power.

But amid the terror, I felt one single blip of different, foreign magic—something intense, yet recognizable. I pivoted toward Noru's still-twitching body. *Something's there.*

Billy, Paddy, and the others had rushed back at the sound of roaring. "We have to go!" Billy shouted, eyes wild.

"One second!" I cried, stumbling toward Noru's neck. My magic flared, guiding me to a jagged shard lodged in the scales. It was half of an arrow, just barely sticking out above the scales. The tip pulsed with a faint, golden light, and recognition rolled through me in a wave. Tink. I tore it free, nearly cutting my hand on the razor-sharp edges.

"Run!" Hook bellowed.

I turned to see a horde of twisted shapes closing in from every direction as their minds pressed in on mine, full of nothing but anger and hate.

"Now!"

"We'll never outrun them!" Garth hollered over the cacophony of growls and snarls.

Xander took Hook's hand, scrambling to his feet as Molly charged toward him. "We have no choice," Hook grunted, his gaze shifting to me. "You good to run?"

I pulled away as he tried throwing an arm under my

shoulder. "You're in worse shape than I am. Let's move."

And he had no time to argue as The Fen began to convulse all around us, tremors radiating through the floor. Chunks of glowing opal rained from the ceiling, fracturing on impact. Steam vents burst, spewing clouds of toxic fog. It was as if the entire realm was collapsing in on itself.

We tore through the undergrowth, monsters at our heels, the roaring of beasts echoing, ever-closer, behind us. My heart pounded, fear fueling my tired legs, but a grim resolve settled over me. This was the end of Noru's reign—and maybe the end of everything else down here, too.

Just as we cleared the final stretch of jungle, the ground shuddered under our feet.

"This way!" Billy led us around a jagged rock outcropping. We ducked through an opening, the roar behind us deafening now—then the world went white with dust and debris.

The minds of a dozen monsters intruded on mine at once, from serpents to wolves to more giant frogs. And all of them were driven by the same, singular goal of taking their place at the top of the food chain now that Noru was out of the picture. The fighting had already begun at the innermost layers, and many more were rushing to join them, as if fear of the massive crocodile had been the only thing holding them back from the quest to become the alpha.

I cast my mind out further, probing at the nearly impenetrable wall of brambles and vines between layers. Monsters poured through by the dozen, ripping holes in their mad rush to get to the center.

Holes for us to run through, before The Fen closed them again. Finally, a bit of luck going our way.

There was a path though, and I could feel it, and I knew it would lead us out.

"Follow me!"

CHAPTER 33

The journey back to base camp was nearly silent aside from the O'Donnelly brothers talking quietly to Billy. The rest of us were still licking our wounds, catching our breath, and coming to grips with our grief over losing Tom.

Moll was a bundle of nerves, as if the trip couldn't go fast enough, and I could hardly blame her. Now that we knew Tink was hurting Caleb—literally sucking his life away— every minute he had to be in her care felt like torture to us too.

"Can you take Garth back home as well?" Hook asked.

He'd already made a deal with the O'Donnellys to take most of the Jolly Roger crew to Blackbriar for a week off. They'd earned it, but more importantly, we were about to face off with Pan and Tink with no guarantee of winning.

371

As dangerous as Noru had been, Pan and Tink were just as big of a challenge in their own way. Maybe bigger. Noru was a killer, but had nothing other than instinct driving him.

Pan and Tink were wicked smart and cunning, to boot.

Hook, Moll, Xander and I were in full agreement. Not one of us wanted any more blood on our hands. We'd go in just the four of us.

"We'll take the old man, too," Paddy agreed as we prepared to part ways. "Got to admit, though, it's a real kick in the prick that we didn't stop and fill our pockets and satchels with opals when we had the chance. We coulda left that place filthy rich."

"Money isn't what makes a man rich, Paddy," James muttered. It was the first time he'd spoken since we'd escaped The Fen. "Be thankful you got your sister back and your family is whole."

Because the Jolly Roger family wasn't.

Paddy looked away, shamefaced, shuffling from foot to foot. "Aye, you're right about that. Tom seemed like a good man."

"One of the best." Xander sat on one of the benches, head hanging low. "It's a hard pill to swallow. I can't believe I'll never see his face again. It's like a bad dream."

Andrew O'Donnelly stepped forward. "Do you think you can get this to Tom's family? They'll need it now that he's not around to support them anymore.

Maybe it'll help some and I'm young, I can always make more money." He stuck a hand down the front of his pants, tugged his fist free and opened it to reveal a Maelstrom Opal the size of an apple.

Paddy let out a gasp. "Fookin' hell, you clever little lad! Good on ya nabbing that. But maybe giving the whole stone away is a bit hasty though, yeah?"

"You can keep it," Xander cut in with a quick glance at Hook, who tipped his head in agreement. "We were Tom's family, and we've no need of it."

The youngest O'Donnelly brother nodded and handed the stone to Billy.

"Good job, boy'o, I'm proud of you." She turned to Hook. "And my thanks to you and your crew for helping get my brothers to the second level. I'd have been stuck there forever if you hadn't come."

Hook stood, reaching for the railing to keep from weaving on his feet. The fight had completely exhausted him, and he didn't waste the last of his energy to respond.

"This is your stop," Scotty said as the skiff pulled up to the dock a moment later and Moll and I made our way over to Garth.

"You were very brave today, sir," Molly said gravely.

"I'm so glad you snuck on board to join us," I added. "We couldn't have done it without you."

He sniffed and waved a dismissive hand. "Ah, go on with the two of you."

Once the others said their goodbyes and Xander

made good on the payment owed for services rendered, we reboarded the Jolly Roger.

It was time to put the next part of our plan into motion. I reached into my pocket and tugged out the arrowhead I'd stashed there. Even stained with dried blood, the fairy dust clung to it, making it seem as if it had been bathed in gold. I'd fastened it to small piece of driftwood so that it would float.

You need to take this and fly West for a while, then drop it in the water. Got it?

He opened his beak and gently plucked the piece of wood from my fingers.

Once you've done that, head back in the direction of Neverland. We'll be there waiting for you. And please...be careful.

We'd suffered one loss already, and even that felt like too many.

Fetch flapped his wings and took to the sky a moment later. Everything was riding on his success, and I watched until he was out of sight.

"And you're sure you can find Neverland, even with Tink shielding its location?" Xander asked as Moll stood next to him, seeming to lean into his body.

"I can definitely sense her magic, and I know the approximate location." I reached out and felt the magic even now as Fetch carried the arrowhead away. "If I can get close enough, I think the power she uses to shield the island will lead me the rest of the way there, like a beacon."

Xander scratched his head, glancing in the direction Fetch had flown. "So odd…her magic is completely untraceable to me. But, if you can sense it on something as small as the arrow, I tend to agree. It's a good plan."

"What do we do in the meantime?" Moll asked, sounding lost and afraid.

Hook stood at the bow of the ship a few yards away, just staring at the moon, shoulders hunched and silent. His shirt was in tatters, covered in blood.

Noru's.

His own.

Tom's…

I wondered if it was just the magic and physical energy he'd expended that had made him near catatonic, or if he was in shock after having to mercy kill his friend.

That would have done me in had I been in his place, and Molly in Tom's.

Why had Tom been so adamant that Hook deal the final death blow? Was it some sort of pirate ritual or superstition? Would it help him travel to the afterlife?

Whatever the case, it wasn't the time to ask. We all needed to process, regroup, and then prepare.

There was still work to be done. I'd looked at the clock with my magical jeweler's loupe and had a sense of how to get it working again. Still, I was afraid to touch it until Fetch lured Pan and Tink away from Neverland to track what they would think was Noru emerging from The Fen early. If I made one false move and the hands started moving before then, they'd be tipped off to the fact that we had the clock in our possession.

That said, being patient while we knew the kids were still on that island and in real danger was tough. Especially Caleb.

"Let's all get cleaned up and change into clothes not covered in crocodile guts," I said to a nervously pacing Molly and the others. "Then I'll see if I can heat us something to fill our bellies with."

Hook didn't acknowledge that he'd heard my suggestion, but a moment later, he wheeled around and marched past us, towards the steps that led down to the personal quarters.

It was more than an hour later, and the sun was kissing the horizon when I headed below deck with a tray in hand. A rasher of bacon, some leftover potato soup, and a mug of ale.

Once I'd bathed and gotten the sweat and gore off and downed a few bites of soup, I was feeling less like a bag of shit. I could only hope the same helped James some, too. James. Hook. I was having trouble deciding which persona I truly saw him as. The man from my dreams? Or the pirate in front of me?

I sucked in a steadying breath when I reached his door and rapped gently. There was no answer, and I was about to leave the tray on the floor and go, but then I heard a snarl.

"Fuck!"

"James?" I turned the knob and opened the door a few inches. "Are you alright in there?"

A groan and a grunt. "I don't want to hurt you, my friend."

My hand shook as I shoved the door open the rest of the way to find him sprawled on his bed, brow bathed in sweat as his head tossed back and forth.

Nightmare.

I could so relate.

I hesitated for a moment and then crept forward. Better I woke him up, because he was reliving something hellish, and that was the last thing he needed right now.

I set the tray beside the softly glowing lantern on the table beside the bed as he rolled fitfully onto his stomach and kicked off the blanket, letting out a low groan.

He was shirtless and his back was covered in ink. Tideblessings. Dozens of them. Small, simple, and almost symbolic, as opposed to fully developed, detailed images, same as Cissy's had been. No color. All were black or had faded to varying shades of gray.

An ear surrounded by three lines radiating outward.

A jagged slash. It took me a second to realize it was a bolt of lightning.

Three wavy lines, faded and barely legible.

I held my breath, leaning even closer, barely

resisting the urge to trace one in particular with my fingertip. It was a tornado, darker and more saturated than all the others, it fairly pulsed with energy. But it didn't feel menacing or scary, just felt...*alive.*

I cocked my head and searched out another, this one a pair of crossed daggers and much more menacing. Despite the simplicity of each design, as I continued to look from one to the next, I realized they all had a different energy to varying degrees.

"There are a dozen more on the front."

I swallowed a gasp and drew back as Hook's gritty voice rumbled through the room.

"Can...will you tell me about them?" I asked gently.

He was silent for so long, I almost wondered if he'd gone back to sleep, but the fresh tension in his body told me different.

"It's okay, you don't have to. It's already been a long and terrible day. Rest, and—"

"I don't need rest. I need vengeance." The fury that had always come hand in hand when he spoke of vengeance on Pan and Tink was gone. Now his tone was bleak and solemn in a way that made me feel cold inside.

Had losing Tom been the last straw?

Suddenly, the thought of using the clock filled me with something like terror. He'd give it to me once the job was complete, and I'd achieve what I set out to. But to what end?

"Is Xander at the wheel?"

"He is. He just had some food and has us en route to Neverland." I pursed my lips and stepped back. "I'm going to go check on the others. Get some rest and I'll be back soon."

I was nearly to the door when his voice stopped me in my tracks.

"The ear is like a sonic boom. The crossed daggers make the user unerringly accurate at throwing knives."

"The three wavy lines?" I asked, making my way back toward the bed.

He rolled gingerly to his back, his expression grim.

"Water. I can call it…control it."

I thought back to the whirlpool caused by the wormhole and nodded. Wind and water. That's how he'd saved the Jolly Roger.

"And you can do," I waved my hand in the direction of his torso, "*all* of these things at will?"

"I can."

"Xander said that it's possible but rare to have multiple Tideblessings, but this is…a lot. How?"

He pulled himself up to rest his back against the wall and jerked his chin toward the edge of the bed. "Sit."

My fingers tingled with the need to reach out, to squeeze his arm reassuringly, because I could feel the tension and pain pouring off him. Instead, I sat and folded my hands in my lap.

"I grew up in an orphanage just like Pan," he began, his words halting at first, like they were being torn from his lips. "The Safehaven Academy for Unwanted Boys and Girls. I never met my parents. But from what I learned later in life, that was probably for the best. They weren't good people. The orphanage was… alright. For most of my childhood, at least. It wasn't until one particular teacher came aboard that things went bad. Hutchins wasn't just violent. He enjoyed causing pain. My time there once he arrived was almost more than I could take. I tried to run away once with a couple of friends. One of those friends was Tommy. The man you knew as Trick-Eyed Tom."

I stared at him. "Trick-Eyed Tom was Tommy? The kid you were in Neverland with?"

He nodded. "Pan and Tink took us from the orphanage at the same time. We met Miguel on the island, and he was already getting sick."

No wonder he'd been so loyal. They'd gone through so much together…

"And who was the other friend? Was it Xander?"

"No. After Tom and I escaped, he was able to heal my wound, and we headed to the nearest island. That's where we met Garth and Xander. Garth was a fishmonger. He'd already let Xander work for room and board and tried to pretend that he needed the extra hands, but truth is, he's as soft on the inside as he is crusty on the outside. He was good to us. We stayed a couple years, until we felt strong enough to make a plan. Then, we took to the seas in search of Noru." His expression darkened. "When Tom and I ran away from the orphanage, it was with a little girl named Sally," he said. "She was younger. Nine, maybe ten. She worshiped me, but I was too old to bother with her most days. Still…something about the way Hutchins had started looking at her…I knew things were about to go from bad to worse. Gods, I was so fucking arrogant. I thought I was strong enough to protect them both." His voice dropped. "I was wrong."

He lifted his head and looked me square in the face and I found myself wishing—not for the first time—that I'd been a true healer instead of a tinker or a fucking bird whisperer. I would have done anything to take away his pain.

"We managed to get as far as the outskirts of the camp," he continued. "But it was slow going. Sally's legs were tired, so I carried her on my back. After a few kilometers, my legs started cramping. I tried to push through, but they caught us." He squeezed the bridge of his nose between his thumb and index finger. His voice was void of emotion when he continued. "When Tom and I finally got out of the hospital a week or so later, Sally was nowhere to be found. It wasn't until years later, after I ran away from Neverland and went back to take care of some…business that I found out what happened from a maid who still worked there. While we were in the hospital, they'd found Sally stuffed in a closet in a dress covered in blood." He exhaled, long and slow. "The maids…they'd pitched in a coin each for a proper burial."

A lump rose in my throat. "I'm so, so sorry." This time, I didn't resist. I laid my hand on his shoulder, pressing my body close to his, offering what little comfort I could. My heart felt like ice in my chest, and I realized with a start that my shirt was wet with tears.

"That's… that's just—" I sniffled, swiping my sleeve across my face. "I don't know why the world has to be so cruel. Especially to children."

The Hollow had been an ugly place, and I'd seen suffering. But when I looked into Hook's eyes at that moment, I knew whatever I'd seen paled in comparison. Part of me wished this conversation was over, but knew that it was about to get worse...

"All that to explain about the tattoos. I've 48 in my lifetime. 24 of them are still with me today. Each of them represents a life I've taken."

So many lives…

My mind reeled as pieces of the puzzle fell into place. "When you kill someone, you absorb their magic," I whispered.

"Almost like Tink, right?" he said with a grim smile. "Disgusting."

"Not at all like Tink," I shot back, shaking my head furiously. "Are you kidding me? No. She chooses to steal from those kids. You didn't ask for this blessing-"

"Not a blessing," he cut in. "It's a curse, I promise you that."

"And that's why Tom wanted you to deal the final blow." The realization shook me to my core. "He wanted you to be able to take his power so you could become a Mend in case you or any of the crew needed healing."

"Exactly."

I let out a low gasp. "When you shot me out of the air, during The Devil's Gauntlet...that was Davy's magic."

"Fresh out of the box, if you will," he said with a nod.

"Why are some of the marks so dark and others so light?"

He tugged the blanket down, bearing his muscled chest. There, over his heart, was a symbol as black and saturated as the tornado on his back, only this one was a pair of bones in the shape of a cross. "Tom. His magic is brand new. If I use it, it'll get lighter and lighter until, eventually, it disappears."

"You don't get to keep the blessing forever?"

"It gets weaker with use."

"And the tornado?"

"Miguel. I've never used it, and I never will."

So he would always carry a piece of his friend with him.

"But there's another part to this curse," he continued. "The part that haunts me more than any other. I don't just get their magic. I also get their memories."

I thought back to his words days before, when he explained how Miguel had died when Pan used him as a human shield. I'd told him it wasn't his fault.

"That's not the way the universe looks at it."

I couldn't fathom how he possibly knew that, but now it all made sense. He felt responsible for Miguel's death, because, to his mind, if he hadn't been, he wouldn't have gained his power or absorbed the boy's memories.

"None of that makes you to blame. Not for Miguel's death, *or* Tom's."

He reached for the mug of ale and drained it before setting it down on the table beside the bed. "I'm not going to argue with you, Harmony. I tell you all of this for one reason and one reason only. I have sympathy for what Pan suffered at the hands of the adults sworn to protect him because I saw it through his eyes. You'd think that suffering would create empathy, but instead, it turned him into something just as bad. Which is why I would go through all of this and more to see him dead and buried. But once that's done? So am I."

My tongue felt thick and dry as I stared at him, dread closing over my chest like a fist. "What does that mean, James? Done how?"

"Done with this world." He held my gaze, his expression solemn. "And when I go, the curse goes with me."

I'd sensed it early on…the disregard for his own life. The relentless darkness inside him. But somehow, I thought that once he was able to complete his mission and stop Pan and Tink, he'd change his mind.

As I stared at his savagely beautiful face, I realized

he wouldn't. And worse? I couldn't even blame him. The only world he knew was one of suffering. His own and that of 48 other souls that had been etched on his body.

"Curse" was too soft a word.

It must've been a lifetime of torture.

I wouldn't try to change his mind, but maybe, tonight, I could offer him some small comfort.

I held my breath and slid my hand slowly across the sheet until I reached his fingertips, and I laced mine with his.

He tightened his grip, his onyx eyes snapping with hidden fire.

I could barely find my voice as I whispered, "Can I…lay with you?"

CHAPTER 34

"You don't want this, Harmony." His jaw flexed and he winced like my words had caused him physical pain. "Be smart and go, while you still can. What I have can't be fixed."

I bit my bottom lip to stop it from trembling as I climbed onto the bed beside him. This was crazy. Absolutely insane. If he rejected me, I wasn't sure I'd ever recover.

And if he didn't?

I knew I never would.

"I can see your wheels turning," he muttered, even as his eyes drifted to my mouth, making the breath catch in my throat. "You already know this can't end well. It's okay. You can still go…"

But he was already leaning into me, that musky scent of soap and sea filling my senses as surely as that silky, hypnotic voice. And when he lifted his arm and slipped that razor-sharp hook between the top two buttons of my shirt, any wheels that had been turning came to a screeching halt.

"I'm not going anywhere."

He flicked his wrist and my top button went flying, pinging off the wall. When his mouth finally met mine, his kiss was soft at first—achingly gentle, as if he was being held back by an invisible rope. But the second my tongue swept out to meet his, that rope snapped, and the kiss unraveled into something wild...something desperate.

I didn't back away. I couldn't. My heart was a thunderclap in my chest, far louder than the warning voice whispering in my head. I dove into the heat and longing and every unsaid thing between us as he cupped my face with his hand, his thumb stroking the edge of my jaw with a tenderness that shattered me.

Whether I died before ever leaving this story, or I lived for another thousand years, I would never forget the way this felt.

Never.

When we broke apart, it was only to breathe. He rested his forehead against mine, his voice rough. "This is wrong. I know it, and I'm not strong enough to stop..."

"You're stronger than anyone I know, and I don't want you to stop."

His low growl only added fuel to the fire, and I

made quick work of my shirt buttons, baring myself to his hungry gaze.

He captured one of my nipples between his teeth, hissing as it pebbled beneath his tongue. I plunged my hand into his hair, pinning him closer.

"Mmm, yes!"

His nimble fingers unfastened my pants and tugged them down to my knees. Then his mouth was on mine again as he cupped my hip and then curled his hand lower. I arched my back when he found my heated center, so wet. So ready.

"Ah!"

I had to blink back the sting of tears as he slid two fingers inside me, so sure, so deep that stars exploded behind my eyelids.

His hard chest pressed against mine, branding me with his heat as he worked me in a relentless rhythm. My heart raced, my breaths turning ragged. Every nerve in my body pulsed like a drumbeat, pounding toward an unbearable crescendo.

"You feel so good," he groaned against my mouth. "Just like in my dreams…"

I tore my lips from his on a gasp. "James, please—" My words caught, my mind barely able to form the thought.

He let out a rough growl before using the heel of his palm to grind against that tight bundle of nerves, enough to undo me completely. My world tilted, shrinking down to a pinprick where only he existed.

The heat of his body, the scent of his skin, the pressure of those torturous fingers, pushing me closer and closer to the breaking point.

His gaze burned into mine, dark and all consuming. "Come for me, Princess."

That was it—the spark that sent me over the edge. My vision blurred, and I heard myself calling his name in surrender.

"James!"

My body clenched around his fingers as I came, the waves of pleasure dragging me under before lifting me to some breathless, weightless place I'd only been to in my dreams.

Our dreams.

I was still shaking with the aftershock when I opened my eyes to find him staring down at me, his onyx eyes glittering with stark need.

"You're so fucking beautiful."

I wanted to say it back, because it was true. Instead, I reached for him…sliding my hand around the back of his neck, leaning in and nipping at his lip.

"Now you." I whispered the words against his mouth, body still humming.

"Captain!"

The shout felt like it had come from another world, and I was content to pretend it had as I pressed closer, my nipples grazing his chest.

"Captain! We've spotted them!"

James let out a groan and pulled back, his breath coming in harsh gasps.

"That's Xander…"

For one, frozen moment, we stared at each other, knowing that everything was about to change. That our stolen moment in the midst of this insanity was over.

I mourned its loss already.

"Harmony, I—"

"Don't say anything."

I didn't want false promises or apologies, and those were all he had to offer right now. We had a job to do, and we'd come too far not to see it done.

I tugged my clothes back into place with trembling hands as Hook stood to grab a shirt from his wardrobe. We dashed up to the main deck just in time to see Xander heading toward us, palming a telescope.

"Pan and Tink. I just saw them from the crow's nest. They're about a kilometer out and headed west, just like we planned!"

I reached into the pouch at my hip and tugged out my loupe as I leaned over the railing. It only took a few seconds of scanning the sky to spot the two fuzzy figures in the distance, zipping around overhead.

"Showtime," I said, nerves suddenly bubbling up inside me. I'd already studied the clock and felt pretty confident, but what if I was wrong? What if I couldn't get the hands moving?

All this would've been for nothing.

"I believe in you." I turned to see Molly standing a few yards behind me, wringing her hands.

If she believed in me, the least I could do was believe in myself.

I ran my hands over the clock. Small divots, tiny rivets, the hands of the clock rusted from being inside Noru for so long.

Opening myself to my magic, I pulled it through me and wove it through the clock, looking for...something. The clock wasn't one of my own creations, and it was far more than just a clock. There was magic curled through it—Tink's magic. Every time her magic brushed against mine, the energy sparked and hissed, like a pair of angry cats meeting in a dark alley.

I closed my eyes and tried to put the world around me away. Noru had taken a massive amount of power, without a lot of finesse.

This was the reverse. All the finesse and very little power.

Carefully, I pressed my magic deeper, looking for cracks in Tink's spell that she'd woven into the clock.

The gears seemed to be jammed, thick with her magic as if it were...stuffed in?

Wrapping my magic carefully around Tink's, I didn't try to break it, but instead pulled it out of the clock piece by piece, cleaning the gears.

Sweat dripped down my face and my palms were sweaty as I worked slowly, methodically until the gears were free and the clock was no longer full of her magic stuffing.

For a second, nothing happened, and bitter disappointment welled up in my chest. Then, the tiniest click sounded and the second hand moved almost imperceptibly.

"Holy shit! It w-"

The clock flew out of my hands and landed on the deck, skittering in wild circles as if possessed. Molly dove toward it, but before she could lay hands on it, a dark blob came shooting out. Moll let out a short scream and Xander pulled her behind him as Hook advanced.

"No!" I grabbed his arm as the black blob began to morph right before my eyes. One second, it was a shapeless mass, the next, it was the silhouette of a lean young man with a jaunty cap.

Pan's shadow...

It turned its head this way and that in seeming confusion. Then, it lifted its face to the sky. A moment later, it was airborne...and headed west.

"You did it! You fucking did it, you beautiful, magical, amazing princess!" Moll crowed, grabbing my arms and dancing me around the deck.

I couldn't deny, I was buzzing with energy and excitement myself, but mostly relief.

"That's my cue," Hook muttered with a grim nod, all business now.

Magic seemed to bubble up from his very soul,

spreading in every direction at once as he strode up to the helm. The winds surged overhead, and the violent roar of the roiling waves below drowned out everything else.

He bellowed, wielding both Tideblessings at once, his energy flaring even higher than it had when we'd escaped the whirlpool. And, as incredible as it was to watch, I couldn't shake the tinge of sadness that tugged at my heart.

The time for his revenge was upon us, and he could hardly wait.

I gritted my teeth, wishing I could've stopped any of this from happening to him in the first place. Revenge could be sweet. I'd seen it firsthand when Moll killed Heinrich, but it could never undo the horrible things that'd been done to her. James would bear those scars for the rest of his life, same as Moll.

Her fingers found my hand at that moment, and she laced her fingers with mine. "We're going to save them, Harm. No matter what."

I dipped my head in agreement, shoving my own fears aside. "Of course. And we'll make sure that no one ever has to go through this again."

I released her hand and picked my way carefully over to the clock, taking extra care not to lose my footing as the ship rumbled and shook from the ever-increasing speed. The magic inside it sent a tingle up my arm as I touched the smooth brass, and I was happy to see that it appeared undamaged.

"Can you tell what it is capable of?" I asked, turning to Xander as I latched back onto the railing.

"Other than act as a home for Pan's shadow to keep him from aging, it's hard to say. Wish I could feel the magic in it the way you can. Maybe I'd be able to tell you more about it."

"Maybe you'll be able to slow down time or something," Molly suggested. "That'd be a good little trick."

I nodded, staring down at it. Whatever it was, I had a deep sense that it wasn't going to come into play just yet. There was something more…complex about it, far different than the loupe. Like a magical labyrinth whose secrets I wasn't yet strong enough to find.

I stuffed the clock into my bag, turning to glance over the railing. Even though I couldn't use my magic in a way that could help Hook get us to Neverland, my role here wasn't done. Magical energy flooded my vision on silent command, and I couldn't help but be a little proud. There was hardly even a dull throb in my temples, and it took far less focus than I'd been expecting.

"Amazin. You've improved so quickly," Xander marveled.

"I think the trip to The Fen unlocked something in me," I admitted, scanning the horizon for any trace of Tink's magic.

"The opals are definitely a catalyst for the monsters that live there. And an improvement with a Tideblessing isn't always gradual. It has happened to me in a flash. Lion tried to attack me once, in the center ring at the circus. I scrambled halfway up the fence before I even knew what happened. That's how I found out what my blessing was."

"Why were you even in the ring with a lion in the first place?" Moll asked with a disapproving frown.

"Because being in the ring with a lamb wouldn't have paid the bills, lass," he said, his shrug visible in my peripheral vision.

I opened my mouth to interject, but a twinkle of light appeared in the distance before I could make a sound. "There! Off the starboard bow!"

The whooshing of the wind slowed as Hook turned to see where I was pointing, then whipped right back up into full force, the ship tilting slightly to the side as he yanked the wheel in the direction I'd indicated. "You sure?"

"Absolutely," I said, the twinkle growing to a full-on glow as I pressed even more magic into my eyes. There was no mistaking it. Visibly bright and sparkly, but now, with my enhanced magic, I could sense the sinister darkness that lay just beneath that surface glow.

Pulling back, I sucked in a breath. "And now, we wait." I spared another glance at Hook, wishing there was some way to lend my own magic to his struggle, but I didn't even know where to begin. Tinkering and the connection with Fetch felt easy, but all the rest of it was like a whole different beast. I was overwhelmed and underprepared.

My fingers dug into my palm as I sent up a silent vow that I'd work like a dog to master all of it if the fates could just see us through this and give me a hot second to breathe before throwing another obstacle in my path.

I pushed a little magic back into my eyes, immediately regretting the decision as the blinding, purplish light of Tink's shield magic came into view, just a few hundred yards in front of the ship.

"We're getting close!" I shouted, gripping the railing.

We were coming in hot, and had no time to slow the Jolly Roger down when it came time to dock. This was a full-on race, and the lives of the three Lost Boys we'd left behind hung in the balance.

The island flickered into view, as if appearing out of thin air, as we crossed the invisible barrier.

"You did it! Now get ready for a rough landing, everyone!" Hook shouted, the ship careening sideways as he turned us toward the side of the island where Pan's remaining ships were docked.

I looked up, sucking in a breath as a sudden new presence rushed up, tickling the very edge of my awareness. Were Pan and Tink really so close behind, despite Hook's efforts?

I let out a sigh of relief as Fetch soared back into view, tucking his wings back to dive directly toward us.

Good job, bud.

A sense of calm flowed over me as his familiar weight settled onto my shoulder.

The team was finally all here and ready to rumble. All that was left to do?

Kill an immortal, soul-sucking hobgoblin and her delusional man-child lover before they killed me and the people I cared about.

Simple.

CHAPTER 35

hen we stepped onto the shores of Neverland, the place was preternaturally dark and still in a way that made the hairs on the back of my neck stand up. It was evening, but surely it wasn't the children's bedtime yet. I would have expected to hear Caleb chattering away or Cissy bossing him around. Instead, there was nothing but the sound of waves lapping against the beach.

"Fuck," Xander muttered, scraping a hand through his hair as he scanned the island, holding the lantern he held in one hand higher. His gaze locked on the unlit house off in the distance.

"Nope," Molly said, shaking her head mulishly. "I'd know if something had happened. They're here somewhere. Maybe they just lost track of time on the other side of the island, picking bananas or something." She marched forward on a mission. "Cissy! Caleb! Tristan!"

she called, before pressing her thumb and forefinger to her lips and letting out a sharp whistle. "Can you hear me?"

I blew out a shaky breath as nothing but silence echoed back.

"We'll split up," Hook said. "Xander, you and Molly take the north side of the island. Me and Harmony will check the house and then head south if they aren't inside."

"Aye, Captain," Xander said, touching Molly's elbow and leading her away.

We'd barely taken three steps when Hook slapped his hand to the side of his face and let out a snarl. "What the hell was that?"

There was a rustling in the trees and my hand instantly went to my side, grasping for my whip. I loosed it with a snap, pressing my back against Hook so no one could roll up on us.

"Moll?" I called, unable to see her behind me now.

"We're okay! You guys?" Molly's voice came from behind me.

"Yup, something hit Hook in the face." I scanned the shadows, squinting. It was almost as if he'd been—

I broke off as a wild *whoop* echoed through the night, followed by a snarl and a shrill screech. Branches snapped and leaves crackled, and a moment later, two small figures shot out from the tree line, hurtling toward us. At first, it was hard to tell what they were— some sort of tiny creatures, maybe adolescent bears? I didn't recall hearing about bears on Neverland, but who knew?

Only when they reached the glow of our lanterns did I realize it was Caleb and Cissy, wearing a pair of sloppily painted masks that covered their noses and eyes, and armed to the teeth. Caleb with a tiny hatchet in one hand and a dagger in the other, and Cissy with her slingshot poised directly at Hook.

"Get away from her, you pestilent scallywag!" she hollered, firing another rock at Hook's head. This time, he dodged the missile and it flew past him, landing harmlessly in the sand with a *thunk*.

"Calm down there, little girl," Hook said, sliding his sword back into its scabbard. "We're not here to hurt you."

"I won't calm down!" she howled, bending low and charging him like a miniature bull. "Until you get away from our friends!"

"Yeah, get away from our friends!" Caleb mimicked, rushing past Hook and me, heading straight for Molly and a startled-looking Xander. When he reached them, he reared back and kicked Xander in the shin with all his might. The first mate let out a sharp yelp and pressed his hand against the boy's forehead, holding him three feet away as Caleb swung his hatchet aimlessly.

"Wun, Molly! I can take care of this guy!"

"Oh, Caleb…" Molly dropped to her knees in the sand and yanked him into her arms. "I'm so glad you're okay." Her chest heaved on a broken sob, and, while I would have loved to see the rest of their reunion, I noticed that Cissy and Hook were currently engaged in what looked like a slap fight.

"Stop it!" Hook snarled. "I said, stop it!" He cuffed her lightly on the side of the head, but she wouldn't be stopped, swinging wildly, kicking, punching, even snapping her teeth.

"I knew Tink had it wrong! They didn't want to leave us," Cissy yelled, not pausing her flurry of blows. "You stole them!"

"Enough!" I shouted. "Please, sweetie, you have to stop. He's not here to hurt you. None of us are. We're here to save you, but you have to listen—"

My words seemed to fall on deaf ears as she took a deep breath and doubled down, stomping on Hook's booted foot. It wasn't until he jammed his hook hand down the back of her shirt and lifted her into the air, leaving her to dangle, that she finally stopped flailing. Her face was scrunched and beet red, streaked with tears.

"Put me down, you big mean bully!"

Caleb broke away from Molly's embrace just then, parroting her words. "Yeah, put her down, you big mean bully!"

"Stop for a second and listen to what Harmony has to say." The voice came from the tree line. I turned to find Tristan standing there with Fetch perched on his shoulder. I hadn't seen the falcon arrive, but he'd clearly found his favorite seat before we got here.

"Why should we listen to you?" Cissy barked. "You might be the oldest, but you're not really my brother, like you always say. That means you don't get to tell me what to do."

"I'm the closest thing to a brother you're ever going to have, so shut up and listen. If they wanted to hurt us, your head would be stuck on that hook, and not just your shirt."

Cissy snapped her mouth shut and slumped, going dead weight in Hook's grasp.

He lifted her close to his face and scowled. "If I put you down, do you promise not to take another swing at me?"

Cissy stuck out her lower lip. "Nope."

"Eh, fine then. You hit like a girl anyway." He set her down on the ground more gently than I'd expected, then took three steps back—which, despite the serious-ness of the situation, almost made me grin.

Tristan padded over and stopped before me, glancing between me and Hook.

"She's making him sick, isn't she?" he asked in a low voice.

"She is," Hook replied.

"And the others before us?" His shrewd eyes flicked to Hook, his throat bobbing.

Hook nodded. "Yes. Dozens. Maybe hundreds."

Tristan winced, his shoulders hunching as if he'd

taken a physical blow. "I saw their clothes, and not just little kid sizes. At first, I didn't think anything of it, but then I realized, why did they leave them behind when they grew up and left? Wouldn't they take them wherever they went? I asked questions about them, but she never gave me a straight answer. So when Molly and Harm went missing last week, I started looking—really looking. Just yesterday I found a little cave on the other side of the island, where Tink always told us not to go. It was filled with bones...some of them old and bleached with time, some of them not. Was still trying to figure out what to do when you guys came back but...they don't ever let them leave, do they?"

Fucking hell. I knew I'd sensed evil there. Carnivorous bats, indeed.

"What are you talking about? You're not making any sense," Cissy said, yanking the mask off her face and tossing it onto the sand. Molly kept an arm looped around Caleb's shoulders as they and Xander moved closer.

"Why don't we go inside the house," Molly suggested gently. "Sit around the table where we can see each other and talk."

"I'm not letting *him* in *our* house. He's our nemesisisis," Cissy snapped, jabbing a dirty finger into Hook's flat belly and then spitting on the ground.

"Come on, Cissy. I'll let you pet Fetch," Tristan offered. "He might even sit on your shoulder if you mind your manners." He gave the bird a quick glance.

Something passed between them, and Fetch inclined his head almost in a nod.

A sizzle of awareness shot through me. So the boy had it, too, the same connection to animals I had—or some version of it. That explained why Fetch was so taken with him.

Cissy sent the falcon a longing look and then shrugged. "He doesn't even like me anyway; he never let me pet him before."

"I have a feeling he will this time. Come on, let's go inside and try."

The little girl puffed out her cheeks and blew a breath, sparing a glance at the sky above the cove. "Well, maybe it's okay for a minute…"

"Yeah, maybe for a minute," Caleb echoed, nodding.

Pan had been telling the truth about one thing. Now that I could see the boy's face close up, he looked worse than the last time I saw him—thinner, more frail, and I could hear a wheeze in his chest.

We had gotten here in the nick of time. Now to make sure we got out as well…

The group of us made our way to the house and stepped inside. It was strange being there. In some ways, it felt like we'd never left; fond memories flooded in. In other ways, it was like we'd never been here before. Now that I knew what it really was—a hotel of horrors—everything felt…different.

Tristan ignited some lamps and lanterns, then waved for everyone to sit at the big table. "They left a day and a half ago and told us to stay out of sight until they got back," he explained. "They told me if they weren't here by Saturday, to use the little boat and take the kids to Blackbriar and find an orphanage that would take all three of us. I got a feeling they were going to face off with Noru."

"They told you all that?" Cissy demanded, flopping into the seat closest to her and resting her chin on her hands glumly. "They didn't tell me any of it."

"I don't understand what's happening," Caleb lisped, brow furrowed in confusion. "Hook is our enemy, Molly. 'Member?"

The adults around the table shared a glance, and Molly pursed her lips. Then leaned forward, looking at each of the kids in turn.

"Every single one of you has been dealt a shit hand," she said. Cissy's lips twitched in approval at Molly's use of a cuss word. "It's not fair. It's not right. Each of you deserves better than what you've gotten so far in this life. And it guts me to tell you that things are going to get worse over the next few minutes before they get better. But I need you to know that I'm only telling you all this because I love you, all three of you. All right?"

The two younger kids nodded. Tristan shot her a dubious look, then inclined his head almost imperceptibly.

"Peter Pan and Tinkerbell are not well," Molly said carefully. "They have something…wrong in their heads that makes them seem really nice most of the time but also makes them do bad things sometimes. And I'm sorry to say they've been doing bad things to all three of you—to you most of all, Caleb." She threaded her fingers with his and gently rubbed her thumb across his hand. "Were you sick before you came to Neverland?"

He narrowed his eyes in thought, then shook his head. "Nope. I was sad, but I wasn't sick."

"That's because Tinkerbell takes the health of others and steals it for herself to make her magic strong. And that's what she's been doing to you."

There was silence as her words sunk in. But only for a moment.

"Take it back!" Cissy cried on a broken sob. She balled her fists on the table, glaring at Molly. "You take that back! Tink would never do that!"

"She would, and she has, girl. She did it to my friends, too," Hook interjected quietly. "I was one of you lot. In fact, you can go check right now, in the second bedroom down the hall on the left, under the windowsill. My initials are carved there: J.T."

"Your initials are C.H., for Captain Hook," Cissy corrected.

"That's what they call me *now*. Since Noru took my hand. But when I was a child—a little older than you— my name was James Tyler. Pan and Tink took me from an orphanage and brought me here. They would have made me sick just like Caleb if I'd let them. But I tried to escape with my friends so they couldn't hurt us anymore."

"Nope! You're a liar. You came to steal Pan's clock!"

"Go look. If you don't believe me, go see for yourself."

Cissy shoved the chair away from the table, its legs scraping across the floor, and the room stayed silent until she returned a minute later.

Tears streamed down her face, but the anger was gone, replaced by despair that felt like a kick to my stomach. I wanted to pick her up and hold her in my lap like a baby; I could tell Molly wanted to do the same. But even if Cissy wanted that comfort, there was no time.

Tristan bent close to her and Fetch extended his head like an offering. Cissy let out a sniffle and a bubble of laughter. "Hey, fella. You look different than last time I saw you," she whispered, scratching his feathers gently.

Fetch chortled in reply, and as much as I hated to break up the moment, the clock was ticking.

For real this time.

"There's still a lot to talk about, but we can't just sit here like this for much longer. I started the clock shortly before we arrived—they're going to be here soon, and we need to be ready."

It took me a moment to realize Caleb hadn't spoken in a while. When he did, his voice was hoarse.

"I could feel it," he said. "When she would read me

bedtime stories at night, she always seemed so happy, so I let her do it anyway. But I always felt worse when she was lying next to me reading."

Cissy scampered around the table and threw her arms around him. "I'm sorry. I didn't know!"She pulled away, swiping at her face. "Why did she only hurt Caleb?"

"She likes to have several kids here, so they stay happy and healthy and don't try to leave," Hook explained. "Your time might have come too, Cissy, but I can't say for sure. I've never heard of a Lost Boy who was a girl."

"They didn't try to take me. I was a happy accident. But I don't care," Cissy said fiercely. "If she hurt Caleb, she hurt me, he's like my brother. What do we do now?" The last of the tears in her eyes dried as a hint of the little spitfire I was used to came shining through. "I can help you catch her. Tink's been showing me how to use my Tideblessing. I can make stuff grow—sorta." She wrinkled her nose. "It's pretty slow at this point, though. I'm not sure how that'd help. Are we gonna take one of the boats and leave?"

"Molly and Xander are going to take you now," Hook said, "so that you'll be on one of the boats and ready to go. But we can't leave yet. If Pan or Tink see you out on the open sea on their way back, they might chase you down before you get away. We need you to stay out of sight while we take care of them."

"You're gonna try to kill them," Caleb said, more a statement than a question.

Hook bowed his head. "I'm sorry, son, but there really is no choice. They'll just keep doing this to other kids if we don't."

It was a hard truth for a child to hear, but lying to them now would only shake their already tenuous trust in us.

"Let's go now, all of you. Grab some of your things, but quickly," Molly urged, standing and motioning for them to follow. But before they even reached their bedrooms, a flash of light illuminated the sky outside the house.

"They're here," James said, drawing his sword.

He led the charge for the door, and I laid my hand on the hilt of my whip as I followed.

"You lily-livered scallywag!" Pan howled as we raced outside.

A flickering light skittered past, doing a loop-de-loop before settling in mid-air a few yards away.

Peter hovered beside Tink, red-rimmed eyes shooting sparks of fury. "You almost had us fooled. But I've come for my clock."

Tinkerbell's smile was a baring of teeth that left me cold inside. "And I've come for your heads."

CHAPTER 36

In spite of their bold words, Pan was breathing hard, and strands of hair stuck to his damp forehead. Even in the moonlight, I could see new lines carved around his eyes. He was already tired and looked older than the last time I'd seen him—the clock was doing its job.

Tink looked the same as I remembered, but there was a tightness to her features that hinted at something brewing just beneath the surface.

I could feel the motion of the clock in the pouch at my waist. So long as it kept ticking, they'd continue to grow weaker.

"You're surrounded," Hook said calmly, saber in his right hand, his iron hook glinting on his left.

Pan gave a bitter laugh. "I've beaten you before."

"I was a child. But then again, those are your favorite victims." Hook's smile was icy as he lifted his sword. "As I recall it, though, I did kill you. It was only your hobgoblin girlfriend's magic and Noru's bad timing that saved you. Killing you a second time is going to be a piece of cake."

Pan let out a guttural scream and lunged at James, blade flashing in the moonlight.

Steel clashed with steel, and Hook swung like a man possessed, using a brute strength that sent the smaller Pan skittering backward unsteadily. He pivoted and danced around, but James parried each blow in the nick of time, advancing on him without pause.

Hook skirted around a thrust, flowing into a counter attack with his sword, then right into a punch, slamming his fist into Pan's chest with a hollow thunk.

Pan gasped, rolling aside, but I had to turn my attention elsewhere as Tinkerbell darted my way in a blur.

"Give it to me!" she demanded.

I flicked my whip, magic sparking along its length. I snapped it forward, forcing her to swerve off-course, right into Xander. She spun midair in a blur, sending a cloud of shimmering dust as she danced right under the tip of his whip. He coughed, flailing to clear his eyes, but he brought his whip back just in time, somehow managing to crack it a second time, smashing it right through one of Tink's fairy-like wings.

She shrieked and a faint ripple distorted her lovely features, her mouth curving into something feral. It was only for a second before her fairy image snapped back in place.

"You're slipping, Tink," I said, setting my feet. "Something wrong?"

She hissed. "I don't need to be pretty to kill you, bitch." She shot toward me again, claw-like nails extended.

I sidestepped and slapped her across the shoulder with my glowing whip, directing its path with magic more than physical motion. Sparks flew as it connected, and she tumbled onto the sand, rolling twice before springing back up. Her wings flickered once again, revealing a pair of ragged, batlike membranes before shimmering back to gossamer.

Near the shoreline, Pan and Hook continued their dance of steel. Pan was still nimble, but the strain was starting to show. Hook exploited it, driving Pan closer to the water. They traded blows—Pan darting in and out with cautious, surgical thrusts, Hook parrying and hacking like he had all the time in the world.

A splatter of greenish blood stained the sand as Xander's whip caught Tink once again, this time in the face, revealing the hideous, elongated features beneath the illusion.

"You dare—?" she spat, floating higher. "I gave you and all the others everything…a childhood full of food and of games and adventure. And *this* is what I get for it?"

She unleashed a stream of fairy dust at me but,

instead of shimmering and gold, it glowed toxic green in the moonlight. My skin tingled, but I pushed through, swinging my whip in a wide arc. The tip glowed bright with energy, carving a searing line across Tink's arm. She tumbled in midair, landing hard on her feet. Her wings drooped, now half-tattered, no longer shimmering. She was taller than before, her limbs thin and angular. Hollow cheeks, large eyes, and beastly fangs.

I heard a furious shout—Hook. Pan was trying to lunge past him toward me, but Hook drove him back with fierce thrusts of his saber. Sand flew under their feet. Their blades locked once, twice, then Pan slipped free, batting Hook's arm aside. Hook grunted in pain, stepping back to steady himself.

"They're not dead. Why are you saying that? Miguel was an accident…"

James roared with renewed fury and reeled off half a dozen blows, backing Pan further and further toward the beach. "Accident? You used him to save your own hide. And the rest of them, they're nothing but a massive pile of bones in that cave she forbid us all from going to."

Pan's expression shifted. "She said—" He flicked a glance at Tink. "She said we released them. She said we only took enough energy to keep going. She wouldn't—"

Hook sneered. "All these years, and you *still* haven't figured it out? Either you're a fucking idiot, or you buried your head because you didn't want to see it."

Tinkerbell snarled. "He's just saying this to break us apart. Finish him and then get the fucking clock before we're out of time. I'm using up all my energy trying to slow your aging, damn it!"

But Pan's resolve was slipping. And, ruthless as ever, Hook seized the chance, sidestepping a half-hearted thrust before slashing his blade across Pan's side, dropping him to one knee. Pan cried out, his sword trembling in his grip as he slapped a hand over the bloody, gaping wound.

Tink howled, shifting her focus away from me.

"Bastard!" She launched at Hook, her now-monstrous features contorting with rage. Her batlike, demonic wings carried her just high enough to dive-bomb him, claws out. Hook twisted aside at the last moment, but she raked his shoulder, sending up a spurt of blood as her jagged claws sliced into his flesh.

I tried to intervene, but illusions sprang up again—this time half-formed shapes of swirling dust. I wasted precious seconds shredding them with my whip as Tink landed at Pan's side, throwing up a magical barrier at the last second to deflect my attack.

Pan struggled to his knees, looking up at her. "Tink?" he rasped. "Is it true? Did you lie about letting them go?"

"Don't listen to him!" Tink shrieked. "I– I love you. He's trying to trick you."

Pan hesitated, sword pointed at Hook, but his hands shook. Wrinkles creased his skin even as I watched and his cheeks had begun to hollow.

The clock was really taking its toll now.

"Think about it, Peter. All the pieces are there…You already know the truth," Hook said, advancing on him again, sword first. Using his first name, drawing him in —smart, it was very smart.

Pan's expression faltered, and he let his sword clatter to the ground, his eyes flitting toward Tink. "We were supposed to be helping them. You couldn't…"

I winced as her hand snapped to his jaw, but it wasn't an attack. Instead, she pulled him closer, leaning in for a kiss. As their lips parted, she swiped a tear from his eye.

"Everything I've ever done has been for us. It's me and you against the world, just like always. Don't let them take that from us."

He turned back to us, his lips curving into a sad smile as his hands strayed to his chest. "It was never supposed to be like this…" He ripped open his shirt, revealing the faint amber light at the center of his chest —the piece of Tink's heart, which she'd shared with him all those years ago. "But, no matter what she's done, I won't let you have her." He plunged his palm into his chest, his face contorting with agony.

Tink gasped, arching her back as a wave of energy flowed from him to her. "Pan, you can't, you'll—"

He dropped to the ground with a thud, his hair

graying, his face collapsing in on itself as he aged a dozens of years in mere seconds.

Tink let out a wild snarl as her hobgoblin body became more solid, her wings mending themselves. A swirl of illusions danced around her again, forming razor-sharp shapes that crackled with energy.

"You see?" Tink said, voice hitching. "He gave it all…he gave me everything. *This* is love." She turned on us, illusions closing in. "And it will be his love that saves me!"

I braced myself. My whip glowed, but I wasn't sure we could stand against her now.

Suddenly, I heard a commotion behind us. The door to the house slammed open, and footsteps began pounding across the sand. Cissy's voice rang out.

"Stop! Please!"

She tore away from Molly's hold and sprinted into the fray, stumbling toward Tink.

"Cissy, get back!" I yelled.

She ignored me, tear-filled eyes locked on Tink. The illusions shimmered, some lunging for Cissy, but Tink waved them aside with a hiss. "Not this one! Leave her alone."

"Please," Cissy said, pressing her small hands together. "No more fighting. You don't have to hurt them, Tink. I know you don't want to."

Tink's expression wavered, and her jagged wings twitched. "You wouldn't accept me," she whispered, voice rough. "None of them ever did."

Cissy shook her head. "I would. I do! What you look like doesn't matter to me." Tink's face once again flickered between that of a fairy and her true form, her expression shifting from fury to despair. "I just need to know…Were you going to hurt me like you did Caleb?"

"Never!" Tink said fiercely, eyes blazing. "Little girls suffer enough in this world. I love you, Cissy."

The little girl reached out to lay a hand on Tink's cheek and the illusions around them faltered.

"Hook!" Xander shouted, sprinting forward in a blur, his whip extended. The lithe strip of leather curled around the little girl's waist and he yanked hard, sending her skittering across the sand even as Hook lunged with his saber.

I watched in horror as he ran her through, piercing the amber glow in her chest. She howled, arching forward, eyes wide with shock. The illusions collapsed instantly as Tink convulsed, wings flapping uselessly. A sickly green energy rushed from her body into Hook, and he collapsed, leaving his sword buried deep in her chest.

Tink sank to her knees. Dark green blood poured from the wound, and her hobgoblin face twisted with pain. Cissy burst into a wailing sob as Tink let out another bloody cough, her gaze shifting toward the near-motionless Pan. She reached toward him, laying her hand on his chest and then slumped, the last shimmer of amber flickering before going dark.

It was over.

Cissy collapsed to her knees beside Tink. Molly and the boys ran up, gathering around her. Xander dropped to Hook's side, feeling for a pulse as I hurried toward them on shaking legs.

Had taking her evil inside him been too much for him to take?

"He's alive," Xander said, voice tight. "But he's out cold."

Thank the gods.

But my initial burst of relief was short lived as I took in the scene around me.

Tinkerbell's body looked pitiful in the moonlight, monstrous features slack in death. Pan's gray hair fluttered in the breeze; his boyish features distorted with wrinkles. And as the moon shone down on the quiet beach, I couldn't shake the hollow feeling inside me.

I took Hook's hand in mine and pressed my face against his chest. The sound of his slow, steady heartbeat kept time with the ticking of the clock in my pocket.

We'd done it. We'd won…So why did I feel so lost?

Maybe it was because part of me knew that there *were* no true winners here. Maybe it was because, in spite of coming out on top, we were all leaving this place with wounds that would become scars.

Or maybe it was because I knew, deep in my heart, that Captain James Tyler Hook had a date with death…

And now that the deed was done, there was nothing stopping him from keeping it.

CHAPTER 37

"That should do it," I murmured as I piled the last of the stones onto the makeshift tombs we'd created for Pan and Tink. Swiping my hands on my pants, I took a step back, surprised that the heaviness in my chest hadn't lifted even a little.

A quick glance around told me I wasn't the only one feeling it.

Cissy's dirty face was streaked with the tracks of her tears, and even Tristan's eyes were red. Caleb pressed his face into Cissy's armpit, while Molly stood over them, her arms wrapped around all three like a mother hen.

"It'll be okay," she murmured gently. "I know it doesn't feel that way right now, but it will. I'm so sorry you had to suffer this terrible thing."

"I would've loved her anyway," Cissy said, wiping her nose across her sleeve with a broken sob. "If she asked me, I would've let her have my energies, too. Nobody was as nice to me as she was…not even Mrs. Crandall at the orphanage, and she used to give me two puddings some days. I know Tink hurt Caleb, but I think she didn't want to do it. Do y-you?"

Her voice broke on a hiccup, and Molly tugged her closer, patting her hair gently.

"I think Tink and Peter had a lot of bad things happen to them when they were young. Things that weren't their fault, just like you three did," she said softly. "And, for a time, they tried to move past it, but they couldn't seem to do it. So to answer your question, do I think either of them truly wanted to hurt any of you? I don't. But they had a choice to take a different path, and they did it anyway. That wasn't fair of them."

"I know! It was so bad. She made Caleb real sick, but…"

Cissy buried her face in her elbow, and I wanted to scoop her up in my arms like a baby. Instead, I hung back. Moll was doing a better job than I ever could at comforting them.

"You can still be sad that they're gone. You can still miss her, and remember the things you loved about her while understanding that she did some very bad things."

"Will we do bad things and hurt people when we get growed up?" Caleb whispered.

"Nope." Moll shook her head and bent low to meet him at eye level. "Because you, young sir, have the sweetest of hearts. All three of you," she added as she straightened and met each of their gazes. "Even after everything you've been through, you're so amazing and kind. You're smart, and funny, and you care about each other, and watch each other's backs. I can't wait to see..." she trailed off and cleared her throat, managing a smile. "I just know you're going to turn out to be amazing adults."

Fetch picked that moment to light onto my shoulder, catching my attention, which was a blessing. I couldn't bear to listen to it anymore.

The plan was to bring the children back to stay with Garth, who would find them each a good home. In the meantime, they'd have three square meals a day and a kind person looking after them. It wasn't the same as having a young mom and dad who could play with them every day and take them on adventures, but it was better than what most kids in The Hollow had, and that would have to be enough.

I let out a sigh and turned to see Hook standing at a distance with his back to me. Picking my way across the sand, I headed to join him.

"Are you alright?" I asked, laying a hand on his shoulder and trying not to flinch as he pulled away.

"Tinks memories," he rasped. "They're so twisted and sad and terrible. She was a madwoman, but what she suffered on the way to that..." he trailed off and pinched his eyes shut, "The things she did afterward? I'm not sure if I can bear the weight of it while staying sane myself. She's a part of me now. Hard to swallow, that."

I covered my mouth with my hand, willing myself not to be sick.

He let out a bitter laugh as his eyes opened and he stared at the burial site. "And now the pair of them get a nice little funeral by the sea, mourned by these poor fucking kids who still care about them in spite of it all, while the countless boys they murdered are nothing but a pile of bones in a dark cave, mourned by no one. And this is the justice I spent half of my life fighting for?"

The pain rolled off him in waves, and I let out a steadying breath as I tried not to let them consume me.

"*We* mourn them."

"You didn't even know them," he shot back, his voice sharp as a whip crack. "But I do. Through Tink's eyes. Watching as they adored her, and did anything they could to win her affection, only to have her suck them dry at the bitter end while they pleaded…She gave each of them a chance, you know, or at least that's how she saw it. Revealed her true form to them, in that boneyard of a cave. And, the moment they screamed or ran, she'd suck out the rest of their life force, shaming them all the while for not knowing what unconditional love was. They died confused, afraid, and alone."

"No." I blinked back tears and shook my head. "They *weren't* alone. They had each other. Just like Miguel and Sally had you."

"Fat lot of good it did 'em." He scrubbed a hand over his jaw and shot me a bewildered look through blood-shot eyes. "This is all I've thought about for the last fifteen years—finding a way to avenge their deaths. Thinking that, if I could make Pan and Tink pay for what they did, maybe it would ease my own guilt for having been the one to get away. Now it's done, and nothing's changed. They're still gone, and this hole inside of me is still there, but blacker than ever, because now I see…I see it all."

"You're wrong." I swallowed past the throbbing ache in my throat and leaned closer, wishing I could take even an ounce of his pain away. "What you did changes so many things. You saved those kids' lives—Caleb's, for certain. Look at him." I tipped my chin toward Molly and the children.

James reluctantly followed my gaze.

"He's so thin he can barely stand. Purple bags under his eyes, and his skin is almost see-through. If you hadn't done what you did, he would've been dead within days, and you know it. Then it would've been Tristan's turn." At the sound of the boy's name, Fetch perked up, turning his head. "You want to go see your friend?" I asked the falcon, stroking his downy chest. "He's over there."

Fetch didn't need further prompting. He took flight toward Tristan, whose troubled face cleared the moment he saw the falcon coming.

"James, you saved an eternity of future Lost Boys,

and the ones in that cave have finally been found. *You did that*," I continued, taking him by the chin and tugging his face toward mine. "Tonight, once we've got the kids to bed, let's have a ceremony to honor the young lives lost. Maybe that will help—"

"Nah." He pulled away with a grim shake of his head, the sadness in his eyes fading to leave nothing but grim acceptance behind. "The only thing that's going to help me right now is a bottle of rum. I'll meet you all back on the ship."

He pulled away and strode off without a backward glance.

I wanted to follow him, but I knew he needed time and space. Instead, I headed back over to Molly and the kids.

"We should probably go soon. It's been a long day, and the kids should eat and get settled for a good night's sleep."

We started for the docks, but Cissy suddenly broke away and dashed back to where Pan and Tink were buried. Pulling a throwing dagger from the pouch at her hip, she laid it gently on the stones. Then, she pressed her fingers to her lips and touched the makeshift headstone before sprinting back to us.

"We can't leave her without a weapon," she said. "Just in case anybody tries to fuck with her."

That got a grin out of me and Molly.

"Ooh," Caleb gasped, eyes wide. "You're not supposed to say that word!"

"Who're you gonna tell? I don't have a mom, so bully for you," Cissy shot back, poking him in the ribs.

The gallows humor was familiar, and the children fell into an easy rhythm, teasing back and forth as Tristan murmured softly to Fetch, scratching the falcon's head and neck.

Kids were so resilient, and these three were tougher than most. They'd be okay. But as I glanced at Molly, watching the children in turn, I couldn't help wondering if she would be as resilient.

By the time we reached the ship and boarded, though, my thoughts had drifted. Molly took the kids to the galley for soup and bread while I went looking for Xander.

I'd done my best not to think about it until now, but once we dropped the kids off in town, our next stop was the edge, where Molly and I would once again leap into the abyss and turn the page. I was getting mighty sick of goodbyes, and I knew this time would be worse than the last.

I was passing by the card room when I nearly collided with Xander as he rounded the corner. He caught me by the shoulders to keep me from stumbling.

"Hey, ho there," he said with a small smile. "Where's the fire?"

"I need to talk to you," I blurted, grateful to see his friendly face. Moll had told him about the prophecy and pretty much everything else the night before when

I'd gone to Hook's room. Knowing I didn't have to lie or hide the truth from my mentor and friend anymore had lifted an anvil of guilt off my chest, making it just a little easier to breathe, although you wouldn't know it now.

Now, it was like the weight of the world was back on me, and I could feel every single ounce of it.

I continued on, barely keeping my voice steady. "I thought once I had the clock, it'd be like last time—I'd just know what to do. But this time I'm not sure. What if I go through all of this, find my way back to my people, and still feel empty inside? I want to be brave and face this next hurdle head-on. I want to leap off that page and into the next story without any fear. I'm just…not sure I can."

"Being brave isn't about being fearless, Harmony," Xander said quietly. "It's about accepting that some things are scary and not letting that stop you. You're all tangled up inside right now. Anyone would be. But that's when you rely on your gifts, yeah? Sit down with that opal in your hand and close your eyes—connect with the power inside you—the right path will make itself clear. I truly believe that."

My eyes welled up, and his face blurred. "I'm going to miss you so much."

"I'm going to miss you too, lass." His green eyes darkened with pain, and he let out a soft hiss. "Both of you."

I squeezed my eyes shut and bit back a groan. How

selfish. Here I was, unloading on him about my problems when he was about to lose the woman he'd fallen head over heels for.

"Xander, I'm sorry. I wish I could tell you we'll be back, but I don't know how any of this works. I hope… maybe someday—"

"Nope," he cut in. "It's alright. Don't make promises you can't keep. No matter what happens, I'll never regret meeting her. Or you."

The thought played in my mind on a loop long after I went to bed later that night. The list of people who felt that way was real fucking short these days. Moll and I seemed to be the harbingers of pain.

That's what revolution was though, wasn't it? Sacrifice for the greater good—The Speaker would've been proud. But if I was the catalyst, why did it feel like the people sacrificing the most were decidedly not me?

The soft snores of the children had me rolling to my side and peering down at the floor.

Molly had made them a bed from feather pillows she'd gathered from the empty crew cabins. She'd used extra blankets and clothes pins to make a fort around them, which even Tristan had agreed was sort of neat.

It was only when I hung my head over the side of my bunk that I realized Moll had left her bed at some point and hunkered down with them. Caleb must've shifted during the night and his foot was firmly buried against her rib cage, but if she was bothered, it didn't show. In fact, she had the most peaceful smile on her face...

My stomach lurched as the word sacrifice floated to the forefront of my mind once again.

And I wept.

"LOWER THE ANCHOR!" Hook called as the ship slowed to a stop.

It had been a long, restless night, and my eyes were on fire from lack of sleep. At least that was my excuse for the tears that flowed down my face unchecked.

Hook had run The Devil's Gauntlet for the first time an hour earlier, in Tom's honor. After securing his trick-eye just above the crow's nest so he could watch over the Jolly Roger in death, he'd buried his hook into the sail and slid down like a right fucking pirate, to the shouts and cheers of all.

But the bittersweet moment had faded fast as we approached the docks, and I swiped the tears from my eyes for Moll's benefit as she stepped up beside me. "So tired. And this stupid pollen is only making it worse."

"Yeah, same here." She let out a loud sniffle and then smiled brightly as she turned away. "Let's go, kiddos! The Captain says it's alright if I walk you over to Garth's house and get you settled in."

Caleb, Cissy and Tristan trudged forward, and the

wary expression on all three faces made my stomach hurt.

"You guys are going to be just fine. Hook has sent more than enough to ensure that you're well cared for."

Cissy's eyes narrowed and she shot a glance up toward the captain, who manned the wheel. Although they knew the truth now, it was going to take some time for them to reconcile the villain Pan and Tink had painted him to be with the person who had saved them.

Moll must've sensed their reluctance because she continued on.

"I know you haven't met him, but I can vouch for Garth, too. He helped me and Harm when we needed a friend. He's a good, kind man." She took Cissy's hand, who took Caleb's in kind, as she led them toward the plank that Xander was setting up to cross over to the dock. "I also spoke to him, and while he doesn't have any pets yet, he did say he would consider getting a kitten while you are all with him if you all agree to take care of it. What do you think of that?"

"And I can stop in from time to time as well and check in on you lot if you like," Xander said as he finished the job and perched his hands on his hips with a smile. "Maybe bring you some gifts from my travels, ay?"

Cissy and Caleb shared a look and nodded, but Tristan didn't acknowledge the first mate's words. His chin had been buried against his chest since early that morning, one hand on Fetch, the other fisted into a ball at his side.

"I'll be back in an hour or so," Moll said as she set to lead the kids down the plankway.

I nodded. "Fetch can go for the walk with you all." I stared at the falcon for a long, quiet moment, the thousands of memories we'd shared flitting through my mind in a dizzying rush, and I could've sworn he smiled. I didn't need to tell him what he had to do. He already knew. Like my father had left Fetch for me, when I was most vulnerable, I would leave him here to protect my heart.

I sucked in a breath and then yanked Moll into a quick, hard hug before shoving her away so fast she nearly toppled over.

"Okay then…" she said with a low chuckle. "See you in a bit."

It wasn't until the four of them had made it halfway down the long pier that I waved a hand to Hook, who was awaiting my signal.

"Help me pull up the plank, Xander," I muttered, my throat on fire as I bent low.

"What are you doing, lass?" he demanded, only to draw back like I'd punched him in the gut a moment later when the realization sank in.

"I'm being brave, what's it look like I'm doing?" I sobbed, snot running down my face as I tugged to no avail. "Don't make it harder on me than it has to be. Help me pull up the fucking plank!"

To his credit, he got straight to work, and we were on the move a few moments later.

"Harm…what the hell? Where are you guys going?" Molly called, tugging the kids to a stop on the side of the street.

"They're taking me to The Edge." I wanted to say more, but it was all I could manage.

"No." She dropped Cissy's hand and broke into a jog back onto the dock. "What about the rest of the story?"

"That's *my* story. This is yours. You're fine not being a rich man's wife, Moll, but I refuse to be the reason you don't get to be a mother."

"Wait!" She was running alongside the dock to keep pace with the ship now, her cornflower blue eyes so wide, I could see them at a distance. "Please…don't do this."

But, unlike the last time I'd left her behind, I could see it in her face already. Mixed in with the same heavy grief that sat on my chest like an elephant;

Relief.

Hope.

Something that felt like the very first embers of joy.

And, for the first time in a story that had almost reached its end, it all finally clicked into place. This page right here was written exactly as it was meant to be.

"We're still like eggs and bacon, me and you!" she sobbed as the dock ran out, and the wind caught our sails.

"We are." I swiped at my eyes, desperate for one more clear look at her gorgeous face. "Amazing together, but still pretty good apart!"

"This won't be the last you see of me, Harmony Marie Fallowell. Count on that!"

I breathed in the words and tucked them close to my heart. Truth or not, I had to believe them.

I was still staring off the starboard bow an hour later, long after I'd lost sight of her. Not for a single second did I question my decision, but my chest felt like an open wound that would never heal.

"She's going to be great."

I turned at the sound of Xander's voice and found him a few yards away with a bottle of rum in hand. He held it out as he approached to lean on the railing beside me.

"And you best believe I'll know it if she isn't. She doesn't have a Da to ask, so I might as well let you know now. I'll be hoping to make her my bride, if she'll have me."

She would. I'd seen the way she looked at him, but it wasn't my place to say one way or the other.

"I hope you're thinking of switching careers, then. She doesn't need to spend her life waiting for James to come to her door with news that you've been sliced in two by some rival pirate gang or eaten by a sea monster."

That probably wasn't my place either, but it was Moll, and she was the only family I had.

I blinked back a fresh wash of tears as Xander took a healthy swig and then handed me the bottle.

"I did what I done to see it through with the Captain. Now that it's over, I plan to retire and buy myself a little farm with some sheep and chickens and a few mango trees. I'm hoping I can reach out to my daughter, Lorelei, and see if she will come visit."

I laid a hand on the whip coiled at my waist, proud that I only hesitated an instant. Xander's fingers closed over mine before I could tug the weapon free.

"Don't even think about it, lass. That's yours no matter what the letters etched on it say. I made it as a way to feel close to her when she was far away. Lorelei is a gentle little lamb with no need of a whip. If she comes to the farm, I'll make her something more fitting."

I blew out a sigh and took a long pull from the bottle. I already felt like I was leaving so many pieces of myself behind, it was a relief to not have to leave this, too.

The liquor burned a path to my gut, but I took another swallow before handing it back over. I couldn't help but note that James had kept himself secluded in the captain's chair since we'd left Neverland. Not that I'd been expecting a declaration of love or anything. I did wish we could spend a little time alone before I had to go. Leaving Duncan back in Alabaster had been hard. Why did this feel ten times worse?

Because you've known this man longer than your mind will even let you remember.

Because he's lived in your dreams for a lifetime.

And the final truth that I hadn't even admitted to myself until right now…the one that blew me wide open, and almost made me go to him, right then and there.

Because you are two sides of the same coin…a coin stamped in C'an Saas.

"We'll be reaching The Edge soon," Xander mused as if reading my mind. He jerked his chin toward the dusky, purple sky as the sun fell off the horizon. "Another few hours and—"

I saw it at the same time as he did. The gaping black holes that dotted the surface of the water up ahead. Dozens of them that seemed to be getting larger by the second. And suddenly my love life faded into the background.

"Wormholes!"

"Shit." Xander rushed headlong up the steps toward the helm. "Hook!" he bellowed. "Trouble ahead!"

"I see it," Hook shouted back, stepping into view. "She's got a bead on us for sure, and she's not going to stop until you're gone." He locked eyes with me. "I have to use all my energy to control the ship and avoid the wormholes, so I can only use the wind to push us so fast. You're going to have to try using the clock and speed up time or we'll never make it."

I narrowed my gaze and let the idea sink in. Almira

didn't actually exist in our timeline, which meant only our progress should be affected. Or at least, that's what my tinker brain told me.

It was a solid plan, assuming I could make it work. And, as much as I hated to use the clock's precious energy, there was no other choice.

I reached into my pouch and yanked it free, holding it in my hand as I whispered encouraging words under my breath.

"You can do it. Just close your eyes and feel the power inside you."

I set one finger on the hour hand and then did just that, reaching for the well of magic that lived inside me.

"It's working…it's workingggggg…"

Everything around me began to stretch and streak. Even sound grew distorted and jumbled. I tried to focus as time and space whizzed past in a dizzying blur. How would I know when to stop?

But I should've trusted myself, because when I instinctively lifted my hand away from the clock face, everything seemed to come to a shuddering stop.

"This is it. This is the spot!" James shouted. "Xander, come help me hold the ship steady. Harmony, head to the plank!"

"Take care, my friend," I called to Xander as he rushed off, resisting the urge to get one last glimpse at James.

There was no time for that. The window was closing fast.

I hurried to the plank, heart hammering out of my chest as I inched my way across it. Had the sea been so choppy before? Surely not...

"You can do it, Harm," I whispered, breathless with terror. "One more stop, then it's off to C'an Saas. And there's no place like home."

I stared down at The Edge, willing my feet to move. *Three, two, one...*

"Fuck!" I snarled, taking a step back. "You're such a chickenshit. Just go!"

Five...four...three...two...

"Stop stalling or the worms are going to eat the ship, and Xander won't be able to get back to Molly."

My stomach took a dive as I wheeled around to find James standing directly behind me.

"What are you doing here?" I managed, the whipping winds carrying my words away almost as quickly as I spoke them. "It's a little late for goodbyes."

"Goodbyes?" His lips quirked into a half-smile. "You didn't think I was going to let you go without me, did you?"

I most certainly did, but my brain was all a jumble as I tried to make sense of what was happening.

"This is my destiny, not yours. You've already given up enough."

His ebony eyes still swirled with a pain so deep, I could hardly fathom it. "What would I be giving up, drinking and gambling my days away? I'd rather see how the story ends."

"I don't even know if *I'm* going to see how the story ends," I admitted with a helpless shrug. "So far it's been dodging one near-death experience after another."

His lips twitched and he inclined his head. "Sounds perfect to me."

My already shaky legs nearly went weak with relief. Not just because I didn't have to go it alone—although I couldn't deny, that was a piece of it. But because James T. Hook would be the one by my side.

Maybe he'd never heal. Maybe we'd both die in the process. Maybe we'd get all the way to the end, only to find that he'd still rather be dead than alive. For now, though, we both still had a chance.

I was about to reach for his hand and count down from three for real this time, but the breath was knocked out of me a second later as he rushed forward, curled an arm around my waist, and dove off the edge of the world.

"No more stalling, Princess. The clock is ticking!"

We tumbled through the air in a freefall, but this time was different than the last, when I'd left the Cinderella story with Molly. The atmosphere shimmered around us—not dark like before, but dazzling, almost blinding, as if we'd been sucked into a prism. Wind howled, tearing at our clothes, roaring in our ears, but just beneath it, another sound…a chime-like singing that seemed to come from inside my own head.

Lalalalala, lalala, lalalahh
Lalalalala la lahhhhhh!

The space around us twisted then, tearing our hands apart as we were swallowed down into a funnel of wind, not unlike what the whirlpool had nearly done.

We were inside a tornado, I realized with a wave of dread. But not a gray collection of swirling clouds. This one pulsed with color, its bands like pulled ribbons of candy. Red, orange, yellow, green...all whirling in a dizzying display.

Hook grunted beside me, reaching for me in slow motion as though the air had thickened into syrup. I moved to make a grab at him and barely caught the edge of his coat.

"Hold tight!" he shouted, his voice stolen instantly by the roaring wind as he managed to clasp my hand.

It was a good call, because a moment later, the world turned sideways, then upside down. Words flickered past, jumbled and disjointed, but this time they weren't completely unreadable—just unfinished. *W E L...O Z* each letter swirled past in streaks.

The pressure built, rising in my ears, squeezing at my chest, and then everything went dead silent. We hovered in the air for one impossibly long moment and I risked a glance down to see endless green fields far below us, a ribbon of yellow winding through it like a scar.

Then gravity remembered us, and we dropped like stones.

I barely held back a scream when a sudden gust of warm, sweet-smelling wind caught us just before impact—Hook's Tideblessing from Davy to be sure. It was enough to slow us down some as we hit the field of grass and wildflowers. Our hands were again pried apart as we rolled and tumbled until we finally came to a stop.

My head spun and my stomach seized with the urge to retch as I tried to get my bearings.

"Holy shit. That was—"

"Stay down and be quiet!" Hook hissed, already pushing himself to a low crouch. "Someone's coming."

"Hello?" a muffled voice called in the distance. "Hello, are you alright over there? I saw the storm and I—"

I blinked furiously into the bright afternoon sunshine that was all-but eclipsed a moment later by the silhouette of a tall, broad-shouldered man, with a snowy-white falcon perched on his shoulder.

He leaned closer, and my heart dropped to my knees as I searched his familiar features, in stunned disbelief.

"Duncan?"

UP NEXT

Turn the page for a preview of Neverthorn,
a dark academia fantasy novel coming in July 2025.

And don't miss the conclusion to Harmony's story.
Inked In Emeralds is coming very soon.

NEVERTHORN: CHAPTER 6

I was just yards away from laying my hands on the crème de la crème of gemstones when I smelled trouble. Literally. The stench of rotten eggs that had me scrambling for cover in the tiny apartment. The foul odor was the hallmark of a particularly shady binding spell. It was cast by a half-assed Dwimmer who probably thought I was too dumb to know the difference between magic and a leaky stove.

Fool.

Moving slowly through the third-story apartment that was most certainly not my own, I kept low to the ground, flicking my fingers around my body, concealing myself in shadows.

Was this the right way of casting this particular spell?

No.

Effective as hell?

You bet.

As long as my luck held, and the spell didn't fizzle out on me.

Untraceable, too, which was rather handy seeing as it wasn't on the Thaumaturgy Senate's list of "acceptable" spells.

Creeping along on my belly, I tucked myself under the ruffled bottom edge of a flowered couch cover that must have been manufactured in the seventies. Then I held my breath. This turned out to be a smart move, as I met the empty gaze of a leathery, mummified rat that had all but melded into the floorboards, right under my nose. I turned my head and grimaced, watching for feet to pass by the couch, wondering who the hell they might belong to.

The old witch who currently lived in this apartment was well known in magical circles as a collector with an odd way of living. Unlike most witches, who tended to settle in areas surrounded by our own – Salem, Asheville, or Triora, Italy – she moved around a lot, certain that someone was after her trash heap of "treasures." She took garbage bags full of junk with her everywhere she went, and regularly burned her homes down – insisting it was the only way to cleanse herself of the spirits that followed her.

Agatha Daisy Faganello was, in short, a weirdo amongst weirdos.

I had followed her here to Rio de Janeiro and had been casing her apartment for the last month, hoping to find the perfect time to slip in, nab what I came for, and get out. Keeping track of all her movements and habits, taking note of the wards she meticulously placed to protect her treasures before she left every night to collect more junk.

I felt like I knew her.

So, I wasn't totally surprised when the shoes that finally came into view weren't the fuzzy bunny slippers Aggie preferred. Nope, scuffed black boots that had to be size twelve or bigger were closing in on the couch.

A crackle of static from a short-wave walkie-talkie burst through the air, then a click of a button.

"No, boss, she isn't here."

Native English speakers, and American, like me.

I ignored the little flutter in my chest as the boots went by again. Maybe some holier-than-thou Runecoat hoping to bust Aggie for practicing unsanctioned magic or some bullshit like that?

"The binding spell brushed up against someone, then . . . nothing. She must have left already," Boots continued.

A second voice, male, a bit raspy, came through the walkie-talkie, and it tickled something at the very edge of my memory. Familiar but . . . not.

"She didn't fucking vanish into thin air; she doesn't have the skill. Find her."

"Yes, boss." Another *click* of the walkie-talkie as the static went silent. "Bastard wizard thinks his shit don't stink," he muttered under his breath.

As he made his way around the room, I slid further under the couch, past the rat, stopping at the pile of crumpled-up papers, with a stash of kindling and a packet of matches perched on top.

Aggie at her finest, prepped to burn and run. I settled next to the kindling and held still, straining to hear every movement.

My mind ticked through the possibilities. So, if Boots *was* a Runecoat, then who was the wizard? Or were the men not magical law enforcement at all. Maybe they were here for the same reason I was?

The Unicorn Diamond was a sweet little piece. Shaped like the eye of a unicorn, it looked purple but gave off every color of the rainbow when held to the light. Legend had it, the gem bestowed luck on its owner. So, while it was worth a cool million plus due to rarity and carat weight, it would command triple that from the right buyer, like the high-stakes poker player who had hired me.

I knew a few things about magical items, but there was magic, and then there were fairy tales.

One you read before bed for shits and giggles. The other could get you killed.

I scrunched up my face as the dust under the couch tickled at my nose.

Breath caught in my suddenly tight chest and my vision began to blur. Pulse pounding, I forced myself to focus on the items I could see and mentally catalogued them.

Dead rat.

Dust bunny.

Pen cap.

The black, scuffed boots came to a stop as the intruder sat down on the couch, the springs poking into my back, pinning me face down to the floor. Sweat slid down the sides of my face as my vision began to flicker, specks of light threatening to pull me under.

Keep it together, Harlow. You can do it. Slow breaths, in through your nose –

"Boss, she isn't here. I've checked everywhere, and the binding spell isn't latching onto anyone."

"She's there. We watched her go in five minutes ago, Brick," the other man said with a heavy sigh. "Check all the rooms, the closets, anywhere she could hide."

Again, that voice tugged at some long-buried memory, and they distracted me for a moment. Long enough to focus on the words being spoken.

They weren't after Aggie *or* the diamond.

They were after me.

Harlow Chandramallika Daygon. Neverthorn Academy dropout in the magical Dwimmer world at sixteen, black market valuables purveyor in the Unlit human world at twenty-nine. Sure, I was an amazing thief out here among the Dims – humans, that is. One of the best. But my work didn't exactly mark me as worthy of attention from magical types unless said attention came with a heavy dose of scorn.

So then, why were they after me?

The question made breathing impossible, and my upper lip broke out in beads of sweat. I had a minute, two tops, before all Carol-the-human-therapist's coping tools went straight out the window and I fully lost my shit.

"I've already been through the whole place . . ." Brick whined, breaking the ominous silence.

"Look again!"

"Roger that." A short pause, followed by a muttered, "Asshole."

"I can still hear you, Brick."

"Sorry, boss."

He didn't sound sorry at all.

"Bring Ms. Daygon in, or don't bother coming back out."

Brick stood, easing the springs off my back. I forced myself to stay still until his footsteps faded down the hall before sucking in a gulp of air. Then, I scuttled out from under the couch and swiped a hand over my clammy face.

I had to move fast. From what they'd said, it sounded like there were more men watching the building, and I needed to buy myself some time before they were called in.

Thieving 101: *Distractions work wonders.*

Grabbing the pile of kindling, some of the crumpled paper, and the matches, I crouched next to the velvet-covered couch and set my fire starters on the cushion. I didn't dare use a spell until I had to, in case they could trace it.

Striking a match, I lit the crumpled paper and used a single piece of kindling to poke at it, burning the tip to a quick char.

Ears tuned for Brick's footsteps, I flipped the raggedy crocheted blanket lying across the back of the sofa over the burning pile of wood. Then, I slid back along the linoleum floor. The crackle of flames was barely audible at first, but with the tinder-dry couch, it wouldn't take long to catch.

Gripping the last piece of kindling, I scooted into the kitchen and pressed my back to the small island.

There was no way I'd be able to get the Unicorn Diamond out now. I frowned and glanced up at the peeling paint on the ceiling.

Unless . . .

Smoke was filling the room rapidly, filtering through the apartment.

"Ah shit," Brick snarled at the fire, stumbling into view. He had his back to me as he used a spell to put the fire out, his focus entirely on the flames.

Moving light and silent, I leapt over the island onto his back, snaking my arm around his neck, and clamping down as fast and hard as I could.

"Lights out, big guy," I whispered into his ear.

He only got out one grunt before he went to his knees, buckling under the speed at which I'd cut off the blood to his head. I held him until he was flat on the ground, then dropped him.

I'd have three to four minutes before he came around.

Which meant it was now or never.

"Brick, why is there smoke coming out the window?"

The question crackled over the walkie-talkie. I grabbed it up and, adjusting my voice as low as I could, I hit the button on the side and said, "Looks like Agatha set a booby-trap."

"Find Harlow; we're running out of time. The Runecoats will be here soon."

So, these guys aren't the magical version of the FBI after all. Who the hell were they?

A new and inexplicable dread spread through me. Still gripping the last piece of kindling as if it were a weapon, I sprinted to the back bedroom where Agatha spent most of her time.

Should I have aborted my mission and just bolted out of there? Probably. But I wasn't leaving without the Unicorn Diamond now that I was this close. The bounty on the purple gem would pay for a house in a safe neighborhood and finally let me turn my temporary shelter for teen runaways into a proper one, with actual beds to sleep on instead of used couches with springs poking through. Better yet, it would be like a real home for me and my sister, Opie.

When was the last time either of us had that?

I flipped the mattress on Aggie's bed, feeling along the edges . . . and there it was. A tiny tear near where Agatha would lay her head, visible from the side window. Every night I'd seen her reach in and touch what I hoped would be tucked inside.

I stuffed my hand in and pulled out a black velvet pouch. A groan from the other room told me my time was up.

Using my forefinger and thumb, I made a swift pinching motion – my own spell, thank you very much, and again, untraceable – shrinking the velvet pouch and whatever was in it to the size of a marble before repeating the maneuver with my last piece of kindling. Who knew when I might need to light another fire?

When I was done, I tucked them into the pocket I had sewn into the inside collar of my jacket.

Another groan, static off the walkie-talkie. "She got the drop on me. She's gone."

No time to waste, I went straight for the window, slid out and climbed up, using the handholds I'd set into the stone the night before. Once on top of the building, I pulled my phone from my back pocket and hit redial.

"Josh, I'm out. I have it."

"Good job!" my getaway driver and partner in crime said with a laugh of relief. "Milkshakes on me."

Just the thought of ice cream blended with strawberries, covered in thick whipped cream, made me feel a little better. I sprinted across the rooftop, the glitter of the night and the hum of the city spilling upward. "I've got a tail, so meet me at the back-up site."

"You got it. See you in five." There was a hum from the engine of his bike, and then the line went dead.

Five minutes.

A crackle of energy spun me around and suddenly four cloaked figures stood on the building in front of me, each with their right hand extended in the classically trained dueling stance. They were prepping to cast Hecate knew how many spells at once.

"I wish I could stay, but I've got people to see and all ..." With a grin, I leapt from the edge of the roof, spinning in mid-air so I could face them as I fell, both middle fingers extended.

Later suckers.

"She jumped, she jumped!"

Before I hit the ground, I wove a quick spell of air, cushioning my fall, praying it wouldn't fail me. My luck held – thank you, Unicorn Diamond.

I landed on the balls of my feet and was moving before the men on the roof had even taken a step in my direction. Of course, I should have wondered why it had been so easy to get away.

Four more figures were waiting for me on the ground and began flinging binding spells my way the second I rounded the corner. I dodged left, then right, but my feet flew out from under me as I felt a telltale slap at my ankles. A second later, I face-planted into the sidewalk.

So much for Unicorn Diamond luck.

Reserve Your Copy
https://books2read.com/neverthorn